JACOB'S BELLS

A Novel

By

Rupert Pratt

Jacob's Bells: A Novel—*the third book of the* <u>*Wine for Tomorrow*</u> *trilogy*

I dedicate this book to the memory of my wife, Millie Pratt, and to my other family members, Greg, Jon, Bobbi, Purvesh, Lizzie, Nathan, and Andy. Special thanks go to Shirley Saccocio, who bugged me unmercifully with, "Show me what you've done," and to Tom and Nancy DeVito, who have a long history of supporting my writing ventures. I am thankful to Barbara Harvey, who suggested the inclusion of charts in the back of the book to keep track of family relationships and the many characters throughout the trilogy; I regret that Barbara did not live to see this completed edition. I would be remiss not to mention the members of my "Monday Lunch Bunch," whom I value for their friendship and encouragement.

Contents

Part One

1972–1976

The Calling

Part Two

1978–1988

The Cross

Part Three

1988–2024

The Bells

Part One

1972–1976

The Calling

CHAPTER ONE

January 1, 1972

The lights were dimmed throughout the hospital hallways, but a sunrise glow filtered through the windows of the tiny waiting room where Obadiah Gainsworthy fidgeted in his chair. A few paces down the hall, Cassie was giving birth; little else was worthy of his interest.

The man across from him had introduced himself as "Joe," and Obie's cursory reply, although not consciously designed to discourage conversation, held that hope.

Joe seemed to miss the subtlety of the response. For the past hour, he had tossed out random comments and questions that had little to do with the events happening a few steps away. He casually announced that he was about to become a father again, but showed no anxiety about it.

"Are you from Tupper Lake?" Joe asked as he stretched out long legs that almost reached the tips of Obie's restless boots. He had asked the same question earlier, but did not wait for an answer.

"I'm from Stafford Rest."

After a short pause, Joe said, "Seems like I know you, Obie. Have we met before?"

Obie studied the man's face. They were about the same age. "If we have, I don't remember where."

"Maybe Evergreen High?"

"Class of forty-three?"

"That's it, then. The fact is, I remember now. Your first name should've been a clue. You're Obie Gainsworthy."

"That's right."

"We were both in Europe during the big one. You was in Italy. I was in Normandy. We marched together in a Fourth of July parade in Evergreen just this past year. You're the one with two Silver Star medals, and you've wrote some books. They had you right up front."

"I don't usually participate in those things," Obie said. Dan had insisted they go together.

Joe reached across the narrow space between them and held out his hand. "I'm Joe Stringer."

Joe's hand was calloused. "Of course, "Obie said, "You're Cora Stringer's brother. She's married to Ernie Boswell."

Obie did not remember much about Joe, but Ernie had been his friend since they were children in the Adirondack community. Ernie's family had owned a sizable stretch of waterfront property on Diamond Lake since the beginning of the century. Ernie improved that property, which now held his marina, store, and restaurant.

Joe laughed. "Yeah, Ernie knocked Cora up while they was still in high school. Chet was who they got, so it worked out pretty well in the end."

Obie did not react to the raw remark, for Joe's expression seemed to hold no disrespect toward his sister.

Joe added, "Chet's a master carpenter and does real well, except for his drinking."

"He worked on my house after I returned to Stafford Rest three years ago. He's the best. You're right, though, about the drinking. He saw lots of bad stuff in Vietnam."

Joe eased back in his chair. "It's funny how what we think are disasters turn out to be blessings, ain't it?" It appeared to be a rhetorical question, and he continued, "My Dad was ready to kill Ernie back in forty-two. When Dad died five years ago, he loved Chet more than anybody else in our family." He paused. "You was once a preacher, wasn't you? Do you think maybe God turns bad things into good?"

Obie wanted to shout that God did just that in his own life—that his and Laura's "sin of the flesh" had given them Dan, a son for whom mere words of praise were insufficient. He controlled himself. "Yes, he does that. And I believe he takes pleasure in it."

A nurse walked up to the station at the end of the corridor. Obie tensed. She came from the general area where they had taken Cassie. The young woman looked toward them but then looked away. He sank back into his chair.

Would the waiting never end? Four hours had passed since they arrived at the hospital, and her contractions were only a few minutes apart. Thank God the roads were not bad. There were slick spots from light snow, but the temperature was not much below freezing except at the higher elevations.

Their plans had gone awry. Obie had insisted they move into a Tupper Lake motel a few days before the mid-January due date to avoid possible bad weather. Yesterday, however, on the last day of December, Cassie complained of feeling poorly and rested all afternoon. Then, just before midnight, she told him to warm up the station wagon.

Now, nearly daylight on New Year's Day, he worried about all that could go wrong. Cassie was forty-five. She had the flu in November. *What if the baby has health problems? That sometimes happens with older parents.*

If anything happened to Cassie, he would not want to live. Finding each other after so many years was not accurately a miracle, for they had squandered numerous opportunities. Still, it seemed a wondrous thing that they were now happily married.

Born on the same day to parents of vastly different circumstances, he and Cassie Hunt quickly became friends. Nevertheless, despite how much he cared for her, it was her older sister, Laura, for whom he lusted. That youthful mistake resulted in Laura's pregnancy when Obie was seventeen.

That might have turned out differently had not Abigail, the girls' mother, engineered a scheme to conceal the pregnancy from Obie and the rest of her family. Abigail's deviousness caused Laura to think Obie had abandoned her, leaving her with no choice but to marry a man "more suited to her position in life." Obie learned of her marriage while in Army basic training, but remained ignorant of her pregnancy. He believed she had betrayed him.

Eventually, his hatred subsided as his love for Cassie matured. While he was still in college in California, they made plans to marry. Sadly, that plan did not work out, and they went their separate ways, with neither endeavoring to heal the rift.

5

In the meantime, the silent animosity between Obie and Laura lasted twenty-seven years, during which Obie remained away from Stafford Rest. When he did return, baggage and all, it was to see Cassie again and to rekindle their love.

Despite her belief that it could bring Obie and her sister together again, Cassie's persistence revealed the truth about Abigail's deception and Dan's parentage. Obie soon convinced Cassie that, although his friendship with Laura was repaired, he no longer had romantic feelings for her.

They had been married over a year—a fantastic year in which Obie engrossed himself in Cassie and his neglected writing. That she might become pregnant did not occur to either; he was both thrilled and frightened. Right now, fright clung to his mind as tenaciously as snow on the High Peaks.

Joe startled him from his reverie. "I've got five children. This one is the last ... but I'm proud of each one."

"Good for you."

Joe clicked off the names and ages of each child; the oldest was twenty-two and the youngest four. "Do you have any other children?" he asked.

Obie squared his shoulders. "A son. He's twenty-seven."

"You like to spread them out, too. What's your son's name?"

"Daniel. Dan. Dan Williamson." *He would get used to saying that.*

"I know him. He has the floatplane. He's Laura Hunt's son. She was in our class in high school."

Joe's face changed as the significance of what he had said seemed to dawn. Obie avoided an explanation: "It's a long story."

Joe grunted and relaxed into his chair with an expression that clearly said, "There's more, but I had better not ask."

Dan had his own sad story. He left Vietnam after the first of two tours, knowing that Ly Yen, his Vietnamese girlfriend, was pregnant, but not that she was carrying twins. He had returned from a second tour, devastated at not finding her.

But happily, Obie and Cassie helped resolve the situation. They went to California to be married but were armed with new information: Ly Yen was living in San Francisco; they quickly arranged to take her and her two children to Stafford Rest to surprise Dan. *What a good memory.*

Dan was unaware of their plan and did not know then that Obie was his father; Laura had made him promise not to tell Dan because it "would upset his life."

Nevertheless, a secret was revealed that brought the truth to light: An old preacher's kindhearted sharing of Hunt family secrets with Ly Yen led her to name the twins after their actual grandparents. The newlyweds brought Ly Len to Stafford Rest along with "Obadiah" and "Laura."

Obie chuckled at the memory; he glanced at Joe to see if he noticed.

Ly Yen and the children had been introduced at a well-attended dinner at Ernie's Restaurant. Dan was overjoyed to be reunited with Ly Yen and to meet the twins. Obie saw his shock at the revelation of his parentage but was pleased that he did not appear upset. After all, they already had a solid friendship.

More than fifty people had attended that dinner party, and they would have talked about the odd coincidence of the children's names. In the days following, it was not uncommon to encounter friends and acquaintances whose raised eyebrows and smiles indicated approval. Ernie Boswell, from whom words often escaped with little forethought, told Obie, "I knew it, you rascal! I always knew there was something off about her marrying Ben Williamson like that."

Despite the apparent discomfort experienced by Abigail and, to some extent, by Laura, Dan's parentage became an open secret. Strangely, Obie and Dan had not spoken to each other about it. Obie hoped to change that.

More time passed in the waiting room. Joe Stringer was called with the news that he was a new father and that his daughter might even be the first birth in the county that year. A few minutes later, the nurse appeared again. Obie gripped the arms of his chair for a moment. She was coming for him.

"Mr. Gainsworthy ... Happy New Year. You have a big, healthy son, eight pounds, four ounces. Cassie is doing fine. She wants to see you."

* * *

Obie's head felt ready to explode. He was not sure which way to look, whether at Cassie's smiling face flushed with perspiration or to the corner of the room where a nurse was holding their son, a wiggling and wailing infant whose red body bore testimony to the trauma of birth.

"He's very strong," the nurse said. "See how he grips my finger?"

Obie could not find words to utter aloud but formed a silent sentence: "Thank you, loving God."

Cassie said nothing as he approached her, but her pale blue eyes radiated love when he took her hand. It seemed one of those intensified moments in a lifetime when reality allowed a mere human to stand on an elevated plane, as though God had reached down to lift him up. But those were ethereal moments, so he tried to burn the scene and the sensations into his memory.

"I love you," he managed.

"And I love you, dear husband."

The nurse waved and took the infant through a door, mouthing words indicating that she would return. Obie said to Cassie, "He's perfect."

They held hands silently for a full minute before she said, "Obie, what's his name?"

"We talked about names a few times, but we never decided. Why didn't we?"

"I don't know. Maybe we couldn't believe this was really going to happen."

"Cassie, you name him."

"No, you choose."

"Are you sure?"

"Yes."

"I don't know. Maybe after our fathers?"

"Would that be Kenneth Pinkerton Gainsworthy, or Pinkerton Kenneth Gainsworthy?"

Obie laughed. "Perhaps this needs a bit more thought."

"What person in your family do you admire more than any

other? I think I know. You speak often of him.”

“Grandpa Jacob?”

“And what friend do you miss and honor every time his name comes up, even after so many years?”

For a moment, Obie was carried back to a battlefield in Italy, to a day when the campaign was almost over, to a battle that should never have been fought. Matt Burroughs, his friend from basic training was by his side throughout the two long years of advancing mountain by mountain up the length of Italy. Matt died while sheltering next to Obie. It was a death he had to explain to Rosa, the waif of a wife Matt met and fell in love with in Naples. Of all the images from three wars that Obie carried in his heart and memory, Matt’s death was the most heart-rending.

“Matt, of course.”

“Obie, our son’s name is Jacob Matthew ... Jacob Matthew Gainsworthy.”

CHAPTER TWO

July 1972

Obie drove down a winding lane toward the familiar stone building beside the lake. The large structure had been the main house on Abner and Claire Gainsworthy's one-hundred-acre farm.

Cassie said, "It seems so long ago that Jacob and Prissy lived here."

But the memories remained fresh. "They lived in that little wood-framed house we just passed," Obie said. "I was twelve when Grandma died … not long before Mom. Grandpa died while I was overseas, but he lived the last years of his life in the big house with Uncle Abner and Aunt Claire."

"I remember." She paused. "We do share lots of memories, don't we?"

"Indeed, we do," Obie replied as he pulled onto the broad expanse of a newly paved parking lot and into a freshly marked parking space.

It was early evening, but several automobiles were already on the lot. Recently planted ornamental crabapple trees ringed the perimeter, and bushes not yet planted with tags still tied to their branches lined the sidewalk leading up to the entranceway. New wooden doors were painted red and seemed out of place.

The restaurant's official name was *Abigail's Lake Inn*, but after a week, the locals were calling it simply *Abigail's*. It was the culmination of eighteen months of interior restructuring and external landscaping. Judging by how customers came from as far away as Saratoga Springs and Plattsburg, it appeared to be a huge success. But he would have difficulty thinking of it as anything other than "Abner and Claire's."

Abigail escorted them to the "best table in the house" beside a big window overlooking Diamond Lake. This was their second time there since the completed renovation. Abigail had thrown a private party last week, the day before the official opening, which was attended by family members, friends, and influential community members and their counterparts from outlying communities: Evergreen, Newcomb, Indian Lake, Tupper Lake, Saranac Lake, Long Lake, and other Adirondack towns were well-represented. More than one hundred fifty people attended.

Obie's father called it "A bash to remember." Ken and Angie were "last-minute" additions to the event, although the couple was unaware of that. Obie was present when Abigail showed Cassie the invitation list with the omission.

Cassie was angry. "How can you even think of excluding them, Mom? They're my in-laws. What were you thinking?"

"He's a drunk."

"Ken hasn't had a drink for years," Cassie said. "He's much different from who he was back in the forties. Angie straightened him out."

Abigail had sounded almost repentant. "Angie is Vi's sister, and I loved Vi. If it were only Angie, I would have put her on the guest list, but I couldn't without inviting Ken."

Abigail's tender words toward Obie's mother were not enough to assuage his annoyance at the offensive ones about his father. Cassie saved him the need for a response. "If you don't invite them," she said, "Obie and I won't be there either."

As his mother-in-law retreated to the kitchen, Obie reviewed that incident with distaste. *When would it end?* He had forgiven Abigail for all the grief she had caused, a breakthrough for him that helped brush aside the enmity that once hampered his spiritual well-being and happiness.

But Abigail had only half-heartedly reciprocated. True, things had improved, but there were times when he felt her eyes on him. He tried to be sympathetic; he had never measured up to her idea of a suitable match for either daughter. Yet, both had given him sons. He was not blameless, but he was not sorry.

The window was open slightly, and the July evening breeze off the lake was warm. Abigail had plans to add an outdoor dining area, but the construction would not start until next spring.

From their table, he saw the well-worn path from the building to the lake a hundred yards distant. In his youth, he traversed that trail in all seasons, either from the boat dock in warm weather or the frozen surface in winter; it was his shortcut from the village. The path was much the same now, except both sides were professionally landscaped.

"It's a beautiful scene, the lake and village," Cassie said.

"It is." Obie used his best "poem voice. "Diamond Lake, its waters tranquil, yet twinkling ... like the facets of a hundred million diamonds."

Cassie laughed. "Did you just make that up?"

"I did," he said. "No, I quoted myself from the manuscript I'm working on."

"About Diamond Lake?"

"Just a little section about the lake and town. Did you know that tradition points to the twinkling you see as the origin of the lake's name?"

"Dad says that, too."

"Pinky knows a lot of local history," Obie said as he looked beyond the lake to the village, a quarter-mile away.

He loved Stafford Rest without any reason he could define, except that it was what he had always known///; "Main Street" was strung along the state road that ran parallel to the end of the lake. No building there was more than two stories high. And homes in the village were modest for the most part, although a few exceeded the norm in value and pretense. The few streets that ran back from Main Street buffered up against three small farms that refused to go away.

Not visible from where they sat, but behind the village proper, was "the Morass," which some called "swamp." There, long-dead trees grasped at the sky like departed spirits clinging to life. And, to the north, beyond the town, Indian Knob and Blackberry Hill were two soft breasts, symmetrical and clothed in the gentle green of summer foliage.

Cassie said, "I can see our house ... just barely."

"We still have the highest elevation on Blackberry Hill."

"And it'll stay that way since we own all the land up to the

State line."

Abigail returned from the kitchen and asked if she could dine with them. The request was unexpected, for she seldom asked permission for such things. After glancing at Obie, Cassie said, "Of course ... do join us."

Obie hid his disappointment. Time alone with Cassie was precious. At six months, Jacob took most of her time, and Julie, her daughter with Down syndrome, would always need care. Obie helped wherever possible, but Cassie insisted he occupy his time writing. This evening, Ken and Angie were babysitting, and Obie had anticipated having his wife to himself. Maybe they should have gone to Ernie's Restaurant or to one of Evergreen or Tupper Lake's eateries.

"I have something to do, but I'll be right back," Abigail said.

Obie studied Cassie's face as they waited. Some people near middle age lost identifying elements of youth, but not Cassie. If he squinted, she looked fifteen again. The only telltale signs were a few gray hairs, almost invisible throughout her golden curls. The tiny crinkly lines at the corners of her eyes even enhanced her oval face.

Both Hunt sisters had aged gracefully. Laura was a little heavier but retained the beauty and coquettish look he remembered. For a moment, he allowed himself to dwell on the image of Laura at eighteen—but only for a moment. He saw relatively little of her now except at family gatherings. Stafford Rest Furniture, the business Pinky started before the Depression, seemed to have become her passion.

Cassie, staring at him, had said something: "What?" he asked.

"You looked like you were miles away."

"I was thinking about you when we were teens." A partial truth avoided hurt.

"I asked you how the book was coming along."

"I'm on schedule for the publisher. I'll finish the first draft in two or three months."

"When can I read the manuscript?"

"Any time you want, but I prefer you wait a bit, until I

polish some more."

"You established recognition with your earlier books, but they had a darker element. From what you've told me about this one, it's different."

She was correct. His first books were filled with war and politics, the "what ifs" of countries and governments. This new one, with the working title *A Rage for Life*, attempted to identify the positive elements that bring purpose and satisfaction to ordinary people. Grandfather Jacob, who grasped those concepts better than most, was prominent in the manuscript pages.

"Yes, it is different, perhaps a reflection of changes in my own life." He placed a hand on one of hers. "Cassie, you've changed everything. Not long ago, I was alone, surrounded by people, but alone, nonetheless."

She laughed. "Well, you're not alone anymore. You have Julie, Jacob, and me, for better or for worse."

"My life, our lives, are as I want them to be."

Abigail returned at that moment with Cassie's father. "Is it okay if Pinky joins us? I found him wandering around the kitchen looking for something to eat."

"Dad, we're happy to have you," Cassie said.

Obie stood to shake Pinky's hand, but the older man put his arms around Obie's shoulders. Obie had never felt animosity from his father-in-law, which was understandable since Pinky had been as unaware as Obie about Dan's parentage. And at eighty-two, he still looked fit, although he had survived a heart attack five years earlier.

"Abigail spends most of her time here," Pinky said, "so I don't get many home-cooked meals. Gladys only comes in twice a week to clean and cook, so if I want to get fed, I come here."

"Or to Beth's Cafe," Abigail said.

"Yes, that, too." Pinky looked away as though wishing to change the subject. "How's our new grandson?"

Abigail said, "He's the sweetest thing." She had been visiting Blackberry Hill three or four times a week. She never stayed long but always played with Jacob and talked to Julie. It encouraged the hope that she had put their differences behind her, as he had. She added, "He's a good baby."

"The best," Cassie said.

"Not like you when you were that little. I can't count the nights you kept us awake, crying."

Cassie's face reddened. His wife could be a tiger, and she hated Abigail's habit of putting her down. "Well, Mom ..." Her voice was steady, a good sign. "I appreciate the care you took of me back then. And I'm sure Jacob will always appreciate the interest you show him."

"He is my grandson. Why would I not show interest?"

The waiter came at that moment. He wore a dark suit and tie and looked frightened. He kept glancing at Abigail as he took their orders.

Abigail said to him, "Herbert, straighten up when you're addressing customers. You're all hunched over like an old man."

"Yes, Mrs. Hunt," Herbert said before he hurried toward the kitchen.

"I never realized how hard it is to get good help until I got into this business," Abigail said.

Pinky glanced at the ceiling with apparent exasperation before saying, "This meal is on me."

Obie protested, but the older man was persistent. "A dinner is a small thing, indeed, after all the good you've done for this community." Pinky raised his water glass in salute.

Obie knew he was referring to the large "Love Fund" gift. I know you'll see that it's put to good use, Pinky."

Abigail's eyes narrowed. "I still think you were a fool, Obie. You had a fortune in your hands, probably enough to buy a town like Stafford Rest, and you just gave it all away."

Obie kept his voice steady. "It wasn't my money, Abigail. It was Annie's. She wanted to give it away. That's the way she was ... pure philanthropist."

Cassie stirred beside him; she was sympathetic toward Annie regarding his less-than-successful marriage but was not shy about pointing out his mistakes. Sometimes, he imagined an element of jealousy. He touched her arm.

Abigail said, "But you don't have to give it all away."

Pinky said quickly, "Abigail, what he does with it is his own business. We should be thankful for the gift. He said it was to honor his grandparents, Jacob and Prissy. Countless young people have been helped." He added, "Jacob would be proud of Obie's decisions."

"Maybe," Abigail said with a look of disdain. She had always disliked Obie's grandfather for no apparent reason. For a moment, Obie thought to enlighten her about the source of the Love Fund. Someday, he would take that pleasure, but for now, it was best to protect that family secret.

As always, mention of his grandfather conjured up nostalgic memories. Now, he observed the massive but little-changed fireplace at the center of the room. Space was needed for the restaurant, so walls had been knocked down, and a second fireplace was backed up to the older one using the same chimney. He had often sat with Jacob at the original one, gathering tidbits of wisdom that later helped soothe the way through periods of darkness.

As a survivor of bloody Civil War battles in the Valley of Virginia, Jacob "eradicated hate from the soul" and made the pursuit of love for God and man his mantra. As a skilled Adirondack guide, it was his good fortune to save the life of a New England manufacturer who left a significant gift from his estate to Jacob. With Pinky as the sworn-to-secrecy administrator, that money had comprised the bulk of the Love Fund.

After Obie's return to Stafford Rest, Pinky informed him that the fund had been diminished. Obie had already decided to give away Annie's fortune to charities, so he donated a substantial chunk to the Love Fund. Although Pinky and Ken knew about Annie's money, it was a pleasant surprise.

"Obie did the right thing," Pinky said.

Abigail seemed unwilling to let go of the subject. "Well, it's not how I would have handled it."

Pinky rolled his eyes. "Isn't it great?" he said, obviously to change the subject, "Who would have guessed that Abigail and I would have grandsons nearly thirty years apart."

Abigail looked at Obie briefly before saying, "Our family is not typical in many ways. But you're right. One grandson is not even a year old, and another just finished his first year of medical school." She added, "Although that came a little late."

"How are Dan and Ly Len doing?" Cassie asked. "I thought they might visit this summer."

Pinky said, "They'll stay in Baltimore. Dan has a job in a clinic. He'll steal away for a couple of days in the fall to go hunting with Ken, and they may come home for a few days at Christmas. It's a long and hard road that Dan has chosen, but a worthy one."

"Danny should have stayed out of the war," Abigail said. "He could be in practice by now."

Cassie said, "I don't think he was interested much in medicine until last year."

Everyone had been surprised at Dan's decision. He loved the Adirondacks and seemed content to work in Abigail's real estate company and train an occasional student pilot. The downside was his frequenting the Diamond Inn and hopping from one sexual interlude to another with such regularity that Obie and Ken considered intervention. The change came when Obie and Cassie brought Ly Len, with Laurie and Obadiah, to Stafford Rest. Dan had believed it was a love lost, and finding Ly Len again revived his spirit.

Abigail said, "His father was instrumental in getting him into medical school."

Obie turned his head away. Abigail's words hurt. Her habit of implying that Dr. Ben Williamson was Dan's father was an insult, especially coming from her.

Cassie's voice rose as she said, "If you mean Ben, he helped, no doubt, but Dan is more than capable of standing on his own two feet."

"Perhaps Ben will take Danny into his practice in Boston when he graduates and does his residency," Abigail said. It sounded more like a hope than a certainty.

Obie could not remain silent. "Dan will come home. He'll come back to Stafford Rest. I know it."

CHAPTER THREE

January–May 1973

It was a peaceful time. Obie worked nearly every day throughout the winter editing *A Rage for Life*. Cassie seemed content. She smiled often, unaware he was looking. Jacob was a healthy and happy baby; if he continued at the same pace, he would soon walk. When they found time, they skied along the ridge. Once, they pulled Jacob on a sled behind them.

Julie was happy anywhere; she was especially eager to spend time with him. She called him "Daddy, a designation that started soon after he and Cassie married.

Sometimes, she came into the barnroom where he worked, sat, and watched him type on his old portable typewriter. Occasionally, she asked a question or made a comment that challenged conventional wisdom about how the human mind worked.

Just last week, she said, "Daddy, why can't we hear fish talk?"

"Fish don't talk," he had replied.

"Yes, they do. Aunt Laura has a fish tank. I watched them all day, once. They move their mouths. When people move their mouths like that, they're talking."

"Honey, that's just something fish do. They don't talk."

"Do you know that for sure, Daddy?"

"Well ... no."

"You told Mommy you shouldn't say things you're not sure about."

"Julie, that's not what I meant ..." He had stopped, for it was an argument he would not win. "Okay, Honey, maybe fish do talk."

Julie had qualities that defied explanation. Once, when he struggled with war memories and prayed for help, Julie had casually told him that "a lady dressed in white" said he must go to Italy to find his "lost parts." That trip eventually led him to Germany, where he found some closure to an incident that had plagued him for many years.

That experience, and what Cassie declared were his own "precognitive dreams," strengthened his belief that there was more to life than is perceived. Perhaps a wall separated the physical from the spiritual, and Julie could peek over it. He would not dwell on the subject but would always listen to her.

It was also a time when he attempted to filter out distractions. National and world events had stolen his attention the previous year: There was the Watergate break-in scandal, the murder of Israeli athletes at the Summer Olympics, and contentious political conventions. Near the end of the year, he rejoiced when it looked like the war might end, but was disappointed when Richard Nixon resumed bombing Hanoi. The war news was confusing, and he was put on blinders. *Only family and work mattered.*

By mid-March, his manuscript was finished, or nearly so. Silverman Publishing, the New York company he ran for over two years, was publishing it. Obie's relationship with Ira Silverman, the owner, had become tenacious when he left the company with little advance notice, so to put a safe layer between Ira and himself, he hired Clark Desmond as his agent.

Obie had a lengthy history with the Silverman family: Adam Silverman, Ira's son, was his squad leader during his two years in Italy and was undoubtedly responsible for keeping him alive throughout that campaign. They later roomed together at Berkeley. Adam's Uncle Hershel Silverman, a professor at Berkeley, had helped pave the way for both young men to attend that school. Adam, married with two children, lived in Israel and managed a farm near Tel Aviv. They wrote often and met whenever Adam visited New York. Obie had called him after the Olympics massacre. His friend was angry and ready to go to war again.

One day, as dripping trees outside his barnroom gave notice about the retreat of winter, Obie paused from rifling through manuscript pages to reflect on where he was in his personal and professional life: Besides finding Cassie again, he had found spiritual peace. His service as a military chaplain in two wars and a two-year stint as the pastor of a prominent San Francisco Methodist church were experiences that both strengthened and tried his faith. And they convinced him that pastoring was not his calling.

His calling? What would his mother think? Vi had wanted, even predicted, that he would serve God in a "special way."

His thoughts often dwelt on his mother and her kind spirit. An experience the previous summer conjured up memories: With Cassie's help, he had expanded the vegetable garden, clearing a section above the original patch. Bushes and young trees required grubbing out. In the process, he discovered his mother's overgrown asparagus patch. He had helped her dig a trench to plant the seeds; she wanted it deep to strengthen the roots. "If the roots are strong, it will last for many years," she said. He was amazed that some plants, although puny, were still alive. *Had God, through her, spoken about more than asparagus roots? Did his roots need strengthening?*

He picked up the six-inch-thick stack of manuscript pages readied for mailing and leafed through it. In this book, he honored God, sought guidance, and tested his themes against scripture. *What would Mom say? Would this satisfy her? Were her predictions fulfilled?* Could he relax now and consider writing his true calling?

Or was there more?

* * *

The Rev. Carl Enslow was retiring—for the second time— and he felt good about it. The first time, five years previously, had been from a Kansas conference of the Methodist Church. His wife, Hallie, had always talked about Tupper Lake, where she grew up in the Adirondack Mountains of New York. Carl's Chicago upbringing was not pleasant enough to draw him back there, so they set off for the East with the dream of quiet retirement.

That had not happened; they rented a house in Tupper

Lake with an option to buy when someone approached him from the Methodist Conference. The pastor of Stafford Rest Methodist had just died; would he take an interim position there? At first, he declined but then received visits from various individuals appealing to his sense of duty; he had always been a sucker for that pitch. The first year, he drove back and forth daily from Tupper Lake.

It did not take long to see that there were problems in the church, but instead of discouraging him, they sparked his combativeness. Satan was rampant in the congregation, and Carl could not turn away from the challenge; he agreed to return for a second year, or until they found someone to replace him. He managed to extinguish most unholy fires that popped up, but by the end of the second year, he was praying for deliverance.

He thought his prayers were answered when Obadiah Gainsworthy came to town. The man seemed a perfect fit. He was educated, well-known in certain circles, and young enough to stand the rigors of a divided and contentious congregation.

Anthony Gladstone, a friend from the Kansas conference, alerted Carl to Obadiah's credentials and put him in touch with George Dulany, a former district officer in California. In a letter, Dulany provided background information and highly recommended Obadiah. However, he warned that he had lingering war memories and might need some persuasion. There was also a hint of something else related to his marriage. Carl needed to know more and called Dulany.

Dulany declined to discuss what he knew about the marriage difficulties but said, "I'm sure he'll tell your Conference about it before he accepts a pastoral position, but it's something that should come from him, not me."

"He's remarried now, and to a local woman here, but perhaps you could tell me if his previous marital problems, whatever they were, might affect his ability to minister to a congregation?"

Without hesitation, Dulany had said, "That's not a problem."

"Thank you for an honest answer."

"Is your superintendent involved in this search?"

"He is. The Conference is always looking for qualified candidates, and he's heard a lot about our problems here. He's anxious to find someone who can deal with them. He told me to go ahead and find out all I can about Obadiah and get back to him. And I understand your reluctance to discuss sensitive details, but maybe you can give me some idea of the kind of minister he might be."

Dulany said. "It's seldom we find ministers who can handle all the administrative duties and meet the congregation's pastoral needs. Sometimes, there's weakness in one of those areas. I think Obie has strength in both. Maybe his Army chaplain experiences prepared him for the administrative end. When he left here, the congregation mourned for a long time."

"He must have faults?"

Delany said, "Well, he is somewhat reserved in dealing with individuals he's not well acquainted with, but that's not a serious problem, if it's a problem at all. He's also somewhat liberal in his thinking, which bothered me somewhat, but he's well-grounded in doctrine. I think he lives his Christian life in a non-judgmental way. He doesn't claim to have absolute answers."

"That might go up against some of our members who believe they have all the answers."

"I'm sure he'll observe the traditional ways. Do you know that he had childhood training in the Catholic Church?"

"Pinkerton Hunt, a prominent businessman here, told me that."

"Have you read his books?"

"One ... his first. I intend to read the rest."

"His writings will give you some idea of his beliefs. But it may also show that he's a work in progress."

"Aren't we all?"

"Indeed. Obie is a complex man and sometimes contradictory. According to my cousin, he's incredibly fearless in the physical realm but hesitant and even shy in dealing with people. If you've been around him for any length of time, you've noticed that he takes his time in conversation, which puts some people off. But I don't consider it a handicap. It's his way of ensuring understanding in communication."

"One problem here is members who take the opposite side no matter the issue. Do you think he can deal with that?"

"Absolutely. But all this speculation could be for nothing if you can't bring him back into the pastoring fold. I hope you can."

That conversation occurred three years previously, and Delany was right; despite Carl's efforts, Obadiah had refused even to consider an appointment.

Partly out of duty and partly because he still enjoyed the challenge, Carl agreed to take on a regular appointment at the church. He and Hallie moved to Stafford Rest and occupied the parsonage, a little house on church property only a few steps from the sanctuary.

Even so, he felt the onset of advanced age and wanted to leave the problems behind. At first, he was determined to renew his campaign to get Obadiah to step up, but relief came when David Gillard, a young minister not long out of seminary, was offered the job.

Carl immediately requested retirement, which would be final this time. He was relaxed, knowing that Gillard would take over by the end of June, and the Enslows would have decided whether to move back to Tupper Lake or buy a house in Stafford Rest. They were leaning toward the latter.

CHAPTER FOUR

June 1974

After several months of intensive edits, the new book was finally in bookstores. Silverman Publishing had arranged a nationwide book signing tour, a new experience for Obie. He left early in June for a three-week trip that started in the Northeast, went south, and then zig-zagged westward. While on the West Coast, he spent two days at his house in the Napa Valley.

Annie had deeded the house to him before her death, and in a letter that accompanied her will, she asked that he keep it. Otherwise, he would have donated it to charity, as he had with most of the O'Shane fortune.

He had not given the property much thought over the past years; it was too far away for frequent visits, but it was a serene spot he had visited during his marriage to Annie. Cassie was enthralled when they went there after their marriage. He had put her "in charge" of the property, and she often goaded him about it, suggesting they go there for vacations.

On the first night at the house, away from the rigors of the tour, he called Cassie and urged her to get on a plane and join him. "That's not practical," she said. "You're on a tight schedule. You'll be in Portland the day after tomorrow. I'd love to be there, but it will have to be at another time."

"You're right as usual," he responded, "but when I get home, we'll make definite plans to come. It's too nice to let it go to waste. I just spent half an hour looking out the back window at the neighbors' vineyards that roll over the hills. I love the view. And our place has been kept up. The flower garden is weeded and cultivated. The grass is brown at this time of the year, but the lawn is clear and tidy. And the inside is dust-free. I didn't expect that after three years of being unoccupied."

"Well, didn't you tell me that Godfrey Lawrence from the

Hartford firm made arrangements for its care, to pay taxes, and the like?"

"That's correct."

"And you said a fund was set aside for upkeep, so you don't have to have a hand in it. That's no doubt why you find it clean and livable."

"A man by the last name of 'Augustine' is responsible for the property's care. But I've never met him or contacted him. I suppose I should look him up while I'm here. I think he owns or manages the vineyard I can see out the window."

Cassie laughed. "You're impossible, Obie. You can run big churches and large companies, and yet you've neglected your duty in handling a little piece of property that could be a source of pleasure for our family and friends."

Obie felt a stab of conscience. "Guilty as charged," he said. He could depend on Cassie to speak the truth—or at least her version.

She said, "And I'd like to remind you that the house is my responsibility."

"I did tell you that, didn't I? You haven't mentioned it lately, but okay, it's all yours."

"And can I run it as I see fit?"

"Of course."

"I'll hold you to that. And I'll be more hands-on than you are. We'll still need Mr. Augustine, whoever he is, to look after things when we're not there, but I see no need to have lawyers in Hartford so involved." He heard her chuckle. "And you're being warned."

"About what?"

"I'm so anxious for that trip that you may not even get to unpack your bags when you get home."

By the time he had completed the final route across the northern and Mid-Atlantic states, he was weary of travel and absence from loved ones.

But the homecoming was marred by the news that Cora Boswell had died. The funeral had been two days earlier. Soon after his arrival, Obie went to the marina to see Ernie.

"She wasn't well for a long time," Ernie said. "In a way, it's a blessing, but I sure do miss her. And Chet's taking it real hard. He's made the Diamond Inn his home for the last few days."

"Would you like me to talk to him?"

"Sure, it might help. I know he respects you." Ernie grinned. "Don't know why."

Obie was relieved that Ernie could still quip; he would be all right. "I'll stop at the village gin mill on my way home," Obie said.

* * *

Chet Boswell came home scarred from the Vietnam War. Despite that, he was a sought-after carpenter and contractor. The common opinion was that "no one in the county is better at his trade." Obie agreed but saw there were days when Chet was seized with moroseness so severe that he shrank from his duties and escaped to some distant plane of forgetfulness. Dan also had war scars but seemed able to ignore them. Obie knew, however, that pushing such pain aside was not the same as shedding it; Chet was trying to drown his demons.

The lights were dim in the Diamond Inn. Chet was seated at the end of the long bar. The stool beside him was vacant. The bartender, Chuck Hinky, was an old friend and classmate of Obie's.

"Hello, Obie," Chuck said, and added, "To what do we owe the honor of this infrequent visit?"

Obie was not going to disguise his reason for being there. "Rescue mission," he said, nodding toward Chet.

Chet was not so drunk that he failed to understand. He said, "Do you come as Mr. Gainsworthy, or Rev. Gainsworthy?"

"I'm no reverend. You know that."

"So you've said ..."

"Chet, I'm sorry about your mother. She was a good woman."

"That she was. Do you know that she wrote to me every day while I was over there?" A tear ran down Chet's nose and dropped onto the polished oak bar top.

"Ernie's worried about you, and I can see why."

"You can, eh?" Chet's speech was slurred, and his tone was just short of combative. "If you think your status as a fellow soldier gives you the right to conduct an intervention, then you're wrong ... as though what I saw over there compares in any way with your experience."

"What do you mean by that?"

"You were a chaplain, and I was a grunt slogging my way through the swamps. Men died right next to me. Calvin Archer was the father of two children. I was three feet from him when his head was blowed off. I picked it up and put it in a body bag with the rest of him." Chet took a deep breath. "You ever see a string of guts trailing out of a man as he runs for cover?"

Obie choked back a retort. Chet's words had brought up ugly memories.

Chuck leaned over the bar top. "Listen here, Chet. You're not the only one who's seen bad things in wars. I was in the Navy in World War II. I saw things, too. But you're barking up the wrong tree if you think Obie hasn't been in the thick of it. He was in three wars. He's seen as bad as it gets, and you don't see him feeling sorry for himself."

Chet groaned but appeared apologetic. "Sorry, Obie. I forgot that. Here, let me buy you a drink." He tossed down a bill.

"I'll pass on that, Chet. I'm still tired from my trip and need to go home and sleep."

"Heard you'd been away. Laura told me."

"How's her house coming along?" Laura had searched for suitable land for the house for two years before Abigail, in a benevolent gesture, gave her five acres from the restaurant property. The strip ran from Lake Road down to the water. Chet started building her eight-room house early that spring.

"It's coming along fine." Chet's eyes lit up. "She's a taskmaster, but we've come to understand each other ... I think."

"Shouldn't you be on the job right now?"

"It's under control. I have two men there, and Amos Adams is handling the kitchen cabinet work."

"Amos Adams? He's a member of our church. I heard he's difficult to work with." Carl Enslow had mentioned the man more than once, and not in a favorable way.

"Don't know much about his character, but he's a good carpenter."

"Cassie says Laura wants it all done before the snow flies."

Chet raised his beer glass. "That's pushing it some, but I'll get back to it ... soon."

"Tomorrow, maybe? They don't need a tipsy supervisor today."

"Maybe."

"Chet, you have friends, don't you?"

"Some. Dan and me were pretty close before he left for Baltimore. We came in here together sometimes. He'd have a couple of beers and leave. I can't do that."

"Can't, or won't?"

Chet appeared thoughtful. "Dad says I'm not addicted. He says if I were, I'd be drinking all the time. It's only when I think too much."

"My point is that friends can help you. You need someone to talk to when these moods strike."

Chet sighed. "I don't have any close friends now, only acquaintances, mostly people I work with, or work for, like yourself."

"You should try harder to make friends." He hesitated momentarily before asking, "Are there any women friends?"

There was a nervous laugh. "Women don't care much for me. They think I'm too rough. But there might be someone out there for me. Who knows?"

"Chet, I'm sure there is someone for you if you actually look. You have a lot going for you. You just need to direct it better. For one thing, you should spend less time in here." Obie glanced at Chuck. "Sorry!" he said.

"Oh, I agree," Chuck said. "I have to make a living, but I hate to do it at the expense of fellow veterans who have drinking problems."

"Now, wait a minute," Chet said. "I don't have a drinking problem. "I can give up the booze anytime I want."

"You could want a little harder," Chuck said as he wiped the bar top with a towel.

When Chet did not reply, Obie said, "I want you to know

you can talk to me anytime you feel like it. Come to church. Our congregation has single women. That would be an excellent way to begin a relationship." He wondered if he was pushing too fast.

"Now you're sounding like a preacher. I'm not much on religion. Our family attended the Episcopalian church when I was young, but Dad doesn't go anywhere now. Thanks, though, for the invite."

Obie stood. "Chet, I need to go get some sleep. Go to Laura's house tomorrow. She needs you there."

"Sure ... I will."

As he left, he heard Chet order another beer.

CHAPTER FIVE

July 1974

Cassie was preparing dinner when she saw Obie's old brown station wagon pull into the driveway. He had been helping Chet Boswell install appliances at Laura's new house.

Julie announced his arrival from the doorway. Jacob jumped up from the kitchen floor and ran to his father. Obie tousled his hair and picked him up.

Obie complained to Cassie, "Your sister always finds one more thing to do."

She could not resist: "Maybe Laura just wants to keep you there longer."

Jacob squirmed, so Obie set him down. "What? No, I don't think so."

Of course, Obie would know that I'm teasing. She enjoyed making him uncomfortable about Laura, but experienced some discomfort of her own while teasing. There was a time when she worried that the flame between Obie and Laura might reignite. After all, their young love had been intense, and Dan, whom they both loved, was the result of that passion.

But that was the past, and Obie loved only her. They both had baggage: she had a failed marriage, and he had lost a wife through death—a wife from whom he was estranged because of her infidelity. But a dark corner of her being whispered that she should be watchful. *Laura may still care for Obie.*

"She's sad," Obie said, "and I feel sorry for her."

"Laura's a survivor and stronger than most people realize."

"She's been through a lot. Her house construction has taken forever. And uprooting herself from Boston to take over the factory management must have been hard."

Cassie was ready to say that some of Laura's sadness might be attributed to her feelings for him, but she controlled herself.

He would deny it and be honest in that belief. A lot went by Obie. That naiveté was one more reason she loved him. "Laura's doing great with the factory, according to Dad. She's toying with opening an outlet store on Main Street."

"I don't think there's anything on Main with room for that."

"She'll find a way."

"She misses Dan and the twins," Obie said. "She talked a lot about them today. They're in second grade in Baltimore. Can you imagine? She says Laurie outstrips Obadiah in reading, but he excels in math."

Cassie laughed. "Do I hear some grandfatherly pride?"

He smiled. "Indeed."

Jacob tugged at her leg; he was hungry. She appeased him with a cracker, but when Obie and Julie went to the sofa in the adjacent living space, he ran to sit beside his father.

After Cassie joined them, she brought up an unresolved matter. "We never made it to California last year, and then we said we would go this year, but we haven't made any plans."

"When would you like to go?"

"Next month, before school starts. A week there would be nice. Two would be even better."

"All right. Two weeks. Let's do it." Despite his words, he looked hesitant.

"What is it?" she asked.

"Cassie, we'll make this a good trip, but I wonder if we shouldn't sell the property. It's so far away."

The Napa house had become a symbol for her, a fairyland prize that simply thinking about had the power to lift her spirits. "Sell it? Why?"

"Let's be practical, Sweetheart. We'll never spend more than two weeks a year out there. It will bring a good price, and the money can be put to better use, as your mother has said."

"So, you've become a responsible money handler? What would you do with this money? Would you give it away? You've already given away almost all of Annie's estate to charity. I've been okay with it because I understand how you feel about it, but ..."

"The house was part of her estate. Shouldn't it also be sold and given to charity?"

It took effort to hold her frustration in check. "No, you're wrong, Obie. The house wasn't part of her estate. She deeded it to you before her death. She also requested that you keep it. You told me that. Where's that letter?"

"What letter?"

"You know what letter." She nearly laughed at his expression. The truth was on her side. "The letter you told me about ... the one Annie wrote ... the one the lawyer gave you after her death. I'd like to see it."

She held her breath as he appeared to digest her request. Finally, he walked to the desk in his workspace and opened a drawer. "All right, I'll share it with you." His voice was barely above a whisper.

She was suddenly ashamed. She had no right. "Obie, I'm sorry. I should not have asked. It was personal between you and Annie. I should respect that."

He held the envelope toward her. "I share everything with you. This is no exception. I should have shown it to you."

She hesitated but took the envelope from him. She removed the letter, unfolded it, and laid it on the desktop. She said, "I don't want to read her letter if it will make you think any less of me."

"Don't be silly," he said as he smoothed the pages to make them lie flat. "I read it first in the lawyer's office shortly after the funeral." His voice held a sadness that touched her heart. "It changed how I thought about her, but of course it was too late to do anything about it."

The letter was dated January 18, 1966, a year before her death. Cassie read it silently as Obie looked over her shoulder.

Did you ever write a letter you hope is never delivered? Well, it seems this one has been, which means you are now thinking of me in the past tense. Oh, lighten up, Obie. Death is something that happens in life. Does it surprise you that I would say such a thing? We never really discussed death, did we? That, and a lot of other things.

There are times when I miss you so much. We loved each other, didn't we? I often long for that feeling, to have your arms around me again. I messed things up and wish I could have undone my mistake. However, it's too late for that and I hope you can at least be happy for me that I went forward and did the things I was intended to do on this earth. Once again, and for the last time, it seems, I ask you to forgive me and put it behind you. Find someone who can be what I couldn't. Be happy, Obie, for me. Please.

Let's get on to more serious matters. You never thought I could be serious, did you? I have to tell you about my finances. That's something else we never discussed because you never seemed interested. I did tell you that my father owned a factory in Connecticut. O'Shane Textiles was quite large and prosperous. It benefited greatly during the Second World War, something that always bothered me. Dad sold the factory while I was in college (colleges, if you will) and set up a fund for me, his only child. I won't go into why he put the money in trust except to say he believed I would run through it in short order. He was right, no doubt. My idea of wealth is to put it where it's most needed. My ideas about that and my father's ideas were at great odds.

The funds I received each month were certainly substantial. I kept only what I needed to live on and gave the rest to charity (Godfrey will supply you with a list of those charities since he takes care of that end of it).

I am leaving it all to you, Obie. Why, you may ask, do I not simply go ahead and give everything to the charities I believe do the most good for humankind? It is because, regardless of what you may think, I love you, and I want to prove my love in this way. I trust you to do what is right. You have many accomplishments, but you are somewhat confused about your life's purpose. If my gift will help you in any way to discover that purpose, I am pleased. I give you a big responsibility, Obie, about how to use the money.

I do have one request I hope you will honor. <u>Please</u> keep the property in Napa Valley. I kept that secret from you for a while. I will not apologize, for it was a good secret, don't you *think? You love the place. I know you do. Remember me when you go there. The property is already in your name, and I have established a fund for its upkeep. I am sure Godfrey will give you details if he hasn't already. A more direct contact is Mr. Lyle Augustine, whom I have placed in charge of the property. He is paid from the fund I mentioned. I have tried to make it so everything can run without involving you, unless you want to concern yourself, for I know you hate to be distracted from your work.*

I place no strings on any of this. You can keep all the money and live a life of luxury, debauchery, or both if you wish. I suspect you won't do that, but you can if you want to. Having said that, I hope you will not forget my charities list.

Once again, Obie, have a good life. I really, really, truly, do love you. I wish we could have found a way.

Your Loving wife, Annie

Obie said, "I cried the first time I read it. It still hurts."

"This time, it's me crying. Oh, Obie, I wish I had known her. We'll keep that property, won't we?"

"Yes, we'll keep it."

"Promise?"

"Yes, Cassie, I promise."

* * *

They planned to go to California for the last two weeks of August. It would be hot and dry, not the best time of the year, but it would not intrude on Cassie's teaching schedule. Although the trip was more than two weeks away, she was excited. There was plenty of time to pack, but there was one thing she must attend to right away.

By his own admission, Obie had neglected practical matters that he should have examined, studied, and resolved. She took him at his word that she could handle the property, so she felt no guilt about invading the files in his cabinet earlier that day.

What she discovered in the legal papers, tax returns, and

letters from his lawyer had floored her. She believed there was some mistake until later that afternoon when she made two phone calls.

Now, after putting Jacob to bed and saying goodnight to Julie, they sat in the glider on the porch. It was pleasant weather, and Cassie had opened all the windows and doors to let in the sweet scent of cut grass, a lingering reminder of Obie's afternoon work. A red-streaked sky, the remnant of the recent sunset, illuminated the hills west of Diamond Lake.

Cassie removed the contents of a big envelope, which she laid on the low table in front of the glider. She had already separated and paper-clipped the papers into related files. Now, she spread them all out into a dozen overlapping piles. It was time to confront Obie with the consequences of his years of neglecting the Napa Valley property.

He was quiet until she finished spreading the papers on the table. At last, he said, "What is this? It looks serious."

"You're an idiot, Obie."

"That's not been clinically confirmed, but I'd bet you're right."

"How, Obie? How could you have taken care of business in such a slipshod manner? A ten-year-old child could have done better."

She saw his annoyance. He said, "I guess I wasn't much interested. It's just a nice house on the West Coast that I don't often see."

"There's more to it. Much more!"

After a moment, he said, "It was Annie's house. I didn't want to be reminded. I've never felt ownership. It's still hers, not mine."

He was being honest, at least. "And I understand your feeling that way, but that's a reason, not an excuse. I've discovered things you should have known about, things I'm sure would have caused you to take an entirely different course of action had you known. Honestly, I don't see how you failed to know what I've learned today."

"Well, get to it, then."

A little suffering was justified. "I want to review some of

these papers with you first."

"I've looked at the deed; I told you that."

"Looked, perhaps, but not studied."

"What is it, Cassie? Have you discovered that I don't really own the house?"

"No, not that. Let me ask you something. Did you get beyond the description of the house and two acres? I think not."

"It's legal jargon ... hard to understand."

"No, it's perfectly clear if you take the time and interest to look. And what about these tax returns? Don't you look at them?"

"I leave it up to Castone, Tomes, and Lawrence. They take care of everything."

Cassie held a sheet up for him to see. "There's your signature. Do you mean to tell me you sign these without reading them? And the name of the vineyard next door didn't attract your attention?"

"Godfrey Lawrence sends them to me. I sign them and send them back."

"Without reading them, obviously."

"I never thought I had to. They manage everything dealing with gifts and the property. Cassie, these returns are different from our joint returns. You know I check and recheck those before sending them out."

"Yes, I know you do, which makes it seem so strange that you don't care about the others. What are these, anyway, business returns?"

"I suppose. Giving away all that money requires a lot of financial transactions. I guess that, in a way, it is a business. But that's what the lawyers handle for me." He paused. "And just what does the vineyard's name have to do with it?"

Without answering his question, she held up another envelope. "Here's a letter from Lawrence from three years ago. There are several more before and since, but I'll draw your attention to this one."

She read a portion that listed a series of debits and profits without any specific reference to what they were. "I suspect you are supposed to know the details," she said. "Then, there's this.

'Mr. Gainsworthy, be sure to include this as income on your personal return.' Obie, the figure is nearly thirty thousand dollars."

Obie's face showed concern. "Oh! I didn't see that."

"I know you didn't. You know what else? I read letters from other years that have similar figures, letters you never took the time to read."

He was quiet for several seconds before saying, "I've botched it, haven't I? We'll have a big bill for back taxes and penalties. But I don't understand where that income originated."

"Yes, it is income, Obie, and as for being penalized, I'm afraid we will take a big hit. I'm sorry. We'll have to come up with funds to pay the taxes."

"There's the money in the account I've set aside for you and the children if something happens to me, but I would never raid that. I have other funds, though. I'll manage it some other way." She saw uncertainty in his eyes. "This is all pretty bad news, though. I've been a fool."

"Yes, it is bad news, but all is not lost. We never spent any of the income listed here. It's all in a fund in your name."

"That is good news."

She did not want to lose momentum. "Let's get back to that deed." This was the moment she had waited for. Even while recognizing her own sadistic nature, she wanted to lift his spirits. She thrust the deed into his hands. "I hope you don't mind, but I called both Godfrey Lawrence and Lyle Augustine this afternoon. We talked about ..."

"More bad news? Have we lost the house?"

"Hardly. If you had read the deed you're holding in your hand, you would know you also own that big house on the hill you so often express admiration for, along with the hundred-acre O'Shane Vineyard." She laughed at his expression; Obie was not easily shocked.

"How could that be?"

"Our trip to California just got more interesting, didn't it, Obie?"

CHAPTER SIX

July–August 1974

"It's not a special occasion," Abigail declared early in the afternoon when she invited everyone to dinner, "just a little gathering of family." Nonetheless, Obie thought it strange; trust issues with Abigail were never-ending.

It was a mild evening, so their party sat on the restaurant's new porch overlooking Diamond Lake. Jacob was in a highchair beside Laura, who had volunteered to watch over him. Pinky had already poured wine for the adults, except for Ken who requested lemonade. Cassie casually informed them about their upcoming trip.

"Wonderful," Pinky said. "It'll do you both good to get away awhile. What's it like, anyway, the house?"

"It's modest, really," Obie said, "bigger than our house here but not as large as yours. It has six rooms, stucco siding, and a red tiled roof. The grandest thing is the surroundings, rolling hills covered with vineyards. Great views."

"Wine country, isn't it?"

"It is," Cassie said. "Dad and Mom, everybody, we have something to tell you, something we're very excited about. We discovered two days ago that Obie actually owns the rolling hills he just mentioned ... and a vineyard."

He heard gasps of surprise. Pinky said, "That's wonderful, just wonderful. Does it have a name? They name their farms and vineyards out there, don't they?"

"O'Shane Vineyard. O'Shane was Annie's family name."

"How did you come to discover all this?" Abigail asked.

For a moment, Obie worried that Cassie would reveal his years of neglect, but she said, "It was buried in the paperwork. With all the distribution of Annie's wealth to charities, the law firm failed to make it clear." He was thankful for the artful circumvention of the truth.

"That's reason to fire them," Abigail said.

Pinky said, "So, is it a producing vineyard?"

"Evidently," Obie responded. "But we know little details. There are some profits indicated by tax return information." He would not go further into that subject. "Most vineyards out there struggle, so we don't expect that ours is any different."

"Wines from California are inferior to French wines and wines from other countries," Abigail said.

"I disagree, Laura said. "California produces some good wines now."

Cassie said, "My guess is that they don't make wine at O'Shane Vineyard, but I'm not sure."

"Obie, tell us more about the property," Pinky said.

Obie painted them a word picture of the lush vineyard and the hilltop mansion that overlooked it. "It's a great place from what I've seen from a distance."

Abigail looked worried. "Might you move out there?"

"Never," Obie said. "Stafford Rest is our home."

Later, while they ate dessert, Abigail said, "Wouldn't it make a lot more sense to sell? It's probably worth a lot. You can use the money for something more profitable."

Cassie cut her off. "Mom, Annie asked Obie to keep the property. He wants to honor her wishes."

Obie added, "Cassie is afraid that if we were to sell it, I would give the proceeds to charity."

Abigail's words snapped like a whip. "And wouldn't you?"

He was annoyed at his mother-in-law but was determined not to get caught up in a verbal battle. "Yes, that's probably true," he admitted.

Abigail, however, was not so inclined to avoid confrontation. "That would be foolish, Obie. You squandered the fortune she left you, and now you'd throw away this last part of what Annie's family worked so hard for? What's wrong with you?"

Laura came to his defense. "Mom, he's not selling it. And Cassie's the one in charge of it." Cassie must have told her that.

"Well, that's a good thing, at least. Cassie will know how to handle it, not give it away ... like Obie would."

Obie bit his lip and vowed to remain silent. He glanced around the group. Pinky was looking down at his plate. Ken's face was red. Angie had her hand on his arm. Cassie was flushed, too, and Obie knew she was about to reciprocate.

But it was Pinky who brought calm. "Abigail, get it through your head that they're not selling the property, so it's pointless to criticize Obie about it. Let's celebrate their good fortune."

"And we can all use the house for vacations," Cassie added.

Abigail's countenance relaxed somewhat. "Yes, I suppose you're right. I've never been to California."

"Speaking of wine, I noticed that this is a California brand," Pinky said as he held up his refilled glass. Obie was relieved that the subject had shifted.

Cassie cleared her throat. "I have a wine story to tell."

"By all means, let's hear it," Ken said.

"When I was seventeen, I came to this farm to visit Jacob, Obie's grandfather. Obie was in Italy. We sat in front of the big fireplace inside," she said, gesturing toward the restaurant's interior. "Jacob talked about wine being a symbol of love. He quoted Saint Paul's observation that love, among other virtues, is 'patient.' Winemaking takes patience ... is an act of love, Jacob told me. He said that Obie's grandmother, Prissy, was his vintage wine. Before I left, he asked me a question that made me cry." Obie saw a tear on her cheek. "See, it's happening again. Obie, you know what he asked me, don't you?"

"I do. He asked me a similar question well before I joined the Army. He wanted to know if *you* were *my* vintage wine. He must have asked you the same question about me."

"Exactly. In his mind, he had paired us up. Now, here we are together. Doesn't it strengthen one's belief in destiny? Jacob may have been something of a prophet."

Across the table, Obie saw Laura's pained expression. He glanced away.

Abigail was quick to jump on Cassie's statement. "Or something of a crackpot." Obie was unsure she meant the remark to be heard, but Ken's expression confirmed that he had heard.

Ken snapped, "Lady, you're talking about my father!"

Abigail paled. "Oh, I didn't mean ..."

Cassie leaned toward her mother and whispered loud enough for Obie to hear, "Mom, you should apologize."

"Yes, you should," Pinky added.

Abigail's mouth was set in a grim line. "Well, I'm not sorry. "The whole town knew what a strange man he was. He had weird beliefs. He wasn't Christian."

Ken rose to his feet and extended a hand to Angie. He said, "Come on, we're going home."

Pinky stood. "Wait, Ken!"

Abigail grabbed Pinky's arm. "Let him go."

"No!" Pinky's face matched his nickname. "Ken's my friend, and your behavior is deplorable. You'll apologize right now, or I'll leave with him."

"No, you won't. I won't let you."

Obie knew Pinky would never let that go by. He glanced at Cassie and Laura; they knew it, too.

Pinky unfolded his napkin and wiped his hands on it, perhaps as a symbolic gesture. He walked around the table and stood beside Ken. He told Abigail, "I'll go home and get some things I need. Someone else can drive you home. When you get there, I'll be gone. You've abused me and all the people around us for most of our marriage."

Her countenance revealed her unyielding nature. "Go then, you ungrateful man. "Go to your whore, and good riddance."

Laura stood. "Mom, Dad, don't do this!" She stopped. "Mom, what are you accusing Dad of? He wouldn't do anything like ..."

"You think not. He's been sleeping with Beth Clarington for years. Isn't that right, Pinky?"

Pinky did not answer her question, but was not finished. "This, tonight, is not by far the worst thing you've ever done. But it's the last straw for me." He turned and linked his arms with Ken's and Angie's.

Every face at the table held a look of disbelief. Cassie and Laura sat with their mouths open. Julie was crying, and Jacob kept saying, "Gran-pa." Obie was numb and at a loss for words. Abigail, though, was pitiful. She sobbed as though a lifetime of built-up expectations had fled, as if she knew there was no chance to get them back.

* * *

"We'll be gone about an hour," Cassie said as Obie walked toward them from the barnroom. Julie was helping Jacob into the Jeep.

"Where are you going?"

"To Mom and Dad's. I need to know that everything is still all right before we leave for our trip."

"Pinky's better, isn't he?"

"Dr. Osborn says he is. He called it one of those three-day bugs, but I'm not so sure. I sometimes see Dad put his hand to the area around his heart. It's been years since his heart attack, but he was told it was a weakness that could give him trouble."

"Cassie, you worry too much. Pinky's tough. He has to be tough to live with your mother."

"Point well taken." She breathed what sounded like a sigh of relief. "But I see that things have changed, even though he was only away from home for two days. Dad has mellowed, and Mom seems more caring. She's quieter. I'm glad he stood up to her. That has not always been the case. I must admit that I was dumbfounded by Mom's accusation at the Inn. So was Laura. I think Mom believed it. I am so happy that Beth straightened it out."

Obie had not been present when Pinky appeared at the Hunt house with Beth Clarington, but Cassie told him what had happened.

"It was comical," Cassie said. "You know Beth. She doesn't mince words. She took Dad by the hand and led him right up to Mom. She told Mom she was tired of him practically living in her cafe. She sat down beside Mom and let loose with an avalanche of advice. It's the first time in a long time I've seen Mom speechless. She listened as Beth told her that Dad was the finest man she had ever known, and the truest."

Obie held the car door open for Cassie and said, "So, it seems that Pinky only went to her for conversation?"

"Yes, Beth told Mom what Dad had said, that when talking to her, all he ever got was accusations and blame. I thought Mom would explode, but her eyes got all teary, and she choked up when she tried to say something. As Beth left, she told Dad that he was not to come back to the cafe alone unless he was still having the same problems, but if that were the case, she would greet him with open arms."

"Beth's a smart woman and a caring one, too, it seems," Obie said as he kissed Cassie on the cheek and closed the door. "But it's hard to believe your mother stood still for that."

"Isn't it? Maybe there's hope for Mom yet. She was attentive to Dad's needs when he came down with the fever the next day."

"Well, say hello to Pinky for me ... and to your mother, of course."

Cassie had just left when an automobile pulled into the driveway. Carl Enslow emerged with another man whom Obie did not recognize. Carl had retired at the end of June, replaced by the young minister, David Gillard. Obie was not favorably impressed by Gillard; he was disorganized and appeared overwhelmed. But maybe, given a little time, he would manage.

"We would like to speak with you, Obadiah," Carl said as he pumped Obie's hand. "This is the Rev. Cal Roberts."

Roberts' tone was apologetic. "The boss would have come himself, but a situation over in Vermont called him away. He asked me to come with Carl."

What was this about? Four years earlier, Carl had tried to persuade him to take an appointment in the conference, specifically at Stafford Rest Methodist. Now, a warning light flashed. He quickly switched it off, remembering that the position at Stafford Rest was filled. Nevertheless, he needed to head off any attempt to recruit him for something for which he had little aptitude or desire.

"Will this take long, Carl? I'm fairly busy."

"Not long, I hope. Can we sit down?"

"Yes, of course." Obie took them to the house and onto the enclosed porch. The two men sat on the glider, and Obie faced them from a rocking chair.

"You probably know why we're here," Carl said.

"No, not really."

"Maybe you haven't heard the news. David Gillard is quitting."

"Quitting? He was just appointed."

"Well, he's leaving. Said it's too much for him."

"This little church couldn't be that much of a problem."

Carl and Roberts exchanged glances. "Roberts said, "Carl tells me you're not on any administrative committees. You may have missed the undercurrents."

Carl spoke softly. "David says he can't stand the backbiting, undermining, and the pure hatred that some members seem to have for one another. He said he would stay if the problems were solvable, but he thinks the church is going 'down the drain.' Those were his exact words."

"So, he'll just walk away?"

Roberts said, "I don't think he's had enough experience to handle these kinds of situations. There's a theological divide in this congregation, traditional versus modern."

"That's not so unusual in churches with a wide age range like ours."

"This is extreme. Amos Adams' name came up repeatedly," Roberts said.

"I'm not surprised," Carl said. "Mr. Adams hounded me repeatedly during my pastorate here. Obie, you must have noticed how disruptive he is."

Remarks from family members and others had confirmed his own observations about Adams, but he had chosen not to make a judgment, at least not aloud. "Yeah, he makes things interesting," Obie said.

"He's an enigma," Carl said. "He wants a 'hellfire and damnation' church but fails, in my opinion, to 'walk humbly before God.' His followers are few but vocal. He does know his scripture. I have to hand him that."

Roberts brought the conversation back to Gillard. "David's stated dream was to bring the church into what he calls 'the modern world of Christianity.' But he's an idealist, so it was best to let him leave without a fight."

"So, why are you coming to me?" *Of course, it was obvious.* "I steer clear of church politics?"

Carl's tone was pleading. "They'll come back for me again unless they find someone. I'm retired. I won't come back again." Obie heard a sigh. "Won't you consider it, Obie?"

"No, Carl. I gave you my reasons four years ago."

"I remember well. You said that you're not worthy. Let me say again what I told you then. None of us is worthy. If worthiness were a prerequisite, no pulpit would be occupied."

"I have my work. I'm a writer. That's my ministry.

"Yes, I realize that's important. It reaches many. But you can also do good by putting yourself into a work that requires a more personal touch."

"We've examined your background," Roberts said. "You're fully qualified. The conference will have to certify you, but that will be expedited."

"Surely you can find someone to replace Gillard."

Roberts said, "Appointments have already been made for the coming year, so we have little room for shuffling. We might find someone to fill the position, but no one with your qualifications. And you grew up here. You know everyone. That's a great plus."

An image of Abigail's face flashed by. "Or it's likely a detriment."

"Won't you do it?" Carl said. "At least long enough to get us through this mess?"

"I'm flattered, I really am, but my answer is still, 'no.'"

Carl said, "David will preach his last sermon this Sunday. And immediately after the service, we'll have a general membership meeting. I hope you'll attend."

Obie wanted to end the discussion on a positive note. "I'm a member. I've been a member here since I was a teen. Of course, I'll attend."

CHAPTER SEVEN

August 1974

Cassie raised her coffee cup and declared, "If you attend that meeting, they'll try to talk you into this. Are you ready for that pressure?"

"As a member, it's my duty to attend. If our church is in trouble, we must all look for solutions."

Cassie's brow was raised in question as she said, "Something in Annie's letter stuck with me. She said you might be confused about your purpose in life. Obie, what if that's true?" You speak sometimes about having a calling as if it were a sacred thing. Maybe your destiny is to be a pastor right here in Stafford Rest?"

He sipped his own coffee and organized an answer before saying, "My belief in destiny goes only so far. Experience has convinced me that there are no simple answers to such questions. Sometimes, we have to …"

"Obie, let's not get into a philosophical debate about this. I'm your down-to-earth wife, and I've heard all your excuses for giving up the ministry. But stop and think a moment about your early life. Weren't you considering ministry at an early age, in your teens? And wasn't that confirmed by your mystic dream experience in a California vineyard? Don't early impressions indicate our purpose in life? I knew from age seven that I was to be a teacher."

The face of the Rev. Charles Lansing, his friend and mentor, flashed before him. Obie's Catholic mother, while dying of cancer and without easy access to a Catholic priest, had begged Pastor Charles to see that Obie was taught "the things of God."

Until he left Stafford Rest for the Army at seventeen, Obie felt a strong attachment to the church and to Charles. Sometimes, he sneaked into the vacant sanctuary and delivered make-believe sermons from the pulpit. He knew what he wanted then—*he had a dream.*

Two years of war and the belief that Laura had betrayed him nearly destroyed that dream. But it came alive again just before his senior year at Berkeley when the mystic vineyard experience led him to attend seminary.

After seminary, there was the Chaplain Corps and Korea, where he broke his vow to "never kill again," an act that placed ministry into some "hold" area of his brain. He eventually relented and took on the ministry of a large San Francisco church, a position that ended badly. His yo-yo career had taken him into uniform again, and after a bitter Vietnam experience, he vowed to return to writing and never again consider ordained ministry. But now, years later, a siren choir was warming up in the distance. Was Cassie, with her prodding, a part of that choir?

He must head it off. "Sweetheart, you told me before we were married that you could be a minister's wife, but you never really encouraged me in that direction. Now, it seems you're doing just that."

She reached across the table and touched his hand. "No, Obie, I want you to do whatever fulfills you. You've seemed content in your writing lifestyle. I merely asked the question because it needed asking. Annie was wise, in some ways."

"I've never been as happy as I've been these last four years. But that's largely because of you, Cassie, and Jacob and Julie, of course. The writing is a bonus."

"I know, Obie. And for you to bow to this request would require a leap of faith."

"Or a leap of foolishness."

Her face displayed serious intent. "I want you to know ... really know, that if you want to return to the ministry, I'll support you in every way I can."

"Being a minister's wife isn't easy. Annie found that out."

He felt her bristle as she took her hand away. "I'm not Annie!"

"Cassie, I know that. I simply want you to realize that it takes a special, dedicated person."

"And I am that dedicated person."

He relaxed and sat back. "Anyway, we won't have to think about it because I'll not let them talk me into it. You'll attend the meeting too, won't you?"

"I'll sit right beside you. But don't forget that we have our bags packed for a trip. At least, I do.

* * *

It was a hot and muggy Sunday morning. Obie and Julie were already in church, having left earlier. As Cassie, with Jacob in tow, exited the Jeep and started toward the front steps, she heard the somber tone of the Baptist church bell. Then, immediately, their own church bell began to ring. She stopped to listen. The village church bells always awakened some nostalgic chord in her heart; they were sounds she had known all her life, a constant.

"Bells," Jacob said as he tugged on her skirt.

"Yes, Honey, it's church bells."

At that moment, the larger and more resonant Episcopal bell began to ring. The three bells ringing simultaneously created a curious medley of harmony and discord.

"Bells," Jacob said again.

She had to smile. It was not the first time Jacob had expressed interest in the village bells.

But today was not about bells. She inhaled deeply; it would be a challenging day.

Young David Gillard's sermon was short and uninspired. Before the benediction, he announced that a "special meeting" would follow the service. No one seemed surprised since word had already circulated that he was leaving.

Two volunteers led the children away to one of the school rooms. Many adults left, but about thirty people remained in the sanctuary. Cassie watched their faces and tried to gauge their thinking, but stony countenances hid any concerns that might have kept them there for the meeting.

She knew more than Obie about what was happening within the church's administrative ranks. Abigail always held high positions in the church and was never shy about expressing her opinions to the family, even about things "off-limits." She wished she had told Obie more of what Abigail had said about the present situation.

Pinky, Abigail, and Laura remained in the second pew on the right, seats the Hunt family always occupied. Obie and Cassie sat well back. She was surprised to see Ernie Boswell in the gathering. Ernie, long a disaffected Episcopalian church member, now attended services at Stafford Rest Methodist. It was sporadic attendance, however.

Frances Gibbons sat on the other side of the sanctuary. She had been back in town for two years after teaching in an exclusive private school in Massachusetts. Frances, a stately, unmarried lady who lived alone, was the librarian in Stafford Rest's new library. When Cassie was growing up, the Gibbons family was the only Black family in town. Cassie became friends with Frances while both attended Syracuse University. She made a silent promise to renew that friendship.

Gillard went to sit beside Carl Enslow in a front pew. They whispered together a few minutes before Gillard rose to speak. "I know this isn't news to most of you. Some of you probably knew it even before I did." A low murmur, possibly statements of agreement, came from parts of the congregation.

Gillard continued, "I'm leaving Stafford Rest Methodist. I'm sorry things didn't work out. Sometimes, ministers and congregations don't fit together. That's the case here. We've had some contentious moments in our administration meetings, and we've all said things I'm sure we regret. I know that I do. I hope we can part as friends." He sat down.

Carl stood, but before he could speak, Roland Kilpatrick said, "Pastor Gillard, I wish you hadn't given up so soon. This church needs someone like you who'll lighten things up. We've become too serious. Why don't you reconsider?"

Sarah Hill clapped her approval, joined by several others. Sarah, a member of the Staff Parish Committee, was soft-spoken but never afraid to voice her opinion.

Amos Adams stood. "Look here," he said. "This preacher's doing the right thing by resigning. He doesn't fit in. He said it himself. He's what's called a progressive thinker, and we don't need that. We need somebody who will preach the true gospel like it was meant to be preached. Let him go, I say."

Sarah turned to face Amos. Her face was red. "You mean the gospel according to Amos, don't you?"

"Well, I know what's right and what's wrong."

Arthur Baines, another church officer, spoke up. "I agree with Amos on this. Some elements of this church don't value our traditions. Their Christianity is watered down so much that it's hard to tell just what they believe."

"Satan is at work in them," Glenda Smith said. Glenda was not a church officer but was elderly, and many respected her opinions.

There was a swell of moans and groans, whether of approval or disapproval, not always apparent. Obie leaned toward Cassie and whispered, "I never realized how bad it is."

"That's because you don't see this in regular church services."

Carl's voice rose above the din. "We're not here to decide whether Rev. Gillard stays or goes. That's settled. As of today, this church is without a pastor."

The noise did not subside until Abigail stood and turned to face the crowd. Cassie knew Abigail's faults as well as anyone, but she was always awed at her mother's considerable presence in such situations.

Abigail's voice was calm. "I know we have differences of opinion about many things, but that doesn't excuse rudeness to our former pastor or our departing one. I'm ashamed of you." She sat down. Cassie felt Obie's nudge. They smiled.

Carl's tone held authority. "I'm here because Rev. Gillard and your Staff Parish requested that I help you through this difficult time. I would be here anyway because I've been a part of this church for several years." He explained the difficulties of finding a new pastor at that time of the church year. "But we do have options," he said.

"And what are those?" Sarah Hill asked.

"Our district superintendent has outlined them in a letter. One is that we can continue without a pastor until one is found. We have lay people perfectly capable of conducting services."

Amos said, "And what about funerals, marriages, and such?"

"And communion," Glenda Smith added. "We'll need an ordained minister for that."

Carl said, "We'd have to rely on visiting pastors for funerals and weddings. I can still serve communion when I'm here, but Hallie and me want to be free of schedules, and we'll not always be available. "He looked toward Obie. "We do have an ordained minister in our congregation who can serve communion."

Cassie felt Obie sink beside her. People were looking at them. Many knew Obie's background, but she was sure some did not. Since his return to Stafford Rest, he had purposely kept a low profile. "Do you want to leave?" she whispered. He looked down and did not answer.

Carl continued, "Another possibility is that a part-time pastor will be appointed. Many churches share pastors. That's easier to arrange than finding a full-time pastor."

"That will never do," Roland Kilpatrick declared. "We've always had full-time preachers." For the first time that day, there was complete agreement.

Carl said, "There's someone else I'd like to hear from. Pinky Hunt, what words of wisdom might you have in this matter?"

Pinky struggled to his feet. To Cassie, he looked frail.

His voice was weak, but he had everyone's attention. "We have troubles. I can see that, as I'm sure we all can. Amos, you want a church like your grandfather's. The God you serve is strict; he doesn't let you have much leeway or get away with much. Sarah, you serve a compassionate and liberal God who forgives easily and even looks the other way at some of your transgressions."

Sarah chuckled. "Thank God for that."

"That's an oversimplification, surely, but you get my point. These differences we have aren't new. We've always had members who disagree on theological points. And we always will. Even the earliest churches had those disagreements. The difference in our church is that we've become polarized to an extreme in the past few years."

"What does that mean, Pinky?" Glenda Smith asked.

"There are more of us taking sides and fewer in the middle who can sympathize with both positions. What concerns me most is that such disagreements can cause splits that can't be reconciled. It happens in denominations, too."

"You mean like when we became 'United Methodists' five years ago?" Roland Kilpatrick said.

Pinky replied. "I'll defer that question to one of our pastors."

Carl said, "That was a merger of the Methodist Church and The Evangelical United Brethren Church, an entirely different thing. But any possibility of this congregation splitting bothers me greatly. We mustn't consider such a thing. We *will* find solutions to our problems. Let's pray often ... and together. But I'm sure that someone, somewhere, has the skills to help us find our way."

Obie stirred beside her. Carl had looked straight at him before sitting.

CHAPTER EIGHT

August 1974

Obie and Cassie headed for California, leaving Jacob and Julie in Angie and Ken's care. They were to be away for two weeks, mixing business with pleasure. In a phone conversation with Lyle Augustine, Obie assured him that they were on vacation and had no agenda except to learn the basics of the vineyard.

Cassie had learned that Lyle, his wife Matilda, and two of their three sons lived in the "Big House." Obie remembered that Annie visited Matilda the first time they went to the Napa House, but he had not known there was a business connection. He hoped that this visit would define the Augustines' responsibilities for the property, as well as their own. There was also the Connecticut law firm connection that needed clarification.

After a bumpy jet ride and a night in Oakland, they drove their rented car to the Napa Valley house, arriving before noon. It was a bright day with no clouds in sight.

Once their luggage was inside, Cassie sighed with contentment. "Obie, do we really own this gorgeous house in this beautiful country?"

"We do, my dear, and far more, it seems."

They had been invited to lunch with the Augustines after settling in, so they drove to the vineyard entrance on the main highway. Two unpretentious stone pillars framed the entranceway. On one pillar was a small hand-painted sign that announced, "O'Shane Vineyard." Its size was undoubtedly why he had not noticed it the numerous times he passed that way."

They motored up the dirt road between row after row of perfectly manicured vines toward the house on the hill. He pulled in beside a battered pickup truck. The house, probably half a century old, was huge and somewhat grandiose but retained the early Spanish style so prevalent in the valley.

A woman exited the front door onto the porch and descended the broad stone steps. She was well past middle age, thin, with deep lines etched into a sun-darkened face. She wore a brightly-colored apron. "Hi," she said. "We've expected you. I'm Matilda. Lyle and the boys are out in the vines but will soon return for lunch."

"Everything is so lovely," Cassie said as they were led through the living area to a large patio. Matilda invited them to sit in longue chairs, and she disappeared long enough to bring back a pitcher of lemonade and glasses.

"I hope you'll excuse me for a few minutes. I have food on the stove, and the menfolk will be here shortly."

"That's just fine," Obie said. "We'll enjoy this spot awhile."

"Can I help?" Cassie asked.

"Oh no, it's a one-person job at this point."

Obie settled back and closed his eyes. He heard Cassie sigh. "What is it?" he asked.

She waited several seconds before answering. "I'm sorry, Obie. A part of me is still afraid you might give all this away. Mom's wrong about many things, but she's right when she says you can be foolish about money matters. 'Foolish' is her word, though. 'Naive' says it better, I think. It's almost like you're afraid of wealth."

"I grew up poor. You know that. I don't dislike money. And poverty is not a condition humans should have to endure. My fear is letting money rule my life."

"Wealth is a good thing when managed correctly. Dad is conscious of that. His factory gave hope to many families, and he treated his employees well. Mom's real estate business contributes to the general welfare, as does the Inn. Yes, I know that for her, it's all about profits. But she knows how to make money, and beyond that, I won't elaborate."

"So, you want me to think like Pinky?"

"You could do worse."

"That's true." He was not surprised by Cassie's words; she was never shy in expressing her opinions, even when it laid blame at his feet. He placed his glass on the metal table between their chairs and took her hand. "Dear Cassie," he said, "Rest your mind. We'll keep the house. And you're in charge of inter-actions with the Augustines concerning the property."

"But we'll confer before making decisions, won't we?"

"Isn't that what we always do? We're in this together."

Matilda called them to the dining area. Four men were seated around one end of the longest table Obie had ever seen inside a residential structure. They all stood as Obie and Cassie approached. The oldest of the four, with white hair stark against a deeply lined and tanned face, stood and reached across to shake Obie's hand. "I'm Lyle," he said. His hand was callused, as were the hands of his sons as he introduced them.

From oldest to youngest were Kent, about thirty, Neal, in his early twenties, and Joel, a late teen. Neal and Joel still lived with their parents, but Kent explained that he and his wife and two-year-old daughter lived in a smaller house hidden behind one of the hills.

"Yet another house," Cassie said.

Lyle smiled. "I look forward to discussing the plans for your property, Mr. Gainsworthy."

"Lyle, call me Obie. Cassie and I are simple folk."

"All right, although I doubt that last statement. We've learned a bit from Mr. Lawrence, your lawyer. He spoke of your accomplishments, and I've made a point to read a couple of your books."

"I read one," Matilda said shyly.

The fare that Matilda put on the table was simple but ap-pealing. There were two large casseroles, one containing beef and vegetables. The other had a white sauce over asparagus and pasta; the pasta looked homemade. There was also a salad with various greens soaked in oil and vinegar. Two loaves of bread, still warm from the oven, one white and one dark, lay on a cut-ting board next to a bowl of butter. Two uncut pies, which Ma-tilda said were peach and apple, sat within her reach. It was more like dinner than the light lunches to which Obie and Cas-sie were accustomed. These were working people.

"Dig in," Matilda said after Lyle finished a short prayer.

Lyle said, "I forgot. You're a minister. I should have let you say grace."

"Oh, no, that's all right. I'm no longer a minister."

"He still has ministry in his blood," Cassie stated.

Lyle looked confused, but Obie did not enlighten him. All in good time. The two younger brothers exchanged good-natured banter throughout the meal, but business seemed off-limits for the present. Cassie was having a private conversation with Matilda about recipes.

As they ate, Obie studied the men. They were much younger than their parents, probably due to a late family start. They all appeared strong, with windblown hair and muscled arms that testified to the rigors of their occupation; he remembered his own demanding work in the Russian River Valley vineyard. Observing these men made him feel guilty for neglecting his body over the past few years. Kent looked the most genteel of this group; he sometimes looked away as though listening.

When Matilda, with Cassie's help, had cleared away the dishes, Lyle pushed back his chair, crossed his arms, and said, "Obie, what will you and Cassie do with your property? We'll help with it in any way you want."

Cassie and Matilda had just returned to the table. Cassie heard the question and said, "We'll add to what we call our 'Napa House' to make room for all our families when they come out here with us."

"Good idea. I supervised the building of that house," Lyle said. "Annie's father wanted it built for easy expansion. I'll help if you wish me to." He hesitated. "But I was asking about the vineyard too, and this house." For the first time, Obie saw worry lines on Lyle's forehead. "We need to know your plans so we can plan our own course."

They had not made it clear enough; this family must have worried for weeks, maybe years. He said, "Lyle, we want you to stay right here, you and all your family, if that's what you want. Cassie and I have our own lives back East. You're the ones who know how to run the vineyard. This is your home as long as you want."

He heard Matilda expel what he guessed was a sigh of relief. "We'll give you a house tour later," she said.

"So, you have no plans to sell?" Lyle said.

"No." Lyle's wrinkled forehead smoothed. Obie said, "We like the idea of having it, though."

"I still miss Annie," Matilda said. "I didn't see her in person much in later years, but we talked on the phone, and she came to see me when she was here." She looked at Cassie. I hope I'm not ..."

"No, it's all right. I'm sure Annie and I would have been friends had I known her."

Lyle said, "I'm amazed that Annie kept it from you that she had deeded it to you."

"Yes, it did come as a surprise."

"This all belonged to Annie's father and his father before that. Her grandfather purchased it before probation ended. The land was much cheaper then, and things picked up after that." Lyle paused a moment. "I should have gotten in touch with you personally instead of doing everything through the lawyer."

"No, I should have contacted you. You can meet us at the house tomorrow to review what we want done there. We will also decide how much the lawyers will be involved."

Lyle's voice was soft as he said, "I expect you'll want to re-negotiate our salaries. Annie was rather generous in that regard."

"Looking at the condition of this place, I can see that you've earned your salaries. If you're satisfied with that arrangement, we can leave it alone."

"Yes, more than satisfied. And this house has tons of room, should you want to use it for an overflow. We've sealed off one whole section that we don't use. It has three bedrooms, a dining room, and a kitchen. We'll open it up."

"No, you don't need to do that," Obie said. "The addition to the other house will take care of our family needs."

"Matilda and I can meet with you tomorrow morning if that's okay with you."

"We'll serve lunch this time," Cassie said.

"We can also map out a schedule for our time here," Obie said. "We'll be free of jet lag by the day after tomorrow. That's when we want to start following you and your sons around the place to see how things run ... how you keep it so beautiful."

"So, you have no knowledge of vineyard culture?"

"Only a little." He briefly explained his summer vineyard job in the Russian River Valley.

"I have none," Cassie said, then added, "Nor of winemaking."

Lyle was quick to respond. "We don't make wine here. We're not that big an operation, although when Mr. O'Shane, the original owner, tore down the old house and built this one, he left the wine cellars intact. Producing wine isn't impossible, but the startup is costly. The grapes we grow go to market. We have good vines with desirable produce for wineries in the valley. We also experiment with new varieties. We think California wines will someday equal French wines."

Without enough knowledge to comment about wines, Obie said, "We simply want to learn something about how you do it all."

Kent had turned to his mother. "I expected to see Alicia. Is she awake?"

"It's time for her to get up from her nap," Matilda said. "I'll go get her." She turned to Obie and Cassie. "Kent's wife, Cara, is a teacher, and she teaches a summer class. Alicia is two years old. I watch her during the day."

Cassie said, "Our son is also two. We'll bring him the next time we come."

Matilda went up the stairs and soon returned with the little girl, who looked sleepy. Dark curls bounced up and down as she walked. When she saw the visitors, she clung to her grandmother's leg. Kent picked her up.

"She's adorable," Cassie said. "Jacob would have a good time playing with her."

"We can arrange that," Matilda said.

Obie felt a growing attraction to this family, as though real friendships had begun. As Kent held Alicia on his lap, he asked numerous questions about Stafford Rest and the Adirondacks. "It's of great interest to me," he said. "Not that I don't love it here, but your mountains are something I'd like to see."

"You're welcome to come and visit," Cassie said. "We have lots of room. You can all come. My parents' house can handle any overflow."

"We might take you up on that," Lyle said. "It'd have to be off-season, though. The vineyard requires a lot of care. Kent and Cara could go most anytime when she's not teaching." He hesitated as though an explanation were needed. "Kent's the organized one in the family. He takes care of the books and a great deal of the organization."

"I'm getting a law degree, but I have a way to go on that," Kent said.

Lyle said, "Me and the other boys do the heavy-lifting part." He laughed. Kent smiled but did not comment.

Matilda said, "Now, let's tour the house. I'm sure you want to see all the nooks and crannies."

"Oh, yes. I've been waiting," Cassie said.

That evening, Obie and Cassie drove to Napa for a quiet outdoor dinner at an Augustine-recommended restaurant. That set the romantic mood that lasted until well after they reached the serenity of their house on the vineyard's edge. Obie basked in the knowledge that their love had grown during the years of their marriage. Cassie's contented sighs showed that she sensed it, too.

* * *

The meeting the following day went well, and Obie felt good about leaving the construction and upkeep details in the Augustines' capable hands. Before leaving, Lyle pulled out a map, which he unfolded and placed on the kitchen table. "This is how things are laid out here," he said. This house, O'Shane Vineyard, everything. You can keep it. Study it and orient yourselves for when we move around the grounds tomorrow. "

The next three days were spent exploring the vineyard, barns, buildings, empty wine cellars, and machinery necessary for the successful operation of the business. The rows of carefully cultivated vines rolled mainly over two hills, but it seemed more like three because of a deep cut in one hill. Obie saw that Cassie was in a heaven of her own: Every new step elicited a question: "Are the distances between the vines always the same?

Where do you get new vines? How long does a vine last? How do you get the extra help you need during busy times?" Lyle was patient, pausing to let her take notes. Obie had questions, too, but Cassie took the lead.

After three days, Cassie and Obie's faces were sunburned, even after wearing the hats Matilda provided. However, it felt good, like a primal need was fulfilled, somewhat like satisfaction following a session in his garden on Blackberry Hill. They enjoyed a two-day break, exploring the area and dining out.

One day, Lyle and Kent came to the house even before the dew dried on the grass. They carried several large hard-backed volumes and a cardboard box full of notebooks. "You want to see the books, don't you?" Lyle said.

"Yes," Cassie said as she quickly cleared the dining room table. "We certainly do."

Lyle said, "I'll leave it to Kent, then. He has all the details."

Kent was modest. "I do the best I can as accurately as possible, but some variables in the operation may get lost in the recording, so if you don't understand something, I'll explain it."

Cassie said, "We don't need to know every jot and tittle. Do you have an accountant?"

"We've never thought we needed one," Lyle said. "I guess we waited for you to request an accounting."

"That's my fault," Obie said as he glanced at Cassie. "I neglected my duty."

Cassie said, "We'll shelve that for now, but we can discuss it later. Right now, please help us understand the major expenses and profits so we can discuss any changes we should make."

Kent said, "You understand that this is a relatively small operation compared to most in this valley?"

"We're aware," Obie said.

The following six hours, with only a short lunch break, were spent conducting an item-by-item survey of O'Shane Vineyard's workings. There were routine matters, but there were also many surprises in the variety of expenses and assets and how they were handled. There were taxes, machine repair, and upkeep. Extra workers were hired each year for pruning and picking, which required feeding and housing. They had not considered such details, and Obie now understood better why the vineyard did little more than hold its own.

After the Augustine men left that afternoon, they sat blurry-eyed on the veranda. Cassie said, "Thirty thousand profit last year is dismal. They're doing their best, but aren't there ways to improve on that?"

Was he seeing a new side to Cassie? "Sweetheart, they know this business. It's what they do. Anyway, the vineyard supports a large family and gives us a windfall. What's wrong with that?"

"Nothing, I guess, but it seems like a challenge. I think this vineyard can do better."

He smiled. "I guess that's the Hunt family's way of looking at it."

Secretly, he hoped that O'Shane Vineyard had not become Cassie's obsession, but he was determined not to worry about it.

During the rest of their stay, they explored the region and visited Napa, Petaluma, Nevada City, and other small towns and villages with their quaint little shops and stores. They navigated dusty back roads through hills whose isolation threatened to swallow them. They even ventured into more populated places around Sacramento and Santa Rosa. Before leaving, they met one last time with the Augustines. Cara was there; she and Cassie, being teachers, bonded at once.

They allowed a day in Berkeley to visit with Hershel and Virginia Silverman. The couple was overjoyed at their visit and begged them to extend it. Obie promised they would stay longer on their next visit to the area.

At the airport, while they waited to board their airplane, Cassie squeezed his hand. "Aren't you glad I talked you into coming?"

"It's the event of the year," he said, smiling.

"So far."

CHAPTER NINE

September 1974

As Obie drove up Lake Road to pick up Laura for the trip to Saratoga Springs, he wanted to say something to comfort Cassie. "Pinky is strong. He can beat this, but we must face the fact that it's serious."

Cassie had voiced her fears earlier that morning, and he downplayed her concern. Now, he eased into the truth—Pinky Hunt was probably dying.

Abigail was already at the hospital; she had been there all night. Her telephone call came before daylight. Since being admitted two days previously, Pinky's condition had deteriorated, and she wanted them to come. Her distress was evident.

On arrival in Saratoga, Obie saw that Abigail's concern was justified. Pinky lay pale against his pillow with an oxygen tube in his nostrils and an intravenous tube dripping liquid into his veins. He struggled to breathe, creating a raspy sound they heard even before they entered the hospital room. "Pneumonia," the doctor told them.

They took turns sitting with Pinky. Worry clouded the Hunt women's eyes. Cassie and Laura wanted Abigail to go home and rest, but their words had no effect. Laura cried silently while Cassie struggled to stay composed. Obie cornered the doctor away from the others and heard his opinion that Pinky would probably not last another night.

Late that afternoon, Obie went outside alone and sat on a bench by a walkway. The mid-September day was warm, and his thoughts were reflective. Pinky was not only his father-in-law but a significant part of his life. His mother worked for the Hunts even before his birth; his earliest memories were in and around that household.

During Obie's early teen years, after Vi's death and while

he struggled to survive, Pinky made light work available for him at his factory. As the Love Fund administrator, he saw that Obie received help through high school. And the help did not end there; at Pinky's instigation, checks went to Obie while he was at Berkeley and in seminary. Pinky always believed in him. He was consistent in his friendship, not only with Obie but also with Ken.

Laura soon came and sat beside him. "Dad's dying, isn't he?"

"I'm afraid so."

Neither spoke as they watched a squirrel scurry around in the leaves near their bench looking for morsels that would add fat to help it through a cold winter. *Life goes on.* That fact, divorced from sentimentality, helped him accept a future without Pinky Hunt. Obie took Laura's hand and held it for a long time.

* * *

Laura waited at a table in a corner of the coffee shop. Only one other customer was in the small establishment, and he sat several tables away. Her last time in this restaurant was with Cassie before either returned to Stafford Rest to live; they had been patching up their latest quarrel over whether Obie was guilty of some undisclosed misdeed.

That issue was resolved, of course; Laura and Obie's hostility toward each other had finally ended after Cassie discovered their stolen wartime letters. Nevertheless, Laura experienced difficult months after that revelation; to her bewilderment, she still had strong feelings for Obie. She had hoped that he might feel the same. After all, they shared so much; *Dan was their son.*

Such hopes were dashed when Obie told her that he loved Cassie and was marrying her. If it were anyone but her sister, she would have fought for him, for she was sure that beneath the surface of his insufferable reserve, he still loved her. She would have won him back had she not stepped aside for Cassie. Still—

Now, she waited in the coffee shop to see what her ex-husband wanted. Dr. Ben Williamson had surprised her by attending the funeral. When visiting Stafford Rest, he was never close to Pinky and spent most of his time with his father. After the elder Dr. Williamson's death, his visits became infrequent. *How had he even known of her father's death?*

Ben had attended the church service, sitting a few rows behind the Hunt pew, and then drove to the Lake Road Cemetery in the funeral procession. She did not speak to him or acknowledge his presence during the graveside service except for a distant nod.

Then, after she helped her mother into Obie's car for the ride home, Ben fell into step beside her as they walked to their vehicles. When he tried to take her hand, she pulled it away. He said, "Meet me at four in that coffee shop on Main."

She had not answered and initially considered ignoring his request, but then decided to meet with him, if only to satisfy her curiosity. He was late, which did not surprise her, for that was one of his many faults.

She did not keep the harsh edge from her voice. "What do you want, Ben?"

"Thanks for agreeing to talk to me, Laura. I wasn't sure you would be here." He sat.

"What is it you want?"

He studied the tabletop, and his finger moved in little circles on the surface. "I want you to listen to me, Laura. We have something important to discuss."

"Like what? Like you finally sent me what you owed me?"

"I'm truly sorry about that. I'm at fault, but we should mend our grievances."

"To what end?"

"Our lives from this point on depend on it."

"What are you getting at? Are you thinking that we have a future together? Not in this universe."

"Of course we do. We're man and wife."

What nerve. "I'm not your wife. We're divorced, Ben. Three years now. You have Simone. Haven't you married her?"

"I'm no longer with Simone L'Amour," he said while bowing his head.

"Am I supposed to be impressed by that?"

"I was simply stating a fact. I still consider you my wife. I know that's a little old-fashioned of me, but I can't help it."

"Well, get over it. I have a new life here. You don't seriously expect us to get back together, do you?"

He enclosed her hands in his before she could draw them away. Despite herself, she studied his beautiful hands. *Surgeon's hands. Hands that healed.*

"I have hope," he said. "Laura, please let me make my plea."

She would not listen; too much ill will had passed between them. It began almost immediately after their marriage: his controlling ways, excessive social demands, and using her as a showcase to advance his practice in the lucrative Boston society. She had fought to gain enough independence to continue her education and make routine household decisions. Now, she felt compelled to make another stand. *She would leave.* She sat still.

"Laura," he said, "things have changed. I've changed. I want you to believe that."

"Why should I? You left me. Remember? Simone was more important to you than either Dan or I." She hesitated. "What happened between you, anyway? Why did you break up? Did you find someone else? Did she?"

"No, nothing like that. She accused me of still being in love with you. When I didn't deny it, she was furious and threatened to leave. I saw that as a way out and gave her my blessing. She's gone, Laura. She won't be back."

"Well, that affects me in no way. You and I have gone our separate ways. I want it to stay like that."

He squeezed her hands tighter. "And I want us reconciled, like it used to be."

"No way! Anyway, was it ever that good?"

"Of course it was, despite our downtimes. Losing our infant son devastated us, but we survived that."

"Barely. And it still hurts. Do you realize that Benjamin would be twenty-eight now?" Her tears welled. His grip on her hands lessened, and she withdrew them.

They were silent until Ben said, "I think you eventually

learned to love me. That's what I hoped for when we married, and I think it became a reality. Don't you think so?"

There was indeed some truth in what he said. Before Dan's birth, she was determined to leave Ben, but then accepted her situation, gradually forgetting Obie and learning to like her life in Boston. There were good years as Ben's practice grew, and he allowed her more freedom. "Love" was just a word, but she supposed she had experienced something of it. Eventually, he became abusive to her and Dan, not physically, but in speech and temperament. Even if there was once love, she was not about to admit it.

"There were too many bad times. I can't forget those."

"I did treat you badly sometimes, didn't I?"

"You did."

"I'm sorry, Laura. That could never happen again."

"No, it won't. That was another lifetime."

After a moment's silence, Ben said, "Are you still in love with your old boyfriend? What's his name … Obie?"

"He's married to my sister. They have a child."

"My question was, 'Are you still in love with him?'"

"Even if I were, it's a hopeless situation." She stopped. "You're still jealous, aren't you? You have no right to be."

Ben had a strange look in his eyes; she was startled to see sadness there. "I want to remind you of something, Laura," he said, drawing out the words as if to give himself more time to compose his thoughts, "and I hope you won't take offense, but I loved you enough to rescue you and your unborn child from what was a bad situation at that time and place. I kept our little secret and raised Dan as my son. I gave him my name, which he's kept, even after he learned the truth."

"What truth is that?"

"I visited Dan and Ly Yen in Baltimore about a month ago."

She was genuinely surprised. "Really?"

"Dan and I had a long talk. We straightened out some issues between us."

"So, he told you that he …"

"That he knows I'm not his natural father? Yes, he did. He

told me about the circumstances that brought it into the open, all about the letters Abigail had waylaid. And that you and Obie avoided each other all those years without reason?"

"I didn't know he knew about the letters, and what Mom did."

"He found out, somehow. Anyway, our discussion broke a logjam of emotions for us. I wish you had let me tell him years ago. We might have avoided some of our difficulties."

"I was ashamed to have him know … and have others know."

"We wouldn't have had to let anyone else know. But Dan should have known."

"Well, it's pretty much an open secret since Ly Len named her children after Obie and me. She told a restaurant full of people that she had named them 'after their grandparents.' Nobody said anything then, but people can put two and two together."

Ben smiled. "Abigail must have been furious."

"Family honor, you know. But she's come around in recent times. She's learned to love her great-grandchildren and maybe even to like Ly Yen."

"How could she not? But, back to the topic at hand. I'm a changed man, and I live with the hope that you can accept that."

"I don't know, Ben." She collected her thoughts while hearing the noise of the window air conditioner in the background. "You may well have changed, but there's something you must accept. We're not getting back together. Not now, not ever. I appreciate what you did for us then, and I always will, but it's a part of our lives that's in the past. I need to get beyond it. You do, too."

"I haven't finished telling you what's going on," he said. "It will change our lives ... and I mean that."

She reinforced her resolve not to change anything about her new life in the Adirondacks but said, "I'm listening."

"I'm coming to Stafford Rest to live."

"What!"

"I've been in touch with Dr. Osborn. He's retiring, and I'm

taking over his practice. I'll be moved here in less than six months."

"Ben, are you out of your mind? You're a successful surgeon with a wonderful practice in Boston. Why on earth would you give that up to come to this little mountain village?"

"Didn't I tell you that I've changed? That's part of it. I'm tired to death of my life there, of the rat race and the eternal pressure to please important people. I'm selling out to Ted Emmons, my former partner. I remember the summers I spent here with Dad. There was work, a lot of it, but rewarding work for him. He served people he would see again, people who were his friends. I long for that kind of life for myself. I'm coming, regardless, but I have hoped you'd be a part of it, Laura. I'm still hoping."

She paused a moment to think. "If you're speaking of us being friends, of course we can be. However, it's a huge change for you. I can't imagine how you'll manage it."

"Dan will help me."

"How?"

"We've had a productive discussion. I'll finance the rest of his medical schooling. I've already helped him through the first years."

"I didn't know that, and I'm not sure he did."

"I funneled help in ways he wouldn't suspect. Now, I'll give him even greater support, which he has said he'll accept. After he finishes his residency requirements, he'll join me in this practice. We'll add to the present office on Main Street to make it a much-needed clinic. It will all be in place within three or four years. We've agreed on it. That's our plan, and I think it's a good one."

"You've agreed on it?"

"Yes, but I wouldn't hold him to it. He likes the idea, though. I think he'll come."

Laura was speechless. It seemed like a good plan, and best of all, it answered a question that had bothered her since her son left Stafford Rest: Dan would not go to some distant city to practice his profession. He would come home. Obie had said he would, and it seemed he was right.

Nevertheless, something bothersome crept into her memory. The first time Ben told her that he loved her was in a rainstorm before she knew of her pregnancy. After she had side-stepped his advances, he informed her that he had "one great quality." When he made up his mind, he never gave up until he achieved his goal. She could not remember a time when he had failed in that endeavor.

CHAPTER TEN

September–October 1974

On the Sunday after Pinky's funeral, Obie was ready to sit in a pew near the back of the sanctuary, but Cassie said, "Let's join Mom and Laura."

He had thought Abigail might not be pleased, but she flashed a "half-smile" before sliding over to make room.

Today, a week later, that seating arrangement appeared to be permanent. Obie sat by the middle aisle, enabling him to go up front later. He had consented to the Worship Committee's request to serve Holy Communion.

It had been a long time since he had performed the sacrament, so he read and reread the order from the hymnal to fix in his mind what he had once recited flawlessly. During the week, he prepared himself mentally through prayer and meditation. Communion was sacred for him, perhaps made more so by his youthful years at Catholic services with his mother.

The committee members tried to get him to conduct the whole service, but he declined. This was a one-time event; it was simply his duty as a church member to help them through a difficult period. Other members had volunteered for various parts of the service. Roland Kilpatrick, a longtime member, a family man, and a student of the Bible, was preaching. It all went well. Roland's sermon was short but grounded in appropriate scripture.

Despite his reluctance to admit it, Obie's relationship with Stafford Rest United Methodist had changed; he had been noticed and was unsure whether that was good or bad. But fixing this church's problems was not something he was going to think about.

After the service, Obie gathered his communion essentials and sought a quick exit. Roland stopped him on the church steps and wrung his hand. "Obie, we need you. I know you've been asked, and I know you've refused, but many of us hope you'll reconsider."

Abigail stood beside her daughters and the children, appearing impatient. They had planned a Sunday luncheon together at the Inn, a ritual that seemed destined to become a tradition. "We're late," Abigail said.

Not answering Roland would be impolite. "That's not likely. You can do much better than me. Besides, I have other interests that take up all my time."

"I heard about you coming into that big property in California," Roland said. "A vineyard, isn't it? Are you and Cassie planning to move there? Some folks think that's why you won't consent to becoming our pastor."

"No, that's not it at all, Roland. We plan to stay right here for the rest of our lives."

Sarah Hill came up behind Roland. Her voice was soft but clear, a testimony to her gentle spirit. "I remember you when you were a little boy," she said. "That was when Pastor Charles was here. I saw how you loved our church and listened to everything he said. You were meant to be a pastor, Obie. God brought you back to Stafford Rest for that specific purpose ... to be our pastor."

Caught off guard by her words, he was momentarily speechless but quickly recovered. "Mrs. Hill, I appreciate your confidence in me, but I've been a pastor, and it didn't work out. I'm a writer. If God has put me here for a purpose, I'm convinced it's for that."

"But maybe you're wrong," Roland said. "Maybe it's God's will that you've been sent to us."

"Yes," Sarah said, "I believe you're wrong."

Unsure how to answer, he excused himself and quickly went to where his family awaited.

* * *

The conversation at lunch covered several topics, including speculation about how soon Ben Williamson's practice would be in place; he had revisited Stafford Rest last week to consult with Dr. Osborn.

"Did Ben come to see you again?" Cassie asked Laura.

"He did, but I've discouraged him. He won't try that again." She did not sound convincing.

"You should see him," Abigail said. "I believe he really has changed."

"Why do you think that?" Laura said. "Have you talked to him?"

"Well, no. I'm only going by what you've told us."

Laura looked annoyed. "If he's changed, I'm glad for it, but I'll not encourage him to think there's any hope of us ever getting back together."

"You should give that some more thought," Abigail said.

"Never!"

Obie tried to gauge the genuineness of the denial. Cassie looked uncertain, too. Laura was always a mystery.

Cassie said, "Mom, Laura needs to make her own decisions. It's not any of our business."

"Thank you, Cassie," Laura said.

The rest of the meal was relatively quiet, but when Pinky was mentioned, Abigail wiped away tears. As they got ready to leave, she was more composed. She said, "Laura, you take Cassie and the children home? I need to talk to Obie alone."

He was surprised. His mother-in-law usually went out of her way to avoid speaking to him. A moment of apprehension came as he remembered the long-ago day she caught him and Laura in the barnroom. Fear had gripped him then, putting him entirely at her mercy. He fought down that ghost memory. *He would never again be intimidated by Abigail.* Nonetheless, he wondered what would prompt her to want a private conversation. Cassie's eyes signaled the same question.

"It's okay, sweetheart. I'll be along later," he said.

When he and Abigail were alone, she ordered their coffee cups refilled, and they moved to a smaller table beside a big window that overlooked the lake. It was a cool day, and a brisk breeze stirred the water.

He waited. For a woman who was usually free with speech,

she was slow to state her mind. Finally, she said, "Obie, I want us to talk about the pastorate at Stafford Rest Methodist."

"Don't worry, Abigail. I'm not considering it."

She studied his face for a moment. "You misunderstand me, Obie. I think you should become our pastor."

If a list of surprises in his life existed, this would be near the top. He muttered, "Why?"

"There's no one else to do it."

There was mixed emotion at being a consolation prize. "Of course, there are others, Abigail. The conference has sent you three good candidates, and your Staff Parish has rejected all three. Carl told me that the superintendent has threatened to override your decisions and appoint someone of his choosing. You are aware of that, aren't you?"

"Yes, I know. And that's why I ... we feel such a sense of urgency."

"Well, I'm not available."

She set her cup down and leaned forward. "I'm going to be brutally frank."

"When have you ever been anything else, Abigail?" he said, even knowing he should not give voice to that truth.

She ignored the remark. "I admit that I've never considered you suitable for the ministry. That stems from our personal history. But you have other useful qualities. Our church is in a precarious position right now. There are theological differences, and we have some money problems. Our membership has seriously declined. You've had experience running companies and have been involved in various other organizations. I still fear your financial decisions, but you might have enough skill to pull us through our present crisis."

"Yes, I might manage enough skill for that," he said, applying a touch of sarcasm. "But then what?"

"I suppose you could go back and do whatever you're doing now."

"I'm writing. That's what I do. I'm a writer."

"Yes, you could go back to writing."

"Abigail, this is unusual, asking me to take on responsibilities in matters so important to you. What's brought on this change?"

She hesitated before saying, "We've buried the hatchet, haven't we, Obie? You told me you've forgiven any hurt I may have caused you."

"And you hurt Laura, too." He would not let her forget that. "But she's forgiven you, and so have I. Forgiveness is necessary."

"I know. I've forgiven you, too." She paused. "But you weren't blameless, you know." *So much for forgiveness.*

"Pinky asked you to talk to me, didn't he?"

Her eyes were still red. "Yes, we had a conversation not long before he died."

"Abigail, I also had a conversation with Pinky." He had not told anyone, not even Cassie, about an early morning visit with Pinky a few days before his death, a discussion Pinky requested.

"Did he ask you to take the job?"

"He asked me to consider it; that's all." It was the truth. Pinky had talked mostly about his love for Abigail and his daughters, as well as his wish for Obie to look after them.

"He made me promise to make this plea to you," Abigail said. "I'm doing this to honor his wishes. He thought the world of you, Obie. He always has. You should honor his wishes. Please think about it."

Had she actually said "Please?" There came a sober moment, a few seconds when moral responsibility and desire were at great odds. He decided to act in self-preservation. "Abigail, I'll pass on this."

* * *

A letter from Anthony Gladstone came the week following Obie's conversation with Abigail. Tony had been Obie's half-blind assistant in Korea. Fearful for his own life on arrival, he went on to perform an act of bravery that helped Obie escape a lethal battlefield situation. Their correspondence since had been erratic, but the soldier-turned-minister reentered Obie's life at crucial times. He had recommended Obie to his church official cousin for the San Francisco pastorate. Tony, who had moved up in the Methodist hierarchy, had tried to persuade Obie to stay in the ministry.

The letter, dated October 2, 1974, filled in recent details of Tony's life; he had abandoned ambitions for a higher church office and "humbled" himself by taking on the pastorate of a small Kansas church in a "backwoods" location. "A step back in ambition and a step up in service," he wrote.

The rest of the letter caused Obie to reflect:

> *I have not written for some time, but that does not mean you have not been on my mind. I pray for you often, and of late, every day. One reason for that is my correspondence with Carl Enslow, your former pastor at the Stafford Rest United Methodist Church. Carl believes you could easily be appointed to Stafford Rest or elsewhere in your conference if you want to. I know what you are thinking at this point: You are bracing for my pitch for you to reenter pastoral ministry. I know you will resist, for you have told me often how you feel about it. And you have given me several reasons for your exit, the main one being what you call your "unworthiness."*
>
> *If only for the absurdity of that excuse, I <u>will continue</u> to make pitches for your return. So, I repeat something I have said to you before and something I am sure you have heard from Carl: <u>We are all unworthy.</u>*
>
> *I want to add one last thought about that, Obadiah. Your awareness of being "unworthy" may be your greatest strength. I think we have too many Christian leaders in all denominations who believe too much in their own goodness. That is a form of arrogance. I have known you since we were together in Korea. You were a caring and hardworking chaplain, and I was a scared young private trying to keep up with you. My knowledge of you then, and what I have learned from your friends and your writing, convinces me that "arrogant" is not something you will ever be.*

Cassie came into the barnroom just as he finished reading. He showed her the letter. She read it slowly, then reread it while he waited. She placed the letter on the table and went to hug him. They stood together like that a long time before she said,

"You're considering it, aren't you?""

"I want to think on it some more. It's a hard thing to contemplate."

"Whatever you decide, Obie, I'm with you ... all the way."

CHAPTER ELEVEN

October–December 1974

From the barnroom door, Obie watched Carl Enslow emerge from his automobile and rest a moment before standing. As he walked toward Obie, he leaned heavily on his cane and dodged puddles left by the cold October rain.

"It's good to see you, Rev. Enslow," Obie said as he held out his hand."

"It's 'Carl' to you, Obie. We're beyond such formality."

They entered the barnroom where Obie directed the retired minister to the rocker. Carl said, "You've been painting. I smell the paint, and I see it on your apron."

"I managed to grab some time for it," Obie said as he sat in the chair opposite the rocker. "Carl, are you here just to visit, or is it something else?"

"I enjoy our conversations, but I do have an agenda."

"I'm not surprised." Obie forced a smile. *There was no question about why he was there.*

Carl sat up straighter in the rocker. "Look, Obie. I know how you feel about joining the conference. You've told me enough times, but I'm here today to persuade you differently."

"Then you've made a pointless trip." Obie was immediately sorry for the caustic words. "Have you and Abigail colluded? She approached me about this last week."

"No, I haven't talked to her, not lately."

When Carl tried, with some difficulty, to rise from the low rocker, Obie assisted him. The older man shuffled over to the easel that held Obie's wet painting. "You're an excellent painter," he said, "and you're gifted in other ways, too."

"Thanks for the compliment, Carl, but I've made up my mind about this. I have other irons in the fire. It would disrupt our lives. Anyway, the job may be beyond me."

Carl turned to face him. His forehead was creased. "Is this

about your worthiness excuse? Some sin you can't let go of? That's nonsense. Put that behind you, accept forgiveness, and move on."

"I have accepted forgiveness."

Carl's voice rose. "Then act like it. Holding on to it and using that as an excuse not to do your duty is a worse sin. And calling it a 'job?' Is that all it means to you?" He pointed an accusing finger. "You're a spoiled brat!"

"What?" Obie had trouble making Carl's words register.

"You heard me." There was firmness in the tone that reminded Obie of times when, as a youngster, he was disciplined by his father.

Carl was not finished. "You're selfish, Obie. I'm sorry for telling you that, but it seems to have fallen to me to set you straight."

Obie was stunned. He studied Carl's face to see if the admonishment was in jest, but saw only earnestness.

Anger rose into his throat. This man, whom he had regarded as a mentor, was accusing him of some act of selfishness. *No way.* His voice felt weak. "I have no idea what you're talking about."

"You're pampered, Obie. Maybe it's because of your personal history, war record, or your writing, but the fact is that you've been gifted with a free ticket on a railway to Easy Street. And you've accepted that without even questioning it."

"I've never been on Easy Street, Carl. Do you think serving as a chaplain in a war zone is easy? I served God as I was called to do, and I think I've earned the right to serve in ways other than pastoral ministry."

"Are you sure about that?" Carl looked smug. "Let's make a list. You quit the chaplaincy soon after being wounded, and you hadn't been in service for even a year. Later, they took you back, with a promotion, no less. You could have made a career serving in the Army then, but left after a year." Carl's eyes were piercing. "And what about that undeserved pastorate in San Francisco? I heard about that through my professional correspondence with Anthony Gladstone, who seems to know everything about you."

"Tony is a friend of many years. It started in ..."

"Yes, Korea. I've heard the story." Carl was not letting up. "And Tony's cousin was instrumental in getting you that pastorate. Yes, I've talked to him, too." Carl paused, but only for a moment. "Don't you know that other deserving pastors were passed over for you, and then you walked away after less than three years. It seems that you quit a lot."

"I had valid reasons for leaving."

"Yes, I was told there was talk in the congregation, but I won't go into that. My point is that you've received favors all along the way, and frankly, Obie, you don't seem to appreciate that."

"I've worked diligently at my writing, which is my calling. And I'm a committed member of the congregation. I pull my weight."

"Your work is appreciated, but your commitment seems to be to what best suits you."

Carl was wrong, but he found no words to tell him that.

Carl said, "I want to remind you of something you may have forgotten. When a Christian takes on the cloak of ordained ministry, he does so with the understanding and the commitment that he'll serve in whatever capacity the Lord asks of him."

"Or, in this case, it would be in whatever capacity the Conference asks of him."

"Don't play word games with me, Obie. You know what I mean."

Obie sat up straighter and took a breath. "Of course, I know what is required in ministry. It's to serve. And I do serve. I've chosen to use the gift of writing."

Carl's voice rose. "Ha, that's it! *You've* chosen."

He had been led into a corner. "Carl, I try hard to listen to what God tells me." Why did his voice feel so weak?

"If you've listened so intently, why haven't you picked up the cross the Lord is asking you to carry?"

Obie struggled to say, "I've done what I thought was right."

Carl smiled, the familiar smile that Obie recognized, but the emphasis remained. "You've assumed you're an exception, but you're not. You may have your hand on the Cross, but you must pick it up."

Later, still reeling from the abrupt lecture, Obie helped Carl to his car. Seated behind the steering wheel, the retired minister sounded apologetic. "Obie, I hope I haven't offended you. I've only said what the Spirit led me to say. You're a fine Christian, but I want you to recognize your true calling."

Obie watched the car disappear over the hill. Carl had left, but his words lingered, stirring chagrin and worry into a brew that threatened to muddy the expectations of his future.

* * *

Obie climbed to the ridge at the top of Blackberry Hill, to a place of retreat since childhood. Weighty decisions were made there; the first, if he remembered correctly, was whether to tell his mother that his black eye was the result of a fight with Ernie Boswell. All subsequent decisions seemed important, too, but none was more pressing than the one he was making today.

Cassie was not much help. When he told her about the conversation with Carl, she merely smiled and made that little clicking sound with her mouth that indicated she was thinking about it. Just this morning, she had said, "Go to your retreat on the ridge, Obie. Maybe that's where you'll find the answers."

The mild October weather had continued, and a brief rain system had moved on. There was the faintest whisper of wind in the treetops. Fall colors lingered, although past their peak. On top, he sat on a large rock that overlooked the town and the Morass. Fragrance from nearby white cedars permeated the air. Leaves from the scattered and less plentiful hardwoods fell randomly, adding to the accumulation on the forest floor. Crows cawed farther along the ridge. For a while, he sat still, letting the serenity calm his mind.

Tony's letter had been on his mind for over a week, bringing his focus to bear on the serpentine direction his life had taken. Carl's list of his failures had prompted him to reexamine his spiritual history. As a teenager, his attention was drawn to the ministry. Under normal circumstances, he might have gone on to that in a straight line, but disastrous circumstances had derailed that future. Then, he envisioned a future in journalism, but God reached him in a dream where his long-dead mother told him, "You must turn your belly up to God." That led him to seminary and then to Korea as a chaplain. After that, he spent years in newspaper work and writing books.

So why had he taken on that pastorate at the San Francisco church? He had tossed it off giddily to Annie that he was "giving the ministry another try." But he came to believe he had found a place he belonged. Had it not been for Annie's indiscretion and his misstep of succumbing to the charms of a Monterey divorcee, he might still serve in that conference. Should he have accepted God's forgiveness, as Carl suggested, and not resigned? But it was a hard thing to do.

It was only after twelve dark years that he returned to Stafford Rest to find Cassie and make writing his life's work—God's plan for him. However, Carl and Tony, friends whom he trusted, challenged that plan.

The rock where he sat was cold, so he moved to a sunny spot. In his mind, he tried to filter out the unnecessary. Perhaps he had deluded himself, as Carl implied. Maybe he really was guilty of seeking the most comfortable. Carl's words, "Your commitment seems to be to what best suits you," still hurt.

He had loved serving the San Francisco church. Perhaps his comprehension of "unworthiness" was the logjam that separated him from the ministry. Tony had declared it an asset, and Carl had kicked him hard in the rear. If his sins were somehow turned to advantages, little stood between him and pastoral ministry.

He knelt by the rock to pray. The gentle breeze in the treetops whispered approval.

* * *

Without ceremony on the last day of October, a quick conference action established the Rev. Obadiah Gainsworthy as pastor of Stafford Rest United Methodist Church. Three days later, he conducted his first Sunday service there. The enthusiastic greeting accorded him and Cassie gave him hope that things would go smoothly.

That hope was soon dispelled. There was an endless procession of loose ends to tie. Disagreement among church officers over nearly everything commanded his attention: Should the parsonage be rented or sold? Should the basement kitchen be modernized? Should new hymnals be ordered? These were legitimate questions, but they soon became fields of battle.

It was apparent that a clearly defined wall divided those who opposed his appointment from those who welcomed him. The former group, vocal but less in number, saw him as "modern " and too liberal, while the latter saw him as precisely what was needed.

He soon realized that attempts to please everyone would not work, so on the Sunday after Thanksgiving, he asked the church leaders and "all other interested parties" to stay after the service. Cassie had to leave because Jacob was not feeling well, but Abigail and Laura attended.

"I won't mince words," Obie stated as he stood before the group of about fifty people. "I'm concerned by what's going on here. We're entering Advent season, and our conduct toward one another is anything but Christlike."

"We're appalled too," Glenda Smith said.

Amos Adams' voice held his usual foghorn intensity. "Well, Preacher, it's up to you to fix it. That's what we're paying you for."

Amos had criticized him at every opportunity. His latest complaints, today in the parking lot before they entered the building, were about Obie's failure to wear a robe during Sunday services and the "scandal" about someone seeing him make the sign of the cross. Amos said about the latter, "That's what Catholics do. We're not Catholics. We serve God correctly."

Obie was determined to have everything in the open. "Yes, Mr. Adams, I'm here to fix it, but ..."

"Amos! Call me Amos! We're not that formal here."

"Okay, Amos. Thank you. I was about to say that I want to address something you said to me before the service."

"About wearing a robe when you preach?" Amos said.

"Well, yes, that too. But ..."

"And the signing sin?"

Obie was determined not to lose patience. "That wasn't what I was about to say, but maybe we should address those two concerns first."

"Yes, please do that." Amos looked smug.

"I'll wear a robe if that's what people want me to do. As for giving the sign of the cross, I hope you understand that it's something ingrained in me by the years I attended a Catholic church with my mother. For me, it's simply a sign of respect for God."

"It's a pagan thing," Amos countered.

Obie could not hide his irritation. "Yes, I'm aware of your displeasure. But something else you said needs addressing. You said, and I quote, 'We serve God correctly.' I assume you were speaking about more than just my signing."

"Indeed, I was. There are tried and true ways of serving God. True Christians follow those ways, especially pastors. Or they should. Pastors can do great harm to a church when they sin. I know that because ..." Amos hesitated before saying, "But that's beside the point. True Christians must serve God correctly, and some of us are called to be watchdogs." There were several nods in the group.

Obie took a deep breath. "I'd like to make something clear for you, Amos, and for the rest of you who might feel the same. I'm not about to change my ways of worship or how I show my respect to God. It's a part of who I am."

He saw some shocked expressions. *Had he been too blunt?* He softened his tone. "Yes, Amos is right that Christianity requires faithful adherence to God's laws. But we all approach God differently. We have our own beliefs about how best to serve God. My concern is that we respect one another's rights. Amos, whether I wear a robe or make a hand sign isn't the slightest indication of where I am as a Christian. For me, that's nonsense."

Amos' face had turned crimson. "I just want us to be a good Christian church," he said.

"As do I, Amos. But I want it to be simple, with all of us

loving and supporting one another while we work to advance Jesus Christ's Church here on Earth."

Obie glanced at faces around the room. Whether minds had been changed was difficult to judge.

Sarah Hill said, "You can help us get along better, can't you, Pastor Gainsworthy?"

Be positive. "I can, and I'll be here for as long as it takes, but you have to help me."

Arthur Baines said in his usual drawn-out fashion, soft enough to give the impression he was speaking to himself but loud enough to ensure he was heard, "Maybe what we'll get is just more modern double-talk."

Obie held his temper. Ernie Boswell did not. "Art, you're a dumb-ass to show such disrespect to Obie. He don't deserve that. Obie's tolerant. We need more of that."

"Amen," Sarah Hill said.

"It's a time of peace on earth," Frances Gibbons said softly from her seat in the back. All eyes turned to the town librarian, who seldom voiced an opinion in public. She continued. "We most urgently need peace in our church."

The faintest of words, again from Arthur, caused Obie concern. He was sure he heard, "She's not the kind to give us advice." There were enough troubles in the congregation without adding bigotry.

Obie had made a mental note to get Frances involved in some church ministry. Level heads such as hers were needed. He said, "Frances, do you have ideas about how we might do that? How we might promote peace?"

"Yes, I do." Her words were still soft but crisp and clear. "One way is to work together on projects that aren't controversial, and do things together to help us understand one another better."

"Would you be willing to come up with some specific ideas for projects?"

"I can do that. And I can give you one right now." Her voice became more confident. "I would like to see the outside decorated for Christmas. I wasn't a member last year but remember no outside decorations. We have several trees and bushes along the side that can hold lights, and the bell tower is seen from all over town."

"Excellent idea," Sarah said.

"I'll work on it," Frances said. "Sarah, maybe you can help, too?"

"I'll be glad to assist you," Sarah quickly responded.

Obie smiled. This was precisely the interaction he desired. "Frances will need more help," he said.

"I'd like Glenda's advice," Frances said. "She's probably done this sort of thing for a long time."

Glenda hesitated before looking at Arthur; he was shaking his head. She turned to Frances. "Well, I guess so. I can't climb anymore, but I can do other things. And I certainly do have some ideas."

"I can climb just fine," Ernie Boswell said from across the room. Obie noted that the words were delivered enthusiastically, even for Ernie. "I'll help you, Frances. We'll put up the best display this town has ever seen."

Several others volunteered. Obie was delighted. Frances would be a valuable asset in his efforts to get things back on track. She had provided the perfect introduction to the little speech he intended to deliver.

"Listen, folks, I'll try not to keep you long, but there's one more thing I need to say. It's true that I'm displeased with some of what's going on, but I want to make it clear that my displeasure is not with your diversity. The fact that each of you has your own idea about what a perfect church should be like is just fine. My displeasure is about how you're acting toward one another. You have every right to believe as you do, even that your ideas are superior to someone else's. But you don't have the right to disrupt the church's operation by insisting everyone else accept your ideas. I won't allow that."

Amos appeared angry. Arthur was also fidgeting in his seat, but it was Amos who spoke, his voice booming against the walls. "You won't allow us to speak God's truth? Well, I'll say what I please in this congregation."

Obie's confidence in openness was severely tested. Looks and murmurs indicated that several people agreed with Amos.

Obie wanted to blast back with a barrage of words, but controlled himself.

Without looking at Amos, he said, "Frances is dead on when she said we should work together on projects that aren't controversial. We need to find areas of agreement rather than wallowing in areas that divide us."

"That might be hard," Roland Kilpatrick said.

Obie could not let the opportunity pass. "We can do it. Let's think about it. The Christmas season is on us. Let's see if we can find just one thing to agree on about the season, one fact we all believe true."

Like a child in a classroom, Sarah raised her hand and said, "God sent his son into the world."

"Excellent, Sarah. Does anyone disagree with that?" The room was quiet. "So," Obie dragged out the words with emphasis, "we have something on which to agree. That's progress. Let's find others."

Roland spoke. "The angels in Heaven rejoiced in his birth."

"Yes! Do we all agree?" Again, there were no dissenters. "That's two," Obie said. *Take a chance.* "Amos, do you have one?"

Amos appeared confused, but only for a moment. "This doesn't tell us anything about the troubles this ..."

Roland uncharacteristically interrupted. "Amos, if you're serious about your love for this church and about service, then give this a chance. Pastor Obie is doing his best to bring us together on something. Anything that shows we're caring Christians instead of fighting fools."

Amos took his time. His face was still red. "All right, I'll give you one." He stood. "'Mary had a little lamb. Its fleece was white as snow.' How's that, preacher?" He sat down, looking smug. There was some muffled laughter.

"That's not funny, Amos," Roland said. "A sick joke's no help."

Abigail had been quiet until now. "Amos, you have the right to address your concerns, but you should address our pastor as Rev. Gainsworthy or Pastor Obie. You should respect his position."

"Respect? What if I don't ..."

Obie stepped in. "Wait a minute. I see what you mean, Amos. That's brilliant." He turned toward the group. "Does everyone see the symbology in that nursery rhyme?"

Frances said, "The Lamb of God! Jesus was the lamb. Mary was the mother of the Lamb of God."

Glenda clapped, and the tribute spread throughout the group. Obie did not doubt that Amos had attempted to disrupt, but he would not deny the man a moment of glory and the chance to negate some of his hostility. "Well done, Amos," he said.

Several others contributed theological truths that had little chance of being disputed. Obie concluded the meeting by saying, "I'll make a list of all these and pass them out so we won't forget. Let's concentrate on them throughout the Christmas season and not be tempted to bring up things we know will divide us. I'll incorporate your ideas into my sermons to keep them before us."

CHAPTER TWELVE

May 1975

"Hello, Ernie."

Ernie Boswell clutched his baseball cap with nervous hands. "Hello, Frances. How are you today?"

"Just fine," Frances Gibbons said as she hooked her cane onto the edge of the library desk. "Can I help you find something?"

It was early, and Ernie was thankful no one else was in the room. He wanted to say something to indicate that he was not there to find a book, but he hesitated. *If he were a fearful man, which he wasn't, he would think his legs were trembling.*

"Well, I'd like ..."

"Maybe something to do with your business. Marinas, restaurants, or maybe you like fiction. We have recent novels that are on the best-seller lists." Her dark eyes revealed excitement as she named a few titles. *He had dreamed about those eyes. She was still beautiful.*

He stood straighter, determined to say what he had planned. Instead, he said, "Something a little harder?"

She laughed, a pleasant sound he remembered. "Ernie, are you trying to impress me?"

"Well, maybe. I want to show you that I've progressed some since high school."

"And I'm sure you have. How about one of Obie's books? I've made a special display of them. You and Obie were always my good friends."

"We still are." He leaped at a chance to delay his planned speech to organize it better. "Obie's doing well at church, isn't he?"

"He's made real progress in seven months. That's not to say things couldn't be better, but they have improved."

"Frances, you did a splendid job with those Christmas displays. I enjoyed working with you. And the Easter egg hunt for the kids went well. It was smart to get the adults more involved."

"Thanks for your help, Ernie. Others pitched in, too."

An awkward silence prevailed. *Get it out.* "Frances, I didn't come here to get a book."

"That's pretty obvious." The gentle words did not condemn.

"We did something once ..."

"You mean in that dark corner in the school library where nobody could see us?"

"Yeah, that spot, at Evergreen High."

That was before Cora, when they were juniors in high school. He had kissed her, something he had wanted to do since grade school. He loved Frances and would have followed up on that school library incident had he not feared alienating his friends. Obie would have understood, and maybe Ed Baumgartner, too, but Chuck Hinky always said insulting things about the Gibbons family. And the larger community sent a message at that time, not spoken except in a few instances, that Blacks and Whites did not mix. He stupidly succumbed to that lie and lost Frances, but had not forgotten the feeling—nor the emotion. *The question was, had she?*

She was still smiling. "Ernie, do you have something you want to say?"

Courage returned. "Are there any dark corners in *this* library?"

"No, everything is open and lighted." Her voice rose. "And we aren't in high school anymore."

"Sorry. Guess I'm too forward."

"Yes, Ernie, you are." She moved to the other end of the big desk and started to stack books that did not appear to need stacking.

"I wanted us to talk."

The silence dragged on until it became uncomfortable. She said, "Ernie, Cora just died."

"It's been almost a year."

"You're still grieving. You must let more time go by before

wooing old acquaintances. Please honor your wife longer."

"Frances, you're not just an acquaintance. Don't you know how I've always felt?"

She was no longer smiling, and her tone held reproof. "No, I don't know. How could I? One kiss, then nothing else ... ever?"

"All through grade school, didn't you see how much I liked you? When you got polio, didn't I camp on your doorstep until you got better?"

"Yes, you did that, to your credit." She hesitated. "So, after that day in the library, why didn't you ever come close to me again? There was never anything more than an occasional 'hello?'"

"I don't know."

"I do." She moved to face him. "It was because of my color." He admired her directness, but it hurt.

"That never bothered me. I would never let ..."

"Wouldn't it, Ernie? Don't you remember all the couples who went through the halls holding hands and stealing kisses? I wanted a part of that, too. Rhonda Patterson and I were the only blacks at Evergreen, and no boy ever asked either of us to attend a social function."

"I didn't know that."

"No, you wouldn't. So, tell me, if you liked me so much, why did you never ask me to do anything with you in public?"

"I don't know." This visit was not progressing as he had hoped.

"Yes, you *do* know, Ernie. So, why don't you say it? Then we'll be good friends again."

"What do you want me to say, Frances?"

"The truth." Anger had gathered in her eyes.

He was trapped. He wanted to turn and run out the door, but too much rested on the moment. "All right, it *was* because you were black."

Her smile returned. "And I still am."

"I'm sorry, Frances. That was the biggest mistake of my life." He felt the beginning of tears, the first time since Cora's funeral. "Please forgive me."

Her gaze never left his face. "I forgive you, Ernie, but that's all a long time ago."

"You've never married."

"No, and I don't intend to. I like my life just the way it is, but we can be friends." She picked up the stack of books and moved off toward the bookshelves. He had been dismissed.

He was disappointed, but there was hope. *He would never give up hoping.*

* * *

Dan Williamson appeared in the barnroom doorway just as Obie stored his paints on a wooden shelf adjacent to the high window.

"What's going on?" Dan asked casually as if no time had elapsed since their last conversation, although it had been nearly five months.

Obie pointed to an unfinished canvas on an easel and answered in the same blasé manner. "Had a little time today."

"Why don't you sell some of your art? People notice the two paintings we have in our apartment."

Obie brushed aside the compliment with, "My paintings are for family and friends, but it's good to see you, Dan. You don't usually get home this time of year."

"We'll go back tomorrow, but we won't leave until after church. Ly Yen and I want to hear your sermon."

"And where *is* your lovely wife?"

"They're all with Grandmother Hunt. Laurie and Obadiah are enjoying the big yard like I used to. Our shared Baltimore yard would fit in Grandmother's garage. Cassie brought Jacob over too, as you probably already know."

"Let's go sit on the porch and talk," Obie said. It was late in the day, and as they walked toward the house, his mood matched the serenity of the sunset painting a red-streaked sky over the western hills. Dan was his son, and although that fact had been kept from them both for many years, Obie now took joy in their time together. What a whirlwind his life had become. Five years ago, he was childless, or so he thought; now he had two sons, although they were many years apart.

They sat in the metal glider on the enclosed porch. "What's the lumber I saw stacked on the side?" Dan asked.

"Chet put the wood there. We had a financial windfall when Cassie sold her house. We're adding two more rooms and a second bathroom. He'll start it Monday."

"You added two rooms last year. This house will be almost as big as Grandmother's."

"It'll give us a guestroom, and I need a study. I'm tired of using a corner of the living area."

"Are you going to California this year?"

"In August, for three weeks this time. Abigail has said she'll go with us, but I doubt she will."

"So, you two are finally getting along?"

"Dan, your grandmother and I live on the edge of uncertainty regarding our relationship, but yes, we manage."

"You're probably right that she won't go with you. She won't leave the restaurant for that long. She spends most of her time there now, doesn't she?"

"Yes, *Abigail's* is a booming business, and I bet she'll want to expand. She might have found a niche she likes better than buying and selling property."

"Grandmother is a real entrepreneur. I admire her for that."

Obie remembered something he had meant to ask. "Would you and Ly Yen like to visit the Napa House? You can go there anytime, and not necessarily with us."

"I'd love that, and so would Ly Yen, but it's out of the question now. I have a year of medical school and at least a year of residency ahead. I'm so busy that getting away for a couple of days like this is nearly impossible. But, after my schooling is complete, we'll certainly do that."

Obie saw an opportunity to learn something he desperately wanted to know. "Dan, will you come back to Stafford Rest? Laura told us that Ben is starting a practice here and that you are a part of it. Is that true?"

"Dad ... Ben has invited me to join him in his practice. He's had difficulty cashing out in Boston, but it's almost done. He'll be set up here by fall. He wants a clinic eventually, but knows he must proceed a step at a time. But, to answer your question, no, I've not formally accepted his invitation."

"You will consider it, though?"

"I will, but I want to keep my options open. I love it here, as you know, but I have a family to look out for. Mom and Grandmother have offered us a place to live until we get settled, but I'm not sure there's room for two physicians in this town. He's paid for most of my schooling, so I owe him consideration, but we disagree on many fronts. I owe you, too, for that Love Fund thing. What's that about, anyway?"

"I'll tell you about it someday. Just accept it and be thankful."

Obie wanted to tell Dan about the fund. He should know it was a family operation and that he might someday manage it. He would tell him that—and many other things—but he must be patient.

"I appreciate all the help I can get," Dan said. "We live close to the belt. I sold my airplane, as you know. Storage was too expensive. Ly Yen is a wonder at making do, which greatly helps."

"She's had experience."

"Indeed. Austere times aside, we're very happy together. Obie, I really do thank you, and Cassie too, for making that possible, and for reuniting me with Ly Yen and the kids."

"Our pleasure. It's great to see the love you have for one another."

Dan's tone turned serious. "Obie, are you and Mom okay now?"

"We're fine." Obie was unsure how much Laura had told Dan about the stolen letters or the part Abigail played. *Perhaps some things were better left untold.* "Your mother has been helpful at church, too. She chairs a committee and serves on others that help bring unity to our congregation."

"I'm happy for her and for you, too, about that." Dan appeared hesitant before saying, "Obie, are we fine, too, you and me?"

"What do you mean?"

"We had a falling out once. Remember? I said some things

I'm sorry for. I understand now why you wouldn't discuss why you and Grandmother hated each other and why you and Mom were at odds."

Obie wondered where the conversation was going. Dan continued, "It was all about me, wasn't it?"

"Dan, this is something to discuss with your mother."

"I suppose some things are hard to say, and nobody in the family has ever said them to me, although I know the truth. Granddad told me about the letters."

So Pinky knew. "We don't have to ..."

"I want the words articulated, Obie. Not publicly, if you wish, but to me anyway. I don't care what people think. If it's discussed publicly, that's perfectly okay with me. Anyway, everybody knew after Ly Yen revealed that our children were named after you and Mom." Dan paused and turned to look at Obie. "I'm babbling, but I want to hear *somebody*, especially *you*, say it *to me.*"

Obie wanted to shout it out, but he controlled himself. "What is it you want me to say?"

"That you're my father."

The words came without effort, "Yes, Dan. I'm your father." A great weight lifted from Obie's soul.

* * *

Obie awoke with an idea he wanted to pursue: Except for the Christmas Community Sing and a few casual encounters, there had been little professional contact with the other two Safford Rest pastors. By the time he reached the office, he knew how to change that.

It was early, but he picked up the phone and dialed the Episcopal Church number. The church secretary connected him to Father Curtis Parker.

"Curt, are you busy?" Obie asked.

"Of course, I'm busy," the pastor responded, but with a tone Obie imagined accompanied with a smile, for the man was always smiling. They had lunched together twice, the first time six months earlier, right after Obie took his pastorate. The young pastor, not long out of seminary, enlisted Obie's help in orienting himself to the larger community. Obie was flattered that he was asked instead of the Baptist minister, Ernest Owens, who had been a pastor in Stafford Rest for many years.

"If you're free, let's have lunch at Ernie's," Obie said. "I'm buying."

"In that case, yes."

"I'll ask Pastor Owens to join us, too, if that's all right with you."

"You have something on your mind, don't you?"

"We'll see, but for now, let's just say we're enjoying a friendly lunch."

After talking to Parker, Obie called the Baptist church. He and Owens had lunched together only once. Owens had a formal bearing, and although they were about the same age, Obie felt subdued in the man's presence. Now, he would overcome that feeling.

"Good morning, Rev. Gainsworthy," the Baptist minister responded pleasantly. They discussed the weather, high prices, and last winter's thickness of the ice on Diamond Lake before Obie extended the invitation to join him and Parker for lunch.

The three men sat at a table in a corner of Ernie's large dining area. Obie's normal lunch menu consisted of a sandwich and a piece of fruit brought from home, but since he was buying, he ordered soup and a chicken sandwich to encourage the other ministers to order whatever they liked. He wanted to use the time and atmosphere to gain their cooperation.

At first, the conversation centered on the common concerns of finances, membership decline, and physical structures needing repair. Finally, Obie raised the subject for which he had brought them together. "Have either of you ever swapped sermons with another minister?" he said, casually.

Parker said, "I preached at several churches while in seminary, but I haven't been here long enough to even think of that."

"I have," Owens said. "Many times."

"And did that pastor for whom you filled in preach in your church at the same time? That's what I meant."

"Yes. Baptists exchange pulpits."

"But have you ever exchanged pulpits with someone from another denomination?"

Owens was quick to say, "No."

"Would you consider it?" *Maybe he had asked the question too soon.*

Parker said, "I like the idea. Obie, are you suggesting we do that here, the three of us?"

Owen said quickly, "I'll have to think about it."

Owen's resistance was expected. "Ernest, I'm not talking about any elaborate exchange, maybe just once a year." He purposely used the minister's first name to break down his reserve.

"I'm not sure what good it would serve."

"Well, I think it's an excellent idea," Parker said with a laugh. "It'd give me the chance to set you Methodists and Baptists straight."

Owens laughed too, but said, "What do you have on your mind, Rev. Gainsworthy ... Obie?"

It had reached the selling point. "Look here, we're a small village on an unbeaten path. Everyone knows everyone. We'd not be strangers in one another's congregations. We can go slow."

"I'm all for it," Parker said.

"What's the purpose of such an exchange?" Owens said.

"Yes, I have a purpose in mind," Obie said. "I think we work in isolation on some common village concerns. For instance, we each have programs to care for the ill and help those who struggle to feed their families. We might do better to work together on some of those programs."

"Our members take great pride in helping others," Owens said. "We work with our Convention in many areas."

Obie said, "And we work through our Conference, but the truth is that we three live right here in this town, and we know the immediate needs. We're in the best position to supply remedies. And we have some resources to share."

Owens said, "That sounds good if we're talking about physical needs. I'm not against ecumenical sharing for those. All Christians need to address poverty and pain. But how we address our spiritual needs is a different matter."

The waiter had started picking up the dirty dishes. Obie wanted commitments. "Ernest, I'm well aware of our differences." He wanted to say that the differences were extraneous and that if you stripped them away, all you would find would be struggling Christians doing their best. He said, "I want us to get together more, both pastors and church members, to address issues we can solve better together than separately."

"And maybe we can have lunch together regularly," Parker said.

"How about once a month?" Obie said. We can set some rules about a pulpit swap if we decide to do that. Curt, you can buy next time."

"Be glad to."

They had agreed. Obie was pleased.

CHAPTER THIRTEEN

June 1975

Despite well-meaning declarations to the contrary, Obie sensed he was making minimal headway against church discontent. The culprits were a minority, but as his father said after listening to his complaints, "Even one bad apple spoils the barrel, and it looks like you have several."

On many days, he longed for the tranquility of the past, for that time in his youth when he had watched Charles Lansing go about his duties here with far fewer difficulties.

Even with the disparity in size, Greenleaf Methodist Church in San Francisco had given him fewer problems. Furthermore, he missed the leisure time to work on the new book he had begun last year. But he had vowed to return the church to good health, which he must do. Beyond that, he was unsure, except that once more he must turn his belly up to God.

Disputes and wrangling had not eased significantly under his strategy of diplomacy and reconciliation. Still, there was improvement regarding his acceptance, evidenced by prolonged handshakes, greetings on the streets, and even whispered encouragement. Amos Adams and Arthur Baines were still his busiest foes and retained a loyal following, although somewhat diminished.

Obie tried to avoid conflict with Amos but found it impossible. The latest incident involved a new stove in the downstairs kitchen. Amos was chair of the Stewardship Committee and authorized to withdraw funds from the church bank account, but he ordered the stove without consulting other church officials. The scene in the church office when the stove arrived was caustic.

"What were you thinking?" Obie asked without keeping anger from his tone.

"It's my right to decide what needs to be done to keep our church in good shape," Amos shouted.

"It's your job to evaluate needs and suggest solutions. It's the Administrative Council's job to authorize them."

Amos's voice had boomed. "There's not a single person on the Administrative Council who knows half of what I do about stoves."

It was true that Amos's knowledge of construction and appliances made him an asset, but Obie could not let him plow ahead without restraint. In his most authoritative tone, he said, "We'll keep the stove because it seems like a good purchase. But, Amos, don't ever do that again with any major purchase."

"And if I do?"

"Then we'll find a new stewardship chairperson."

Amos had stalked out, muttering to himself. Obie spent several minutes devising ways to remove Amos from all church business, but finally realized that, for now at least, he was stuck with the man.

Glenda Smith was linked with Amos and Arthur to some extent, but hers was a different threat. Her lack of presence on any administrative committee blunted her influence, but her strength was her sway over others in the congregation, especially the younger women. Her advanced age, which many assumed brought wisdom, gave her exalted respect. Her secret was her ability to express ideas to individuals in engaging ways and to make the listener think theirs was a great secret shared. Amos shouted his way to attention, and Arthur's role was to affirm Amos's proclamations, but Glenda's quietly whispered words fell on receptive ears that verbal bombardment could not reach. Obie met a shortcoming when he found it difficult to pray for those three people.

Despite the turmoil, or perhaps because of it, Obie yearned for the peace of nature more than he had at any time since his return to Stafford Rest. A boyhood spent in the open had left its imprint. He still skied and took snowshoe jaunts on the ridge with Cassie, but interaction with the nearby wilderness had been sparse in recent months.

Obie was surprised, then, when one warm June afternoon

cried out for him to join it. Although next Sunday's sermon was unfinished, he could wait no longer. He told Roberta Barnes, the church secretary, that he would be gone for about an hour. He had already had a lunch break, so she raised an eyebrow under her towering beehive hairdo, her usual reaction to unexpected events. She nodded and went back to stenciling bulletins for Sunday's service.

With hands in pockets, he strolled up White Pine Street, the thoroughfare he still called "White Pine Road," toward the Morass. He passed Cassie's old house and stopped next door at Ken and Angie's. Ken sat in a rocker on the porch, sanding a small table.

"I'm going over by the Morass," Obie announced. "Want to walk with me?"

"Sure. Give me a minute to tell Angie."

There had been good times on the trail with his father during his youth. Ken's love of the forest and mountains helped to instill that love in Obie. At eighty-eight, Ken was restricted to a once-a-year deer hunt; Dan had made quick trips home the last three hunting seasons for that outing. This was an easy walk.

Obie let Ken set the pace. "Looks like you're playing hooky," Ken said, sounding more congratulatory than condemning.

"It's too nice a day to stay in a hot office. I miss being able to step outside whenever I feel like it."

"It's the price you pay for taking on that thankless job. Speaking of such, why did you?" It was a subject not previously discussed with his father. "You were doing fine writing books."

"I don't see it as just a job, Dad. I'm open to what God calls me for, and right now, this is what I'm asked to do."

"Seems like it took you a good while to get to it."

Obie had often smarted under Ken's forthright observations, and this was no exception. But to let his father's words upset him served no purpose.

"Dad, it may seem to you like I live without purpose, but I think it's all part of God's plan." Obie stopped and faced Ken. "I've learned from all the places I've been and the things I've seen. I bring that learning to this mission."

"In other words, God has groomed you for Stafford Rest?"

"Well, yes, you might say that."

Ken stopped again and crossed his arms. His voice rose an octave. "Let's see now … you were a chaplain in a war zone. That nearly got you killed. Then you were a writer. Then, you were a minister of a big church in a big city. Then you edited a magazine. Then, you went off to war as a chaplain again. To cap it off, you ran a multi-million-dollar company in New York City. That seems like moving up a ladder of success."

"Some might think of it as success."

"If God led you, he must have given you greater responsibilities as you went along. Don't you think the next step would be up again, like as a bigwig in some church hierarchy?"

"I have no bigwig desires."

"Tell me this, Son, why has he placed you here in this little Adirondack village, in a little church that, from all I hear, is on its way down, and even in danger of dissolving? Did God bring you along all this time just to dump you here?"

"Dad, I haven't been dumped. I'm here to get the church through this crisis."

As they continued to walk, Ken said, "I said that badly. Your return was something I waited a long time for. And I don't mean to play down the importance of what you do. I guess it's more to do with me and my trying to get my head around my own faith issues. Your mother thought you were destined for something great in the religious world. I pooh-poohed her ideas at the time, but I've matured some since then, although I still can't think of myself as a religious man. I wish I could accept everything the churches teach."

Obie laughed. "You'd be a mighty confused man."

"I guess I already am confused. My father, your grandfather, was a progressive thinker. I tried to understand his point of view and lack of respect for organized religion, but my thinking was sidetracked by other issues that didn't require such deep thought. There was the war, my war, and as you know, wars scar you. And, making a living during the depression was hard." Ken looked down. "And, of course, there was my drinking."

"Dad, I'm thankful that's all in the past."

101

"After your mother died and I married Angie, I got involved with her in the Catholic Church. Religion doesn't get much more organized than that, what with all the rituals, saints, and such. I try to take it all in, but I have trouble. If not for my respect for Angie, I wouldn't keep going to Evergreen."

"You can always come to my church, you know."

"Be a Methodist? Would I understand their beliefs any better?"

The question seemed tongue-in-cheek, but Obie saw that Ken was serious, and his pastoral responsibility surfaced. "Look here, Dad, the Catholics in Evergreen are good people, just as the people here are good." He fought down doubts about Amos and Arthur. "Catholics are big on form and ritual. I was a part of that, too, while Mom was alive."

"But which is best?"

"There's no best. Differences, yes, but I refuse to say that one denomination is better. Who's to say that one way of worship is better? You're fine with the Catholics. It means a lot to Angie. The important thing is that we worship … that we serve."

"I'd like to know more about your religious beliefs."

The plea sounded earnest. They had never talked in this vein. Introspection was not readily associated with Ken Gainsworthy.

"My beliefs are pretty simple," Obie said, "and I work to keep them that way."

"I'll bet not as simple as Papa's."

"It's true that Grandpa never thought of himself as a church family member, but he did good things. He established the Love Fund and attended church services with his family. It was all about love. Love for God and for one another. And he lived that life. But I need fellowship, and I suspect you do too. I'll not judge Grandpa. I'm sure he's right now with Grandma in God's Heaven. I'm merely saying that my way differs from his, just as churches differ."

"Papa was the kindest, gentlest man I ever knew."

"I think the love Grandpa lived by is simply God's spirit in us, the essence that moves through all faiths. It's the framework.

But we also need faith, and we need to walk humbly before God."

"That's all?"

"Pretty much. The Spirit will teach us. And we should be faithful to our ways of worship. As a pastor, I must concentrate heavily on worship, but my private way is simpler. Worship, study, service, all lubricated by ..."

"Love?"

"You've got it."

They walked past the furniture factory, now a two-story structure with two smaller adjacent buildings. The fenced-in factory grounds covered more than half an acre. Several cars were in the parking lot. Obie saw Laura's Lincoln Continental in her reserved space.

A footpath trailed down from the factory to the Morass edge. It led onto a wooden walkway that extended fifty yards out over the water, an addition Laura had designed and constructed soon after taking over the company. The structure was secured by sturdy wooden posts driven into the earth beneath the water, and railings were on both sides of the walkway. They went out to the end and sat on a bench.

"Well, Laura did get this right," Ken said.

"It's a good place, the Morass," Obie replied. "You brought me here when I was very young?"

"That old boat always leaked. It's a wonder we didn't sink."

"We gigged for frogs at night. And you taught me all the routes through the maze."

"Will you bring Jacob here?"

"I will, when he's a little older."

"Lots of folks still call it 'swamp.'"

"Their loss. But I sometimes see busloads of people. I assume they're college or high school groups."

"Yeah, they still come. That's because there's no other location around with such a variety of wildlife. I used to guide groups, but I finally gave that up. I think these classes walk the path around it now."

"Laura has it in her head to preserve the Morass, and that's a good thing," Obie said.

Ken was watching him. "You still think about her, don't you?"

"No!" He had answered too quickly. "Not the way you probably mean. Laura and I have settled into a comfortable friendship. It's a family thing now."

"She's also the mother of your older son."

"That's true. I can't deny that we have that connection, but I'm married to Cassie. *I love Cassie.*"

"Cassie and Pinky are the jewels of that family ... and Pinky's gone now."

The stern set of Ken's jaw reminded Obie of his father's inability to let go of some things. Since Obie's marriage to Cassie, his father tolerated Laura, but Abigail was another matter. Combined family gatherings brought contentious behavior between the two, worse since Pinky's death. Obie's attempts to bring peace had led nowhere.

He was tempted to try again. "You and Abigail must bury the hatchet, you know. Neither of you is getting any younger."

Ken removed his cap and rubbed his nearly bald head. "What does age have to do with it?"

"Not much, but time does run out."

Ken snorted. "Time for what?"

"Forgiveness."

Ken blew out a puff of air. "Some things are impossible to forgive."

"Hard, but not impossible. Dad, you asked about my beliefs. I gave you a simplified explanation. I had the most trouble with forgiveness, even though Jesus has told us that we must forgive if we expect to be forgiven. I tried to forgive for years."

"For what Abigail and Laura did to you?"

"Yes, for what Abigail did, and for what I believed Laura did. I would think I was good with it, but then it would come back like a reopened wound."

"So, how did you stop hating?"

"I learned about true forgiveness from an unlikely source. God's intervention, I believe. Do you remember the trip Angie and I took to Italy five years ago?"

Ken laughed. "I cooked for myself while Angie was gone. I

nearly starved."

"And you no doubt remember that I stayed longer? I never told you much about it except that I had visited old battle sites."

"Well, I want to hear about what you didn't tell me."

Obie put his head down as he told his father the story known to only a few, of his killing a young German prisoner of war in Italy because Obie thought he had a gun, of discovering that the "gun" was a Bible, and of suppressing the incident from family and friends for years, thinking of it only when it surfaced in troubled dreams. Ken listened intently as Obie explained how he revisited the battle site where the man who lived there told him about the recent visit of the dead man's brother, himself looking for answers.

"And you learned about the family?"

"I learned that I had killed Günter Erdmann, a seventeen-year-old German soldier who had planned to become a minister."

"You said you'd kept his Bible?"

"I had hidden it away, out of sight. It was simply on impulse that I took it to Italy with me."

"So, what did you do with it?"

"I took it to Germany and returned it to the Erdmann family."

Ken emitted a soft whistle. "Damn, that must have been hard."

"I feared it would be, and it was, but only in the beginning. Dad, they forgave me. Can you believe that? They treated me like a long-lost friend. I was humbled."

"Are you saying their forgiveness caused you to forgive Abigail?"

"When I felt the joy and relief of being forgiven and saw their delight in forgiveness, it inspired ... no, it compelled me to forgive. It changed my life."

Ken stood and leaned on the railing. "Thanks for sharing that, Obie. It explains a few things about you that I've never been able to put my finger on."

Obie rose to stand beside his father. "I'm sorry, Dad, for all the years I stayed away, and for neglecting you."

"And I forgive you for that, son." He chuckled. "About forgiving some others ... well, I'll have to work on that."

Obie slapped Ken on the shoulder. "This is a start, though."

* * *

"I simply don't know what to do," Laura said as she collapsed onto the overstuffed couch in the church office.

As people left the sanctuary after Sunday service, she had whispered to Obie, "I need to talk to you. I'll wait in your office."

He pulled up a chair to face the couch. She looked stressed; her hands kept brushing her skirt, and her eyes were red, as though from crying.

"You have to give me a little more to go on," he said

"It's Ben."

"Ben?"

"Has Cassie told you what he's doing?"

"You mean the clinic that he wants to build?"

"That too, but I meant what he's asking of me?"

Cassie had told him that Ben Williamson was trying to win back Laura's affection, but after all that had transpired between them, Obie had dismissed it as inconsequential; Ben's chances were about as favorable as Ernie Boswell's winning Frances Gibbons' attention. But there was more to it, judging by Laura's present state of mind.

"No, I don't know anything about his plans." He scooted his chair closer—but not too close. As with all interactions with Laura, he needed to set parameters. "Are we having this conversation because I'm your pastor, or because I'm family?"

"Oh, both, although I could use some of your pastoral wisdom."

"So, what's going on?"

"He's asked me to marry him."

"Really? Out of the blue?"

"It all started right after Dad's funeral. I was surprised he attended. We talked. He swears he's changed, that the affair that broke up our marriage was a huge mistake on his part. Begged my forgiveness, even."

"Forgiveness is a start, but evidently, that isn't enough for you?"

"Not nearly enough. We had issues even before his indiscretion. I give him credit for raising Dan as his son, even though he became distant with Dan as a teenager. He had a way with words, too. Ben was never physically abusive, but he hurt us, both Dan and me, not only with put-downs but also with long periods of silence anytime we protested."

Obie hesitated before asking, "Did you love Ben?"

She was not meeting his eyes. "Yes, I think I did. I learned to love him. But, Obie, remember the times." He heard her sigh. "My feelings for you were so mixed. Love and hate. I was simply numb until after Dan was born. After that, I believe I did love him."

"So, couldn't you still?"

"Maybe if he really has changed, but ..."

"You need proof, is that it?"

"I guess that's what it is. He seems sincere, but I'm struggling with trust."

He waited for her to look at him. When she did, he said, "Laura, I don't know how I can help you with this. Don't you know that I'm too close."

"Please, Obie, I need your help."

"How?"

"Talk to him. Please get to know him. He'll be here permanently in about two weeks. I trust your judgment."

"I remember him from when I was a teenager. He was often with Dr. Williamson when he saw Mom during her illness. I also saw him at Pinky's funeral, but I don't remember ever speaking to him."

"He plans to attend our church. His going to any church is a change. You'll have opportunities for private conversation."

"And any such conversations are just that, private."

"I understand, but you could at least give me some idea of the person you believe him to be."

"So, if he really has changed, will you marry him again?"

"Oh, I don't know. I don't know, Obie."

"That would be a big step, of course."

"I'm settled into a lifestyle. I don't know if I want all the problems that go with marriage, especially marriage with Ben."

"What about love? He obviously loves you. You deserve that."

She reached out and touched his hand. The effect was electric. "Talk to him, won't you?"

He must say it. "Laura, are you seeking my validation to marry Ben? If you are ..."

"Obie!" She stepped back, her eyes angry. "Don't even think such a thing."

"I'm sorry. I should not have asked that."

Her countenance softened. "Don't you remember what you told me when we went our separate ways? You said we were relatives by marriage and friends by choice, and we could be nothing more? I honor that, and I know you do, too." Her lips trembled.

He struggled to meet her gaze. He had overstepped. He said, his voice a little unsteady, "All right, Laura. I'll give you my opinion of Ben based on casual conversation, but I won't discuss you with him unless he requests it, and I doubt he will, knowing our history."

"Thank you, Obie. You're a good friend, in addition to being an exemplary brother-in-law."

He prayed silently, "God, help me."

CHAPTER FOURTEEN

July 1975

Ernie Boswell sat across the table from Obie in Ward's Coffee Shop. His boyhood friend was no longer trim but looked fit. Judging by how his left eye twitched, a quirk Obie remembered, Ernie had something important on his mind.

"You're buying the coffee," Obie said. "And why did you want to meet here? You have your own restaurant, and I have an office."

"Just supporting the other locals. We look out for one another, you know. Speaking of such, I worried at first that *Abigail's* would take business away from the other food joints, but that hasn't happened. Mine does better than ever, and Beth says the same about her café." He paused a moment. "Did you know that Beth is retiring?"

"I didn't, although she's up there in years, and she's not well."

"She's closing the café and selling the building."

"Doesn't she have relatives who could take it over?"

"None I know of. I heard that Bert Larkin over in Evergreen is interested, but that might be a rumor. The café would be missed. Beth is the best cook in the village. I tried hiring her years ago, but she wanted no part of that. I think she misses Pinky."

"They were good friends." *No more to be said about that.* "Ernie, you didn't ask to meet me to discuss eateries."

"Nope, I didn't." His eye still twitched. "I need your help."

"Is this church-related?"

"Nope. Matter of the heart."

More of this? He might have guessed. Matchmaking was not the role of a minister, nor was he suited for it, as evidenced by his failure to check out Ben for Laura as he had promised. Ben Williamson was settled into the refurbished office on Main Street, so there had been opportunities.

As for Ernie, Obie was sure this was about Frances Gibbons. Everyone knew he was in love with her and that she repulsed him at every turn, a fact he was not accepting. He sympathized, but it was Ernie's problem.

"Well ..."

"I can't get Frances to go on a date with me."

"And what am I supposed to do about that?"

"Well, you're my friend. You can persuade her. You're good at persuading."

"Not nearly that good."

"You know how I've always felt about Frances, even way back?"

"Ernie, you need to face facts. She's not interested in a romantic involvement. Don't you see that? Be satisfied with being her friend." The statement was purposely blunt, but they communicated that way.

"I want her to be my wife?"

"I know she's told friends she isn't interested in marriage. Clara Benedict heard her say it, and Clara told me."

Ernie snorted in disgust. "Bunch of clucking hens around here. You're the pastor. You shouldn't listen to that kind of gossip."

"I try to avoid it, but that's hard. Anyway, I can't talk to Frances about this."

"All right, you don't need to talk to her, but maybe you can advise me on how to convince her."

Obie laughed. "You're asking the wrong person for that advice. It took me over twenty years to figure out how to ask Cassie to marry me."

"Yeah, but you did figure it out. Are you my friend or not?"

Ernie would not let up until he had some weapon to take to the fight. Obie's sigh was involuntary; he had compassion for his friend because any help he might give would be insufficient.

But this was Ernie, his boyhood pal. "What does she like?" Obie asked. You should find out what she likes and make those your tastes, too."

"She likes books. Likes to read. I already tried that, though."

He already knew, but asked, "Where does she live?"

"She has that little house that sits off Clearwater Road, close to the Baptist Church."

"If you can get invited there, you can judge her tastes."

"What kind of tastes?"

"Furniture. Knick-knacks. Paintings. Look in her book-cases. That's where you'll find her greatest interests. You get the idea?"

"How in hell can I get invited to her house?"

"That's something you'll have to figure out."

"You're not much help."

Obie remembered something. "Did you know that Frances has started leading a women's Bible study?"

"I didn't know, but I'm not surprised."

"They meet in the library on Thursday evenings, but some-times they meet at her house. If you could get into that ..."

"Obie, do I look like a woman? Hell, that won't work."

This was a chance to get Ernie involved. He never partici-pated in such groups, although he would undoubtedly benefit. "I'll approach Frances about opening up that group to every-one."

A gleam lit Ernie's eyes. "That might work." He scratched his chin while Kelly, the waitress, refilled their coffee cups. "Once a week, eh? I might find time. Yeah, I just might."

* * *

It was not the way he would have chosen to have a discus-sion with Ben Williamson, but the opportunity came after Obie's axe bounced off a knot and put a gash in his leg.

"I'll have to stitch it," Ben said, "but the good news is that it's a clean cut and will heal quickly." While sewing the dead-ened wound, he said, "I've attended a couple of your church services, but we haven't talked before, have we?"

Obie tried to suppress his discomfort, a feeling not leg-injury related. *Ben knew precisely who he was.* "No, we've never talked." After a moment, he added, "But we should."

It was a perfect opportunity to critique Laura's former husband's sincerity. He had rehearsed what he might say, but before he could speak, Ben said, "Can I call you 'Obie'?"

"Of course, you can."

"And I'm Ben. Yes, you and I need to talk. And we need to be honest, too?"

"We do. We have a great deal in common in our personal lives."

Ben was not looking up as he continued to sew the wound. "Is it really over between you and Laura?"

It was a razor-sharp question, and Obie responded in like manner, "Just why do you want to know that?"

"I'm sorry, Obie. I shouldn't have been so direct. It's just that I'm a little desperate."

"Ben, it's been over since I was seventeen years old. I'm happily married to Cassie."

"Yes, it was explained to me how all that bad stuff happened. It was unfortunate for you both, but what I really want to know is whether Laura is over it."

"Oh, I'm sure she is. What happened between us happened a long time ago, and we were very young."

"Love can last a long time."

"Yes, that's true, but we're simply good friends now, as well as in-laws."

Ben chuckled and looked up from his work. "What about that Abigail? Isn't she something? There's not an honest bone in her body."

"A surgeon would know." Their agreement on that subject was a step toward friendship. "Ben, about Dan. I'm grateful for your ..."

"Look, Obie, I loved Laura. I considered it my good fortune that she consented to marry me. Taking Dan as my son was an honor. I love him, although I haven't always shown it the way I should have."

"We both have regrets."

"You and Laura were victims, which turned your love into

something else." He stopped a moment as he placed his instruments on a table. "But I deserted Laura and Dan for that foolish interlude."

"That was later in your lives, after you raised Dan to manhood."

"I still love Laura, Obie. I want to marry her again, but she won't forgive me."

Obie was unsure if it was the right time, but said, "I think she wants assurance that you really have changed."

"How can I give her that assurance?"

"Laura's an intelligent woman. She must see that you came to Stafford Rest to be near her. Doesn't that show your love?"

"She should see that, but I'll remind her." Ben had finished dressing the wound and stood. "Obie, I have changed."

"I believe you have."

"Laura asked you to talk to me, didn't she?"

"Yes."

"That's a good sign, isn't it, her wanting to know if she can trust me?"

"That's an excellent sign."

"Will you put in a word for me?"

"I will, and please come to church Sunday. Laura's helping serve communion. It's a good chance to look her in the eye."

"I'll be there."

* * *

Chet Boswell exited the Diamond Inn as Obie left the coffee shop following a light lunch with Tommy Matthews.

"Reverend, I'd like a talk."

Obie was in a hurry. "I have a meeting I can't miss," he said. "Come to my office later, anytime after two."

On the walk down White Cedar Street, Obie speculated about what Chet might want. Ernie's son was a laid-back contractor who worked on his own schedule, between bouts with the bottle. This might be an opportunity to swerve Chet from his self-destructive path.

Chet arrived shortly after two, entering the narthex door as

Obie happened to exit the office hallway. Obie directed him to a pew near the altar. Chet smelled of liquor but looked under perfect self-control. The sanctuary was dark, but enough light came through the stained-glass windows to illuminate the pew where they sat.

"I won't take up too much of your time," Chet said.

"We'll take as long as you like."

"It's about Dad. I know you two are good friends. I'm worried about what he's up to."

"And what's that?"

"His chasing after Frances Gibbons."

Obie braced himself. "Yes, I know about that."

"I hope you don't approve."

"Chet, I neither approve nor disapprove. It's Ernie's affair."

"He said you gave him some advice about how to win her attention, which he's been following."

"He asked me for help. Ernie is my lifelong friend and a member of my congregation. I can't refuse to help."

Chet's voice rose slightly. "Even when it's wrong?"

"I'd never advise anyone to do something I consider wrong." The last few months had taught Obie never to tiptoe around controversy, especially if it involved prejudice. He sometimes saw subtle evidence of bigotry in his congregation, not widespread but visible enough to know he must stand up to it. *He must confront Chet.* "Tell me why you think your father is doing something wrong."

"He wants to marry her, of course."

Obie said firmly, "Ernie has every right to happiness, Chet. I've known Frances Gibbons since we were children. She's a good person." Obie wanted Chet to state his objections in specific terms he could rebuke. "What is there about her that you don't like?"

A gasp escaped Chet's mouth. "Good lord, Obie, I don't dislike Frances." There was genuine surprise in the utterance. "I've known her for a long time, myself."

"Then what?"

"It dishonors my mother. It's just too soon, that's all."

Obie was pleased with his new understanding of Chet's thinking. "Well," he said, "in that case, I want to tell you something you may not know."

He proceeded to explain Ernie's early fascination with Frances, going back to elementary school. The thought occurred that it was Ernie who should be giving his son this private history, but he judged that Chet's need to know outweighed any potential embarrassment to Ernie.

"So, you see, Chet, your father hasn't suddenly lost his head over someone new who could replace your mother. He loved Cora, and he grieved."

"Maybe not long enough."

"Perhaps from your perspective, but people handle grief differently, just as they handle recovery from other trauma. War, for instance."

Chet nodded in agreement. "Yeah, I know about that. So, are you going to lecture me again about my drinking?"

Obie smiled. "Not today, but we can discuss it when you're ready."

"Hmm, maybe."

"Anyway, even if you had reason to worry about your father's feelings for Frances, you shouldn't."

"Why not?"

"She's a mature woman. She owns her home, has a job she loves, and has settled into a comfortable lifestyle. I'd say Ernie has little chance of winning her affection, except as a friend."

Chet sighed. "That's good news." He waited a few seconds before saying, "Now I feel guilty. Who am I to want my father not to find love? Everybody needs someone to love. Right?"

Obie recognized the cry for help. "Chet, what about you? Is there someone in your life?"

"Oh, no, not really." He hesitated. "There is someone, though. Someone I know. Shelly Gonzales. She works in the office at the furniture factory."

Obie had overheard a conversation between Cassie and Laura that cast a cloud over the young lady. He was curious about why Chet was attracted to her. "Tell me about her," he said.

"We've been out a few times. She has boyfriends, a lot of them, if you know what I mean." Obie was glad to see that Chet was not naive. "She likes me but doesn't want to settle down."

"Do you want to settle down?"

"I'm not getting any younger, so I suppose I am thinking about it. I'm not sure who'd take a chance on me, though. Shelly won't."

"Chet, you may be looking in the wrong places. I'll give you the same suggestion I gave you once before. There are several unattached women in our congregation, and that's probably true for the other two village churches."

Chet laughed. "Do you think I'm the kind of man who'd draw the attention of churchgoing ladies?"

"You might be surprised." He glanced at Chet's dirty trousers. There were wisps of sawdust in his hair. Some personal care might be in order.

"Are you trying to convert me? Get me to come to your services?"

Obie chuckled. "Well, that's a good objective and one I'll work to achieve, but I'm sincere when I tell you there's someone for you, Chet. There's a woman made just for you, but you have to look for her."

Chet stared at the cross over the altar for a long time before he said, "Shelly might like it if I bought a car. My truck smells of oil and grease. She mentioned it."

His obsession with Shelly Gonzales was apparent. Obie saw no good in that, but now was not the time to pursue it. He would, however, place himself in Chet's way at every opportunity.

He also needed to work with Ernie on his obsession. *Would he ever have time to write again?*

CHAPTER FIFTEEN

August 1975

On their return from a two-week vacation in California, they found a letter from Israel. Obie had counted the days and the hours until now and could barely control his excitement as they waited for their visitors. When he saw their car pull into their driveway, he called to Cassie from the doorway, "They're here!"

The man got out first. His distinctive long face with high forehead was little changed, but his slender body was no longer so thin.

Obie pumped his hand. It had been five years since their last meeting. "Adam, it's so good to see you."

"Likewise, Gainsworthy. You look fit."

Adam's wife emerged from the passenger side as Cassie arrived, holding Jacob's hand. Julie was only a step behind.

Dr. Rachel Silverman's short hair was dark with scattered gray. Her face was plain but unlined, and her smile was engaging. Although they had talked on the phone, this was their first in-person meeting.

After introductions, Adam knelt to speak to Jacob, who clung to his arm like they were old friends. "You're much better looking than your father," Adam said. "How old are you, Jacob?"

"Three." Jacob held up three fingers.

"A lot smarter, too." He hugged Jacob before he stood. Julie sidled up close and grabbed his hand.

Obie slapped his friend on the back again. "You said you're in the country for a month. So, how long can you stay with us?"

"Three days, maybe four if it's convenient with you and Cassie."

Cassie said, "Of course, it's convenient. We've waited years for this visit."

Adam took her hand. "Cassie, you're as beautiful as I remember." Cassie was blushing. "How long has it been since I came here and gave you that lecture about this idiot being in love with you?"

"A while ago," she said.

"Twenty-seven years, "Obie said, "and you're right to call me an idiot."

"I'm glad you finally got everything squared away."

"We have a good life," Cassie said. "We're content."

Laura's Lincoln pulled up behind the Silverman car. Cassie had invited her that morning after she expressed interest.

Adam bowed to Laura. "Aw, yes, Cassie's sister. Good looks seem to run in your family." Obie saw Adam's eyes on him. Adam knew the whole story from the earliest days to the present, but Laura knew little of his and Adam's history except that they were good friends. He hoped Adam would be discreet; ugly words had been vented about Laura during those war years.

Laura said, "Cassie tells me that you and Obie were in the war together in Italy."

"Yes, we were. We helped each other through some difficult times."

Cassie said, "You're in the presence of two war heroes, Laura. Highly decorated soldiers."

"Well, I know that Obie has a couple of medals, perhaps deserved, but Adam, what's your claim to fame?"

Obie cringed at what seemed her casual indifference. He gritted his teeth to keep from setting her straight.

Cassie was not so kind. "Laura, men who risk their lives to serve their country should be held in the highest regard. Adam served nearly the full length of the Second World War, and Obie has served in three wars."

Adam sounded benevolent as he faced Laura. "I have no part of fame, Mrs. ..."

"Williamson. I kept my married name. But please, call me 'Laura.'"

"All right, Laura." Adam, as usual, was gracious.

They went inside. After a quick house tour and a catch-up

talk session on the porch, they gathered around the big oak table in the dining area. Since they knew the Sivermans' approximate arrival time, Cassie had prepared a simple meal. Laura and Rachel helped her distribute the dishes.

"This table is like ours at home," Rachel said.

"We have lots of guests," Adam explained. "But I think this one is a bit larger than ours."

"We got it just last year," Cassie explained. "It's heavy. It took four strong men to carry it in."

Obie said, "It was in this house as I was growing up. Dad gave it to the elementary school to use in their cafeteria, but I got it back."

Laura laughed. "Yes, he bought them four new tables in return."

"Sentimentality," Rachel said. "I'm sentimental too, unlike Adam. Our country is new, and most of our inhabitants arrived with little more than they could carry. For those, sentimentality is a strange concept."

"Unless it's for historical antiquity," Adam said. "And we have much of that."

Obie sat next to Adam. Cassie meant to give Rachel a seat on the other side of her husband, but Julie slid quickly into that chair. "Julie," Cassie said, "I saved a seat for you on the other side."

"Mommy, can I sit next to Uncle Adam?"

Adam said, "You sure can, Julie. I'm honored to have you sit next to me." He patted her hand.

"It's perfectly all right," Rachel said. "I'll sit by Jacob."

"You'll have to excuse her," Cassie said quietly. "She takes liberties sometimes. And Adam, we've never referred to you as 'Uncle.'"

"Maybe it's time you did," Adam said with a smile. "How can I refuse a term of endearment that will make me part of your family? From now on, I insist on being called 'Uncle Adam' by Julie and Jacob."

"And I'm Aunt Rachel," Rachel said.

"Uncle Adam," Jacob called from his chair at the end of the table, "you've got big ears."

Adam roared with laughter. "So, I do! The better to hear you with. And you'd better be careful what you say, young man."

"You could hear our bells?" Jacob said.

'What bells is that, Jacob?"

"Cassie said, "He means our church bells here in the village that ring on Sunday mornings. He talks about them a lot."

"Well, Jacob," Adam said, "we won't be here on Sunday, but I'm sure those bells are beautiful to hear."

Julie was tugging on Adam's arm. "You remember Italy, too," she said.

"Obie's been telling you tales, Julie."

"I haven't," Obie objected. With some hesitation, he explained. "Julie seems to have some perception outside the realm of our understanding. She comes up with these little insights that often astound us. She once told me that I had to return to Italy before I had even decided to go. There are other things, too."

Adam took Julie's hand in his large ones. "Julie, you're right. I often remember the many adventures your father and I had together."

Obie blinked. It struck him that this was the first time anyone had referred to him as Julie's father. *But it was true.* She was his twenty-year-old daughter in every way except biologically. He loved her, and she loved him. He had *three* children, not two. Although he must have told Cassie that, he would tell her again.

Julie basked in the attention. "A woman with white hair talks to me sometimes," she said.

Rachel leaned forward from her chair. "I've heard of such experiences. I know it's not scientific, but our faith acknowledges the possibility."

Adam said, "Gainsworthy, you told me once about a vision you had in California. You insisted it was only a 'dream.' Isn't this the same thing?" Without waiting for an answer, he said to Julie, "Tell us about the white-haired lady."

"She's pretty," Julie said.

"And she talks to you?"

"Yes."

"What does she say?"

"She says she loves us. She tells me things I should do. And sometimes she says what other people should do."

"Do you always do what she says?" Rachel asked.

Julie laughed. "Oh, no. Only sometimes."

Obie had never questioned her extensively about her strange experiences. Now, he was curious. "Honey, did the woman ever tell you her name?"

"I asked her once. She said it didn't matter. She only wants to help people."

"How interesting," Rachel said. "It seems that Julie may be in touch with God's hidden world."

Laura said, "I don't believe in such things. Some people have overactive imaginations." She turned to Obie. "Man of God, what about it?"

He hesitated. "I don't know," he confessed.

"Isn't it against scripture?" Laura asked.

"No, it's not, but it may go against some church doctrine."

"That's a fine line, isn't it?" Adam observed.

Rachel said, "I've had a couple of patients who believed they passed briefly into the spirit world. They were good and decent people, not given to exaggeration. Anyway, it's food for thought. There's much we don't know."

Wishing to leave the subject, Obie said, "Rachel, our Dan is more than halfway through medical school. It's too bad he isn't here, for I'm sure you two could have an interesting conversation."

"Yes, I'm sure we could. He's at Johns Hopkins, isn't he? I'm attending a medical conference in DC next week. We could get together if he has time."

Laura said, "I'll call him. Maybe it can be arranged." She hesitated. "My ex-husband is also a physician. He has recently set up practice in Stafford Rest. You might enjoy a conversation with him."

"Why, yes, I would. Will you introduce us? I suppose practicing here is not so different from my situation."

"I'll take you to his office tomorrow morning."

Obie had watched Laura's face while she spoke. She and Ben had sat together in recent church services. Ben appeared to be a reformed man and sincere in his feelings for his former wife. *It might work.* Laura deserved happiness.

* * *

Ken and Angie often seized opportunities to supervise Julie and Jacob, so Obie was not surprised when Ken told him the day after the Silvermans' arrival, "You go and enjoy your friends. Me and Jacob will do some exploring." Ken had already taken Jacob for brief walks along the Morass.

Relieved of child-care responsibilities, Obie sat with Adam on the enclosed porch. He heard Cassie and Rachel in the dining area, comparing daily life in their home environments. He and Adam talked of many things, trivial and profound. The day was warm, so the windows were open, and a breeze stirred the curtains.

"It's peaceful here," Adam proclaimed as he set a nearly empty glass of lemonade on a side table. "Our home is also peaceful right now, but there's always the dark thought that we must watch over our shoulders."

"Will it ever improve?"

"We're making progress. Yes, it's better, but the conflicts with our neighbors will last my lifetime and beyond. We take two steps forward and slip back one, and sometimes it's two or three steps back."

"You handled the recent conflict with Egypt and Syria quite well."

"With your country's help. That victory has changed everything."

"From what you said in your letters, I gather you had a part in the conflict."

"I'm no longer in the military, but I act as an advisor when asked. That's all." Adam picked up his glass and took a sip. "You have your own problems, don't you?"

"Indeed. Watergate, a disgraced president, and a gasoline shortage, to name a few. At least we're out of Vietnam. Not the way we wanted, but now it's done."

"How are you handling the gas shortage?"

"Long lines at the pumps. We make do since we don't travel much, but it's a big problem nationwide. Dropping the speed limit has helped, I suppose."

"On another subject, Father's not well. Did you know that?"

"I didn't." Obie had not had personal contact with Ira Silverman since leaving Silverman Publishing; his book deal was handled through his agent and editors. They did, however, see Ira's brother when they went to California, but Hershel had not mentioned Ira.

"What is Ira's health problem?"

"Besides old age, he has a heart condition. He says he's retiring, but you know Father. In case you don't realize it, he'd like to have you back. He told me he would place the company in your hands in a minute. But, of course, he tells me the same about Silverman Financial, should I go back."

"Would you even consider that?"

"No, of course not. Would you?"

"Good heavens, no."

"I guess we've found our niches," Adam said. "Do you find time to write?"

"Not to any extent. All my time is spent whipping this church back into shape, or trying to. Once that's accomplished, I'll get back to it." Obie did not want to think about church duties; this was a day to spend with an old friend. "Tell me about David and Sarah," he said.

"Sarah still pursues her journalism career. She's becoming well-known in the Middle East, which has good and bad aspects since she's very outspoken. And Rabbi David sends greetings. He feels he knows you, having heard your name so often."

Obie had to smile. Adam was blasé about religion during his military and college careers, but that changed after his move to Israel. It seemed that Rachel and David had a significant influence.

The women came onto the porch. Cassie said, "Rachel is interested in our education system. I'll take her to the school and show her around. School doesn't start until two weeks from now, so there'll be no children there, but she'll at least have some idea about our physical layout."

"I'm on the education board in our equivalent of your school district," Rachel explained.

"And after that, we're meeting Laura at the clinic," Cassie said. "She's made an appointment with Ben for him and Rachel to discuss doctor things."

"I understand he's a skilled surgeon," Rachel said. "I want to pick his brain."

"He's a family doctor now," Cassie said. "My nephew Dan, Laura's son, will join him in the practice in a few years."

"I look forward to talking with him," Rachel said.

"Yes, Ben is always informative," Cassie replied, "but first we'll go to the school, and right after that to *Abigail's* for lunch. Mom and Laura will join us there."

* * *

After lunch, Laura, Rachel, and Cassie left for Ben's office. Obie needed to repair a forgotten matter at church, so Adam went with him.

He led Adam through the sanctuary and into the secretary's section of the church office. Roberta Barnes was bent over her desk, stapling sheets of paper together.

After introducing Adam, Obie said, "Roberta, I forgot to change an item in this week's bulletin. Is it too late?"

"No, I haven't run it yet. You're just in time. Where have you been all morning? The phone's been ringing off the hook." Her tone indicated exasperation.

"I told you I was taking today and tomorrow off." He must be patient; Roberta had a troubled relationship with her alcoholic husband. "That date I gave you for the retreat is incorrect. Please change it." He wrote on a notepad and handed it to her.

She looked at it and set it aside. "What are you going to do about Amos Adams?"

"What about Amos?"

"He's sitting back there in your office. He's been there nearly an hour."

"Didn't you tell him that I'm not in?"

"I guess I forgot that. I'm sorry, Obie."

"It's all right. I'll talk to him. But please remember that I'm unavailable the rest of today unless it's an emergency."

"Brad Blanchard is in the hospital in Saratoga Springs. His wife called."

"Is it his heart again?"

"Bertha thinks it's something he ate."

"Call Bertha and tell her I'll find time to see him tomorrow morning if he's still there."

"And that wedding you scheduled three weeks from Saturday ... the bride wants to move it up an hour. Is that possible?"

"Write down the information. I'll deal with it tomorrow. What does Amos want?"

"Didn't say."

Adam had a wry smile as he listened to the dialogue. While in the hallway between the two offices, he said, "Day off, eh? I'll wait in the car while you take care of this."

"All right. I won't be long. No, wait. Come in with me. You're a good judge of character. I want you to tell me what you think of this man. He's a thorn in my side."

"In what way?"

"He bucks me in nearly every project I initiate. He's not ignorant, but he's vocal."

"Well, bust him down for insubordination." He was grinning.

"Adam, this isn't the military, but I know what you're saying, that I should find a way to get rid of him. That's not the way churches work. It's not the Christian way. Not my way." He added, "At least not yet."

"Why do you think he acts the way he does?"

"I have no idea."

"Maybe you should learn more about him?"

"It's true that I don't know much. I avoid him when I can. He's a contractor and cabinet maker, and evidently is good at what he does. He owns a shop on Main. I've never been there, but I understand he deals in antiques, too."

"Know your enemy. That's something I've learned."

"I just want to see him changed."

"If that's possible."

"I don't want to give up on him or on any member of my congregation. But come in with me and see what you think of Amos."

Amos rose from the chair behind Obie's desk as they entered the room. He placed a spiral notebook on the desktop, a logbook Obie had used since his appointment. The book had been in a desk drawer. Obie felt his blood pressure rise. "That's private, Amos," he said.

"Pastor, if it's in this church, it's not private. As trustee chair, I have the right to know what's going on."

"You have the right to see that the boiler works and the roof doesn't leak. Stick to that." Obie picked up the logbook and put it back in the drawer.

"Anyway," Amos said with a smirk, "I've come here on behalf of a group of us that want some changes made."

Obie was not surprised since most of their conversations began the same way. He was sorry to have invited Adam to his office; his friend would see the difficult task he had taken on himself.

Obie controlled himself. "Let's put off this conversation until another time. I'd like you to meet …"

Amos had already turned to Adam. "Who are you?" he asked bluntly as he held out his hand.

"Adam Silverman, sir, a longtime friend of Reverend Gainsworthy. I'm glad to meet you."

"Silverman? Is that a Jewish name?"

"Yes, sir, it is."

Amos turned back to face Obie. "I've been here over an hour. I hope your absence was for church business?"

"I've been with friends I haven't seen for years. I worked the last two Mondays to have two days off. Staff Parish approved it, which was announced in the last two Sunday bulletins." He was losing patience.

"Well, I guess I can put off what I came for, but you can expect my visit in two or three days, and you'd better be on call today and tomorrow in case there's an emergency."

"I have it covered, Amos. Now, I'd appreciate you leaving

my office."

"In my good time."

"No, Amos ... now!" Obie motioned toward the door.

"What the hell! You have a lot of nerve kicking me out. I'll speak to Staff Parish about this."

"Speak away! Now, just leave."

As Amos moved toward the door, Obie was surprised to see Adam block his path and say authoritatively, "What, exactly, do you want from your pastor, Amos?"

Amos paled as Adam towered over him. "You know ... things," he sputtered. "Church things, something a Jew wouldn't understand."

"Try me."

Although the situation might have gotten out of hand, Amos recovered. "We want him to stop using the pulpit for his own personal beliefs. Beliefs most of us don't have."

"Be specific."

"He talks against war. He does that in his books, too. He would have our country be weak."

"You've read his books?"

"Well, no, but that's what they say."

"Mr. Adams, your pastor knows a great deal about war? He fought in the Second World War and the Korean War, and in this last one?"

Obie saw Roberta standing in the doorway, possibly brought by the raised voices. Amos said, "Everybody knows he was in three wars. So what? A chaplain? A desk job, likely. And I'm sure you can get medals pretty easily if you know the right people. A real soldier goes and does his duty without complaints."

"And which war did you fight in, Amos?"

"I was 4-F for the Second World War. But I was ready to go if they called me."

Adam's laugh was scornful. "You don't know a thing about your pastor's years of service to his country. I do because Obadiah Gainsworthy was in my patrol in Italy. We endured two years of hellish fighting up Italy and into the Alps. He was one of the bravest soldiers I've ever known."

"Well, of course …"

"Did you know he received a Silver Star for saving the life of his platoon leader while calling down artillery fire on positions only he knew about? He also received another Silver Star in Korea when he saved the lives of several men. All this is a matter of public and military record, so I would be careful of accusing him of shirking his military duty."

Adam stepped aside to let Amos pass. Obie expected retaliation in some form, but Amos was subdued. But he said over his shoulder as he slipped past Roberta in the doorway, "I still want that appointment."

"Roberta," Obie said, "please schedule Amos for Friday morning at ten."

"Yes, sir." He heard heightened respect in her voice.

After the door closed, Adam said, "I'm sorry to have interjected myself into your church affairs, but I couldn't help myself."

Obie laughed. "You got me through our war. I guess you're still protecting me, aren't you?"

"I believe you're doing a pretty good job of it yourself."

"So, what do you think about Amos?"

"He must have a bad past of some sort. Obie, you can't save everybody."

"I can try, though."

CHAPTER SIXTEEN

September 1976

Obie had enlisted Abigail's help the year before, soon after the Silverman visit; the blowup in his office with Amos made him realize that he must be more proactive toward the man. He was unsure how Abigail had quietened Amos's bluster but asked no questions.

He needed her help again. They met on her turf at *Abigail's*. He held off on church business, making small talk while eating a ham and cheese sandwich while she dabbed at a Caesar salad.

"You should have gone to California with us this year," he said. "Family" was a safe subject for the moment. "Even Dan and Ly Yen came for three days. All the kids had a ball. They explored the whole vineyard. You would have enjoyed it, Abigail."

"I'm getting too old for that kind of travel. There's too much to care for here to go gallivanting all over the country."

"Looking after everyone's business, including your own?" He made sure to smile.

In recent years, he had employed humor to smooth the delicate layer of their new trust. Sometimes it worked, and sometimes not so well.

Abigail smiled and said, "I feel like things are coming together in my family."

"Laura's marrying Ben, isn't she?"

"I'm hopeful. I've prayed for it."

Problems in that relationship still needed to be worked out, so he thought it best to remain silent on the subject. "And Danny may be returning to Stafford Rest."

"At last."

"That's almost a year away, and after he finishes his residency in Boston. He could go on to a specialty."

"I believe he'll come back here next year. Ben can teach him everything he needs to know."

"I don't think that's how it works, Abigail, but I hope you're right about his returning."

"They'll live with me."

"They will eventually want a home of their own?"

"I'm all alone, and my house is much too big for one person. I want them to live with me."

This was the woman whom Cassie had quoted as saying, "The last thing I would want is to have a little Asian bastard running around my living room." *There was hope.*

Despite his good intentions, he could not keep from saying, "There'll be little folks running around your living room."

If she recognized the jab, she did not show it. "The house is big enough for that," she said. "I want them there. It's so lonely without Pinky."

He saw her sincerity and regretted his words. "We all miss him, Abigail."

"Yes, but we were talking about Danny and his little family." She waved a hand. "They'll live with me, and after I die, the house will be theirs."

"You'd do that?"

"Danny's my grandson. I've already arranged it."

He was surprised, not only about her plans but that she was telling him. He was pleased, but it begged the question that he put into spoken words: "You haven't forgotten that you have another grandson and a granddaughter, have you?"

She laughed. "Obie, I have enough to make Jacob and Julie happy, too. How I divide it up is my business." She sat up straighter. "Now, what did you want to see me about?"

"Amos Adams and Arthur Baines will try to load Staff Parish with people who think like them. They want me out."

"Obie, I gave up my position on that committee last year. I need a rest. Anyway, I don't think they'll find that many people displeased with you."

It seemed a compliment, a rare thing from Abigail. "They'll try," he said. "Those two, with Glenda Smith and some other newer members under their influence, might manage a majority and get the ear of the Conference."

"I think you worry too much. Those new members haven't a clue about governing a church. And Glenda has never served on a major committee in her life. Why would she now?"

"Amos is good at organizing such things. I would like it if you rejoined and assumed the leadership again. You could do that, Abigail."

She stared at him a moment before speaking. "Why do you even care? You took the job reluctantly over two years ago, and I know you want to return to your writing. There are plenty of candidates now who can step in. This is your way out."

"I'll finish the job I started."

She smiled. *She was playing with him.* He should expect that from his mother-in-law.

She said, "I'll go back on the committee to give you my vote, but I'll not be chair again. That job belongs to Lucille Epps. She's young enough and has a friendly face."

"I know exactly what to expect of Amos and Arthur, but I still worry about Glenda. She has followers among the women. If she joins the committee, she might bring others with her."

"Find a job for her, something else that'll keep her so busy that she'll avoid other church duties."

"That's a good idea. And I think I know just the thing."

Abigail stood abruptly, saying she needed to supervise the kitchen staff. The meeting was over.

Later, he sat in his station wagon in the restaurant parking lot for several minutes. It had been a productive meeting. He needed her help and was grateful, but it was a bonus that she helped him of her own free will. One of his goals, set years ago, was to chip away at the wall between them. Maybe today, they had thrown a few chiseled wall fragments on the growing pile, but he was not yet sure how best to use the chisel.

He prayed aloud, "God, that's where you must help me."

* * *

It was a warm day, and the hills surrounding Diamond Lake were taking on their familiar fall attire. Ernie Boswell wiped greasy hands on a towel after lubricating the wheels of a dolly used to move large objects around the docks. However, his thoughts were not on dock tools or the scenery.

He had decided that tonight he would ask Frances Gibbons to marry him. It had never been a question of if—only when. For over a year, he had mulled over how to do it, whether to present her with the ring in a fancy restaurant in front of a crowd of people or take her to a private place, maybe a simple spot like the little-used path that connected his marina with the town beach. Or a picnic might do; she liked picnics. She had invited him to one during the summer, an outing for the library volunteers. Privacy was not an option at that event.

Her asking him was a surprise. For months, he had tried to get close. Obie's idea of joining her Bible study group had not worked well. He was the only man in the group for several weeks, a harrowing experience. In addition, he seldom knew what they were talking about, which made the meetings agonizing. But one night, after a session at her house, she asked him to stay a few minutes. His soaring hopes were dashed when she suggested that if he were to get anything from the "study," he would have to "actually read" the Bible.

He never mastered the nitty-gritty of Bible study, but it was a good sign that she reached out to him. A few days later, when she told him she would like him to attend the picnic and help carry the picnic baskets, he almost cried for joy.

For two months after that, he had enjoyed the uncertain elation of believing she had begun to like him again. Finally, he managed the courage to call her. He used the phone because he was not sure he could look in her eyes while asking for a real date. He told her, "I'll pick you up in my truck, and we'll go wherever you want and have the best meal you've ever had."

She had agreed but said, "We could go to your restaurant, but I would really like to go to *Abigail's*. I've been there only once."

This morning, he had taken his grey suit to Evergreen to have it cleaned and pressed, paying extra to have the job completed while he waited. He should have shopped for a new tie;

all his old ones were too wide and had dull colors, but he had chosen one that would do.

Ernie put his hands on the dock railing and looked off to the High Peaks in the north. He would take the "far view" and gain control of his life. *Cora was gone; she would not be back.* He loved Frances and would marry her, no matter what people thought, even if Chet objected. He would convince her to marry him. Absolutely.

* * *

"Did you like the salmon?" Ernie asked.

"Delicious. The wine was good, too."

"And the chocolate mousse?"

"Divine."

"Abigail said it's the best menu they've offered all week."

"Ernie, everything was just grand. I don't know when I've had a finer dinner. Thank you."

"I'm glad." *Of course, he was glad.* He was a stupid man who said stupid things.

Their private spot was by a northern window that offered a clear view of the water and village. It was getting dark, and lights had appeared in the village. He could still see his restaurant and marina on the near side.

Frances was watching him. "It's beautiful, isn't it?" she said.

"Kinda like Heaven."

"Yes, I guess it is. We're so lucky to live here."

"Except when the black flies come in early summer." *Why did he keep making idiotic comments?*

She laughed. "That's a small price to pay."

He paused to breathe. He must turn the conversation toward his intent. "Frances, there's something I'd like us to talk about."

"You sound serious, Ernie."

"Well, I am serious. I want to talk about us. About who we are to each other?" *Best to get to the point.*

"I value our friendship, Ernie. I really do."

He remembered that day when he was twelve and was, for the first time, about to jump off a north side cliff into water forty feet below. He had hesitated then, but now he made the leap. "Frances, I want us to be more than friends. I love you, and I want you to love me. We could ..."

"Ernie, I'm not ready ..."

"I want to marry you, Frances." He struggled to find the ring box in his pocket.

"Please, Ernie, be sensible. It would never work."

He found the little box and opened it. "Look, I have this for you." He removed the ring and held it toward her.

Her dark eyes were, for a moment, unreadable. She said, "It's a beautiful ring, and I feel honored that you'd want to give it to me, but what you want isn't possible. I'm sorry, Ernie."

Hope was slipping away. He eased the ring back into the box, which he set on the table between them. "I think you're wrong," he said.

"No, Ernie, I'm not."

"You don't have that kind of feeling for me? Is that it?"

He saw her hesitate. "Please, Ernie," she said, "just accept my decision. We can still be friends."

His head was aching. "Tell me why, Frances. Please tell me why. You do care for me. I've noticed little things, like how I catch you looking at me when you think I'm not looking at you."

"I don't do that."

"Yes, you do. There are other things, too. You pay more attention to me in Bible Study than the others."

She laughed. "You need it more than the others."

"Tell me that you don't love me." It felt like taking that plunge off the cliff and seeing a fat boulder directly below. He waited. When she hesitated again, he said, "I think we've loved each other since we were very young. I know I've loved you all this time. That's not to say I regret marrying Cora or having Chet and Linda. I can't imagine them not in my life. But this is now, and we have a chance to make our lives better. So, tell me how you don't love me, and why you don't."

A tear ran down her cheek. She took a tissue from her purse and dabbed at it. "I'm touched. I really am. You're elegant sometimes in what you say."

"You haven't answered my question, Frances. Why don't you love me? Is it the Black and White thing? I don't think anybody cares about that anymore."

This time, she responded quickly. "No, it's not that. It never was. And I haven't ever said I didn't love you."

"Now you're confusing the hell out of me."

"You must give up on me, that's all."

"I can't do that."

"You must, Ernie."

"Why?"

She signed, sat back in her chair, and did not resist when he reached across the table and cupped her hands in his. "Frances," he said, "You must tell me what's going on. You won't tell me you don't love me, but you won't consider marriage. You owe me an explanation."

Painful seconds passed before she said, "Yes, I suppose I do. I want to be fair, but this is hard for me."

"I'm here to listen."

"I think you'll understand when I tell you something only a few know about."

"Tell me."

"I don't want anyone else to know. Promise me, Ernie."

"I promisc."

This time, she took his hands in hers. "You went through some bad times when Cora was ill," she said between sighs. "I don't want you to go through something like that again."

"That's all over ..." He recoiled as if a knife had stabbed him in the ribs. "Frances ..."

"Ernie, I have cancer. I've known about it for two years. Chemo seemed to get rid of it, but it came back, and I'm scheduled for an operation. I don't know what my future holds."

Ernie's world stopped, but for only a few seconds. He said the words he must say. "Whether you marry me or not, I'm with you, Frances. Whatever comes, I'm with you."

*   *   *

Dan Williamson stared at the streetlight-illuminated ceiling as he lay beside Ly Yen in the bedroom of their small apartment in downtown Boston. He was exhausted after a double shift at the hospital, but could find no comfortable sleeping position.

Ly Yen stirred, then turned toward him and placed a hand on his shoulder. "Dan, you are restless. What bothers you?"

"Sorry, Honey. Things are rattling around in my head."

"I thought I heard clanging," she said. He grinned. Her innocent humor was always refreshing.

"I'm trying to be quiet. Don't want to wake Laurie and Obadiah."

"Don't worry. Ten-year-olds sleep like our forefathers long gone.

"Yes, I guess you're right. Ly Yen, I'm trying to make a big decision. I know you say you'll go anywhere with me, but I want it to be our decision, not mine alone."

"All right, my dear one. Let us decide." She had not called him that for a long time. She had become Americanized in many ways, but when she slipped back into the mode of her Vietnam days, he was reminded of how they had met and how he had fallen in love with her then.

"Do you want us to decide right now?"

She switched on the light by their bed. "Yes. Let us decide our future now so we can go to it."

"There are only two possibilities I want to consider."

"Perhaps you want to study some more? Specialize?"

"I could do that. At the least, I need more surgery skills."

She said, "It will mean staying in Boston much longer, maybe for the rest of our lives."

"But we would secure our future, send the twins to the best schools. and contribute to this community." He remembered discussions with his mother in which she had presented that case. He had argued the opposite. Times change.

"They are good things."

"And you can continue your schooling once I start to earn a living salary," he said. "Ly Yen, you've talked about going to a seminary. Is that still something you'd like to do?"

"It is, but it is not what I must do. It is a like, not a must."

"The other possibility is to go back to Stafford Rest. Dad is holding open a position for me. He needs someone, and he's patient, but I have to let him know, and soon."

"When could we go?"

"Next summer."

"What will we do, then?"

"I don't know. That's what's keeping me awake."

"A nun once showed me how she made decisions. She pinned two pieces of paper on the wall. On one, she wrote 'advantage.' On the other, she wrote 'disadvantage.' She said it was to see which list was longer and decide from that."

"I guess that makes as much sense as anything. Okay, get the paper."

They went to sit on the sofa. Ly Yen wrote, filling both sheets as they expressed the pros and cons of various possibilities. Nearly an hour passed before Dan said, "That's enough. Clearly, it's more favorable to stay in Boston. We must think of our children and of advancing our professions. It's no contest."

"It is decided, then?"

"We'll stay here. Now, let's go back to bed. I'm ready to sleep."

Sleep did not come. Eventually, Ly Yen turned the lamp on again. They lay quietly as their eyes adjusted to the light. She said, "The nun spoke other words too. She said that happiness overturns ... no, that is not the word."

"Overrides?"

"Yes, overrides everything. She said that God gives us the happiness. 'What the heart feels' is the words she said."

It came then, knowing without a doubt. *List be dammed.* He said, "Ly Yen, we're going home to Stafford Rest."

"Yes, dear one, I know."

Part Two

1978–1988

The Cross

CHAPTER SEVENTEEN

June 1978

Lacinda Grandcastle, weary from several days and nights in state campsites, approached the village from the north. "Awesome" was the word that came to mind as she viewed the midday panorama of town, lake, and sky spread before her. The sign at the bottom of the hill announced, "WELCOME TO STAFFORD REST AND DIAMOND LAKE."

She said aloud. "God help me, I think I've found it."

A green metal bridge was ahead, but she turned her ragged Volkswagen bus into the parking lot on the right. An oversized sign on a long, low building announced, "Caleb's Diner." Her empty stomach begged for attention.

She could have sat at the counter alongside three other customers, but chose a table a few steps into the dining area. The waitress came before she was seated and said, "Lunch special today is butter and garlic-glazed trout, fresh from the lake."

She wanted to say that she doubted that "fresh from the lake" part, but asked, "What's your soup?"

"Beef barley."

"I'll have that. I get bread with it, don't I?"

"Of course. The rolls were made this morning. Cup or bowl?"

"Bowl, and a glass of water."

"You passing through?"

"Don't know yet."

"My name's Dorothy."

"Mine's Lacy." She would give no more identification than that, and probably should not have given that much. She watched as Dorothy spoke to a big man at the grill, whom she guessed was Caleb. He glanced in her direction. *She really should be more careful.*

When she was sure no one was looking, she withdrew a small zippered bank pouch from her larger cloth bag. The pouch was rescued from a garage sale somewhere in Pennsylvania. Inside were three five-dollar bills, four ones, and a handful of change—less than twenty dollars—her entire net worth, not including the doubtful worth of her motor vehicle.

She was sure she smelled; she had bathed at night in the stream that bordered the last campsite but had no opportunity to wash her clothing. With dwindling funds, she could not continue to pay even the small campsite fees. Her gas tank was nearly empty, so going farther was not an option. She liked the looks of this town and wanted to ask more questions.

When Dorothy brought the soup and rolls, Lacy said, "Any work around here?"

"Not much. You'd need to go farther south, to Glens Falls or Saratoga Springs."

"This is a pretty town."

"There's also an Air Force base over at Plattsburg. It's a better economy there."

"What is there here?"

"Restaurants, mostly. Supermarket. The furniture factory is the biggest industry, but I don't think they need anyone now."

"How do you know that?"

"I hear things from our customers. Everybody here knows everybody else."

Lacy had no experience in the furniture world, but thought that having pursued the goal of an industrial designer might translate. As always, there came regret about leaving college after three years. She had been drawn away from her ambition, captured by the glamor of a different profession. That venture ended in disaster and had forced her to run. *What a fool she had been. No more!*

She must not let her feelings show. She asked, "If I wanted to apply for a job at the furniture factory, who would I contact?"

"I suppose Laura Williamson. She runs it."

"Do you have her phone number?"

"Wait a minute," Dorothy went to the front and returned with a phone book.

The book was thin. That was good. Staying away from larger cities and towns will make it less likely that she could be found.

Dorothy said, "Stafford Rest Furniture. That's the name."

"Thanks, Dorothy," Lacy said, forcing herself to smile. Interaction with people had been erratic lately, the result of always being on the move. Now, she must polish her manners and be extra polite with this Laura Williamson if she were to get work at Stafford Rest Furniture—and she was confident she would.

*   *   *

As Laura placed the phone back in its cradle, she wondered why she had consented to interview a stranger she had no intention of hiring. The deep southern accent, refreshing in its sincerity? That was it—the sincerity. The woman was not a carpenter, and there were already more sales staff than needed. She would speak to this Lacy Grandcastle, but would make quick work of it.

Later, she stood at the window that overlooked the parking lot. When Miss Grandcastle arrived, Shelly would greet her and bring her to the office.

To make matters worse, today was not the best of days. *What had gone wrong with her life, anyway?* There were too many miscues lately. It was not only her lapse of sanity this afternoon concerning this interview; there was a forgotten dinner date with Cassie and Obie, a fight with her mother over nothing, and worst of all, she had told Ben that she would seriously consider marrying him again.

She thought he had given up on that. His notable lack of attention for several months was undoubtedly because he and Dan were so busy with the final stages of opening the clinic. That was done, and he appeared to have renewed his pursuit. His persistence was admirable. *Should she ask Obie's opinion again?*

A battered Volkswagen bus with hand-painted flowers on every available space pulled into the lot. The young woman who emerged confirmed her suspicions: *Hippy.* Her hair was long and probably unwashed. She wore white slacks, dirty even from a distance. Laura went to sit at her desk and called Shelly.

It should have taken only two minutes for them to arrive, so after ten minutes, irritation set in. By the time Lacy Grandcastle entered the door, Laura had decided she wanted no part of this girl. She would, however, be polite.

With a raised eyebrow, Shelly said, "Sorry we took so long, Mrs. Williamson. Miss Grandcastle wanted a quick tour of the facility."

"Thank you, Shelly. Sorry to take you away from your work."

"And it's impressive," Lacy said as she held out a hand to Laura.

Lacy's hand was unexpectedly soft. "Have a seat, please," Laura said. The girl eased herself into the overstuffed chair in front of the big desk.

"Yes, we've been in business a long time," Laura said. "My father started it in the twenties. At first, we only made rough Adirondack furniture to fit the décor of most homes here and for those who like the style. But in the last few years, we've branched out to include many other styles. Rest assured that 'Adirondack' will always be at the core of our business."

As the girl nodded, Laura wondered why she was telling her these things; she would be gone shortly.

Up close, Laura saw that although her clothing was filthy, Lacy was clean. She was attractive enough, her smile engaging. Her hair was damp as if she had just washed it; that was a mystery, for she said she had just arrived in town.

Lacy sat up straighter, seeming aware she was being scrutinized. Her eyes flashed annoyance for a moment, but then softened. "Mrs. Williamson, I want to apologize for my appearance. You see, I've slept in campsites for several nights now."

"And why were you doing that, Miss Grandcastle?"

"I'm fascinated by the Adirondacks. My father, who worked here a long time ago as a lumberjack, painted a wonderful picture ... not of lumberjacking ... he hated that, but of the beauty of the forest. I'm looking for a place to settle, you see, and the images he painted have stayed with me. So, here I am, exploring all the little towns and villages."

"Yes, the area is unique."

"Y'all have a nice town, but I do apologize for my appearance. I planned to stay in motels, but my car was broken into and my clothes and money taken. So, I'm a little destitute right now. I hope you understand."

Probably a lie. "You've had some bad luck."

"This job will put me on my feet again. Ma'am, perhaps I can have an advance to ..."

What gall. "Miss Grandcastle, this is an interview, not a job offer."

"Of course. I'm sorry." Her face displayed little remorse.

"Most young people leave to find work in the cities, not come here to work."

"I know, but I grew up in the city, and now I want something different."

"This is a relatively small furniture factory and outlet in an out-of-the-way town. What qualifications do you have that set you apart from other young women looking for work?" *That will separate her from her illusions.*

"Ma'am, I have three years of industrial design from the University of South Carolina."

Laura hid her surprise. "So, you didn't finish?"

"I took a break to pursue another career."

"And what was that?"

"I sing. Soprano. I was offered a job in a nightclub. It was the chance to pay off some of my debts."

"I see. How long did you do that?"

"Several months."

"And did you quit that job?"

"I did." For the first time, Laura saw hesitation; there was something the girl was not revealing.

"Why are you not going back to school?"

"I need to work in the world for a while. I may go back someday, but for now, I want to gain experience in an organization like this."

Better to end it now. "Lacy, I don't think you're a good fit for a job here. First of all, I'm not looking to hire right now, and second, your education makes you overqualified for any position I might have."

Lacy sat up straighter and said with a new level of confidence, "And I think you're wrong about that, Ma'am."

The girl had brass. "And why do you think that?"

"I see possibilities that other people might not see."

"After a ten-minute walk-through?"

"Yes, Ma'am. I can help you push through to a better business."

Laura's defenses kicked in. "There's nothing wrong with this business."

"No, of course not." She crossed her arms. "But I can help make it better."

This was getting ridiculous. "Oh, and how will you manage that, Miss Grandcastle?"

"Your outlet is in the wrong place. I can help you move it to where your sales will burgeon."

Perhaps the word "burgeon" made Laura turn a corner, or maybe it was because she had already thought about outlets. "All right, I'm listening."

"You're way back by this swamp with one little sign on Main Street to guide you here. Main Street *is* where your outlet should be."

"Miss Grandcastle, our outlet is a small part of our business. We make most of our sales by placing our furniture in retail stores all around the region. We have salespeople for that."

"And that's fine, but that doesn't mean you shouldn't expand sales. To start with, it would increase your cash flow tremendously."

"There's no space available on Main that's as large as we have here."

"You're wrong about that, Ma'am." She saw Lacy's eyes brighten. "Dorothy, at the diner, gave me a general idea of your layout here, so I took the liberty of looking at Main Street. Dorothy said she heard that the food market by Garnet Creek, Cam's Supermarket, I think it is, was going out of business ..."

"Cam's going out of business? I haven't heard anything about that."

"I checked it out. I couldn't speak to the owners, but one

clerk was quite talkative. They are closing. The building will go up for sale in about a month. It's the right size for your outlet, with tons of room for expansion."

Laura was impressed. "You did all that? You were here less than an hour after our phone call. That's pretty quick work."

It was focused work, too. There was more to Lacy Grandcastle than she had first thought.

"I need this job, Mrs. Williamson."

Laura folded. "All right, but you'll start in the billing department at beginning pay. Then, we'll see how that goes."

"About that advance ..."

"Don't push it," Laura said, but she opened her purse anyway.

* * *

Lacy had landed the job on Tuesday. As she parked on Main Street Saturday afternoon, she congratulated herself on her good fortune. The work was easy and the people were friendly. Stafford Rest appealed, but her real success hinged on keeping her location a secret from the man who wanted to harm her.

The sign over the door of the red brick building said, "Diamond Inn." She had purposely delayed coming here. With time off until Monday morning, she would relax and get to know more people.

It was dark inside, and she stopped momentarily in the doorway until her eyes adjusted. A half dozen people occupied the room; two couples sat at tables off to one side of the bar. A man sat on a bar stool. The bartender had slicked-back hair and wore a slightly soiled apron.

The patron at the bar was elderly and drinking beer. Lacy sat on the stool farthest from him.

"What's your pleasure, miss?" the bartender asked.

"Bourbon on the rocks, please, and do y'all serve food?"

"We're not a restaurant, but we have several kinds of sandwiches."

"Ham and cheese?"

"Sure." He called the order to someone in the back before saying, "You're that new hire at the factory, aren't you?"

"Why, yes, I am." She had heard that same question in different forms for three days. She would have to get used to the speed at which news traveled in small communities.

"Well, welcome to our kingdom." He offered his hand across the bar. She took it and tried to smile. He said, "I'm Chuck."

"Lacy."

"Good to meet you, Lacy. Where are you from?"

She expected it—the questions. To not answer would cause suspicion. She could not hide her accent, but the South was big, and she could choose an origin far from any place that gave clues to her present whereabouts. "Birmingham, but I've been around, too."

From the look on Chuck's face, she expected him to say, "I'll bet you have," but he nodded and said, "We're happy to see new faces around here. It seems like more people leave than are coming in."

She had her drink, ate her sandwich, and ordered another bourbon. During that time, the couples at the tables left, and one man came to sit next to the man at the bar. Their conversation was in soft tones.

"Is it always like this?" she asked. "So quiet?"

Chuck laughed. "It picks up considerably at night. Fridays and Saturdays are my best days. Seats tonight will be scarce. I have an extra bartender coming on later today."

"I see a piano over in the corner. Do y'all have live entertainment?" She had saved the question for the right time.

"We have some local talent we draw on occasionally, but not this weekend, unfortunately."

She was startled by a voice behind her. "Cowboy and country music. That's it."

The man had entered without her noticing. "Honky-tonk stuff," he said as he sat beside her without asking.

He was several years older than her, but ruggedly handsome, and well on his way to intoxication.

148

Chuck said, "Lacy, this here's Chet Boswell. He's harmless."

"Howdy do, Miss. I'm Chet." He extended his hand. It was callused.

"Yes, I know. Chuck just told me."

"Oh, yeah, and I'm harmless, too." His grin was broad. He said to Chuck. "I was over at Evergreen. They cut me off."

"And you drove over here? Dammit, Chet, you've got to stop doing that. You're going to kill yourself, or somebody else."

"I'll have a beer."

"No, you won't. Not in here. I'll get you a soda or coffee."

"Well, can I at least buy the lady a drink?"

Lacy was unsure to whom he directed the question, but she answered anyway. "Chet, I've had my limit. Why don't you have something to eat? The sandwiches are good."

Chet put his face up close to hers. "Miss Tracy ..."

"Lacy."

"Lacy, why don't you and me go somewhere and have a good meal together? There's the diner, or *Abigail's,* if you want something fancy."

"Oh, no. But thanks anyway, Chet. I just ate a sandwich."

"Later, then?"

She would not encourage him, no matter how appealing he was if you imagined him sober. "Maybe," she said, knowing she should have used stronger words.

Chet grunted something unintelligible before he excused himself to go to the men's room. When he had gone, Chuck said from down the bar where he was washing glasses, "Lacy, Chet's not usually like this unless he's had too much to drink. He's shy around women."

"What's his problem?"

"He's a war vet. He won't talk about it, but he saw some bad things in Vietnam. He drinks to forget."

I believe I will have another," she said before adding, "But it's his life, and it's up to him to turn it around."

"Yeah, I guess you're right."

This was her chance. "Chuck, you mentioned earlier that you sometimes have entertainment on weekends. Do you have any groups or singers lined up?"

"Nope. Sometimes, they just show up. I don't make a big thing of it. They bring in business, so I give them a little something from the till. Why do you ask? Are you a performer?"

"Singer."

Chuck set her drink on the bar. "What kind of music?"

"I have a wide range. I can adjust to whatever your audience wants."

"Tell you what … come in tonight. If no regulars show up, you can give it a go for a couple of numbers. Even if they do show, you can squeeze in. Bernie is always here. He's a piano player."

"Thanks, Chuck. I'll be here."

Chet looked more subdued on his return. He slid onto the bar stool and said, "I was a little forward with you. I'm sorry if I offended you. I meant well about asking you out for a meal."

"I'm not offended in any way, Chet. I've been eating at the diner since I arrived and probably will until I find an apartment. What was that restaurant you suggested? *Abigail's?* I'll have to try that sometime."

CHAPTER EIGHTEEN

August–September 1978

Rain fell in streaks against the corner window of Obie's office; it made a dreadful day even more bleak. A mid-morning phone call had come from his father in Saratoga Springs with the news that Angie had died.

Ken had taken her to the hospital the previous evening. "It's only indigestion," he said in a late-night call; she would come home soon, and Obie "need not drive down."

Angie's death came on the heels of yesterday's letter from his cousin in Italy, in which Teresa Hazen informed him of the recent death of his Aunt Maria. The two sisters had died within days of each other.

Obie spent several hours performing the hurtful task of informing family members and making arrangements for his aunt's funeral. Except for a few cousins in Italy, his mother's family had dwindled. He had called Angie's son, Martin, in Hartford, and her daughter, Cleo, in Buffalo. Angie had a brother, too, but Gerardo had left the family at an early age, and no one had heard from him again. Angie and Izzie believed their brother was dead.

Obie had also called Father McNeal in Evergreen; he would handle the funeral Mass. Angie's body was already on the way to a funeral home there. She would be buried in the cemetery above Lake Road, where Obie's mother and all the elder Gainsworthys were buried.

It was late afternoon when Ken called to say he was back in town and was coming to the church. He soon arrived, shaking his raincoat vigorously in the hallway before hanging it on a coat rack near the office door. They hugged. Except for Obie's initial "I'm sorry, Dad," neither spoke for half a minute.

Ken broke the silence. "Can you send a message to Maria's family?"

"It's already in the mail."

"How about Cleo and Martin?"

"I've called them. They're coming."

"You'll have to postpone your vacation in California."

"I'm canceling it altogether. It won't hurt to miss a year."

Ken went to sit on the couch. Obie joined him.

"Does Cassie know?" Ken asked.

"I called the school right after you told me. She'll tell the rest of her family."

Ken's eyes were red. He sighed. "Isn't it strange, Angie and Maria dying so close together and neither knowing anything about it?"

"Well, I suspect they know now," Obie said.

"Do you believe the Heaven thing, that we go to that better place after we die?"

"Yes, Dad, I do."

"And not into some purgatory?"

"I'm not sure about the mechanics of it all, and the Bible isn't consistent on the subject, but I think that if we are worthy, we go at once to live with our loved ones in God's Kingdom."

"So, Angie is right now with Maria, Izzie, and your mother?"

"I believe that. Mom and her three wonderful sisters are together."

"I'll try to keep that thought uppermost, but right now, it's tough to do anything but cry."

Obie put his arm around Ken's shoulder. "Dad, you can cry as much as it takes ... and I cry with you."

They were quiet as rain splattered with added intensity on the corner window panes.

* * *

Medical practice in an Adirondack village was harder than Dan had imagined, but rewarding. Although Ben was a task-master, he was also a brilliant mentor. More than that, he had changed from father to friend status. Dan marveled at how different it was from his growing-up years in Boston, when constant friction existed between them. The man really had changed, and he was not the only one to recognize it; his mother told him that she had finally consented to remarry Ben.

What will his relatives think about that, especially Obie? The undercurrent of family feelings remained an ongoing mystery; maybe that was a permanent situation. *But he wanted to know more.*

On a warm day in early September, he invited Obie to lunch at *Ernie's*. It was their first time together since Angie's funeral two weeks previously. They spoke of various things, including their children's lives.

"I can't believe Jacob will start first grade next month," Dan said.

"He breezed right through kindergarten," Obie said, sounding proud. "And what about Laurie and Obadiah? Sixth graders. Have they chosen their career paths yet?"

Dan laughed. "They would have if it were up to Ly Yen. I keep reminding her that they're still children."

"She wants the best for them. She's a gem, that wife of yours."

"Indeed. I lucked out."

"We all did. I hear that she even gets along with Abigail. So, it still works out, living in the same house?"

"It's manageable. Ly Yen is quite adaptable." He imagined Obie was thinking that she would need to be.

"In the year you've been back, Ly Yen has made herself an indispensable member of our congregation."

"Did you know that she attended classes at a seminary in Baltimore? That was hard with the kids and me in med school, but she managed. I think she wants ordination, eventually."

"She's mentioned the classes, but I didn't realize the extent of her ambition. That's wonderful news. Now that you're settled in, she can continue on that path. I'll help in any way I can."

"Actually, she said she wanted to talk to you about it." Dan sighed. "She takes her faith seriously, much more so than me, I fear."

"I'm happy that you joined our church, Dan. I know it's a family thing with Ly Yen, but your association with people of faith won't do you any harm."

Dan wanted to get to the subject. "I suppose you know that Mom and Dad are remarrying." He watched Obie's face for a reaction.

"Yes, I heard." It was said with the same detached look that might be displayed after the announcement of a distant cousin's birthday party. "That's months off, isn't it?"

"New Year's Eve wedding at Grandmother's. It will be on the patio if the weather permits. That's where they were married the first time."

Obie had looked away and was clenching his jaw. *A nerve had been struck.* However, when Obie turned to face him again, his expression was inscrutable. "I'm happy for them," he said.

"Nothing fancy, just a simple service. Father Parker will marry them. Then they'll go away for a week to Bermuda. Dr. Carson in Evergreen will help me cover Ben's patients while he's gone."

Laura had told Dan that Curtis Parker, the Episcopal priest, was asked to perform the marriage ceremony after Obie declined her request. She also revealed that she was upset initially but accepted Obie's explanation that it did not "feel appropriate."

"I'm happy they've finally reconciled," Obie said.

"Mom says you helped pave the way for that."

"I did little. Ben and I talked briefly, but we discussed other family and church matters. And we've become friends."

"Well, I'm sure your words had an impact."

Dan felt guilty about probing Obie's feelings for his mother; it was the same tactic he had used on her. *Was he being unnecessarily cruel, or was it simply to validate his own existence?* From the insight he had gained, he believed Obie and his mother had been in love when he was conceived. Would that not make it possible for them to feel some of that emotion now?

Love made impossible things possible. He and Ly Yen had loved each other from their first time together. And even with all the barriers in their way, that love never faltered. Obie often spoke about love in his sermons, and although "love" had several meanings, there must be some overlap, a congruence where one kind was hard to distinguish from another. According to Obie, love in all its forms comes from God. Ly Yen said that, too.

He did not doubt that Obie and Cassie would stay happily married and that his mother and Ben would make a new beginning, but he hoped they would handle any bleeding-through of emotions with maturity.

Without meaning to reveal his thoughts, Dan said out loud, "It's all okay."

"What?"

He recovered. "This day. Beautiful."

"Yes, it is."

* * *

Obie was laying an undercoat on his canvas when Ernie came through the barnroom door. For a moment, he was annoyed. Monday was his day off.

"Painting, eh? Ernie said as he came into the room. "What's it going to be?"

"This is just the base. I'll climb the ridge to catch the early fall colors."

"Do you have time to talk?" Ernie sounded in good spirits.

"Of course."

"It's about Frances." Obie would have been surprised had it been about anything else. Frances had been Ernie's main topic for the past two years. She was recovering from her second operation. Hope soared after the first surgery, but plummeted when the cancer came back. Her friends were concerned, but Ernie worried the most.

"How's she doing?" Obie asked.

"Good. No, excellent. They think that this time they got it all."

"I'm happy about that, Ernie. She's a sweet person."

"Ernie's voice boomed through his smile, "And that sweet person has finally told me that she'll marry me."

Obie stood to shake Ernie's hand. "That's wonderful, Ernie. Just wonderful!"

"And I give you a heap of the credit."

"I didn't do anything. I've never talked to Frances about you. Never."

"You showed me how to get her attention."

"That wasn't ..."

"And one of your sermons not long ago changed things. She said it herself, said the way you explained love made her realize that we can't pass up the real thing. That part about love being a gift from God that we should gift to others is something she's repeated over and over."

"I'm glad it helped."

Ernie had not stopped smiling. "She said that my sticking by her through this cancer thing shows that my love is my gift to her and that she'd be foolish not to love me back."

"So, when is the wedding?"

"Today, if you've got time."

"What! Ernie, I can't ..."

"I have the license." He held out a document toward Obie.

Reason must prevail. "Ernie, I'm sure Frances will want to do this differently, announce it in church, and invite folks to a service. We can't possibly get all this together today."

"Sure, we can."

"I'll talk to Frances tomorrow."

"You can talk to her right now. She's outside in the truck. She's okay with it."

Obie was floored. "Are you sure?"

"Well, go ask her yourself. And make it quick. I've made reservations at Niagara Falls, and we want to get there before dark."

Obie discovered in the next few minutes that Ernie was correct; Frances was not only willing, she was eager. Painting could wait.

Cassie gathered a few people who had an hour free, including Dan. Obie went to the Diamond Inn to inform Chet of what was happening. Drinking but still sober, he said, "I guess I'm happy for whatever makes Dad happy. When and where is it?"

156

"*Abiligails*', an hour from now. Abigail has offered the terrace on the lakeside for the ceremony and said she'd provide hors d'oeuvres as a wedding gift after the service."

The terrace had a cool breeze from the lake that caused the small group to gather close around Ernie and Frances as they took the vows that joined them "for better or for worse." Obie prayed that it was "for better."

Later that evening, as he sat on the porch in the fading light, he reminisced about his and Ernie's long friendship. There was youthful sparring, but his friend was always trustworthy, a trait Obie was sure carried over into every aspect of his life. Ernie had always loved Frances but had married Cora and was faithful to her because it was the honorable thing to do.

Ernie always approached him in a carefree manner and said what he thought. His Christian faith was neither sophisticated nor displayed, but it seemed somehow purer than his own.

He could not suppress a sigh. *Would he ever be truly at peace with himself?* After four years as pastor of Stafford Rest Methodist, he was still struggling. He had hoped to know himself better—identify his true purpose. Was he a writer or a pastor? Or some hybrid of the two? Answers seemed distant. He sat through the dusk until it turned dark.

* * *

Obie was surprised to see Chet at his office door two days after Ernie and Frances's marriage. It appeared to be a working day, for sawdust was in his hair, and he was sober. "Can I have a little of your time?" he said.

"Of course."

Chet sat on the couch. "There are a couple of things I want to discuss. But the first is simply something I want to say. We talked once about my dad's relationship with Frances. You thought my reason for objecting was that I'm prejudiced."

"No, Chet, I didn't think that. You explained that you thought your father was moving too fast after your mother's death."

"Okay, I just wanted to make that plain. Frances is a good woman, and they're both happy. But I've got to say, that was one whirlwind of a wedding."

"Indeed, it was."

Chet leaned forward. "Obie, I have a problem. It's not a huge problem, just a situation I want advice about."

"Shelly Gonzales, I bet." That was an off-again-on-again romance. Chet probably wanted to settle down, and Shelly was not the settling-down type.

"No, Shelly and I are quits. That's over. Has been for some time now. But this situation is something like that."

Obie feared where the discussion was going. "Chet, I'm not Ann Landers."

Chet grinned. "I know," he said, "but Dad said you gave him some good advice along those lines, and I happen to know that you helped Dr. Williamson get back together with Laura."

"I never ..."

"I also remember your part in bringing Ly Yen here and hooking her up with Dan. You're good at bringing people together. Real good."

The conversation had become ridiculous. "I'm a pastor, Chet, not a spokesman for the lovelorn. I don't have any special ability along those lines."

"You do talk about love a lot in your sermons."

"How would you know? You don't attend church."

Chet ignored what he could easily have considered a put-down. "Dad told me."

"There are more kinds of love than romantic love."

"But romantic love is one of them. If you preach about it, you should be willing to talk about it."

Chet had backed him into a corner. "All right, what's it about if it's not Shelly? What's going on?"

"Have you met that new girl Laura hired at the factory?"

"I've seen her around. I don't know her. Is she your new interest?"

"Her name is Lacy Grandcastle. She's much younger than me, but to be honest, I'm head over heels. We've dated almost since she got here."

"Well, congratulations. Tell me about her."

"She's from down south somewhere. I can't pinpoint exactly where. She's a singer, too. A good one. She's already making a name for herself locally. And though I'm older by a stretch, we've hit it off."

"So, what's the problem?"

"She dates other men, too. At least, I think she does. Nothing like Shelly, though. The thing is, I can't stand for her to do that."

"So, you'd like her to make a commitment to you?"

"Yes, I would like that, very much."

At the risk of insult, Obie struck at what he thought was a reason a young woman might reject Chet. "Maybe Lacy doesn't like your drinking problem."

Chet took no offense. "That's not it. She drinks, too. We drink a lot together."

"Well, that may be a problem in itself."

Chet was silent momentarily. Had he pushed too hard? Chet said, "I want to get her away from the drinking, but her singing takes her into bars."

"Chet, do you think she's addicted to drink? Or drugs?"

"I don't know about the drinking, but I've never seen her take drugs. Maybe she does, but I don't know."

"I'm giving you the same advice I once gave about Shelly. You didn't follow through on that, but I hope you will this time. Bring Lacy to church. It will do you both some good, and since she's a singer, it might give us a much-needed addition to the choir."

"I'm not much on religion, Obie. I'd sit there and wish I was someplace else. Anyway, I don't know if she'd be interested in church. That subject has never come up."

"Well, that's my best advice. Incidentally, two weeks from this coming Friday, there's a roast beef dinner at church. Why don't you bring Lacy?"

"I might do that. She should get to know people other than the ones she meets at work and in bars ... and I like beef."

"I'll expect to see you there, and I look forward to meeting Lacy."

"You'll like her. Everybody does."

After Chet left, Obie felt energized by their conversation. He had long puzzled over ways to turn Chet from his destructive lifestyle. Lacy Grandcastle might be the answer. He crossed himself in a gesture of gratitude for the insight.

CHAPTER NINETEEN

March–April 1979

Laura surveyed the hollow interior of the old Cam's Supermarket that Stafford Rest Furniture had purchased the previous day. The building held more space than needed for their outlet store, but Lacy said they would need room to grow.

Lacy met her at the door. "Isn't it great, Mrs. Williamson? It's just what we need."

"It's big and somewhat overwhelming."

"We'll get things sorted out soon enough, Ma'am."

"You will, Lacy ... you'll sort it out. That's why I've put you in charge."

That administrative decision had not gone smoothly. Laura still smarted from yesterday's barrage of accusations from Shelly Gonzales, who thought she should have been appointed manager of the new outlet instead of "a barhopping hussy who's been here less than a year." Shelly threatened to quit until Laura soothed her by pointing out that she was Laura's secretary and, as such, was a vital part of the whole operation. The promise of a pay raise helped.

Nonetheless, Laura expected contention between the two women; Lacy was dating Chet Boswell, and Shelly was livid about it, even though she had broken up with Chet before Lacy arrived in the village.

Lacy Grandcastle was a valuable addition to the business, something Laura had not imagined the previous summer when she hired the young woman. Besides being self-assured and intelligent, she saw with "business eyes." Her recognition of the potential for the empty grocery market had led to its purchase. She rewarded Lacy by putting her in charge of the renovation and management.

But a mystery surrounded Lacy. *Where is she from, and why is so little known about her background?* When questioned, she gave answers that seemed adequate at the time but led in circles. Laura worried sometimes about giving her so much responsibility.

Laura asked Obie to use his fact-finding skills to track her past, but he had found nothing. She sang in bars on weekends and, according to Shelly, drank "like a fish," adding that she slept with any man who was handy when Chet was not around. It was an accusation that Laura thought was suspect.

The secretary was silent when Laura asked her how she knew all that. Had Lacy's work suffered, Laura would have investigated her private life further, but she was always efficient and focused.

For an hour, the two women took measurements and discussed improvements such as lighting, lowering the ceiling, painting, and exterior renovation. Laura was ready to leave when she remembered a request Obie had made of her. "Lacy," she said, "Our minister, Obie Gainsworthy, is extending a special invitation to you and Chet to come to services. He's known Chet and Chet's family for a long time."

"That's the Methodist church, isn't it?"

"Yes, on White Pine Street. My husband and I are members there."

"I don't know, Mrs. Williamson. I've never attended church except for weddings and a few funerals. Anyway, I'm out late on Saturday nights and sleep in on Sunday. It wouldn't work out, even if Chet wanted to go, and I doubt he would."

"Well, anyway, the invitation is open. And I wish you'd call me 'Laura.' We're beyond formality."

* * *

Obie and Cassie sat at a table in the Diamond Inn well back from the entertainers. The room was packed, and cigarette smoke was so thick that Obie thought he might choke. They nursed their wine glasses while they waited for the entertainment to start.

"This feels strange," Cassie said.

"How so?" He had noticed it, too, but wanted to let her

voice her opinion.

"All through my growing-up years, I was told to avoid the Diamond Inn at all costs. I imagined all kinds of sordid happenings within these walls. Now, it looks benign. I even see some of my former students."

"It seems a much more acceptable part of the community than in previous years."

"Still, I feel like people are staring at us, a teacher and a minister in a den of sin."

"Relax, Cassie. We're here for the entertainment, and I suspect many others came for the same reason. This is not a sophisticated audience, just common faces we see around town. I understand Lacy does songs from the fifties and sixties, as well as contemporary numbers. And, according to all reports, she's good. That draws in a range of folks."

"We've been here for thirty minutes. You said they would start at seven o'clock."

"I think they're ready now." The four-piece band was assembled, and Lacy Grandcastle stood in front. He had seen her a few times, but at a distance.

"She's beautiful," Cassie said.

Lacy wore a short, light blue dress cut low in the front. Her long blonde hair was tied back with a red ribbon. *She was extraordinary.* No wonder Chet, who sat at a table next to the stage, was so enamored. "Yes, she is," Obie said.

Cassie tapped his arm. "Obie, tell me again why we're here."

"To learn what we can about Miss Grandcastle. She's the key to changing Chet's lifestyle."

"And why are you so bent on that? He's only doing what he's been doing for years."

"He's a vet, and you know my empathy for vets. I also think Chet has the potential for much more than he is."

"He's an excellent builder."

"That he is, but I'm speaking of his personal life, particularly his spiritual side."

Cassie remained silent momentarily before saying, "So, who is engineering this rescue? Is it Obadiah Gainsworthy, the minister, or Obie, the friend?"

"It's both. My pastoral responsibility is to invite Chet to become a practicing Christian, but he needs to be lifted from the gutter first."

"So, what is the plan?"

"Invitations to come to church haven't worked. Lacy can get him there. But first, we need to get her there."

"And how will you do that? Her reputation isn't stellar. I've heard talk."

"So have I, but that's why we're here, Cassie. We'll learn something about her and find a way to make her want to come."

"Reel her in?"

"Well, yes, that's accurate. Don't you remember how Lisa Goodrow came into our congregation? She makes a living organizing parties and planning banquets. When we hired her to organize a fundraiser dinner, she had no religious affiliations. Mingling with our members attracted her to our church. Then, when I asked her to organize a smaller project, she was drawn in. Now, she's one of our most active members."

Cassie laughed. "Obie, you have a diabolical streak."

"And I don't apologize for it. Whatever works."

Lacy's first number, a Sinatra version of *"My Way,"* revealed that Lacy was talented. "Wow!" Cassie said. The audience clapped and cheered.

Chet plopped down in the extra chair at their table. "Isn't she great?" he said.

"She has a beautiful voice," Cassie said. "And I envy that long hair."

Chet grinned. "She's wonderful in every way."

Cassie said, "Chet, I believe you're in love."

"Head over heels," he admitted. The grin faded, and he revealed a more serious look. "I don't know what my chances are, though. I'm older than her, although she says that doesn't matter."

"It shouldn't," Obie said. "Dad was many years older than Mom when they married."

"We aren't in shouting distance of marriage."

"Chet, you told me once that you're ready to settle down."

"Yeah, eventually, but Lacy and me have an agreement." He paused as Lacy stepped up to do another number.

"What kind of agreement?"

"We'll continue to date, but we can see other people too."

"Is that your idea or hers?"

"Hers, I guess."

Obie was appalled but held his tongue. Now was not the time. Cassie looked away; Obie could only guess what she was thinking.

They stayed until a break made their exit easier. On the drive up the hill, Cassie said, "I think we need to worry about Chet."

"It does appear bleak for that romance, but let's not give up on it. Love can yet win out."

"I think you're forming a plan."

"A part of my ministry does seem to have become match-making." She laughed, no doubt at the improbability. "But, yes, I have a plan. I'll get them to attend our church services."

"How?"

"I don't know yet."

* * *

Lacy was met with a current of stale air through the open door of her second-story apartment. The day was warm for that time of year, and she was tired. She opened all four windows.

Her apartment, on the lakeside of Main Street, was small and needed paint and repair, but had the saving grace of an excellent lake view. Laura said her sister, Cassie Gainsworthy, once lived there. That was a tiny grain of information, but such tidbits of village lore would tie her closer to the community. She was right that first day she drove into Stafford Rest. This truly was "the place."

She was not hungry. Having worked so late, she grabbed a sandwich from the Stewart's Shop by the bridge and ate it in her vehicle. She should have something healthier, so she made a salad and ate it in the nook next to an open window. There was enough breeze to stir the curtains.

Chet had said he would stop by. Perhaps he already had and left without leaving a note; he seldom wrote notes. She sighed. *What was she to do about Chet?* He loved her, and she was unsure how to feel about it. She could easily love him if she let herself go, for he was a good man—except for his excessive drinking.

The many uncertainties in her life could derail a serious relationship. It was not fair to him. She must hold him off, as much for his sake as her own. She had let him think she dated other men, and lying about it bothered her. There had been opportunities; the drummer, Harold, tried wooing her, but she had fended him off.

She was aware of the gossip, but she had never been promiscuous. In the year and a half with Dave, she never strayed, although that may have been more out of fear than fidelity. *Why was she pretending with Chet? Was it to keep from getting too close?*

The phone rang. Thinking it was Chet, she said, "It's about time you called. I'm sorry we missed each other."

Someone cleared their throat and then remained silent. Fear gripped her. "Who is this?" she asked.

Uncomfortable seconds passed before she heard the throat-clearing sound again and then a dial tone. She shuddered. *Had he found her? Would she have to run again?*

She jumped when the phone rang again. She picked up the receiver and waited a moment before she found her voice. "Dave, is this you?"

"Who's Dave?" Chet said.

She breathed easier. "Just somebody. Not important. Was that you who just called?"

"No.

"Someone called and hung up."

"Probably a wrong number."

"Yes ... probably."

"Can I come over?"

"Chet, I'm exhausted. I've had a long and brutal day. Setting up this new store is much harder than I imagined."

"People are talking about it. Most think it'll boost the economy, especially since it's on Main Street."

"Can we get together another time?"

"Tomorrow night? I'll bring pizza."

"That's fine. I'll look forward to it." She started to hang up, but remembered something. "Chet, how well do you know Rev. Gainsworthy?"

"Obie? I've known him personally for almost ten years, but he and Dad have been friends for as long as either can remember. I built the addition on his house right after he returned to Stafford Rest, plus two additions after that. Why do you ask?"

"He came into the store yesterday to talk to Laura, but before he left, he came to me and started a conversation."

"What about?"

"He said that he and his wife ... yes, I know ... she's Laura's sister ... said they heard me sing at the Diamond Inn and wondered if I'd do a couple of numbers at something called an 'outdoor barbecue dinner.' I guess it will be held outside at the church in a couple of months. He didn't mention money, so I'm guessing that I would be doing a freebie."

"Yeah, that's the way it usually works. They'll give you a free meal, but I'd insist on payment if you're asked to do more than one or two."

"Do many people attend these events?"

"They're popular. They pull in town people and folks from other churches, too."

"What do you think?"

"The publicity can't hurt."

"I'm not familiar with church music. My parents never took me to church. I guess 'Pistol Packing Mama' wouldn't go over well."

"You can ask Obie for a hymnal. Or better yet, go to their services to get an idea about what to sing. Keep in mind that if they hold this event outside, there won't be any accompaniment. But you can use your guitar."

"I guess I can do a couple of numbers. Chet, will you go to a service with me so I can explore the music?"

Chet laughed. "Dad would have a heart attack if he saw me inside a church. I attended the Episcopal church with my grandparents when I was little, but except for funerals and weddings,

I don't go near churches."

"Please make an exception for this. I'm on unfamiliar grounds and need someone to lean on."

"Obie has tried to get me there for ages. I don't think I'd better ..."

"I guess I can ask Harold."

"We'll sit way in the back."

CHAPTER TWENTY

May–June 1979

Due to a coincidence of nature that Cassie and Obie were born on the same day, Laura and Abigail organized a May fifteenth "party" at the Hunt residence on Garnet Point. For Abigail, of course, it was a celebration of Cassie's birthday, not his. Considering what had transpired over the years, he was lucky to be there. Yet, here he was, on the Hunt patio on a lovely spring evening, surrounded by his family of in-laws and descendants. *God is kind.*

Laurie and Obadiah, the Williamson twins, were fifteen. They sat at the table with Obie and Cassie, ignoring their elders as teenagers do. Their teachers at Evergreen had said they were at the top of their classes and "well-liked by their peers." In time, they would assume their responsible places in society.

Dan and Ly Yen had their heads together at a nearby umbrella-covered table, whispering as if no one else existed. Not far away, Laura sipped wine and waited for Ben to arrive. Abigail had been up and down continually for the past hour. Jacob, over by the patio edge, made realistic engine noises as he maneuvered the green Hess tanker truck back and forth along the road he was forging through the grass.

Ken was late; he had reluctantly agreed to attend. *He might not show at all.* There were still issues Ken needed to work out with Abigail. Obie sighed; he also needed to work out problems with her.

Abigail came from the kitchen with a pitcher of fresh lemonade. "The food will arrive in ten minutes," she said while placing the pitcher on the table where they sat. She had arranged to have a smorgasbord assortment delivered from the Inn. "You can help yourself to drinks," she announced. "I'm all tired out."

169

She looked anything but tired. Obie was awed at her constant energy. Even after placing her real estate business into other capable hands, she often made unscheduled appearances at the Evergreen office to ensure everything was "going well." And she was usually at the Inn from midmorning until late evening.

Laura said, "Sit still awhile, Mom. "We'll get the food from the truck when it arrives."

"I'm happy the weather is permitting us to eat outside. I hate dependence on the weather. We should have gone to the Inn as I suggested. Don't you agree, Obie?" she said, startling him with the unexpected familiarity.

"I'm afraid I must side with Cassie and Laura, Abigail. It's a family affair, and they want the privacy we couldn't enjoy at the Inn."

"Ly Yen wanted to help, but people don't like her cooking much." She waved her hand in dismissal. "In any event, we'll have all the fixings, so we don't have to cook here." She looked toward the driveway. "Where's Ken, anyway, Obie? Isn't he coming?"

"I'm not sure." He would not say what he thought. "Maybe something came up."

Abigail said softly but loud enough for Obie to hear, "Yes, something always comes up with that man."

Cassie said, "Mom, he'll be here."

Obie whispered to her," How do you know that?"

"It's our birthday. He loves us both. He'll show."

After several minutes had passed, Obie said, "I'll call him." As he started to get up, a truck pulled into the driveway.

"It's the food," Abigail said.

Then, as a large box of food was carried onto the patio, Ken's truck pulled in beside the inn truck. Cassie said to Obie, "Didn't I tell you?"

Everyone rose, either to help with the food or to greet Ken. Jacob ran to him and grabbed his hand. "Grandpa, we waited for you. Come and see my truck and the road I made."

Ken followed Jacob and attempted to kneel beside Jacob's play site. Obie saw his difficulty and went to steady him. Ken waved him off and said, "I'll see it long distance."

As Ken spoke to Jacob, asking questions about the important project in the grass, Obie observed his father. Ken was aged now, a fact evident in the man before him. He had recognized it intellectually but tried not to dwell on negative thoughts. Now, it sank in; his father would not be around forever. Obie vowed at that moment to spend more time with Ken.

"You made us wait," Abigail said, apparently forgetting that Ken and the food had arrived simultaneously.

Ken's tone was gruff. "Don't look like you've starved any."

She made no response but continued distributing items from boxes onto the two long wooden tables that Obie and Dan had brought from the indoor section of the patio.

Cassie said, "We knew you would come, and we're glad you're here. We were getting worried, though."

"Sorry about that, but I have an excuse. I'll explain in a little bit."

An hour later, after Laurie and Obadiah read their birthday poems aloud to Cassie and Obie, and Jacob had presented them with several pages of his latest creative artwork, a cake with lighted candles was brought out. And still later, when stomachs were full and daylight was fading, Ken said, "I was late for a reason. I have some news that's not so pleasant, and I didn't want to spoil the party."

"What's it about, Dad?" Obie asked.

"You know, that new girl who sang at your outdoor event and attended your church services the past few Sundays?"

Laura said, "You mean Lacy Grandcastle? She works for me. Has something happened to her?" Her concern was evident.

"She's not hurt if that's what you mean, but she is in trouble."

"I knew it!" Abigail said. "I knew she was bad news. A lot of other people think that, too. What's she done?"

"She was arrested for driving drunk. She's in jail in Saratoga Springs."

"Was there an accident?" Obie asked.

"Not with another car. A state trooper followed her and

saw her weaving back and forth on the road. I guess she scraped a guardrail at one point. That's when she was arrested."

"I'm not surprised," Abigail said.

Obie was perturbed. He had been pleased when Lacy came to church, accompanied by Chet. Not only that, they came again the next two Sundays. Last week, Lacy sang a solo, and her beautiful voice caressed the farthest corners of the sanctuary in a way he was sure had not happened for many years. She would sing again next Sunday. He wanted her to become a regular choir member. *Would this news derail all that?*

Ly Yen said in her soft voice, "She sings so beautifully. I have looked forward to hearing her again."

Dan said, "Maybe there's some mistake."

"Or maybe not," Laura said. "She does stellar work, but I've heard from more than one source that she has a drinking problem."

"Dad, how did you find out about this?" Obie asked.

"Larry Ogden, a state trooper I know, called me. We were on the phone a long time. That's why I was late. Actually, he wanted to talk to you."

"Me?"

"Larry called first to get your home phone number. When he couldn't get you, he called me back. Miss Grandcastle asked *you* for help. Larry was only relaying the message."

"And a pretty face helps," Abigail said.

Obie asked. "Did he say why she wants to talk to me?"

"According to Larry, she told them you were her minister, and she didn't have anyone else to turn to, Anyone with influence, I mean."

"Influence to do what?"

"Arrange bail, I guess. I don't know. He didn't say."

"It sounds more like she needs a lawyer. Do you have a phone number for me?"

"I wrote it down." Ken pulled a slip of paper from his shirt pocket and handed it to Obie.

"She's not a church member," Abigail said. "You don't have to help her."

"Christian duty, though," Obie said quickly.

Cassie broke her silence. "Mom, Obie feels obligated. It's true that she's not a member, but she's made a substantial contribution through her music and will probably do so in the future. She has a problem, evidently, and that needs addressing, but right now, she needs a different kind of help."

"She may be trouble," Abigail said. "She gets drunk. Works in bars. It has a bad influence, especially on our young people. When she sang last week, I watched their faces. Freddie Littleton ... he's fourteen. I saw the look in his eyes. It was lust."

The twins were snickering. Freddie was a classmate in Sunday School and probably in public school.

Obie said, "I'll go down there right away. I don't know what I can do, but I must try."

Abigail, as usual, managed a last word. "You may be sorry."

* * *

"You have a beautiful voice, Miss Grandcastle," Obie said to the young woman who sat on the couch across from his desk. "We can use that in our choir." He watched her face to judge her reaction.

He had asked her shortly after Sunday service to meet with him. She reluctantly detached herself from Chet to join him in the office. "Is that why you wanted to talk to me, to ask me to join the choir?"

"I've been caught," Obie responded, forcing a laugh to lighten the mood. Her demure expression did not change; she would not make it easy. "I find it a chance to spread joy through music, and I hope you feel the same way."

"Music is a big part of my life," she said.

Bringing her into the fold would also bring in Chet. First, however, he must convince her. He should probably have guilty feelings for using the leverage gained three weeks before, but he shoved that emotion aside for the greater good. "What's the status of your court appearance?"

"I paid a fine, and they've impounded my van for a few days because of violations, but they're not suspending my license, thank goodness." She smiled for the first time since entering the office. "And thank you again for your help, Rev. Gainsworthy. Vouching for me saved me a lot of misery."

"I was glad to help." He felt compelled to don his counseling hat. The choir appeal could wait. "And please call me 'Pastor Obie,' or simply, 'Obie.'"

"All right, if you call me 'Lacy.'"

"That's a deal. Lacy, can we discuss what happened? Concerning your arrest, I mean."

After a moment of hesitation, she said, "Not pleasant to think about, but yes. I guess you're entitled to further explanation."

He was direct. "I wonder if you have an alcohol addiction. There's an AA group in Evergreen." His encouragement to get Chet into that group was never successful. But maybe Lacy was the key to helping them both. He added, "What you tell me here is confidential, Lacy."

"I'm not addicted." She sounded confident. "I drink. I admit that, but it's not like I have to drink."

"When I talked to you that evening in Saratoga, you seemed, excuse the expression, hung over."

"I was still very tired."

"Lacy, you were arrested at five in the morning. What was that about?"

"I had a Monday night gig in Albany that went very late. I don't usually have engagements during the week, but it paid well." She paused. "Rev. Gainsworthy ... Obie, people buy me drinks. I nurse them as best I can, but it's hard to refuse."

"I suppose it would be, but you should try." *Was he pushing it?*

"I will be more careful. I don't want another cell visit."

"How do you get around with your car impounded?"

"Chet, mostly, and sometimes band members when he can't go with me."

"When you get your car back, you must be doubly careful." He wrote a phone number on a sheet from his notepad and handed it to her. "This is a contact number for the AA group. You might benefit from talking to them, Lacy. Chet could go with you."

She put the piece of paper in her small purse. "I doubt he would, but anyway, that's not the help I ..." Her hand went to her mouth. "I mean, it's not help with drinking that I need. I'm not addicted to drugs, either, if that's what you think." Her tone had turned defensive.

There was still that mystery surrounding Lacy; Laura and Cassie agreed that things did not add up. His research had revealed no records of her in places she said she had been. This could be a chance to bring her past into the open. He mulled a moment before asking, "Lacy, are you in trouble of some kind?"

Her hazel eyes sought assurance as she shifted positions on the couch. He waited. Finally, she said, "Are secrets safe with you?"

"They are, unless a serious crime is involved."

She hesitated again. "A serious crime *is* involved, but it's against me."

He went to sit on the couch beside her. "Lacy, if you need help, I can give you counsel as your pastor, but you may also benefit by confiding in a friend, someone you've become close to since your arrival."

"I've not made many friends, the kind I think you mean."

"What about Chet?"

"I think too much of him to get him involved."

"Don't underestimate Chet. He's crazy about you, you know."

"Yes, I know. But I also know he'd want to protect me, which could endanger him."

"So, this situation is a dangerous one?"

"It is." She moved to get up. "I think I've said enough."

"Wait, Lacy. I do want to help. I'm sure Laura and Cassie will feel the same. We want to help you. And Chet will help, without question. You've been here a year. You're among friends. Please let us help you."

She let out a deep breath. "You might not want to help if you know the details. Anyway, I don't know what you can do. I'm not sure what anyone can do."

"Does someone want to do you harm?"

Tears appeared in her eyes. "Someone wants me dead."

"Why don't you go to the police for help … and protection?"

"They would arrest me."

"Why, Lacy?"

"I'm wanted for attempted murder."

He saw her tear-filled eyes and trembling hands and wondered how this lovely young woman could possibly be wanted for such a crime; there had been some terrible mistake. He expressed his thoughts. "Impossible!"

"No, it's true. The state of South Carolina wants me. I'm a fugitive. I've lived in fear the past three weeks, thinking that law enforcement here will learn about me, for sure. And I'm still in fear."

Obie tried to think. This was unexpected. If he took it further, he would involve himself in a situation with unknown results. He said, anyway, "Lacy, tell me about it so we can help you."

"I shouldn't."

"Go ahead. I'm listening.

She started to speak, fast at first, then slowly. She explained that while in her third year in college, she became involved with a man several years older than herself. He was a divorced businessman to whom she was sent as part of the university's apprentice program. She blushed, saying she had dropped out of school to be near him.

"What's his name, Lacy?"

She hesitated before saying, "Let's just stick with 'Dave.' That's safer for you, and for Chet."

"If you prefer, although I'm not worried."

"You might be if you knew him. He has an import-export business. He put me to work in his office, a mistake on his part because I learned through studying day-to-day transactions that the company was a front for drug dealing. I didn't believe it initially, so I asked him about it. My mistake. He was furious, and he threatened me."

"What kind of threat?"

"Told me I'd better keep my mouth shut or … and that's

when he did that hand slash across the throat thing. I didn't want my throat cut, so I told him it was none of my business and that he could operate his business as he liked. But he changed after that. I knew he was watching me. I had moved in with him sometime before, but now he told me to get my own place. When I resisted, he kicked me out. He threw my belongings on the curb and told me not to come to work again. I was angry at first, but later realized that I was actually relieved."

"Being free from him?"

"I was putting it behind me. I made plans to go back and finish college, but not even a week passed until he came to my new apartment. I don't know how he knew where I was because I took pains to hide from him, but all of a sudden, there he was, and he was angry. He said an FBI agent had called him and asked questions. Said I'd betrayed him. Of course, I denied it. We were in the kitchen when he grabbed a knife from the counter and put it against my throat. I was terrified; I asked him if he was going to kill me, and he said he didn't have a choice, that he couldn't allow me to testify against him. His eyes convinced me that he meant it."

"But obviously, he didn't hurt you."

"He tried to. As he slashed with the knife, I pulled away and backed up against the counter where I was able to grab my iron skillet. He was off balance when I hit him in the head. He just crumpled to the floor. It all happened in seconds."

"I hope that's when you ran?"

"It's what I should have done, but foolish me, I called the police and told them someone was hurt and to send an ambulance."

"Although he'd just tried to kill you?"

"He wasn't moving, and I didn't want him to die. The police and medics arrived at about the same time. As they loaded him onto the stretcher, he revived and pointed at me. Said to the officers, 'That bitch tried to kill me.' I told them what had really happened. They took notes and called me later that day. They said they had talked to Dave and wanted me to go to the station to answer a few questions."

"And did you tell them about his drug business?"

"I didn't go."

"What happened?"

"I ran."

"Lacy, why did you do that? Why didn't you tell them what you knew about his illegal actions, not to mention the fact that he intended to kill you?"

"As I got ready to go, he called me. What he said I won't repeat, but the gist was that if I went to the police, he would send someone to kill me before the day was over. I asked him if he would leave me alone if I promised not to press charges or testify against him. He was quick to say that one way or another, my life was over, that I could run and hide awhile, but he'd find me wherever I went."

"So, you didn't go to the police station?"

"I panicked, I guess. I was afraid. I had already told them what happened, but he must have given his version. It was my word against his, a successful businessman against a college student. What chance did I have? I packed and ran that evening. I saw a newspaper the next morning; the police were looking for me as a suspect in an attempted murder case, but there were no details given. I kept moving around for months and took odd jobs to survive."

"How long ago did all this happen?"

"It's been almost two years. I've been here nearly a year, the longest I've stayed anywhere."

"Well, if no one has found you in all this time, it's likely they never will, don't you think?"

Lacy's sigh was audible. "Reverend ... Obie ... I think Dave's found me. I received a phone call some time back. No one spoke, but I think it was him."

"But nothing since?"

"No, but I can't rest. I look over my shoulder all the time. I'm going to move on."

"Lacy, don't do that. You have evidence against this man or know how to get it. Don't you see? You have leverage?"

"Evidence won't help me if I'm dead?"

"We can look out for you and help you contact law enforcement there." He was unsure how that would work, but added,

"We'll find a way."

"I'll have to think about it."

"You should tell Chet. He'll want to be involved."

"I'll tell him. But I'm not sure I can stay here."

CHAPTER TWENTY-ONE

June 1979

A week after the conversation with Lacy, Chet barged into the church office and pounded on Obie's desk. "I'll find that bastard and kill him!" he bellowed.

Having found no public records concerning Lacy's incident in South Carolina, Obie deliberated about how to proceed. Her protection was his primary concern. Apparently, Chet had heard her story, or maybe the parts she wanted to divulge.

"Chet, you must calm down. Let's think this through."

Chet stepped back from the desk and exhaled a blast of air before flopping onto the couch. Obie watched his face gradually regain normal color.

Chet said, "How can I keep her safe? Tell me that!"

"Well, certainly not by going to jail for killing somebody."

"If I can find him, I'll make him pay for his threats. But she won't tell me where all this happened. Only that his name is 'Dave.' Said it happened down south. Do you know where, Obie?"

He weighed the consequences of a lie against those of a disaster. "I don't have that information to give you," he said in compromise.

"So, what are we going to do?"

Obie drew up a chair to face Chet. "We must convince Lacy to contact the police."

"She's wanted for attempted murder, Obie. That man has stacked the deck against her. We can't let her go to jail."

"She may not have to go to jail, Chet. Over the last two days, I've checked and rechecked police records for areas she's supposedly from, and I can't find any evidence of a warrant for her arrest."

"You mean she's not wanted?"

"I can't say for sure. I'm simply saying that there's no evidence that she is."

Chet let out a long sigh. "Well, that's something."

"But it doesn't mean she's out of danger. She has evidence against this Dave, or knows where to find it. He's undoubtedly part of a group with no qualms about violence against anyone who threatens their illegal business."

"So, it's a pretty sure thing that someone will try to hurt her if she's found, either Dave or some other lowlife?"

"She's in danger if they discover she's here, but I'm not convinced they will. That phone call might have been just a wrong number."

"She shouldn't go to the police," Chet said. "Nothing turned up from the drunk driving thing, and you didn't discover anything. If she's not wanted, why drag it up?"

"Maybe she should have police protection in case someone really is looking for her."

"Obie, we don't need the police. I can protect her. I've already asked her to move in with me."

"Did she agree to that?"

"Sort of. She said she didn't want to put me in danger, but I think she'll move in." Chet's anger flared again, and his voice rose. "I'm not scared of these bastards. She'll be safe with me."

"Chet, you must know that you can't always watch her. You have your business, and she has her job at the factory. And I'm sure she'll want to continue her musical gigs."

"Well, that's true, but friends will surround her, and I'll go with her when she travels ... like I did when she didn't have her minibus."

"I suppose ..."

"Obie, don't encourage her to involve the police. Maybe later if things change."

Against his better judgment, he said, "All right ... for now."

"Should we bring anyone else in on this, like Laura? She's with Lacy most of the day."

"Talk to Lacy," Obie said. "If she's agreeable, we'll keep Laura informed."

* * *

"Pastor Parrish wants to meet with you after the service," Lucille Epps whispered to Obie as he waited in the back of the church to begin the procession for Sunday service. We'll be in your office."

Obie was annoyed by the request; he had planned to take Jacob for a walk around the Morass. "Why are we meeting?"

"I'm sorry, Obie," Lucile said. "This is not my doing, but I can't ignore what's come up."

Obie softened his tone. If he had a true friend among church officers, it was Lucille. "What's it about?" he asked.

The procession, with the choir leading, moved forward. "No time to explain now," Lucille said. "I just got the request myself from three church members. I'll get word to the other committee members right after the service." She turned and moved quickly to one side.

Amos Adams, in the choir line, looked back at Obie. His snug smile identified him as the most likely suspect for this sudden assembly request.

During his sermon, Obie tried to stay focused on the theme but was distracted by concerns about the meeting's purpose. Some issues did need addressing: the budget was behind expectations, a new secretary had to be hired to replace Roberta Barnes, who was moving away, and the joint picnic of the three churches needed planners. Or maybe it was about his annual report which was a few days late. But none of those items required an emergency meeting.

After the service, the receiving line in the back slowed him, but when the last person was out the door, he whispered to Cassie that she should not wait for him.

The day was warm, so he removed his coat and loosened his tie at the office door. He glanced in to see that all the Staff Parish members were there except Abigail, whom he knew was home nursing a sprained foot, and Sarah Hill, who was absent because of illness.

At least a dozen people were present who were not committee members. None of his close friends was in the room. *What was going on?*

There were not enough seats in the office, so folding chairs had been brought up from the kitchen. Amos, who sat at Obie's desk, spoke first. "Nice of you to finally show up, preacher."

Obie turned to Lucille, "This is a Staff Parish meeting, is it not?"

"Yes, Pastor Obie," she said.

"It's more than that," Amos said. "As you can see by the attendance, this is a whole church matter."

Obie ignored Amos. "Lucille, if this is a formal meeting, you should call it to order."

Glenda Smith said from the couch, "Obie, can't we keep this informal? Just let us speak?"

Obie asked Lucille, "Is that all right with you?"

"Yes, it's fine if that's what you want. But I want to say something first."

Lucille faced the group. "I want Pastor Obie and everyone here to know that this is not a planned meeting, at least not by Staff Parish. Amos and Arthur approached me just before church to request that we meet. Amos said they had talked to several members who wanted it. When they told me about the emergency, I told them it was a matter better taken up at our regular monthly meeting. But I relented when Amos said he would take it to the district superintendent. I respect their right to discuss it, but I still think it's a matter for a regular Staff Parish meeting."

Amos was quick to respond: "Lucille, you'll have to deal with it now or later. I say 'now.'" There were several nods of agreement and a few verbal assents.

"It appears I'm the only one in this room who doesn't know what this is about," Obie said, not hiding his irritation. "Somebody please enlighten me."

"It's that Grandcastle woman," Glenda said.

Obie had noticed some members' unspoken coldness toward Lacy in recent weeks. "What about Lacy?" Obie said, purposely using her first name.

Arthur Baines uttered the condemning words, although Obie knew he was echoing Amos. "Preacher, this woman is ripping our church apart. She sings like an angel, but she ain't one. She's the devil's tool if you ask me."

"I agree," Amos said, "and everybody knows it's the truth." He waved a hand toward the assembled group. "Isn't that right, folks?"

Murmurs and nods came from several people, but no words were uttered aloud, so Obie was encouraged that the frontal attack came from only three people. He almost admired the ability of the obstructive three to organize this protest so quickly. It was likely, however, that they had planned it for some time.

He did not often wish for Abigail's presence, but her acidic words could silence a union hall full of steelworkers. Even if she agreed with this crowd, she would keep Amos in his place.

Amos continued, "It's bad enough that she spends her weekends in bars and beer joints, but ..."

Obie interrupted. "Amos, Lacy's a singer. She performs in reputable places."

"You mean like the Diamond Inn?"

"Yes, like the Diamond Inn. And incidentally, that was where I first heard her sing."

"I'm not surprised that you frequent that joint. But anyway, she's not really that good a singer." At that, a few howls came from around the room. Obie was pleased that, on this one point at least, Amos was not about to win.

"Anyway," Amos said, "her singing ability is not what this is about. Our concern is how her presence in this church influences our young people."

"And how might that be?" Obie asked.

"Can I answer that?" Glenda Smith said. "Miss Grandcastle was recently arrested for drunk driving. I believe you got her out of jail."

"I spoke to the authorities on her behalf," Obie replied.

"You should have left her there," Amos said.

"I aided one of our church family members. I don't apologize for that, not to you, Amos, or anyone else in this room."

"She's not even a member," Arthur said.

Faces were solemn. "That's true for now," Obie admitted, "but I've asked her if she wants to become a member, and she's considering it. But that misses the point, Arthur. Membership doesn't mean you have special rights that nonmembers don't have. Our Christian job is to save lost souls, not simply make church members."

Glenda's groan was audible. "Preacher, do you mean that someone like me, a member for over fifty years, doesn't have any more rights than somebody like this woman? I'm offended by that."

"As am I," Amos said. Sounds of agreement came from around the room.

Obie soothed his tone. "Glenda, of course, no one disputes your place of honor in our congregation. You *are* our oldest living member." Glenda smiled and nodded. "But we must make room for the future generations as well, as members fifty years ago made room for you. Don't you agree?"

"Well, I guess if you say it like that ..."

Amos said quickly, "That was then, this is now. Let's not get sidetracked."

Obie wanted to make the meeting less tempestuous. "Look here, folks, I know Lacy isn't perfect. None of us are. She has issues. There are also people right in this room who have issues, including me." He made eye contact with Luther Gordon, who was trying to decide whether to leave his wife, Sally. Obie had counseled him for several weeks.

He continued, "Even the earliest Christian church members had issues, but they went about making new Christians anyway. That's what our job is. But yes, there are souls who hover at the edges. We must nurture them with kindness and offer help for their troubles. That's our purpose." He could not help adding, "Or it should be."

The room was quiet for several seconds before Amos said, "You haven't heard the worst part, Preacher."

"I'm sure you're about to tell me."

"She's organizing a group of teenagers, teaching them to play the guitar and sing her godless songs."

"They're love songs, Amos. I encouraged her to form that group."

"There are boys in the group, too."

"I should hope so."

"She wears short dresses. They stare at her."

Obie laughed. "Boys do that. It's a natural reaction."

Arthur said, "Tell them what we know."

"Preacher, this is more than boys looking at girls," Amos said. "One incident was reported to me yesterday that I had to tell others about."

"So, you went first to members of the congregation instead of coming to me?"

"I consider it my duty. You're too involved with her. You brought her to the congregation. You even put her in the choir without consulting us choir members. We think you're too sympathetic toward her."

Obie's anger had grown. "What is this incident you heard about?"

"Tom Gaither passed by the downstairs recreation room one evening last week, where Miss Grandcastle was conducting her session. Tom said she had her hand on the shoulder of one of the boys, whom I won't name. She was massaging him. Tom said the boy looked like he really enjoyed it."

"Just a minute, Amos." Obie turned and pointed to Tom Gaither in the back. "Tom, you should be the one telling us about this."

Tom stood and said in his drawn fashion, "The boy was sure enjoying her touch. I guess I would, too. My old lady never does anything like that." There was muffled laughter. Tom took no notice and continued. "I'd gone into the kitchen to check out a gas leak that John Neal reported. I'm a certified plumber, you know. Been doing that for ..."

"Tom, about the young man," Amos said.

"Oh yeah, after I left the kitchen, I went to the restroom down there. That boy who had the massage was in there. I won't say in this group what I think he was doing, but when he saw me, he left real quick."

"That's enough, Tom," Obie said. "I think we get the picture."

Glenda said, "That behavior isn't acceptable, especially in a church. Preacher, what are you going to do about it?"

Obie said, "Amos, you give me the boy's name in private, and I'll talk to him, and possibly his parents, but Lacy is not to blame for a teenage boy's fantasies."

"I agree with that," Roland Kilpatrick said. "She's a great addition to our choir."

"Well, I don't agree," Amos said. "She shouldn't touch young boys like that. I figure she does that to all the boys."

"There's no proof of that," Lucile said. "Unless someone in this gathering has something they want to tell us."

When no one spoke up, Obie said, "I don't see the need for further discussion. I'll speak to the boy, and with Lacy, so that she understands our social rules. She wasn't in church today, but the next time ..."

"She may not be back," Amos said.

"And why is that?"

"I told her to stay away."

Obie's anger erased his sense of caution. "You *what?*"

"She was coming in this morning with Chet Boswell. I met them on the front steps and told her she wasn't welcome. They left then, but she stuck up her middle finger at me. Shows what kind of person she is."

It had been a long time since Obie was angry enough to strike anyone, and knowing he was near that point, he rushed from the room. He needed to find Lacy.

* * *

"She's gone, Obie," Chet said from the doorway of his Main Street apartment. His eyes were red, although he did not appear intoxicated.

"What do you mean?"

"She left a note." Chet handed Obie a sheet of stationery before sitting on the stone steps of the building.

Obie sat beside him, the hot steps searing his backside. The note was in neat handwriting:

Dear Chet,

I'm so sorry to leave like this, but you must have known it would happen eventually. I fear for my life, as you know, and have concluded that I must vanish altogether. I don't yet know how that will be accomplished, but I'll find a way.

I know you love me, Chet, and I love you too, but we'll never know how that would have turned out.

Please apologize to Laura for me for leaving her in the lurch. The new store is almost ready to open anyway. And let Pastor Obie know I don't hold it against him that a few of his church members don't want me there. Maybe he'll be pleased to see that he's opened my eyes to many things. Anyway, what happened in front of his church this morning may be a good thing, for it has prompted me to move on with haste.

I'll always remember you with love, Chet. But just a word of advice—find someone else to love—and quit your drinking.

Lacy

"I only left her for a couple of hours," Chet said. "When I returned, she was gone. I tried the road in both directions, but she must have had a good head-start."

"Chet, I heard about what Amos Adams said to her this morning, that she wasn't to enter the sanctuary."

"I'd like to strangle him."

"I know the feeling, but tell me ... what was Lacy's reaction?"

"She was calm. A lot more than me. I told him off on the spot, but she just walked away. I should have known what she was thinking of doing. I'm going to find her."

"You can't blame yourself, Chet. Lacy came with baggage, and you tried to help. We all did, but we might make it worse for her if we keep looking for her. Maybe someday she'll get her life straightened out and come back."

"I love her."

"I know."

"The church don't want her. I guess it don't want me, either."

"That's not true, Chet. Only three people instigated this, and maybe a few were influenced by their blather. Our congregation has good and caring people who will welcome your presence."

Chet sighed as he folded Lacy's note and stuck it in his shirt pocket. "Obie, you're a good man and a good friend, but I'll not be coming back to your services. I came because of Lacy, and she's not here anymore."

CHAPTER TWENTY-TWO

August–October 1979

It was nearly noon when Obie, Cassie, and Jacob arrived at the O'Shane Vineyard in the Napa Valley. It had been two years since their last visit.

The Augustines were hosting a Sunday lunch in the spacious dining room of the "Big House." As they gathered around the long dining table, Matilda said, "We look forward to your annual visits, and when you miss a year, it's a big letdown."

"You're part of our family now," Lyle said as he pumped Obie's hand for the third time.

Their association with the Augustines had become more than a business arrangement: Obie saw Lyle's love for the land while following him and his sons as they performed the various duties required to raise and market a grape harvest. The women had bonded, too; Cassie, Matilda, and Cara never tired of conversation. Jacob and Alicia played together, alternating between conditions of cooperation and rivalry.

Kent Augustine had finally obtained his law degree. Obie's prediction that he would leave the farm had proved wrong. The middle son, Neal, was engaged to a local woman; they would live on the farm. Joel, the youngest son, was a carefree spirit who made promises to no one.

Early talk at the table centered around family matters. Cassie explained why Julie had stayed home: "Our daughter loves many things, but travel isn't one of them. She chose to stay home with Laura."

"Blizzard stayed with Aunt Laura, too," Jacob said.

"He's the newest addition to our family," Cassie explained. "Jacob has wanted a dog for a long time."

"I bet there's a story about that name," Lyle said.

Jacob said, "He's white, and the man who gave him to us said he was born during a blizzard."

"He's a mutt," Obie said, but added when he noticed Jacob's scowl, "He's a good mutt."

Matilda said, "I'm sorry Julie won't be with us this time. I love the way she's so curious about everything."

At Kent's probing, Obie and Cassie brought them up to date on Stafford Rest affairs.

"Obie, we're so sorry about your aunt," Cara said.

"Yes, we do miss Angie. It's been hard on Dad, but he's managing it."

Later, Kent said to Obie over dessert, "And how are you handling that difficult church of yours?"

"It's under control, although there are always problems. But we manage."

"He hops around putting out the little brush fires," Cassie said.

"I've been a pastor there for almost five years. But the Conference may want to move me somewhere else. In that case, I'll resign and go back to writing, something I'm better at."

Lyle said. "Why would they want to move you?"

"It's just what Methodists do. They don't want pastors to get too comfortable."

"We're Catholics," Matilda said, "all except Kent and Cara. We like to keep our priests in one place until they die."

"It'll consider it my chance to move on, knowing my mission is complete."

Cara said, "But isn't pastoring a lifelong thing?"

Obie hesitated; it was not the first time he had to defend the position that he was more writer than pastor. He said, "For personal reasons, I once chose to leave pulpit ministry and establish a career in writing. I haven't abandoned that position."

"And you are a good writer, Obie." "I've read *Ultimate Conflict* and *Discourse of Nations,* plus some of your lighter things, and I see a progression from an expository style to a more personal tone."

There was more to Cara than he had suspected. "You're right," he said." My writing has changed. Evolved, I hope."

"And, from what I know of you, I believe you're a good and caring minister of the gospel."

"He is," Cassie quickly said.

He pushed back his plate, which held remnants of Matilda's homemade peach pie, hoping they had reached the end of that conversation.

Cara, however, said through a smile, "It seems you're a reluctant minister?"

"You might say that." He laughed, but her words echoed Carl and Tony's unsought but stinging counsel. He was relieved when Cara turned to Cassie and initiated a conversation about teaching.

Neal and Joel excused themselves while everyone else settled into canvas chairs on the patio. "We'll take care of the dishes later," Matilda announced.

Lyle said, "We have an abundant harvest this year, and as you know, we've made several new hires. I'll show you around and introduce you later."

Where do they stay? "Cassie asked.

"Mostly in the migrant apartments in the processing barn, but some locals live at home. We did a major revamp of the living quarters. It's all inspected, as required."

"Lyle and Kent," Cassie said, "I have a question. Obie saw her pause; he knew what she would say, for they had discussed it on the way, with some disagreement. "I know you said you aren't in the winemaking business, but what would it take to inch into that arena?"

Lyle mumbled something to himself. Kent answered the question: "'Inch' is a good word, Cassie. You and I have had many phone calls about our finances, so you know that we operate on a shoestring. Offhand, I'd say it's not something we should even consider."

"I don't mean a huge production, just something that could grow over time. Something that might encourage a conversion later."

Kent's tone suggested resistance. "Do you know what it takes to run such an operation? Anyway, we already supply fruit to local wineries. They're satisfied with what we give them."

Obie had questioned Cassie's wanting to get too involved in a business they knew little about. Now, he said, "You supply a good service. We should concentrate on ways to improve that."

Cassie looked annoyed as she turned to Kent, "It's a business, not a service, and I'm not completely ignorant on the subject. I know, for instance, that although we grow good wine grapes, there are better vines out there. Can't we cultivate a few of those? Wouldn't that be a start?"

"We don't have the space," Kent said. "We'd have to dispose of producing vines."

"There's a little room on the south slope," Cassie said. *How did she know anything about a "south slope?"*

"A thousand square feet, maybe," Kent said.

"That's a start."

"Well, if you're only thinking on that scale, we can, as you say, 'make a start.' It's expensive, though."

Cassie was smiling. Obie said, "Kent, we'll talk seriously about this in the coming months." Maybe the subject would be forgotten by then.

Cara said, "Cassie, you two can talk in person. Kent and I would like to visit Stafford Rest, maybe this winter. I have time around Christmas."

"Wonderful," Cassie said. "I'll have time off, too. The whole family can come."

"We might," Lyle said.

"Sounds great," Obie said. "Kent, have you ever been snowshoeing?"

"Not yet, but I look forward to it."

* * *

On a Saturday morning in late October, Obie looked out the corner window of the church office and wondered why he was having such difficulty polishing his Sunday sermon. Perhaps it was the beautiful day itself; fall weather hung on tenaciously, revigorated after several days of rain.

The phone rang. Ken sounded cheerful. "Son, why on earth are you in that office instead of out enjoying this marvelous day?"

"Dad, I have work to do. Do you want me to stand in the pulpit tomorrow with nothing to say?"

"You'd think of something. This day's too good to fritter away. Let's you and me go walking on the ridge."

"I really shouldn't."

"We haven't done that for a long time."

They had walked together in the village and by the Morass, but a longer and more strenuous trek was not a recent occurrence.

In his youth, Obie loved tramping through the woods with Ken. Had they lost that desire somewhere along the way?

He made a quick decision. "I'll be at your house in ten minutes. We'll pick up Jacob and Blizzard on the way up the hill."

"Now, you're talking! And don't worry about your sermon. You'll have several in your head by the time we return."

*   *   *

Obie noticed Ken's heavy breathing as they climbed the upper section of Blackberry Hill to reach the ridge trail. Even so, he was still more agile at ninety-two than most men his age.

The woods were quiet today. Most leaves from hardwood trees had fallen, leaving bare areas throughout the dominant evergreens. Snow cover would soon arrive. Obie enjoyed the seasonal changes, even with their often-ragged dividing lines. He loved the West Coast, too, but seasonal changes there were smoother and less extreme.

Obie stayed one step behind Ken, letting him set the pace. Jacob ran ahead on a zigzag path with the big dog at his heels.

"Do you need to rest?" Obie asked as they neared the incline that led up to the cliffs on the eastern end of the Morass.

"Why? Are you having trouble keeping up?"

"You've set a blistering pace, but I'll manage."

There came the memory of another trail, one from a long time ago. Obie was young, six or seven, and they were trailing deer in the dark. "Dad, do you remember when we hunted over on Canner Meadows?"

"Which time?" Ken had not slowed, even as they approached the cliffs.

"Let's stop here to rest," Obie said. "This is the highest point on the trail."

"All right. We can go sit on that big rock over there."

Ken was breathing hard, but his voice was steady as they seated themselves on the smoothest surfaces of the glacial boulder. Jacob and Blizzard continued to explore the perimeter.

"We hunted together a lot," Ken said. "Which time do you mean?"

"You shot a doe in the dark after I dropped the flashlight. It was wounded, and we chased it. We packed it out. To top it off, we had to push the old truck to start it. Remember that?"

"Sure do. Good-sized doe."

"Illegal, though, wasn't it?"

Ken smiled. "We needed the meat. Those were hard times."

"It was cold that evening, and I remember trying to keep up on the trail."

Ken looked down at his boots. "Obie," he said after a pause, "I pushed you too hard, didn't I ... back then?"

"You wanted to make me strong. I understand that now."

"Well, that was my aim, but maybe I overdid it. It became an easy way for me to be a good father. I was away a lot, and I drank too much. I took shortcuts to make things in my life work. Obie, I'm sorry. I'm real sorry."

Ken's head was lowered, and his shoulders shook, but Obie saw his wet eyes. Jacob saw, too, and came to lean against his grandfather's arm.

"Dad, even if we had troubles earlier, and I think you're seeing it out of all proportion, it turned out well."

Ken sat up and placed a hand on Jacob's head. "I have many regrets, but it has turned out pretty well."

"You're forgiven, Dad. You're in the clear."

Ken laughed. "The preacher emerges."

"I just wanted you to know that no one holds anything against you."

"Have you forgotten about Abigail Hunt? She can't look at me without scowling."

"Ignore it. Abigail has mellowed."

"Well, maybe. I guess we've learned to slide right by each other. Still ..."

"Dad, you must forgive her. Whether she reciprocates isn't a factor."

"She did some awful things to our family."

"I know, but that's in the past."

"So, you've really forgiven her?"

"I have. And I think she leans toward forgiving me."

"Forgive you for what ... giving her two grandsons?"

"Dad, I'm not blameless. You know that. Laura and I brought about the actions that led to all the intrigue and deceit."

"You were just kids."

"We knew better. But all that's beside the point. Our lives are intertwined now, and we have to get along. Love is better than hate, isn't it?"

Ken sighed. "I know that, Obie. And I want to feel it, but I have trouble with it. And there's my own guilt that I need to deal with. I loved your mother, but I could have treated her better, made more effort to get my sorry life in order."

"That's behind us. Let's look to the future."

"My future isn't that long."

"Dad, how many men your age can climb mountains like you do? You'll be around awhile."

Ken became quiet, and Jacob went to sit beside him. "Grandpa," he said as he rubbed Ken's arm, "Why are you so sad?"

Obie saw Ken smile again as he put an arm around Jacob's shoulders. "I'm not sad, Jacob. Fact is, I'm the happiest I've ever been."

Why is that, Grandpa?"

Well, I suppose it's because, in my old age, I've found a family to love. I've had your father a long time, but now I have you and your mother to love … and also Dan and Ly Yen, and your cousins, Laurie and Obadiah. They're all part of the big family that I love."

"Don't forget Grandma Hunt and Aunt Laura," Jacob said.

Ken glanced at Obie, and a moment passed before he said, "Yes, Jacob, it's important to love everybody."

Ken said, "By the way, Jacob … what's this I heard about you climbing up in the bell tower at your church? Why did you do that?"

"Don't worry, he's been appropriately disciplined for that," Obie said.

Ken patted Jacob on his shoulder. "Oh, I thought it sounded like fun."

"Don't encourage him, Dad. He has this strange fixation on church bells. We like that he appreciates the sounds … so do we, but such close interaction with these big bells is out."

Ken laughed. "If liking bells too much is my grandson's greatest fault, I'll die happy."

On the way back along the ridge toward Blackberry Hill, Ken told Obie, "I'll try to forgive her. I really will. You can pray for me that I can do it."

"Dad, I don't remember you ever asking me to pray for you. But you must know that I do pray for you, and I will."

They slowed, for Ken was breathing hard. "I would have come to your church, but you know that Angie and I went to Evergreen all those years, and I still have friends there. I haven't gone back since she died, but I think I will. Father McNeal still sends me church mail."

"He's a good man. Will you go to a Sunday Mass?"

"I will, but I want to see him privately too, and talk about things I've kept too long to myself."

"Confession, you mean."

"Yes."

"Dad, that's exactly what you should do. You should go to services, too."

"I will. And I'd like you to go with me."

Obie was surprised. "Dad, you know what I do on Sundays."

"Just once. That's what I mean. Think about my history of churchgoing. I went with your mother, but only occasionally. It was with Angie that I started to go regularly. And I've never been to the Methodist church."

"Yes, I know. You've never attended even one of my Sunday services."

Ken stopped and turned to face Obie. "I'm sorry about that. That's what I'm getting at. There's a disconnect in our religious lives. Let's do this: You attend one service with me, and I'll attend one at your church. Would that work?"

"It's a marvelous idea." They had never raised such issues about religion before. "I'll find a free Sunday. In fact, the Sunday after next will work. "I'll get a layperson to conduct our service."

They walked slowly the rest of the way. Ken was exhausted after they descended the upper section of Blackberry Hill. He said, "Thanks for going with me. I needed this. And I'm sorry that I took you away from sermon-writing."

Obie laughed. "As you predicted, it has given me material for several sermons. It's me thanking you, Dad."

CHAPTER TWENTY-THREE

December 1979

The Augustine family arrived in Stafford Rest four days before Christmas, except for Neal, who stayed behind to oversee the vineyard. Fatigued by the season's preparations, Obie saw their presence as an enhancement of the holiday spirit.

As they sat around Obie and Cassie's dining room table for a pancake breakfast the morning after their arrival, Lyle asked, "Where's the snow? We came all this way to see an Adirondack winter, and it's not even cold."

"Colder than home, though," Cara said.

"I wanted to ski and go snowshoeing," Joel said.

Alicia, seated next to Jacob, said, "Ice skating, that's what I'd like."

"I can teach you," Jacob said quickly. "Mom and Dad take me skating down on Cedar Creek under the bridge."

"Not yet," Cassie explained. "It has thawed lately and isn't safe."

"I apologize," Obie said. "I'm afraid I raised your expectations. This weather's strange, and people are worried because the Winter Olympics are coming in February, and for that, we need lots of snow."

"How far away is Lake Placid?" Lyle asked.

"We can drive there in an hour or less. It's too bad you're not staying for the games, but we'll show you the village and the surrounding area."

"Obie, you're not to worry about the weather," Cara said. "We're just happy that we're here. It's like a dream come true."

Lyle laughed. "That's because we've never been anywhere before. I'd never been out of California until now."

Kent said, "Dad hates to turn the vineyard over to anyone else."

Lyle said quickly, "Neal is perfectly capable of looking after things."

Kent explained, "My brother is taking over more of the daily duties. And Dad's stepping back some."

Lyle bristled. "Not stepping back that far ... yet."

Cassie said, "We're happy to have you here for a few days. And I'm sure it won't be the last time."

Later that day, Obie and Cassie took their guests to nearby sites and introduced them to family members and friends. The factory was empty because it was Saturday, and Ken promised to take Lyle there later. Laura said, "I'll go too, and I'll show you our outlet on Main Street."

Kent and Dan had bonded. "We'll go flying," Dan said, "I sold my plane when I was in med school, but we can rent something for a few hours at the airstrip in Evergreen. Maybe by the time you come back again, I'll have a new airplane."

"We're definitely coming back," Kent said. Cara nodded.

Obie gave them a church tour. "Tomorrow is Sunday," he said, "I would be honored if you attended our service." He knew Kent and Cara were Protestants but was unsure how strict the rest of their family was in their beliefs.

"We'll attend," Matilda said, smiling. "And we'll critique."

"We certainly will," Cara said.

Obie laughed. "I welcome it."

* * *

The plan was to hold a Christmas Eve celebration at the Hunt house on Garnet Point, but first, they gathered for dinner at *Abigail's* following an early church service.

Abigail had arranged the seating so they could sit close together. Obie watched her flitting around, alternately giving orders to waiters and entering the kitchen to supervise the cooks. She was trying to be gracious, he conceded, but whether to impress the visitors or from genuine hospitality, he was unsure. He would not allow himself to have negative thoughts about it during this joyous season.

The lights were dimmed inside the restaurant except for flickering Christmas decorations. Through the windows, Obie could see the darkened waters of the lake and beyond to Main Street. *The scene was always familiar yet always new, constantly reminding him of how fortunate he was to have returned.*

He had much to be thankful for: Ken was sitting with Jacob at his side, his beautiful grandchildren, Laurie and Obadiah, were between Dan and Ly Yen, and Laura appeared content next to Ben Williamson, her "recycled" husband. Even Abigail, now taking her seat, had shaped the life he enjoyed. And there was Cassie, of course; her hand found his with familiar frequency.

The restaurant had other familiar patrons. He was surprised to see Ernie and Frances Boswell at a nearby table; they should be helping with the Christmas Eve crowd in their own restaurant. Ed Baumgartner was over by the fireplace with a man Obie had seen him with before. There had been disapproving gossip about that relationship; it was not his job to judge. Ed was a longtime friend. He would always be a friend.

Right now, everything was going well in his life. He hoped for that to continue.

* * *

As they gathered around the big fireplace at Grandma's house, Jacob was determined to ignore Alicia. It was not easy; she followed him every time he moved to another seat, and it had been like that since her arrival.

He did not dislike Alicia, but she was a shadow, ever ready with an idea about where they should go or what they should do. *He would make his own decisions about that.*

The massive mound of presents under the giant blue spruce in the corner was eventually reduced to piles of crumpled wrappings and discarded boxes. There were more presents this year. The Augustines gave good presents. His parents' gifts were usually limited to clothing, books, or educational games. He went to bed that night feeling good.

Christmas Day was festive. The Inn was closed for the day, and everyone gathered for breakfast at Grandma's. Lunch was to be at Aunt Laura's, and they would return to Grandma's house for dinner.

After lunch, Jacob went down to the dock to watch for fish in the frigid waters. He was only there five minutes when Alicia joined him.

"Is the water cold?" she asked.

"Well, of course it is. It's December. It's not frozen over yet, but it will be soon."

"Are there fish?"

"Sure. That's what I'm looking for."

"Why don't you try to catch them? Don't you like to eat fish?"

"We eat lots of fish. Dad and me go fishing all summer, mostly on lower Cedar Creek and sometimes out on the lake. And after the lake freezes over, we take our fishing shanty out on the ice."

She said, "I like it here. We're leaving before New Year's, but my father says we'll come back sometime, maybe in the summer. You can take me fishing, then. I've never been."

Jacob was unsure how to feel about her future visits. "How old are you, Alicia?" He knew her age because his mother had told him, but he needed something to say.

"I'll be eight in two months."

"Me too, about a week from now." It felt good that he was older than her. "Mom said I'll have a party. All the kids in my class will come."

"I've never had a party, except with a few friends. We live really far from town."

Maybe Alicia wasn't so bad after all. He started toward the end of the dock. "Come on, I'll show you the best place to see the fish. They come up real close."

They watched for several minutes without seeing anything except a few darting minnows. "The water's rough. That's why we can't see them," Jacob explained. *Her eyes were brown.*

Eventually, they tired of watching for fish and went to sit on a bench by the path to the house. The short bench required them to sit close together, which was weird but pleasant. He knew little about girls. His sister, Julie, had her strange but sweet ways, and his cousin, Laurie, was nice, but she was older.

They sat quietly awhile before she spoke. "Jacob, we don't see each other often, but our families have gotten together for as long as I can remember." Her brown eyes stared straight at him. "Why don't you like me?"

The question startled him because it was not true. He did like her, even if she was pushy sometimes. And she was almost as pretty as Carrie Summers in his class. He stared down at the ground. *Had he mistreated her?* His father talked about treating people "as you would like to be treated."

"I do like you, Alicia." Without further thought, he added, "I like you a lot."

She was smiling. "I like you, too, Jacob." After a moment, she added, "But I'm really confused about your family."

How was he supposed to answer that? "I don't know what you mean."

"My dad says that Dan is your brother. How come you have a brother that old?"

"I don't think he's my brother."

"How do you know?"

"My Aunt Laura is his mother. Wouldn't that make Dan my cousin?"

"So, who is Dan's father?"

'Well, Uncle Ben, of course. They both have the last name of 'Williamson.'"

"I heard your father call Dan "son" last night as they exchanged gifts. He said, 'Thank you, my son.' If your father is his father, then you'd be brothers."

"I think you heard wrong, Alicia. Anyway, lots of people call people 'son.' Last week, my teacher, Mr. Clark, caught me helping someone on a spelling test. He said, 'Son, you shouldn't help people cheat.'"

"You just made that up, Jacob." They laughed. Alicia was hard to fool.

She had not finished her attempt to unravel his family relationships. She said, "And what about Julie? She has a last name different from yours."

That was easy to answer. "My mother was married years and years ago to someone else. I forget his name, but he was

Julie's father. Julie's my half-sister.''

That night, he thought about their discussion. His family had confusing relationships—whispered conversations that ended when he got too close. He made up his mind to have his parents explain it all to him. Alicia was smart to ask those kinds of questions. *She was really pretty, too.*

* * *

Obie and Cassie had discussed business only briefly with Kent during the Augustine visit, but the day before their departure, Kent took them aside. They sat in the enclosed porch room. He seemed hesitant. "I've put off telling you this," he said, setting his coffee cup on the low table between them.

Was the vineyard in trouble? Obie braced himself.

Kent cleared his throat. "I'll just say it. You know I have a law degree that I've barely used except for dealings in our business. But I've recently decided to leave the vineyard. I'm going to practice law the way I've always wanted." He sat back in his chair, expelling a sigh of relief.

This was major. How could the vineyard run without Kent's help? Neal was ambitious but not ready for that responsibility. It was not a matter of profit, at least for Obie; he was unsure about Cassie. They gave most of their earnings away to charity, anyway. The bigger question was whether the Augustine family could still make a living from the vineyard. Lyle and Matilda were excellent tenders, but their business aptitude was questionable.

Cassie asked the obvious question. "How is this going to affect us ... and your family?"

"It will, some, I guess. Dad and Mom know. I told them before we left. Dad was angry and hurt initially, but after I explained it all to him, he seemed to accept it."

"Maybe you can explain it to us," Cassie said with an edge in her tone.

Kent looked more relaxed as he sat back in his chair. "I've trained Neal for years. He's perfectly capable of handling the nitty-gritty of the business. And he's far surpassed me in his knowledge of vines and wines. Cassie, you'll be glad to know that he's interested in your idea of introducing some new vines."

Obie hoped that "new vines" would not be a topic of discussion since it had become a sore subject between him and Cassie.

She said, "That's good news, but will we need to hire a legal firm now?"

"Well, yes, in a way, you will. But the good news is that you'll hire *me*. I can still manage O'Shane Vineyard's legal affairs."

Obie was relieved. "So, you'll set up practice close to the vineyard?"

"No, we won't even be in the Napa Valley. But it doesn't matter. Most legal affairs can be handled by phone and through the mail."

Cassie asked, "Where, then, are you going? You and Cara love the Napa Valley?"

"Yes, we do. But we've also found another place we love, and we want to live there awhile. Cara and I have discussed it for a long time, but we made a final decision just last night."

"Is it far?" Obie asked. "From the vineyard, I mean?"

"Yes, it's about as far as we are right now from the vineyard. Obie and Cassie ... we've decided to come to Stafford Rest to live."

CHAPTER TWENTY-FOUR

March–April 1980

At first, Obie thought it was part of a dream, but he soon realized that Julie was shaking his shoulder. Her voice was quivering. "Daddy ... wake up!"

Beside him, Cassie stirred. "Julie, Honey, it's five o'clock. It's too early to get up."

"What is it, Julie?" Obie asked.

"That lady with white hair was in my dream again."

Obie tried to clear his head. The "beautiful white-haired lady" was a recurring phenomenon in Julie's life. She believed the woman talked to her. He saw no harm in it and had not tried to dissuade her. After all, she had been right about Italy.

"Did she tell you something in your dream, Julie?" Obie asked.

"Yes. She said to go see Grandpa."

"We will, Honey. We'll go right after breakfast." It was Saturday, and he had planned to see Ken anyway; visits with his father on Saturday mornings for coffee and friendly discussion before work had become a ritual.

"No, Daddy. We should go now.

Cassie said, "I'll call him."

"It's early. I'd hate to wake him up."

"We're talking about Ken," she said. "He'll already be up."

"Call Grandpa," Julie said, sounding desperate.

"Okay, Honey, I will. Just let me get up and get dressed."

"Hurry up," Julie said as she rushed out the bedroom door, nearly bumping into Jacob, who stood sleepy-eyed and confused.

Obie let the phone ring several times, but there was no answer. *He might have stepped out the back.* Five minutes later, there was still no answer. Obie was worried. "I'm going down there," he told Cassie.

"We'll come too," she said. "I can fix breakfast for all of us. He has all the fixings. It'll be a treat."

Dawn was breaking as they pulled into Ken's driveway. The door was not locked, and the house was silent. Obie hurried to the bedroom and knew immediately that something was wrong; Ken's breathing was labored, and he was pale. Obie could not rouse him.

He told Cassie, "Call Dan, and call for an ambulance, too. We'll need it."

Dan was there in ten minutes, and the ambulance arrived from Evergreen shortly afterward. Ken was conscious now, but incoherent. Obie helped where he could as they loaded him into the ambulance for the trip to Saratoga Springs.

"I'll drive separately," Dan told Obie. "I must come back, but you'll no doubt want to stay."

"How bad is this, Dan?" Obie asked.

"I believe he's had a heart attack, but we must get him into professional care to know more."

"We'll meet you in Saratoga."

Cassie told Obie, "We'll take the Jeep. You may have to stay longer."

Obie experienced waves of despair while on the way. *How bad was it?* Ken could have been like that for hours before they found him. He was awake as the ambulance left, but did not respond to their questions. *It was serious.* He was ninety-two. *He could die.* His father was such a part of his life that he could not imagine a world without him.

It had not always been like that, of course. He did not blame his father for a lack of parenting in Obie's growing-up years; the hard times of that era had a brutal impact on many relationships. And it was on himself for his "lost years" when he was away at wars, at schools, and wallowing through self-imposed periods of disillusionment. Father and son had grown close only after Obie's return to Stafford Rest.

Ken had changed. Angie managed that; she was responsible for his father's new attitude toward faith. She had convinced him to become part of a Christian community, something Obie's mother was unable to accomplish. And his and his father's Saturday morning chats and frequent walks on the ridge were healing events.

There was also the exchange of church visits, made at Ken's suggestion. Despite his worry, Obie smiled as he approached Saratoga Springs, for that first visit to the Catholic church in Evergreen had unexpected results. Not only was Ken greeted with enthusiasm by friends he and Angie had made over the years, but some older members remembered Obie, as well, from the time he and his mother attended there.

Father McNeal pumped Obie's hand after the service and said, "I'm glad you came. I've talked to your dad, but frankly, I never expected you to come."

"It sneaked up on me, too," Obie said. "But you'd better get used to it because we've agreed to visit each other's congregations occasionally."

"What a marvelous idea," the priest had responded. "I might get a sermon out of this."

The result was that not only had Ken and Obie exchanged visits, but a few members of each congregation did as well.

Obie was surprised, for he knew something of Catholic tradition, but Father McNeal said, "I'm considered a progressive, I suppose, but like you, I want to see greater communication between churches. We have our differences, but we're all children of God."

Obie and Father Thomas McNeal became better friends that day. However, not all Stafford Rest Methodist Church members liked the idea; Amos was the most vocal.

Obie managed to calm his mind as he pulled into a parking space at the Saratoga hospital. He and his father were at peace; they finally understood each other.

* * *

Ken's heart attack had been sudden, and the week following was stressful as his condition slowly worsened. His death, although expected, brought shock and grief to family and friends.

It was a cold and windy March day as they gathered for

burial at the cemetery above Lake Road. Among the friends were several from the Evergreen church where Father McNeal had conducted the Funeral Mass. The priest had just concluded the graveside service, and Obie stood silently with Cassie, Julie, and Jacob, feeling both sorrow and thankfulness.

Friends eventually drifted away, but family members braved the harsh weather conditions and lingered. The grave was still open, and three funeral home workers waited respectfully on the side.

Julie had cried throughout both services, but now was silent. Jacob's eyes were wet; Obie had heard him crying during the night. The twins' faces were somber.

Laura, Ben, and Abigail soon left; they sat with the other family members at the church but had remained in the background at the graveside service. As she was leaving, Abigail said," Obie, I'm sorry for your loss. Ken and I had our differences, but we finally learned to get along better."

He wondered if he should tell her what Ken said the night before his passing. Obie had believed that death was near and stayed at his father's bedside throughout the night. Toward morning, Ken emerged with clarity of purpose from the jumble of hospital hoses and apparatus Dan said was keeping him alive. His hand, with a tube attached, reached for Obie's hand. "Son," he said, "I'm going to let it go now."

"Dad, I'm here."

"I'm at peace, Obie, but there's one thing I need to get off my mind."

"What, Dad?"

"Abigail."

"Do you want to tell her something?"

Ken coughed and then remained silent for a moment before he said in a raspy voice, "Tell her that despite all our harsh words toward each other, we were faithful in our love for our children and grandchildren. We share that, and it's more important than any issues we had against each other. That's all over now, and I wish her all the best."

Those were his father's last words; he died later that morning. Obie would tell Abigail, but this was not the right time.

He turned his attention to the gravesite. At Ken's request, he was being buried between Angie and Obie's mother. *That was appropriate.* Close by were the headstones for Grandfather Jacob and Grandmother Prissy. He had almost forgotten that her given name was "Priscilla." It was long ago, but he could still see their faces.

Ly Yen, standing with Dan and the twins, brought him back to the present. "Pastor Obie, I am so sorry. We have loved Ken very much. There have been many prayers already, but I want to say another prayer for him now, with your permission?"

"Of course, Ly Yen. I'd like that, and I'm sure Dad would, too."

She came to stand beside him. What was there about this slender Asian woman that was so appealing? Beauty? Honesty? Grace that defied explanation? Surely those things, but if defined in a word, it was "faith."

He had seen it during their first encounter in Vietnam. As a dutiful chaplain, he delivered the news of Dan's wounding. She noticed the cross on his collar and asked, "Is that a cross of Jesus?" She followed the question with, "I follow way of Jesus, too."

Those were hard times, but she never lost faith. Obie patted her hand. He wished she would stop calling him "Pastor Obie."

"Say that prayer for Dad, Ly Yen. He's probably listening."

She did not hesitate. "Father of us all, please accept our most reverent entreaty." *She had learned some new words.* "Please to welcome Mr. Ken to your timeless and endless Kingdom that welcomes all who say your name with love. He has taught us through his strength and courage to win hard fights. He has helped to make this village where we live a better village. Father of us all, we ask in the name of Jesus that you give wonderful rest to this good father of our family. Amen."

"Ly Yen, it was a beautiful prayer," Obie said as he patted her hand again.

As they turned to go down the path to Lake Road, Dan said, "I wish I had known sooner. To have known that I had a father and another grandfather would have made a great difference in my life."

"And in mine," Obie responded. "But that's the past. We know now, and that's what matters."

* * *

Ly Yen wanted to tell him something, and it was not like her to hesitate; her opinions were free-flowing, although usually on calm waters. After Ken's funeral, Dan had noticed her reluctance to speak of anything beyond the mundane, and now, a month later, that was unchanged.

Was she ill? Had he done something to offend? He must address the matter.

This might be the right time; kitchen clean-up after the evening meal was complete, Laurie and Obadiah were doing homework at the dining room table, and Abigail had retreated to the section of the house she called "my space."

It was an unusually warm evening, and Dan suggested they sit on the patio. Streaks of red illuminated the sky in the west and cast that color onto the lake waters. They turned their chairs to face the view.

He was ready to ask her if there was anything she wanted to tell him when she spoke. "Dear One, I am sorry I have been so silent in all the recent days."

He reached for her hand. "What is it, Darling? What's on your mind?"

"There is something I must say." She hesitated. "I think you will not like it."

"What affects you affects me, Ly Yen. Anyway, I think I know what's bothering you. It's our living conditions, isn't it? After three years back here, we still live with my grandmother. It bothers me, too. We've talked about buying or building our own place, but that hasn't happened yet."

"No, we should not worry about that. Grandmother Hunt is lonely. She needs us. Someday, we can make a place of our own. I do not worry."

"Ly Yen, Sweetheart, what is it if it's not that?"

"I have a desire."

"Yes, a desire for what?" This was becoming a full-blown

worry.

She moved her chair closer. "You know that we follow the way of Jesus?"

"I know. Ly Yen, we're Christians, although I'm not as good at it as you."

"We worship God through Jesus. Jesus takes us close to God. To know Jesus is to know God. That is how Pastor Obie explained it when we became church members."

"Yes, I know, and I try to live up to that ideal."

She said with familiar firmness, "I want to follow Jesus way more."

"Honey, you do as much as anyone. More, really." He shook her shoulder. "Why, you're a Christian dynamo."

They laughed, but he saw the seriousness in her expression. "For me, it is not enough," she said. "That is why I worry."

"You know I'll support you in whatever you want to do, don't you?"

It was the truth. He had loved his beautiful wife almost from the moment he met her, and she loved him unconditionally. Now, she wanted to assume even more responsibility in church matters. *Obie will be pleased.*

"You do not understand, Dear One. I want to do more, like Pastor Obie."

While relieved that she was not ill, he realized this was a more serious matter than he had imagined. He remembered that while in Baltimore, she expressed the desire for seminary training and even took some religion courses. He had asked her to wait until they were settled in Stafford Rest before she pursued further education. *Is that what this was about?*

"Do you want to be a minister?" he managed.

"Not a minister. Not until a long time. But I can teach about Jesus or be a good influence. But I cannot speak well. I try, but language is hard. I am what Mr. Amos tells me ... ignorant."

"That man isn't qualified to call anyone that," Dan said, his anger rising. "You've done well with language skills in the time you've been in America."

"I want to be educated," she said with such firmness that

he was surprised.

"Well, that's not so hard. We can get a tutor for you. Cassie knows educators who do that on the side."

Ly Yen sat forward in her chair. "No, that is not what I mean." He heard her catch her breath. "And that is why I worry. I want real education."

"College?"

"A school like that. I would go away, and it would upset our lives."

"Yes, I'm afraid it would. I don't know how we could do that. I have my practice here. Sweetheart, it's a noble ambition, but I don't see how we can accomplish it right now."

"I would much like to find a way."

Should he mention an obvious problem? How could she pass an entrance exam to an institution of higher learning? She had attended the equivalent of high school in Vietnam, but had that prepared her for this?

"Dear one," she said, "I have kept something from you, and I am sorry."

"What, Ly yen? What is it?"

"You will think me not a good wife."

"Never, Darling. I will never think that about you."

"I have heard the 'calling.' That is what Pastor Obie says it is. I wish to learn more about Christianity ... the way of Jesus."

He feared what was coming. "Are you talking about the seminary?"

"Yes." She bowed her head. "I want to go to seminary."

"You might need a college degree to get into a seminary."

He heard her long sigh. "Some seminaries admit students with less," she said. "Pastor Obie has helped me to find one of those."

He was surprised again. "You've talked to Obie about this?"

"Yes, we have talked much since Grandfather Ken's funeral."

It dawned on Dan that things may be out of his hands. "Ly Yen, what have you done?"

"Dear One, I am enrolled in a seminary. I will go to

Pennsylvania in the fall." There were tears in her eyes. "If it is your good will."

It was almost dark now, but the light from the kitchen window cast a shallow glow on Ly Yen's face. In their nearly ten years of marriage, she had never asked such a difficult thing. To deny Ly Yen anything was difficult. He struggled with conflicting thoughts. *He must give her an answer.*

He sighed. "It seems impossible ... but maybe we can find a way. No, we will find a way."

CHAPTER TWENTY-FIVE

July–October 1981

Obie quickly agreed when the Rev. Ernest Owens requested a lunch get-together of the three Stafford Rest ministers; the warm early July day did not encourage work. Curt Parker, the Episcopal pastor, was always ready for a break from the routine.

Still, it was unusual. Owens was not antisocial but quite reserved. He had never initiated a meeting in the six years they had lunched together.

At *Ernie's*, there was the usual complaint airing session and critiques of their recent pulpit swaps before Owens said, "Did you miss our bell last Sunday?"

"Actually, I did," Parker said. "I thought I imagined it."

Obie had noticed, too. The church bells of Stafford Rest were familiar sounds, each with a resonance that reverberated throughout a village surrounded by high ridges. Sounds carried well within that configuration; some wit had said that a cat purr on Indian Knob could be heard on Garnet Point.

The peals of Sunday morning church bells were etched into Obie's memory even before he had seen the inside of a church. He remembered his mother saying, "That's the Episcopal bell," or "I hear the Methodist bell." The Baptist bell, closest to Blackberry Hill, rang loudest in his memory. He missed the bells during his years away. It was as if their sounds opened gateways to some inner clarity—a connection to the divine. Jacob's fascination with church bells had reawakened some of those feelings.

Their Methodist bell, high in the bell tower, rang before services, activated by a rope that hung a few feet above the narthex floor. Teenagers so coveted the bell-ringer's job that they drew lots for it each month.

"Our bell is broken," Owens said. "I wanted you to know that."

"What happened?" Obie asked.

There was genuine sadness in Owen's tone as he explained. "We have rotted timber in the tower. A support broke Saturday night and caused the bell to fall onto a platform below. We were lucky it didn't crash onto the main floor."

Parker said, "So you'll need to fix the supports before you can put it back up?"

"That's being accomplished even as we speak," Owens said. "But the bell has a crack."

Obie said, "Will you replace it?" *Maybe they were looking for financial aid.* Owens and Parker knew about the Love Fund, but not his association with it. Nevertheless, they might suspect.

"No, we'll put it back up. It will work just fine with a little welding, but the sound might be changed. I thought you might wonder about hearing a different tone."

"We'll let you know," Parker said.

"Some churches are using chimes instead of bells," Owens said. "I guess that's easier once you get the system installed. Some of our members would like that."

Obie said, "There's no sound quite like our bells on Sunday morning. It's a tradition, and we'd miss your bell."

"I love our bells," Parker said, "even when they ring simultaneously." He snapped his fingers. "We should stagger times so we don't interfere with one another."

"Not a bad idea," Owens said.

*   *   *

Kent Augustine and his family arrived in Stafford Rest with little fanfare. No one in the village except members of their families, seemed to notice, but it was a big deal for Jacob. The huge moving van nearly blocked White Pine Street, where he and his dad were helping them move into Grandpa Ken's old house. His mother and Ly Yen also helped, but would soon leave to cook dinner. Cara directed the placement of every item that entered the house. Alicia helped, too, but spent more time sitting in the rocker on the porch than carrying boxes into the house.

Jacob did not understand all the details, but from overheard grown-up conversations, he concluded that they were renting the house to the Augustines until they had a home of their own. Mr. Augustine, a lawyer, was also renting office space on Main Street to use after he heard from something called "the state bar."

His parents talked a lot with Mr. Augustine about the vineyard in California and seemed to worry about it. But Mr. Augustine said it would all "be taken care of."

Jacob's only worry was about what he would say to Alicia when they were alone. She had sent him a note tucked inside a letter from her mother to his parents; she should not have done that because now everybody knew about it, and he had been teased. He kept the note safe in his pocket. Her handwriting was much better than his. The note was not long, a half-page about all the girl things she was bringing—as if he cared about that.

But the last words in the note kept prodding at his brain: *"I can't wait to see you again, Jacob. I'm making a list of all the things we can do together. Love, Alicia."*

"Love? What did she mean by that? And what were the things she wanted them to do together? It might be fun to do some things, but he would not take time away from baseball or hiking in the woods whenever he felt like it.

When they first arrived, Alicia kissed him on the cheek and then turned her head so he could kiss her cheek. *That wasn't so bad.* She smelled like Aunt Laura did sometimes. He would do "some things" with her, but would not give up time for the things that mattered.

After the furniture was in and the moving van had left, they took the Augustines to Blackberry Hill for dinner. His grandmother had offered to treat everyone at the restaurant, but after the four-day drive from the West Coast, they were exhausted and wanted to relax in a home setting.

His mother had set up tables outside. His grandmother and the twins soon arrived, followed by Laura and Ben. Dan was delayed twenty minutes by a medical emergency. "Just a few stitches on a careless hand," he explained once he arrived.

Dinner was fun. The grown-ups laughed a lot. Alicia sat beside Julie and across the table from him. *She was really pretty.*

217

Kent said, "Obie, you and Cassie put on a good feed. Are these vegetables from your garden?"

"Most came from our garden right up the hill." His father said, pointing.

Jacob had picked the beans and cabbage early that morning. The tomatoes had only started to ripen, but he had found enough for the dinner table. It was too bad that the strawberry season had passed; Alicia would have liked their strawberries.

The Augustines had brought wine. Obadiah and Laurie sampled it, but Jacob and Alicia were not allowed even to take a sip. He did not care because he had not liked it when he and David Gerder tasted some from David's father's cellar.

Jacob was only marginally interested in most of the conversations. They were quizzing Ly Yen about her classes at the seminary in Pennsylvania. Everyone was surprised last year when she enrolled there, all except his parents. He had learned that his father, more than anyone, helped her to get into "a really good school." She came home often, having learned to drive, so she did not interfere with Dan's schedule. And Dan flew down there frequently in his new floatplane.

"She's a super student," Dan said, looking proud. "She makes excellent grades."

"What classes are you taking, Dear?" Cara asked.

"Religious courses," Ly Yen replied. But I take basic English, too. There is much to learn."

"She's doing great," his father said, echoing what he had told his mother.

Jacob eventually grew tired of sitting at the table and excused himself. As he started to walk away, Alicia said, "Where are you going, Jacob?"

"To the barnroom." He hoped she would not want to go with him; the barnroom was his private space.

His fear was justified. "Wait! I'll come with you."

"Okay." His voice was weak. He should not have encouraged her.

She followed him to the small Dutch-style barn that, according to his father, was once a stable. His grandmother, who died many years ago, had made the end facing the house into the space they called "the barnroom."

It was cool inside, and there was the faintest scent of hay despite there being no hay in any part of the barn. The other section of the barn held tools and winter equipment such as skis and snowshoes.

"This is a wonderful room," Alicia said.

"It's my favorite spot to be by myself."

"Do you like to be by yourself?"

"Sometimes. It's a good thinking place." His mother called it that.

He hoped Alicia would stop asking so many questions. She said, "What are those covered-up things by the window?"

"Dad's paintings."

"Is he an artist?"

"He says he isn't, but he really is. Some people want to buy his paintings, but he won't sell them. But he does give some away."

"Can I see them?"

He removed the burlap from two canvases. "These are his latest ones. He doesn't paint often since he doesn't have much time for it."

"I like them," she said as she rubbed a hand over the edge of an unframed canvas. "I wish I could paint like this. Would he show me how?"

"You can ask him, but he doesn't have much time. He's a writer, too, you know?"

"Yes, my parents talk about that." She turned away from the paintings. "What do you like to do? Do you paint, too?"

"I'm not very good at it. I like to write, though. And I like baseball. I play third base. I'm really good at that. Uncle Dan is one of our coaches. He says I'm the best player on our team." He hesitated. *He had told her too much. She would just ask more questions.*

She went to sit in the rocker by the wood-burning stove. He took the chair next to her. "What do you think about?" she asked.

"What do you mean?"

"You said that you come here to think. Well, what do you

219

think about?"

It was private. He would not tell her anything about it. "Well, I ..."

She quickly said, "I had a place to go to, to think. But I guess I'll have to find a new place now that we live here."

He was pleased because if she had her own space, she would stay out of his. He did not really want to know but asked anyway, "What do you think about?"

"Lately, I've been thinking about leaving my old friends behind. I didn't have many friends there because we lived so far away from town, but I had two very good friends." She was silent for a moment. "But I hope I can have friends here too."

He tried to imagine what it was like to leave home and friends. Charlie Cook moved away from Stafford Rest last fall and cried when he said goodbye. Charlie promised to write, but no letters ever came.

He studied her face; it was a sad time for Alicia. "You'll make friends quickly," he told her. "There are lots of nice girls in our school."

Her brown eyes pleaded. "You'll be my friend, too, won't you, Jacob?"

"Of course I will." Suddenly, he meant it.

* * *

It was Saturday morning in mid-October, and Cassie was worried. Obie was on call today rather than going to the office, so it seemed a good time for a serious discussion about their future.

She served pancakes with blueberries and a side order of scrambled eggs, Obie's favorite breakfast. After Jacob had consumed a second serving of pancakes and left to play baseball on the school playground, she set Julie up with a sewing project so they would have privacy.

She carried two mugs of coffee into Obie's study, where he sat silently at his desk, staring at his typewriter. She had chosen to approach him there because it provided an atmosphere favorable for discussion.

"Having trouble?" she asked as she handed him his coffee.

"Sometimes I wonder why I continue these writing sessions. I'm so obstructed by thoughts of other things that the words won't come."

"Obie, please put your writing aside for a few minutes so we can talk."

His face revealed that she had his attention. "What shall we talk about, Sweetheart?"

"The state of things in our lives. Where we are, and where we're going."

"Honey, what's bothering you? What is it?"

"Do you remember our last building project, with so many things in progress and most only half done? That frustrated you. You said that nothing felt complete. Well, that's how I feel now. Our lives have loose ends."

"Yes, but those projects turned out just fine, and I'm not worried that our world is falling apart."

"Obie, you don't worry much. That's your nature and a blessing in many ways, but we must discuss an issue that will soon impact our lives. If I'm to have peace of mind, we need to address it."

Obie sat up in his chair, the lines on his forehead more pronounced. "Cassie, I'm so sorry. I should have known you were worried. Yes, let's have this discussion. You're right to say that we have loose ends."

"Of course I'm right." She was immediately sorry for not softening her words; she wanted to engage him, not accuse him.

"Is it us? Are we good?"

"Oh, Obie ... of course we're good. It's not that. I love you, and I know you love me. It's really only one thing, but it's big in my eyes."

"Tell me, Sweetheart."

She started with a question: "How many years have you been pastor of our church?"

"Seven years."

"And what is the average length of a pastorate in the Methodist church?"

"I don't know. Five or six, I guess. Some go longer, some

shorter. I know a pastor in Vermont who's served in the same church for twelve years. And remember Pastor Charles? He was here a long time. I still miss him."

She would not let the discussion get sidetracked. "Obie, what will happen when they decide it's time for you to go? Aren't you concerned about that?"

"Cassie, don't forget that they begged me to accept this position, even though I didn't want it. They chose me for a specific job. The church was in turmoil, and I believe I've turned it around. Not that there aren't still problems, but I'm confident they'll be solved."

"Yes, you've done wonders. But that doesn't answer my question." *It was time to clear the air.* "If the conference says it's time to move on and assigns you to a new pastorate, what will you do?" She moved her chair next to him and touched his arm. "Will we move? This matters greatly to us, and it's something we must prepare for. If pulpit ministry is your true calling, you'll eventually have to move to another church. Obie, is this your true calling?"

He took time. "Cassie, I'm a writer at the core of my being. God gave me the gift to express my fundamental and religious beliefs that way, but having said that, my 'calling' is to humbly work where God places me."

"Humm ... so, if you had a choice, you'd write full-time?"

"Yes."

"So why not resign and do the thing you want most to do?"

"I thought you liked being a pastor's wife?"

"Obie, these years have been the happiest of my life. I'll be beside you in whatever you want to do, but you must decide what that is, don't you think?" She purposely raised her voice a little. "Just give me a straight answer."

"Cassie, am I a good pastor?"

"You're the best. I mean it. You advance God's Kingdom with love and good works. People love you."

"Maybe not Amos."

She laughed. "He's an exception. Maybe even he will come around."

"Or perhaps he's a reminder that I still have work to do."

"Obie, if I had to name one fault of yours, it would be that you expect big things of yourself."

"That I value myself too highly?" He was smiling.

"No, not that. But maybe your true calling is to take care of the little things. Look at how you helped Ernie and Francis. And there was Lacy …"

"That didn't turn out well."

"We still don't know how that will turn out." *Enough of side talk; she needed an answer.* "What if you're sent to another church?"

Obie moved his chair close enough to put an arm around her shoulder. They sat like that a minute before he said, "Cassie, the answer to your question is that I'll decide when my time at Stafford Rest Methodist is finished."

This man to whom she was married was eternally frustrating. She tried to remain calm. "To put off making such an important decision gives me no relief at all."

He took her hands in his. "Cassie, listen to me. I'm giving you a straight answer. Stafford Rest is our home. We'll not leave it. I will *not* take a pastorate position that's not close enough to allow for that." He motioned toward his typewriter and added, "I can go back to that … with great pleasure."

She was relieved—provisionally. He had said that Blackberry Hill would always be their home. Good, but she wished his "straight answer" was not just slightly bent.

CHAPTER TWENTY-SIX

July 1982

Obadiah Williamson barely contained his excitement as he walked the last few steps to the end of the Hunt dock, where the floatplane sat on choppy water. His dad had escaped the clinic for a few hours and waited on the pier beside the brown and yellow aircraft.

Obadiah was to have his first flying lesson—the first "official" one. He had flown with his father all his life, even in Baltimore and Boston, where they rented airplanes. He bragged to his friends about that and about his father having been an Army pilot in Vietnam.

He had been disappointed last year when, even though he was sixteen, his dad had made him wait a year to begin formal training. *But today was the day.* He would have that license before the summer was over.

He was confident, having learned so much from his father. His dad was never stingy with explanations—and demonstrations. Many flights ended with words still in his ears, such as, "Obadiah, this is what happens when you climb too steeply." Or, "Son, to get out of a stall, you must put the nose down like this." While sitting in the right-hand seat, he was often allowed to handle the controls "just so you know what it feels like."

They called this airplane "new," but it was nearly twenty years old, "refurbished and in excellent shape." Obadiah had taken the train with his father to Buffalo to purchase it and to fly it home.

His sister, who expressed no interest in flying, told him she had overheard their father tell their mother that, "He's cocky, and I'm going to make him earn his wings." Obadiah did not believe that; Lauri was jealous. He was fully qualified to sit in the left-hand seat.

Bring it on, Dad! He climbed into the cabin and began to buckle himself into the pilot's seat. "What are you doing?" his father said as he knocked on the window. "Get back out here and do your preflight check. If you're not serious about learning to fly, I'll do the check myself, but you'll go back to the passenger side."

Obadiah hopped out quickly. "I'm on it, Dad. Sorry! I misunderstood."

"If you're the pilot, you'll check the airplane over before every flight. Every time."

Obadiah, still smarting, circled the airplane, testing every part on the pre-flight checklist that he had long since memorized. Satisfied, he started to climb back into the cabin.

"What about the Pitot tube?" his father said. "If it's stopped up, how will you know your airspeed?"

Obadiah was annoyed; his father was uncharacteristically strict in speech and attitude. "Dad, you checked the Pitot tube before the last flight, which was no more than half an hour long, and you know that little tube isn't stopped up by anything."

"Is that right?" The instructor voice increased in volume and emphasis. "And what if a tiny spider has crawled in there at night and spun a web, or an insect has laid an egg? Those things have happened, Obadiah."

"Well, maybe."

"There's no 'maybe.' To be a good pilot, you must attend to all the details. And if you're my student, you will. Always."

Maybe Laurie had told the truth.

* * *

As Dan tossed the tie-downs to the dock and climbed from a pontoon into the right-side door, he experienced some guilt about the hard-rock way he had introduced Obadiah to flying school. It was not substantially different from how he handled any student; it was how he had been taught. But this was his son whom he loved more than his own life. Still, he needed discipline.

Before and after Obadiah started the engine, Dan had him review every checkpoint and repeat them aloud. The boy knew the routine without a doubt. Leaving the dock area was tricky, so Dan took the controls. Obadiah could practice that later.

A light wind came from the west. After they cleared the dock area, Obadiah took over and made for deeper water, deftly handling the throttle.

"Everything looks clear," he said as he pushed the throttle forward. "No boats or swimmers in the way."

The floatplane moved forward with increasing speed. Dan waited until they were nearly at takeoff speed before saying, "Pull the power back, Obadiah."

"What!"

"Kill it, or I will!"

Obadiah obliged, and they slowed to idle.

"Dad," Obadiah protested. "I was perfect for takeoff. Nothing was in the way, and the water is only a little rough. Why'd you do that?"

"Today's not just a flying day. We're going to work on fundamentals, too. We'll apply things you've studied in your manual. You'll do takeoff runs and practice docking skills later, but there are other fundamentals, as well."

"I could have taken off perfectly, Dad."

"Yes, I'm sure you could have, but, tell me, what would you have done if a speedboat suddenly crossed in front of you?"

"They don't allow speedboats on this lake."

"Do you think that's a smart answer?"

Obadiah did not respond. Dan saw his disappointment and said, "I didn't mean to surprise you with something unexpected, but we're going to take this in little steps. Little steps are surer. We'll practice maneuvering around out here and at the dock. And we may do a takeoff and landing, but we'll work up to it. Does that sound okay with you?"

"Yeah, Dad, it'll do ... I guess."

A couple of hours later, after securing the airplane, they crossed the road and sat on a bench Dan had placed at the foot of the stone stairway leading up to the Hunt house. He wanted to talk with his son about something other than flying.

He had neglected his children. The practice required his time, but that was no excuse. He needed to make more time for Obadiah and Laurie. They were nearly grown and would not be with him and Ly Yen much longer.

Obadiah initiated a conversation. "Dad, Laurie and I were talking recently about our family, or maybe I should say, 'our families.'"

"What about it, or them?"

"You and Mom have told Laurie and me about how you met in Vietnam and came back here together. But we were five years old when you married. Why did it take so long?"

"Obadiah, the war separated us. Didn't I explain all that to you?"

"When we were younger, but I would like to hear it again."

Dan took several minutes to explain the situation in war-torn Vietnam that made it so difficult for them to leave and how Ly Yen struggled to survive in San Francisco while trying to locate him. "We didn't know how to find each other," he said. "That happened to other people, too. It was a bad time."

"So, you got married as soon as you found each other?"

"Within days. It was the happiest time of our lives."

"I know, Dad. And I know how much you and Mom love each other. I hope I can love someone like that someday." Obadiah paused. "There's something else, though. Laurie and I know all our family members, and we get along well, but it seems like something is missing. Something that we should talk about. Maybe secrets?"

Dan knew how his son must feel; he had experienced his own disconnection until he learned the truths as an adult. He had been careful to explain family connections to his children, and he knew Obie would tell Jacob at an appropriate age.

Obadiah was right. More discussion was needed, but among all the family members. Everyone had their version of events, which was not readily shared with the others. The only way was to discuss it together.

"I understand your confusion, Obadiah. You're right to suspect that there are family secrets. But they aren't so much secrets as simply things family members know but don't talk about, at least to one another."

"I want to know everything that's part of our heritage, and I'm sure Laurie would, too. And Jacob will want to know when he's a little older."

"Yes, Obadiah, you do deserve full and open explanations. Some family members are reluctant to talk about certain subjects. But, maybe it's time to speak aloud of things only whispered about in the past."

"That would be great, Dad."

It really was time. "I'm going to call for a family get-together."

* * *

Obie mulled questions as he parked their Ford Explorer in the Hunt driveway. Dan's invitation had sounded like a command; maybe he and Ly Lyn would announce their long-delayed departure from the Hunt house. Jacob and Julie were simply happy to be attending another family patio dinner.

Laurie met them by the gate. Her long, dark hair streamed to her waist. "Grandpa," she said, "you have a new car. I almost didn't recognize you as you pulled in."

He kissed the top of her head. She was tall, like Obadiah. *Like me,* he thought, although he would not say that. "It's not new, but it's a late model. We just purchased it this week."

"I'll miss the old Brown Cow," she said. She had named the venerable station wagon soon after their arrival in Stafford Rest.

"Didn't have a choice. It gave out ... finally."

Cassie hugged Laurie and said, "We heard you're starting to look at colleges. That's wonderful."

"Just looking, Aunt Cassie," Laurie said as they walked along the pathway to the patio. "I still have a year to go at Evergreen High."

"Is Obediah looking, too?" Obie asked.

"Who knows? He does his own thing in his own time. Right now, all he talks about is flying. Dad's giving him lessons."

"So we heard," Obie said. "I'm sure he'll tell us all about it."

"It's all he talks about. He bragged yesterday that he had made the flight to and from Lake Champlain without any assistance from Dad, but Dad didn't confirm it."

Family members on the patio were seated, except for Dan,

who was cooking steaks on the grill, and Obadiah, who was adding wood to the fire pit. It was early, barely past sunset. The sky was cloudless, but Obie's artist eyes observed that the western hills were painted with a subdued vermilion brush, framing a perfect summer evening in the Adirondacks.

Eventually, Abigail passed out paper plates onto which Dan slapped steaks grilled to each person's requirement. Other food items were available on a table beside the grill. Greetings were noisy, but the atmosphere was quieter while they ate. The younger members returned for seconds, but Obie settled into a chair beside Cassie.

It surprised him that the Augustines were not present; They had been invited to all the family gatherings since their arrival the previous summer. *Something unusual was going on.* As darkness settled, fire in the pit cast back flickering light on the circle of faces.

Dan said, "You may wonder why I invited you all here. Of course, we don't need an excuse to get together, but this time, I have a specific reason for it."

"I thought so," Obie whispered to Cassie.

"Obadiah inspired me to call us together. A couple of weeks ago, he commented that our family has things to discuss, some past secrets that aren't really secrets but need open discussion. I've long known that the family has secrets, but ..."

Abigail's voice rang out with familiar authority. "Danny, every family has little secrets, and it's usually best to ignore them."

It was apparent that Dan was stirring the pot. *How will Abigail handle this?" Was it right to feel some pleasure about it?*

Dan continued, "Us older family members understand all the history, but the younger ones have questions, and rightly so."

"Dan is forcing us to talk," Cassie whispered into Obie's ear. "And it's about time."

Abigail said, "There's no need to bring up these things."

"I have questions," Obadiah said.

Laurie said quickly, "Me too."

"A lot of what's happened in this family is quietly discussed between individuals," Dan said, "but we've never sat down to-gether and talked about it. We should, and that's why I brought us together. It's a healthy thing to do."

"It is," Obie said.

"Well, I don't think so," Abigail said. Her desperation was apparent.

Obie was not surprised at her resistance. This would em-barrass her. *Why did that not bother him as much as it should?* He had forgiven her; he was her pastor. *He must try harder.*

Laura had remained quiet. She and Ben sat where Obie could not see her face. He wondered what she might be think-ing. His and Laura's actions had set in motion the web of secrecy that was not unraveled, even to them, until a decade ago. *Maybe Dan should not be doing this.* The grown-ups all knew the truth, but perhaps it was unfair to Laura to discuss this openly.

Laurie said, "Mom and Dad have explained a lot to Oba-diah and me. We know that Grandma Laura and Grandpa Obie had a son and that he's our father."

"And Dad married our mother," Obadiah said, "although it was five years after we were born." There seemed to be no enmity in the statement.

Laurie continued. "Mom and Dad explained that they were separated and couldn't get married sooner. I understand that because such things happen in wartime, but ..."

"They finally made us legitimate," Obadiah said.

There was shocked silence until Dan said, his voice rising, "Obadiah, that's uncalled for, and it's disrespectful to your mother and me."

Ly Yen said quickly, "Find other words, Obadiah."

"Sorry!" Obadiah said. "I was trying to be funny. I didn't mean any disrespect."

"As usual, your mouth got ahead of your brain," Laurie said.

Jacob, who sat close to the fire pit, said, "Good one, Lau-rie." Cassie's stern warning quickly followed.

Dan said firmly. "Laurie, Obadiah interrupted you. You were about to say something."

"Yes, I understand everything about how we came to

America and how we got our names, but there's something I don't understand. It's about Grandpa and Grandma."

Obie tensed. Maybe this was not such a good idea after all.

He was surprised when Laura said, "What would you like to know, Laurie, Dear?"

Laurie paused. "It might be kind of personal, Grandma?"

Laura moved closer to the fire pit, where nearly everyone sat. Obie saw her face now; it revealed no anxiety.

"Honey," Laura said, "it seems we're here to clear the air. I'll gladly answer your questions."

"Laura, what are you doing?" Abigail asked, her voice soft but holding worry. "These are not matters to be discussed openly."

"Mom, I'm tired of tiptoeing around my grandchildren and the rest of you, too. We've all made mistakes, and it doesn't help to hide them. Don't you see that?"

Abigail did not answer. Cassie stirred in her chair before she said, "Laurie has a question. Let her ask it."

"What I wonder about," Laurie said, "is how it came about that Grandma Laura and Grandpa Obie never married, as our father and mother did."

Obie took Cassie's hand; he could feel her tenseness.

Laurie paused again before saying, "Aunt Cassie and Uncle Ben, I love you both very much, and please don't think that I value your marriage any less, but this was never explained to me. Grandpa and Grandma are excellent friends now, so there's not a lack of love." Obie waited for the question he knew would come. "So, Grandpa and Grandma, why didn't you marry?"

It seemed to Obie that nearly half a minute passed, with the only sound being the crackling of the fire. But the heat he experienced rose from deep inside himself. *What was he to say? How could he explain without hurting?*

Cassie broke the silence. "Laurie, do you mind if I answer your question?"

"Of course not, Aunt Cassie."

"Please do," Obadiah added.

Obie still held Cassie's hand as she said, "I'm answering because I'm the closest link between Obie and Laura, and I know the truth about what happened between them. Laurie and Obadiah, something did happen to prevent your grandparents from marrying, and it's time that you hear about it."

Obie heard Abigail gasp from behind him. He expected words of protest, but they did not come. Cassie continued, "Here's the story ... and Jacob, you listen, too." Obie saw his son nod.

Cassie said, "Your grandparents were very young. And they were in love. You know, the love you feel about a girl or boy you can't stop looking at."

"Like a giant crush?" Obadiah said.

"Yes, exactly. I remember seeing you watch a girl in the hallway when you were in grade school. Yes, I was spying on you. What was her name?"

Obadiah did not hesitate. "Clara. Clara Hunter."

"Remember how you felt? Well, as you get older, that feeling becomes even more powerful."

"He likes a girl at Evergreen," Laurie said. Obie saw her smile.

Again, Obadiah did not protest. "Jane Paxton. She's the prettiest girl in the school."

Cassie said, "Laura and Obie, your grandparents, were caught up in that kind of love that they weren't ready for, and things got away from them."

"Like how?" Obadiah asked.

Laurie said, "You mean Grandma was pregnant?"

"Yes, that, but ..."

Cassie was looking at Laura, who nodded, signaling assent. Cassie continued. "Things might have been different if they could have had a normal courtship."

"Why didn't they?" Obadiah asked.

"Because someone didn't approve of it." Cassie paused.

"Who?" Laurie said. "Who on earth would not approve of two people loving each other?"

Obie turned enough to see Abigail's face. Her lips moved, but no sound came. At that moment, he felt pity for her. Her sin, known to most in the family but never publicly articulated, was about to be put into words. How would this affect Obadiah and Laurie, her great-grandchildren, and her grandson, Jacob? How would they feel toward her, knowing something like that? *This was serious.* He pressed Cassie's hand. He should ask her to stop.

"But I won't get into that," Cassie said. "It was just an interested party with misguided principles who caused them to think they needed to hide their love."

Obie breathed easier. Cassie had defused a family crisis while at the same time expressing her long-held disdain for Abigail's covert actions.

Cassie said, "But, Laurie, your question about why they didn't marry still needs an answer. You know your Grandmother Laura married Uncle Ben before your father was born. And ..."

"And Grandfather Obie went into the Army," Obadiah said. "But why did he? He's a good man now, a minister of the Gospel. I love him. But ... did he run away?"

Laura's voice broke an awkward silence. "Obadiah, he didn't run away from me."

Obie found it hard to breathe. But he must say something.

Obadiah gave him no other choice. "I want Grandpa to tell us what happened."

Obie cleared his throat. He was unsure whether to stand or remain seated. He remained in his chair. Dan had accused the family of remaining silent instead of communicating. Of that, Obie was guilty. Sweeping things under the rug was his ally in many aspects of his life.

Now, he was challenged to stand naked before them. Should he speak preacherly, or as a wounded seventeen-year-old? He sought a path between those extremes. "I know you kids have many questions, and I'll answer them as best I can. But I want you to know before I begin that all the secrets among the adults in our family have been exposed and resolved." He said a little prayer, asking forgiveness for any lie he was forced to make to protect Abigail.

"Yes, Laura and I had strong feelings for each other. We were close, all three of us. I loved both Laura and Cassie, but for whatever reason, Laura and I were thrown together." He nodded to Laura; she smiled. "We don't make excuses for being stupid, but ..."

"Stupid, in this case, was good," Obadiah said. "Grandma had Dad, and Dad had us, with Mom's help, of course."

Ly Yen said sternly, "Obadiah, you must learn to speak with respect."

There were giggles. Obie forced a smile. "Yes, Grandson, some things turn out for the good." He felt more at ease. "Yes, I went into the Army. There was a war. That's what the young men did, either being drafted or volunteering. I chose to volunteer. But I knew nothing of your grandmother's condition, and she didn't either at the time."

"But you must have known later?" Laurie said, then turned toward Laura. "Grandma, didn't you tell him?"

Laura's voice was subdued. "I wrote to him. Several times."

"I never received her letters," Obie said.

Laura said, "He wrote to me, and I never received his letters."

Obie heard Laurie gasp. "You both wrote letters that never arrived? How could that happen?"

Laura's words came this time as smooth as glass. "Our letters were taken from the mail by someone who didn't want us to marry."

Laurie and Obadiah's questions came simultaneously. "Who?"

"Doesn't matter who," Obie said. "The same someone your Aunt Cassie mentioned is the one who stole the letters. And that caused Laura and me not to know that we wrote to each other until we found out just a few years ago." He added, "Until then, I didn't know Dan was my son."

Dan spoke from the shadows. "And I didn't know that Obie was my biological father until after you and your mother came to Stafford Rest."

Laura said, "It was my fault that your father didn't know for so long. I thought knowing would upset his life. I was wrong."

Ben spoke from the back, "I raised Dan as my son, and I still consider him as such. And Dan, it's a good thing that you've done today. It makes me feel better, and I'm sure it feels better for the rest of you."

"Indeed," Obie said.

As he turned to search faces, he realized that Abigail had quietly slipped out.

CHAPTER TWENTY-SEVEN

July–October 1983

Through the corner window, Obie saw Chet Boswell's pickup tear up White Pine Road and pull into the church parking lot. Obie prepared himself. Less than a minute later, Chet charged into the church office like a rodeo bull released from the bin.

Chet was loud but not angry. "She's back!"

"Who?"

"Lacy! Lacy Grandcastle. She's at the factory right now. Laura just called to tell me.

It had been four years since the young woman who stirred up the church community had fled Stafford Rest to escape a drug lord she believed wanted to kill her. No one had heard from her in all that time.

Chet trembled with excitement. "I'm on my way to see her," he said. "Laura said Lacy wants to talk to me."

"Chet, that's wonderful, but we don't know the circumstances. Maybe she's only passing through."

"No, Laura said she wants her job back."

"Well, what are you waiting for? Go see her."

"Seeing as how you're so involved, you might want to go with me."

Obie did not wish to impose himself on what might be a joyous reunion, but he was curious. "Okay, then, let's go."

The familiar Volkswagen Beetle was in the Stafford Rest Furniture parking lot; its painted flowers were faded but visible. Obie could hardly keep up as Chet ran up the stairs toward Laura's office.

Lacy sat in a straight-backed chair facing Laura at her desk. Both women rose quickly when Obie and Chet entered the room.

Obie expected Chet to grab Lacy, but he stood before her

with his head down. Neither spoke, but the look between them was powerful. Lacy said, "Don't I at least get a hug?"

Chet enveloped her in his arms. They stood like that for a long time, swaying gently from side to side. Finally, Lacy pushed him back. "I need to breathe," she said. "Let's sit down. I have a lot to tell you."

"I've been asking," Laura said, "but she wanted you to hear it first."

"Well, I'm here," Chet said. He held her hand as they went to sit on the couch. "And, what I want to know, first, is that you're back to stay?"

"Yes, Chet, I expect to make Stafford Rest my home."

"That's wonderful," Obie said, "And I hope the problems you were encountering are resolved."

"Tell us," Chet said.

"There's bad, and there's good. Which do you want to hear first?"

Chet said, "Both, but let's get rid of the bad first."

Laura came to sit beside them. "I'm happy to have you back, Lacy," she said, "but I'm dying to know all the details."

"Yes, Ma'am, I'm happy to be here. I'm sorry it's been so long."

Chet said, "Lacy, Sweetheart, tell us where you've been and what you've been doing. Are you finished running? Was that drug dealer arrested? What's ..."

Lacy pushed Chet's arm away. "Please let me tell the story my way. Just sit and listen. Some of it is hard for me to tell."

Chet sat back, subdued. "Okay."

"When I left here, I had two emotions: I was angry because of how the church people treated me, and I was scared because I was sure the man who had sworn to kill me had found me."

"I'd have protected you," Chet said.

Lacy continued. "The danger I faced came from the town where Dave was. I should have avoided that place, but that's exactly where I headed." She stopped. "I can't account for why I did that, but I did."

Obie said, "Sometimes we realize we must face our problems head-on."

237

"If that's the case, then maybe I faced the problem by deciding that my only course was to kill Dave before he killed me."

She paused, and except for Laura's little gasp, they were silent. Finally, Chet said, "Honey, did you kill him?"

"I had a gun I'd bought before I came here the first time. I wanted to lure him into a place of my own choosing and shoot him. I intended to put an end to his threat on my life."

"That was foolish," Laura said.

"Yes, Ma'am, I know that now. I acted in desperation." She paused. "Haven't you ever been desperate?"

"I know something of desperation," Laura said. Obie saw her glance at him.

"Did you kill him?" Chet asked again.

"My plan was simple. I checked into a motel and called him to tell him I was ready to see him. I knew he would come. I hinted at a reconciliation. But I knew he wouldn't want that. He would come to kill me."

"Didn't you take precautions to protect yourself," Laura asked, "to not get caught? A motel is a public place, and someone there could identify you."

"I chose a room at the end of the building. It was early afternoon, and there were only a few motel guests. The room next to mine was empty. I put a pillow around the gun, so I was confident. My biggest fear was losing my nerve."

Chet lost patience. "Lacy, did you kill the bastard?"

"I was determined to. I set myself up against the wall facing the door. I held the gun in my hand and waited for the door to open."

"What happened?" Obie asked. His greatest worry at that moment was that a fugitive with a murder charge was sitting in the room among them.

"I was nervous, and by the time the door opened, I had lost my nerve. I didn't mean to fire the pistol. It went off in my hand. I'll never forget how it sounded and how it jumped back from my grasp. I didn't mean to fire it. I really didn't. It just went off too quickly."

"Did you hit him?" Obie asked.

"I did, but the 'him' I hit was a police officer."

"You shot a policeman?" Laura's tone was one of disbelief. "Did it kill him?"

"No, it didn't. The bullet hit him in the arm. It wasn't severe ... at least the wound wasn't, but my having shot a police officer was serious. Very serious."

"Why were the police there?" Obie asked.

"They had watched Dave for some time because someone had tipped them off. They were watching for me, too. They still thought I was an accomplice. They followed him to the motel and expected to catch us both there. When Dave arrived at the motel, he saw the police cars and ran. They chased him, and he crashed his car several blocks away."

"So, they caught him?" Laura said.

"He died in the crash."

"Good!" Chet said. "So, you're free of him?"

"Yes, Chet. I'm free of him."

"Well, that's not the bad news we were expecting."

"No, the bad news is that I didn't get off scot-free for shooting a law officer. However, my knowledge of Dave's business led to the arrests of several drug dealers. They were able to take out an entire supply chain. The court took that into consideration, and I spent only eighteen months in jail." She smiled. "So, the bad news is that I'm an ex-con, but the good news is that I'm back here to stay.

"What about the drug lords up the chain?" Obie said. "Is there still danger from them?"

Lacy exhaled what sounded like a sigh of relief. "The authorities believe they eliminated any criminals with a connection to Dave, and thus to me."

"Thank God," Obie said.

Chet said, "Lacy, you should have contacted me during all this. I would have come to you."

"I didn't want to drag you into my troubles. I thought it best to do my time and start over. And here I am." She hooked her arm with his.

Obie said, "We're just happy that you're back."

They stood and took turns hugging Lacy. Chet was ecstatic. "You left things in a closet at my apartment," he told her.

"They're all still there, waiting for you. And my new house is almost ready to move into. You will come to live with me, won't you?"

"Chet, I don't know. Let's not push it. A lot has happened."

Obie saw the disappointment in Chet's eyes as he said, "Lacy, Honey, I understand. I'm here for you, whenever you want."

Laura smiled, "I've never hired an ex-con before, so this is a first."

Obie was astonished by Lacy's account but managed his own smile as he said, "We have a new choir director, and I know that she's looking for members."

"Pastor Obie," Lacy said, "I'm not going to hide anything from anybody. I'm what I am, and people will know it. Your people didn't want me before, so I'm sure they won't want me now. So, let's just be friends and stay out of that treacherous territory."

There was no choice but to agree. Nonetheless, he promised himself that he would find time for another appeal.

*   *   *

Obadiah waited in the parking lot at *Abigail's* for Jane Paxton to arrive. He was nervous. They had dated a few times during his senior year at Evergreen High, mostly at school events, although he had taken Sara Blake to the senior prom, having foolishly promised her a year earlier.

Jane was popular; she had dated other boys, a fact that annoyed him, but it was not something over which he had control. He had graduated, and she still had a year to go at Evergreen. *He would be away. What will happen to their friendship?* "Friendship" was what she had called it, but he wanted to make it more. That was what today's "date" was about.

He parked his bike under a crabapple tree and waited. When she arrived in her family's older model Oldsmobile, he opened the door for her; he wanted to do this right.

"Thanks for being a gentleman, Ob," she said, calling him by the name most of his classmates used. He liked that.

"Obadiah" was too formal. It was also his grandfather's name, but people called him "Obie."

As they entered the restaurant, he hoped his great-grandmother was not present. She would make a big deal of it. She was there less often but still kept a firm hand on the business. His dad had used that "firm hand" phrase.

Their waiter was a classmate working there for the summer. He greeted them by name as they seated themselves.

"I work here, too," Obadiah told Jane. "Three days a week. Last summer, too."

"I know. You told me yesterday when you called."

They ordered soft drinks and sandwiches. He was anxious to express his concerns to Jane, but wanted to start slowly. While they waited, he asked, "What have you been doing all summer?"

"I work at the factory outlet. I was supposed to work today, but I took it off." Her blonde hair fell onto her shoulders in soft waves, and her voice was beautiful. She sang in the choir at the Episcopal Church. He should invite her to their church.

"I didn't know you worked at the outlet." Had he known, he could have worked there instead of at *Abigail's,* to be near her.

"I enjoy it. I wanted to work there last summer, but Laura said I was too young. Lacy's the boss now. She's great to work for."

"Yeah, Grandma likes her, too." *Jane's eyes were green.* "Did you take today off?"

"I did so that I could have lunch with you."

Her words pleased, but also left him a little embarrassed. Her family was not wealthy; she probably needed the money. "I'm sorry. I didn't think that you'd take time off. Today is one of my regular days off."

"Yes, you told me that, too."

"I'm sorry," he said again."

She laughed. "It's okay. Lacy lets me be flexible."

She was teasing him. He should have expected that. Her playful ways were part of her charm.

Their food came, and they ate quietly, unlike when they had eaten together in the noisy school cafeteria. *It was time for a serious talk.* "I'm going to Cornell in two weeks," he said.

"I know. And Laurie's going to Buffalo. That's wonderful. I wish you both the best."

"I plan to major in biology or physics. Laurie wants to become a teacher."

"Dad and Mom want me to go to Syracuse. I'm more inclined to attend a state school, but I haven't decided yet. That's a whole year away."

Enough about schools. "Jane, there's something I want to talk about."

"Yes, Ob, I thought this was more than just lunch." She was still smiling, a good sign.

"Jane, I want to know what you think of me?" He had planned carefully how he would ask the questions, and this was not the way. He tried to recover. "What I mean is, do you think I'm good enough to be more than your friend?"

She reached across the table and took his hand. "Why don't you think you're good enough?"

She had not answered his question. He gathered confidence. "We've known each other for years, and I know we're good friends. We do things together, and we kinda date."

"And I enjoy our 'kinda' dates."

"But don't you ever think that we could be more? You know ... more to each other?" His right eye was twitching, and he was sweating.

"I suppose anything is possible, but I haven't thought a lot about that. Have you?"

She had tossed the question back to him. She was smart. He needed to focus on their discussion. She still held his hand, a good sign.

"Jane, we won't see much of each other this next year, except when I can come home. What I wonder is ..."

"Ob, tell me more about yourself."

"What do you mean?"

"Something I don't know. Something we've never talked about."

Obadiah pulled his hand back. Why had she diverted the conversation? A horrible thought came, one that was against everything he knew about her.

"My mom is Asian, but I thought you already knew that."

"Yes, of course I know that."

He asked, "Does that bother you?"

She grabbed his hand again, tighter this time. "Ob, dear Ob, you don't know me if you think that."

"Some people think like that, even here in Stafford Rest."

"Well, they're fools." Her angry words sounded genuine. "If I'm hesitant to discuss this, it's not because of anything like that."

So, she was hesitant. How was he lacking in her eyes? It may be best to get it out in the open. "Jane, you know what I'm trying to say, don't you?"

"I believe so. You want us to commit to each other to be exclusive? Isn't that what you want?"

"Yes, Jane, that's what I want." *There, he'd said it.*

"Ob, I've known this conversation was coming. I intended to initiate it myself. I'm not a fool. I see the way you look at me. And I want you to know that I enjoy having someone ... having *you* see me like that."

Her beautiful lips had a red tint; she must have used lipstick. "I've thought about you like that for a while," he managed.

"I know. But now we must be sensible. You're going away, and not just for this year. I'll also go away in another year, probably to a different school from yours. There will be at least five years of our 'being away.' So, Ob, being exclusive doesn't seem like something we can do. I don't think I can."

Obadiah could think of nothing to say about how he felt. Their waiter came to pick up the dirty dishes. Jane was quiet, too. He voiced his disappointment only after they were outside and seated on a bench by the entrance. "I like you far more than I've ever liked any girl before," he said.

She grabbed his hand, "And I feel the same about you, too. But I guess we're adults now, and adults act reasonably. When we're apart, we can't live as if we're attached to another person. We have our own things to do and to learn."

"Like seeing other people?"

"I suppose like that, too."

He sighed. This was not what he had hoped, but the logic

was easy to understand. "But we can see each other when we're home, can't we?"

"We'll always do that." She laughed. "I remember that you never really answered my question about telling me one thing about yourself that I don't know."

"I did, too. I told you that Mom is Asian."

"I already knew that."

"Well, I have my pilot's license now."

"Congratulations."

"I've been meaning to ask you if you'd like to go flying with me."

"That would be fun. Let me know when."

* * *

Three months after her return, Lacy was experiencing a sense of well-being not felt for many years; Laura had welcomed her back with open arms. The outlet had performed well during the years of her absence, and they were discussing ways to make it even better.

To cap off her good fortune, Chuck Hinky asked her to return to the Diamond Inn for weekend performances, leading to requests from other area night spots. She had found "her place."

The only question now was what to do about Chet. He was coming to see her and would ask her again to move in with him, a request she had deflected since her return. This time, however, it was different. After last night's performance at the Diamond Inn, he cornered her and insisted that they sit down and talk.

"I love you, Lacy," he had said as he held her hand, "but this can't go on forever. I need an answer." He would be here this morning, and she had promised him that answer.

Her cramped two-room apartment on White Pine Street near the Methodist Church seemed insignificant to Chet's spacious new home on Lake Road, but she would not decide based on that comparison. Did she love him? That was the crucial question.

He arrived at nine o'clock, half an hour later than they had planned. "Old Lady Nelson in the Epps Development had a broken window where a blue jay crash-landed," he explained. "Her daughter has cancer, and she worries about everything, so I had to go."

"Do you want breakfast?" she asked. "I'll make us some pancakes."

"Sure, why not?"

They said little while they ate, except to make small talk. After Lacy removed the dirty dishes and refilled their coffee cups, Chet pushed his chair back from the small table. "Honey," he said, "I didn't mean to put you on the spot by asking you to make a decision, but I love you and ..."

"You *are* asking me to decide, Chet, and I understand. It isn't fair to delay such an important decision."

"You were gone so long I was sure I would never see you again. When you came back, it was like a miracle. I think we're meant to be together."

"A miracle, eh? That sounds like something religious." She smiled.

"I haven't been inside a church since you left, and certainly not that church."

"Chet, I must tell you exactly how I feel. When we lived together ... no, it was more like we roomed together. I had a lot on my mind. You know what that was all about. I want to be honest. I clung to you because you were my protector. It wasn't love, although you may have considered it so, and for that, I'm sorry."

"So, you're saying you can't love me?"

She grabbed his hand. "No, Chet, I'm not saying that. I feel closer to you than I've ever been to anyone. In my way, I love you, and want to be with you, but I have doubts."

"About what?"

"About you. About your ability to be what I need."

His confusion was apparent. "I don't understand."

"I'm talking about commitment."

"Lacy, you're everything I've ever hoped to have in my life. I can commit. I have committed to you. How could you think differently?"

She scooted her chair to face him and placed both hands

on his arm. "Chet, you're broken. You were broken in Vietnam, and you haven't healed."

He was looking down. "You're mistaken. Yes, I had a terrible time there, and I have nightmares about it, but that has nothing to do with my commitment to you."

"Tell me, are you still drinking?"

"Well, some. But you know I can handle it. You drink, too, so you know it's possible to handle it."

"I haven't had a drink since I left here four years ago."

"I saw you with a drink just last night."

"That was soda pop. I've stopped drinking. Completely stopped."

"Really? Is that true?"

"It is. And I did the AA program while I was in jail."

"What about drugs?"

"Contrary to what people think, I've never done drugs, except for smoking a little pot in college."

Chet was smiling. "Lacy, that's wonderful. I'm proud of you."

"You need to have some pride in yourself. You must stop *your* drinking."

His smile faded. "My drinking is not a problem."

"Of course, it is. We were talking about commitment, so I'll lay it out for you, Chet. Here's the truth. I love you and want to commit to you, but I'm not sure you're ready to commit to me."

"I am, Lacy. I am. A few drinks now and then don't have anything to do with love or commitment. Sure, I drink. I have for years. Lots of people drink moderately and still manage their lives. I'm not rich by most standards, but I manage my business and am financially comfortable. I can take care of you if that's a worry."

She laughed out loud. "Chet, that feels like an insult. I don't need anyone to take care of me. I want commitment from you, not your money."

"You think I don't love you enough? Is that it?"

"I know you love me, but you're on a downward spiral. I would try relentlessly to save you, which would change your feelings for me."

"It wouldn't, but tell me, anyway, what must I do to get you to share your life with me? Marry you? You know that's what I want whenever you're ready. What ..."

She squeezed his arm. "Chet, I want you in a recovery program like AA. And I want you to have counseling. You have demons that need to be exorcised."

"I guess you're right about the demons." He looked down at the floor. "Obie told me something like that, but he thinks I should talk to God about it. Can you imagine that, me talking to God?"

"I'm not against talking with God or whoever can help you. But here's my deal. You quit drinking, do AA, and get counseling, and I mean to really immerse yourself in those things. You do that, and I'll move in with you."

"You will? Honey, that's what I want to hear."

"To hear and not do is like building a house without a foundation. You'll take this seriously. And you'll stay out of the Diamond Inn."

"I'll only go there to hear you sing."

"I'll hold you to it. And stay away from the other dives, as well."

They stood, and he held her in his arms. She felt the soothing sensation of his breath near her ear. "I hear music," he whispered.

"Yes, it's coming from the Methodist church. It's Sunday morning. I hear it every Sunday."

He held her hands but stood at arm's length. "Lacy, let's go visit."

"The church?"

"Sure. But only if you want to. I remember how they pushed you away. But that wasn't Obie. It was just some mean folks."

She laughed. "We'd shake up those mean folks."

"I think we'd enjoy that?"

"This is my town, now," Lacy said, feeling purposeful, "and I have the right to go wherever I want. But your suggestion surprises me. You don't like church."

"I like wherever you like, Lacy. And Obie's a good friend,

even if his sermons are a little long."

She grabbed his arm. "Well, what are we waiting for?"

CHAPTER TWENTY-EIGHT

April–August 1984

Obie received Abigail's early morning phone call at the church office; she wanted him to come to Garnet Point, a request he could not remember ever coming from her. *What did she want?*

Dan's car was not in the driveway; he would have left for the clinic. Ly Yen was in school in Pennsylvania, and Obadiah and Laurie were away at college. Abigail was alone in the house; he was not comfortable with that.

The door was unlocked, so he announced himself and went in. She was in the new spacious living area that Chet had renovated a few months earlier.

"Thank you for coming," Abigail said. "I know you're busy, but I want to discuss something with you."

"Abigail, my time is yours, at least for the next half-hour." He needed to put bookends on his time with Abigail.

She pointed toward the kitchen. "There's coffee in the craft, so help yourself."

"I'm fine, Abigail." He seated himself on the couch that faced her Queen Anne chair. "But let's take care of business because I am busy. With Easter coming soon, I need to prepare special sermons." There was a mild sense of guilt, for he was already fully prepared and would never make such an excuse to anyone else. He and his mother-in-law had a unique relationship.

"I must tell you something," she said. Her face revealed uneasiness. There were rumors that upcoming ministerial appointments would likely affect Stafford Rest Methodist—and, therefore, him. That was probably the subject of today's discussion. She had told him she was on his side—but was she? He braced himself.

"What is it you want to tell me?"

Her voice was calm as she said, "I'm ill."

The unexpected words caught him off guard. "What? What illness?"

He heard her draw in a breath. "I have cancer. It's in my pancreas."

"Are you sure?"

"Yes, of course, I'm sure, and it's advanced. Stage four."

He knew the seriousness of the disease. The church had lost two members in the past year to the same killer. *But this was Abigail.* "I'm sorry. But I'm sure you'll have good medical treatment with two doctors in the family." That sounded dispassionate. "Abigail, I'm so sorry."

"No one else in the family knows except Ben, and I've asked him not to tell Dan."

"Cassie certainly doesn't know, or I would have known."

"You probably wonder why I'm telling you?"

"Well, yes, I suppose I am."

"Obie, we've had our difficulties, that's true, but despite what you may think, I respect you for what you do. I admit to having my doubts, but I've moved past that. You also occupy the central position in our families, and things move through you."

There came a teenage memory of sitting on a cold beach with Cassie and Laura and hearing them recite Abigail's words. "He's beneath us." And there was the time, when he was seventeen, when she had told him, "You'll never amount to a thing." This woman had threatened to kill his father and him, too, if he did not do as she told him. *How was he to respond?*

"You should tell Laura and Cassie," he said. "They need to know. You can't expect me to keep this from Cassie."

"I've told you this in private, so as my pastor, you're obligated to honor my wishes."

"Abigail, if this disease progresses, you'll need care, care from your family. They'll all want to help." He weighed his words before saying, "We'll all want to help."

"Of course, I may need help in the future, but for now, I want to keep it private. I want only you and Ben to know. Give me your word."

"Against my better judgment, I'll keep it secret for now, but I want you to know that I strongly disagree with your decision. Her resolute expression did not change. He said, "You believe in prayer, don't you, Abigail?"

"Yes, you know that I believe in prayer."

"Our church members are praying people. Their prayers will benefit you. People in our church and community should know about your illness. You *will* need prayer."

A rare sign of humor curled the corners of her mouth. "There are some in the community who will welcome the news of my illness and possibly of my demise."

'Abigail, you're a pillar of our community and a leader, especially in our church. I've depended on you in ways too numerous to count." That was true; she was rigorous in handling administrative issues and confronting troublesome people.

"Look," she said as she sat up straighter in her chair, "I'll tell everybody when the time is right. For now, you do your part and keep this to yourself."

No matter how he felt toward Abigail, he respected her power. He would have saluted her if she had been a superior officer in the wars he had known.

* * *

Jacob needed to talk to Alicia because she had told other girls that he was her boyfriend and had kissed her in the dark behind the school cafeteria. That 'boyfriend" idea was hers— and he had never kissed her, even though he almost did once.

During the two years Alicia had lived in Stafford Rest, their families enjoyed time together. She even came to watch his baseball games. They were in the same grade in school but in different classes. In church, however, they attended the same Sunday School class. She had lots of ideas about God and other religious things, which interested him, too.

She had climbed mountains with him and their parents twice last summer. On Algonquin, Alicia had been fascinated by his father's story of being lost there in a snowstorm and thinking he might die. That story was one of his favorites, too, since his father said it may have been what led him to the ministry.

On the summit of Algonquin that day, while they looked out over the Adirondack Park's vast wilderness, Alicia tugged on his arm and said, "Your dad listens to God, doesn't he?"

Unsure how to answer, he mumbled, "I guess he does." Her dark hair, blowing in the wind, brushed his face, a good feeling. "But I heard him tell Mom that he didn't always know what God was telling him."

"He must have listened after he was lost up here. Didn't he say he promised to do whatever God wanted?"

"I guess so. My dad has done a lot of things in his life. Good things. He was a soldier and a chaplain. He has medals."

"You're proud of him, aren't you?

"I'm real proud."

That conversation with Alicia was often in his memory. According to his mother, his father had "worn several different hats," but Jacob could not remember when he was not the pastor of Stafford Rest Methodist Church. Recently, he had overheard conversations between his father and mother about the Conference wanting to move him, but that he might be unwilling to go. Was that something to worry about?

If his father were no longer a minister, what would he do? He could be a writer. He painted beautiful landscape pictures, but called it "a hobby." He could not imagine his father as anyone other than the Rev. Obadiah Gainsworthy.

His father had been forced to make hard decisions all his life. Jacob wondered if he would ever have to make decisions like that for himself. If God were to show him what to do, could he do it?

Family gatherings with the Augustines ensured that he saw Alicia often. He had taught her to ski and walk on snowshoes. For two winters, they had taken snow-blown trips along the ridge that circled the town. She always kept up, sometimes leading the way.

They had talked yesterday in a corner of the library away from other listening ears. She had surprised him with the question, "Jacob, do you think we'll always be friends?"

"Well, of course. I'm not going anywhere. Are you?"

He had watched her face as she appeared to consider an answer. There was a big curl that covered half her forehead. Her eyes were dark. "You know that we'll grow up someday, don't you? What kind of friends will we be then?"

She was smart and pretty. But sometimes, she made no sense at all.

* * *

"Mom doesn't seem well," Cassie said as they placed the last dinner dishes into the dishwasher.

For four months, Obie had worried about avoiding the truth. "What seems to be her problem?" he asked.

"She sleeps a lot. When I went there this morning, she was still in bed after nine o'clock. Dan says she has been like that for some time. She won't let him examine her, not even take her temperature. She said she would talk to Ben. But I think that's just Mom's shyness. Ben is not a blood relative. I go to him for medical treatment for the same reason."

"Dan is okay with us having Ben as our doctor. He told me that."

"Obie, you don't ever seem to need a doctor. You're indecently healthy."

"And for that, I'm grateful." He hoped the conversation would move away from Abigail.

"When Ly Yen was home recently, she told me that Mom had lost hair. She finds it in the sink drain. And I've noticed it, too."

Obie was not surprised, for he had known for some time that she went to Saratoga Springs for treatments and would lose hair. Abigail had given Ben permission to "tell Obie whatever he asks of you." She had ordered a wig to "use at the proper time."

"I'm worried about her."

Why not tell Cassie the truth? She and Laura should know. His promise did not seem as important as the good that would result from the family knowing. *Abigail needed help.* Was it not his duty to aid her however he could? It was troubling.

Thankfully, Cassie did not pursue the subject, but the next day in the church office, he could not get it off his mind. Even a contentious visit from Amos was not enough to divert his worry. He must talk to Ben.

Ben was between patients at the clinic, and Obie asked, "What should we do? If this disease isn't cured, she'll need all the help she can get. It's not right to keep this from Cassie and Laura. And from Dan, too."

"Yeah, it bothers me, too," Ben said. "Dan and I share information when we make medical decisions unless patients ask us not to. He knows I see Abigail and suspects there's more to it than routine visits, but he also understands I can't talk about it. And, because it's family, it's more complicated. Frankly, it has become increasingly challenging to divert his questions. As to what we should do, that's probably more in your domain than mine. I can't violate Abigail's wishes. You'll need to decide your own course of action ... or inaction."

Ben had tossed it back into his lap. "I guess I'll have to convince her to tell the family."

"Good luck with that." It was said with a wry smile. Obie was sure it matched his own.

He left the clinic and went straight to Garnet Point. A mild and cloudless day, one free from treatment, found her on the patio.

At first, he said nothing; he just seated himself in an Adirondack chair facing her. She wore an old-fashioned bonnet, the kind you see in vintage photographs of farm ladies who work in the fields. This one was white with a floral pattern.

"How do you feel today, Abigail?" he said, trying to sound casual.

"I feel well, considering."

He would not dance around the conversation he was determined to have. "Cassie told me that Ly Yen told her that you're losing your hair."

"Some is coming out ... yes."

"Abigail, do you know how hard it is for me to hear things

like that from my wife and not tell her the truth?"

"You promised."

"Yes, but I'm having trouble with it. I think your family should know. It's in your best interests."

"My best interests are what I decide they are." She paused. "And I look out for *your* interests, Obie."

"What do you mean?"

"Don't you know that the Conference considered moving you to another church?" I sent them a petition that I circulated for members to sign."

"Someone told me there was a petition, but I wasn't aware you started it."

"I'm sure it brought results. You're here for at least another year. I did that for you, Obie, so you'd better keep your promise to me."

She may have been ill, but her long-held quid pro quo mode of operation appeared intact. He could tell her that the district superintendent had told him "not to worry" even before her petition arrived. He decided against it.

"I thank you for that, Abigail. You've always been a big help in my ministry." It was true, and it always amazed him. Privately, she held him over the fire in church matters, but against adverse odds, she had supported him. It was apparent that she wanted him to know that.

"I try to do what's right," she said.

Abigail was a proud woman; he would use that to convince her to inform her family of her illness.

He scooted his chair as close as possible without invading her space. He wanted the conversation to be intimate but not invasive. "Aren't you cold? There's a little breeze. I can go get you a blanket if you want me to?"

"No, Obie, I'm fine." She turned her head to face him. "Why did you come here today?"

"To convince you to let your family know that you're ill, and that you may soon need help." There was no harm in revealing the goal, just not the method.

"I don't need help. I can get along fine."

"I'm sure you can. For now."

She bristled. "When I can't, I'll let them know."

He waited a moment before he said, "On another matter, I hope you'll help me with a project I want to start but don't have the time or expertise to handle."

There were signs of interest in her expression. "What's the project, and I hope it doesn't have anything to do with convincing me to tell the world that I'm sick?"

She was an intelligent woman, and it was useless to try to separate the project from his goal of helping her. "You have the expertise to help me begin this worthy project."

"Which is?"

"Providing help to people in the community who have cancer."

"You mean people like me?"

"Well, yes, but also for other kinds of cancer, and perhaps even other cancer-related diseases."

"And just when did you start this new project? Obie, is this your way to get me to bow to your wishes?" She gave him a smug look.

"No, I've had this on my radar for several months." He was happy to speak the truth. "You know that we lost two members of our congregation to cancer recently? And I'm sure other people in the community have the disease right now. Many families need financial aid. You have the knowledge and experience to get things done."

There was a tiny uplift at the corners of her mouth. "Yes, I know people, and I do know how to get things done. And you're right that, with the high cost of medicine, it's difficult for many families. I assume you're thinking of raising funds for needy families?"

"Yes, exactly. As a church, we must also look to their spiritual needs. Finance is a big part, but stricken families need other help. They need rides to appointments. They need meals served to families. They need comfort when people die … you get the point. Organizing such a project is right up your alley."

There was a smile now. "Yes, I can do that. And the fact that we have two doctors in our church can't do any harm. I have a question, though. We're talking about major expenses, and our church members aren't wealthy for the most part. Where will the money come from?"

It was time to enlighten her about the Gainsworthy family secret. "Abigail, did Pinky ever give you information about the Love Fund?"

"Not much. He mentioned it a few times. And I know about all that money from the O'Shane estate that you contributed to it. The fund gives money to needy young people. In fact, you were a recipient of funds after Vi died. Pinky may have helped distribute it."

"He was the administrator of the fund from the beginning."

"Who started it? Do you know?"

"I do." He purposely waited a few seconds before he continued. "It's a family secret. Cassie and I are the only living persons who know the details."

"What family?"

"The Gainsworthy family. Abigail, I would like to tell you a little more about it." He paused. "But, as I said, it's a family secret."

He hoped to arouse her interest, and her expression told him he had. "I'd like to know more," she said.

"I'll share this secret with you with the understanding that you'll tell no one else about it."

She nodded, and he told her the story, taking his time, about how Grandfather Jacob acquired a large inheritance from a wealthy New England manufacturer and then set up the Love Fund to give it all away.

After he finished the story, he said, "Pinky managed it, Abigail. He distributed funds to scores of needy people, including me, but I wasn't favored over anyone. That was my grandfather's wish. I want you to know that some money is available from that fund for this project."

"I wish I had known all this." She hesitated. "I wasn't kind in the things I said about Jacob. I didn't know."

I administer the fund now, and someday, I'll pass it on to Dan or to Jacob if Dan doesn't want it."

"I'm sure Dan will want it."

He held his breath. "So, you'll take on the organization of

this project?"

"Of course. I'll need some helpers, though. Let's announce it at next Sunday's service. But we'll have to plan even before that." She struggled to get up. "Let's go in where I can get my notebook."

He was ready to help her, but her stride matched his as they went from the patio through the kitchen and into the living area. She was still smiling.

As they seated themselves at the dining table, he said, almost as an afterthought, "So, you'll make it known that you're receiving treatment for cancer?"

"It's how I'll create the empathy needed to get this project off the ground."

CHAPTER TWENTY-NINE

June–December 1986

Chet Boswell was perspiring, and Obie suspected that the reason was less the warm June day than what his friend wanted to say. Lacy looked at ease as she sat on the couch beside him. The words came out in a choked but firm declaration. "We're getting married."

"Chet! Lacy! That's great news."

It was what he hoped to hear. The couple had lived together for over a year. His hope for their return to church services had failed, except for one brief appearance near the end of a Sunday morning service when they sat in the back and behaved like two lovebirds unable to stop touching each other. During the closing hymn, Lacy's voice rang through the sanctuary with such power that heads turned. She had been making a statement. He caught up with them after the service to invite them back.

"We're only here because we heard your music," Chet said, adding, "And Lacy couldn't resist improving on it."

Lacy had been more tactful but direct. "Pastor Obie, I like you, and there are others in this congregation that I like, but how we were treated several years ago shows that we're not welcome."

"And I'm sorry about that, Lacy," he had replied. "It wasn't Christian. Please forgive us."

Chet had said, with uncharacteristic emphasis, "Obie, I see that Amos Adams is still in your congregation. We'll get along just fine without his kind of Christianity."

Their words had hurt, but now he wondered why they had come to the church office to give him this news. Lacy provided the answer: "We want you to marry us, Pastor Obie."

"You mean a church wedding?" *There was hope.*

"Not in church," Chet said. "Well, maybe in the building if

we have to, but not in a service with people here."

"I can marry you anywhere, but surely you'll want friends present."

"And family," Chet said, "We've already told Dad and Frances. I have other relatives, too, who'll want to see me get hitched."

"Us, Chet," Lacy said.

"What?"

"It's *us* getting married, not just you."

Obie had to smile. That little exchange might foretell the tenor of their future together. "We can have a private ceremony in our sanctuary," he said.

Lacy said, "We prefer to be married in the Diamond Inn."

Chet nodded. "We've already cleared it with Chuck Hinky and hope that's okay with you. We just need to set a date."

Obie found it hard to hide his disappointment. He had hoped it was a chance to bring them back into the church family in a welcoming way. *But when God gives you opportunity, you had better grab it.*

"Okay," he said. "I've never married anyone in a bar before, but I remember that Jesus went to sinners to eat and drink. So, I'm good to go with it."

* * *

When Obadiah came home near the end of his third year at Cornell, he had not only decided to apply to medical school but had made another decision based on pure interest: He would learn all he could about winemaking. Cornell had experts on the subject; he would ply information from them.

Family trips to the vineyard in the Napa Valley had inspired him. He had roamed the O'Shane Vineyard, which Grandpa Obie owned.

Earlier today, he had quizzed his grandfather, asking questions about grape varieties, their sources, and cultivation methods. Grandpa Obie answered his questions freely, but it soon became apparent that he was no expert. Their conversation revealed that Cassie was the most informed family member.

Obadiah went straight to her.

"It's an interest of mine, too. We'll go see Kent Augustine," she told him. "He knows more than anyone."

They spent most of that afternoon with Kent, who canceled some "unimportant" appointments. Although the details of bookkeeping and legal matters were boring, Kent's knowledge of the vineyard's history was fascinating. But, he, too, was no expert; that knowledge would have to come from other sources.

As they left Kent's Main Street office, Obadiah said, "Aunt Cassie, can we talk more about this?"

She led them to a seat on a bench at the park beach. At first, she teased him about spending so much time with Jane Paxton when they were both home from college, but he steered the conversation to the California vineyard. "How come you know more about it than the other family members?" he asked.

She laughed. "Your grandfather is good at what he knows, but there is much he chooses not to know about. I chose to know more about the business, even though it's his name on the deed."

"So, how did he come by the vineyard in the first place? Great Grandpa Ken wasn't wealthy, and you and Grandpa don't seem to have a lot ..." He stopped. "I'm sorry, I didn't mean ..."

She smiled. "Obadiah, your grandfather and wealth are like water and oil. He deals with it because he must, but he's uncomfortable about it. You know that he was married before. Annie, his wife, died, and since she had no living relatives, she left everything to him."

"So, there was more than just the vineyard?"

"Yes, much more. Her family was wealthy, but Annie was austere and gave away to charities and organizations she championed. And except for a tiny portion set aside into what Obie calls a "disaster fund" for Julie, Jacob, and me, everything else is in a trust that feeds Annie's charities and many more that he's added. On his death, the trust will be divided among all the charities."

"Wow! Grandpa is a generous man. But he kept the house and the vineyard. Why?"

"Because Annie asked him to. He honored her wishes." Cassie looked sad. "But let me tell you the whole story," she said.

He listened silently as Cassie told him about his grandfather's first marriage. She spoke candidly about the marital difficulties and Annie's tragic death. Obadiah was surprised that so many years had passed before his grandfather discovered his vineyard ownership. "Why?" he asked.

"Obie knew he inherited the smaller house and property from Annie, but didn't know that the O'Shane Vineyard was part of the inheritance."

"But how could he not have known that?"

"He had other interests and turned the business dealings over to a law firm that didn't keep him properly informed. Of course, he should have kept on top of it, but he didn't pay enough attention."

"So, now you and Grandpa run it?"

"By no means. Kent takes care of legal matters, and Lyle, his father, grows the grapes. I, and sometimes Obie, make minor decisions."

"Does the vineyard make much money?"

"Not as much as it should. It's enough to support the Augustine family and give us a little, but the expenses are enormous. I'm trying to get them to experiment with growing better wine grapes."

"That interests me, too. I want to learn more about it."

"I'm happy about your interest, but you should know that there's resistance from the Augustines about changing anything."

"Why is that?"

"As good as they are at what they do, they lack knowledge about wine types and wine-making. They're content to grow and sell to wineries and food companies. It's what they've always done."

Obadiah wanted to nail down an obvious fact. "Aunt Cassie, it sounds like you want to produce wine?"

"I do have an interest, but it's more dabbling than serious intent. I'm under no illusions. Anyway, Obie doesn't like me to study winemaking." She laughed out loud. "I bring it up often just to annoy him."

He laughed, too. "Aunt Cassie, you're a troublemaker, aren't you?"

"I am what I am, but I love the man. Anyway, winemaking may be beyond the capabilities of O'Shane Vineyard. We're losing money, and the Augustines won't change."

"Kent told us a lot, but how much do you know of the vineyard's history?"

"It started as a winery before the O'Shanes bought it. The basements are filled with equipment from that era. Turning it into a winery again is possible, but only with a lot of work and expense."

"Lyle and Matilda are pretty old, aren't they?"

"They are, and Lyle wants to retire. Their son, Neal, already manages most day-to-day stuff, and Kent's settled here. I'm worried about the vineyard's future."

"Is there nothing you can do?"

Cassie sighed. "I suppose we could sell it. Obie talks about that, but passing it to the next generation, or maybe your generation, would please us."

He hoped he was not being too bold as he said, "If what I gather about the size of the O'Shane inheritance, you and Grandpa could use some of that to turn the vineyard into whatever you want."

He heard that sigh again. "That money is locked up, Obadiah." Some frustration was evident in the statement.

They were quiet for a while as they stared out at the lake. He was disappointed. He might never have a chance to chase after the wine gods.

He had learned new facts about his grandfather. But he wanted to know more. "Why is Grandpa like that about money? Is it a religious thing?"

"I think it has more to do with his early years. Your Great-Grandmother, Vi, died when Obie was only thirteen. And because Ken was away so much, Obie depended on himself. The Gainsworthy family didn't have much in the way of earthly goods."

"You'd think that would make him value money more."

"He developed an independent spirit early on. And it's a really stubborn spirit." Obadiah liked the way she laughed. *Jane laughed like that, too.*

He asked, "So, you don't feel like that about money?"

"No, I don't. I want to be generous with people in need, and I am, but Obie and I differ about how to use money. We even argue about it sometimes."

Obadiah turned to face her. "Aunt Cassie, I think you would like to turn the vineyard into a profitable business. Am I right?"

This time, she was quick to answer. "I would like that, but I don't want you to think it's a problem between Obie and me because it isn't."

"No, Aunt Cassie. I would never think that. Anybody can see how much you and Grandpa love each other."

She sighed again. "My upbringing was much different from his. My mother's financial enterprises made our family wealthy. And Dad built the factory, which is now a thriving business. I suppose a lot of that entrepreneurial spirit has rubbed off on me. I grew up privileged, so my views about money differ from Obie's. But that doesn't mean I won't support him in every way I can."

"Does religion have anything to do with it? He's a minister. And doesn't Jesus teach against money?"

"No, Obadiah. Jesus doesn't teach against wealth, only about how we might wrongfully use it. Obie controls a lot of money, and that responsibility falls on him without his wanting it. He's a Christian and a minister, so in that sense, religion is involved, but he's also a humanitarian. He doesn't use Christianity as a prerequisite to dispense help. And, as I said, I support him without reservation."

"Well, if he ever changes his mind about the vineyard, I would like to help."

"Obadiah, you'll be a physician like your father. That's your purpose."

"Even a physician can have other interests."

Obadiah's father flew him back to Ithaca two days later. Throughout the flight, he thought about the conversation with

Aunt Cassie. He would go to medical school, but he would also entertain his dream about the vineyard in California, a companion dream to the one about a future with Jane Paxton.

* * *

Obie found Dan at the Stewart Shops' gas pumps, and after filling their tanks, they went to Beth's Café for breakfast. His son needed company; the twins were back at school after the Thanksgiving break, and Ly Yen had just left for Pennsylvania.

They sat across from each other in one of the ancient wooden booths. Bert Larkin refilled their coffee mugs for the third time. Bert had purchased the café from Beth not long before her death and elected to keep the restaurant's name and décor.

"Haven't seen you to talk to since the wedding," Dan said.

"Really? That long? That's nearly three months."

"The bride and groom seem to be getting along okay. I imagine Lacy's not that easy to live with."

Obie laughed. "I was about to say the same about Chet."

"They are a strange couple, but they love each other." Dan appeared pensive. "Has Lacy given any indication that they'll come back to church? I miss her voice. She'd be a great addition to our choir."

"I'd love to get them back. Chet will come if she does. They need some work in the spiritual department."

"Don't we all?" Dan hesitated. "Obie, I want to ask you something concerning our past."

Obie hoped it was not about Laura. That chapter of his life was closed—a door not to be reopened. "Okay, I'm listening."

"It's about Grandmother. Yes, we've talked, and I know all the details of her illness, and I've consulted with Dad ... with Ben ... and we agree that there's no recourse for further treatment. She's in decline, and she knows it."

"I know, Dan. I talk with her, too."

"She's worked hard the past two years for our drive to help cancer patients. She told me that you're responsible for her involvement. But I fear she no longer has the strength for that project."

"I believe you're right. Are you considering nursing home care?'

"Two physicians in the family can certainly make her comfortable. We want to keep her at home as long as we can."

"I'm happy about that, but you had a question, I think."

"Yes, it's about your history with Grandmother, which also involves your history with my mother."

"Dan, we shouldn't go there."

"Yes, we should. You owe it to me to fill in some details."

"Dan, I'm your biological father. You know that." Behind the counter, Bert's head jerked up. Obie spoke more softly, "Isn't that enough?"

"Many things have been explained, but there are still raw edges. Most of us have heard about the letters Grandmother withheld and how she made everybody think Ben was my biological father, but ..."

"That was a long time ago, Dan. The younger family members don't know her part in it, nor should they."

"You loved my mother. You told me that you did. So, I'd like to know why so many years passed before you talked to each other. If you had, you would have discovered that you had been deceived and that neither of you was to blame."

"But we finally did."

"For God's sake, that didn't happen until after you learned that I was your son. I'm talking about all those years of silence."

Old anger crept back in: *He had tried.* There was that time in San Francisco at Cassie's wedding; he had almost begged Laura. Now, he tried to remain calm. "Dan, it was something neither of us wanted to discuss."

"Over all those years, either could have picked up a telephone, called the other, and simply attempted to talk. You even walked away from the opportunity dinner I organized to bring you together. I don't understand it."

"Are you making this same appeal to Laura?"

"I will."

"Of course, we should have made more of an attempt. We know that now." Obie drew in a deep breath. "I'm a stubborn man and accept my share of the blame. I acted much the same way with Cassie for years."

"I'm sure some blame belongs with the sisters."

'We've learned, and we've forgiven. Dan, your mother and I are on good terms. We've resolved all our ill feelings and are in happy places in our lives. It's good now."

Dan smiled. "Yes, and I'm happy that's the situation with Mom, but I still have concerns about you and Grandmother."

"I think we're okay."

"How did you resolve things?"

"Again, forgiveness. We forgave each other, simply that."

Dan turned his empty coffee mug in his hands. "Obie, I've given this some thought. Your anger toward Grandmother predates your finding out about the letters. Did she do some awful thing to you?"

Dan was not giving up his quest for truth. Peace had been made with Abigail, although negative images about that long-ago night on Blackberry Hill sometimes crept in. But that was behind him and not something to tell Dan about; some secrets must remain secrets. Cassie and Laura knew, and that was enough.

"Not really awful," Obie said. "I guess I simply suspected that she steered your mother toward Ben."

"Yes, she probably did. And stealing those letters is a real sin, but I think she's sorry. But what I want to know is that all the differences between the two of you are resolved."

"I think she's sorry. And, yes, our differences are resolved. But, Dan, it's our duty now to take care of her."

"Yes, you as a man of God, and me as a grandson and physician." Dan set his coffee mug on the table and rose. "Speaking of doctoring, I need to get to the clinic. I'm probably half a dozen patients behind."

As Obie watched him go, he felt the weight of having withheld a truth, but also knowing it was a truth whose disclosure served no purpose. He said a silent prayer, one often repeated, that he genuinely held no resentment toward Abigail Hunt.

* * *

Jacob relished the wind in his face as he skied along the ridge trail with Alicia close behind, having no trouble keeping up. The day was mild, but a recent light snowfall provided sufficient base for their skis. They were near the east end of the Morass, the halfway point of their trek to Garnet Point. The trail ahead led up to the familiar mass of rocky cliffs that overlooked the area.

"Can't you go faster?" Her words came between giggles.

"If I do, how will you keep up?"

Jacob grabbed every opportunity to be near Alicia. He sat beside her on the school bus, walked with her in the school halls, and most recently worked with her on the church Christmas decorations. She never resisted his presence, sometimes even initiating encounters.

The trail up to the cliffs was steep, and they were both puffing when they reached the top. He slowed and put his parka hood down to indicate a rest stop. She did likewise and skied to his side.

"It's a beautiful spot," she said. "You can see the whole town and the lake behind it."

He did not respond; he was still thinking about what to say. For days, he had practiced using the right words. He had even looked up some in the dictionary to verify their meaning.

He had chosen to bring her to this location only last week after skiing here with his parents. He had always been drawn to the spot, so when his parents told him what had happened to them there, he knew what he must do.

His mother had said to his father, "Don't you remember that this was where you first kissed me?"

"Well, you asked me to."

They had laughed about it, arguing about who asked who, before they kissed again right in front of him.

"We were only fifteen years old," his mother told him.

He would be fifteen in a few days, so it made sense to use this outing with Alicia to let her know his feelings.

"Yes, it is a beautiful spot," he said as he moved closer. He was happy that she did not move away.

"I'm glad you taught me to ski."

"I was here just last week with Mom and Dad."

"I would have come with you if I had known."

He sucked in his breath. "Today, I wanted us to come alone." He waited for a comment. When she remained silent, he said, "Alicia, you're my best friend."

She turned toward him, smiling. "Jacob, of course, we're best friends. I knew that from the first time your parents brought you to California to visit. You're in my first memories."

"I was really happy when you came here to live, and I'm glad our families get along so well."

"Do you realize that we've lived here for over five years? I feel like I'm more a New Yorker than a Californian."

"Mom says your father has a good law practice now."

"We're building a house on Lake Road."

"I know. Dad knows he'll have to find another tenant for Grandpa Ken's house." He kicked at a rock beside the trail. *Why were some words so hard to get out?* "Alicia, what I meant to say, about being friends ..."

"You like me, don't you?"

"Of course, I like you. Didn't I just say so?"

"You have lots of friends. Do you like me better than them?"

"Well, yes, I do like you better, but in a different way." This was not going as he had planned.

"What way is that?" She had turned, looking away, but was laughing. *Was she teasing him again?*

Her voice became softer. "You want us to be more than friends? Is that it?"

"I'd like that. I'd like it a lot."

"Like boyfriend and girlfriend?"

"Yes, that's what I mean." He was overjoyed that they had reached this point in their conversation. He had expected to use more words.

"You're not old enough," she said while putting her hood up.

"I'm older than you, Alicia."

269

"Not by much. Anyway, I mean that, at our age, boys aren't as mature as girls. Miss Devers, our biology teacher, told me that. I would always have to tell you how to act and behave, which would embarrass you."

He was shocked into silence. *What was she saying?* He found his voice. "I don't know what that means, Alicia. I was just hoping you'd want to be my girlfriend."

She laughed so hard that her hood fell, freeing her dark hair to blow in the wind. "Jacob, I'll be your girlfriend if that's what you want, but I need to know it's something you'll take seriously."

"Of course, I'll take it seriously." He put a hand on her arm.

"So, you'll tell all your friends that we're going together?"

"Well, sure."

"And our families?"

"They won't care."

"Jacob!"

"Okay, I'll tell them."

Her mittened hand grabbed his. 'Will you hold my hand in public?"

He took a breath. "If that's what you want." She was laughing again. If she were not so beautiful, he would be angry.

She turned to face him and grabbed both his arms. "If you're serious about all this, you'll have to kiss me. That's part of the deal."

Right there, on the spot where his dad first kissed his mom, Jacob did the same to the girl he loved.

CHAPTER THIRTY

March–September 1987

"It's not looking good," Obie said to Dan, who sat across from him on the office couch.

There were worry lines on his son's face. "It's sad, but she's failing," Dan said. "She will soon need more intensive care."

"Cassie says you've ruled out nursing homes. How will you handle it?"

"Grandmother wants to stay at home. Ly Yen will take time off from her schooling."

The phone rang. Lacy Boswell sounded desperate. "I need to talk to you, Pastor Obie. Please!"

"I'll be in the office all morning."

As Obie cradled the phone, Dan said, "I see you have church business, and I'm needed at the clinic, so I'll just scoot on out."

"No rush. It'll take Lacy a few minutes to get here." Time with Dan was precious.

Dan turned from the doorway. "I think Chet and Lacy are having difficulties."

"Oh?"

"I don't know all the details, but word gets around."

"And what is that word?"

"That he's upset about her singing gigs. She's attached herself to Denver Boyles' band, and Boyle has a reputation."

"Lacy would never do anything to hurt Chet."

"Obie, there's a lot of talk about her. About her reputation, and some of it's coming from right here in our church."

"I've heard some of it. Amos Adams again, isn't it?"

"Yes, and he has a following, as you know."

"It's not a large following."

"He's made no secret of his wish to see you go."

"I know that. And a few others may feel that way. But that's another matter. Our job, right now, is to concentrate on making Abigail as comfortable as possible."

Lacy arrived half an hour later. She entered the office un-announced and closed the door behind her. "I don't know what to do," she said.

Obie studied her face. She was a beautiful and talented woman. But what was he to think about her? He had dismissed most of the rumors, but some came from more reliable sources than Amos' consortium. She had resisted his efforts to bring her back to church, but he would not stop trying.

"What's going on?" he asked.

"It's Chet. He's drinking again. He quit AA." She sobbed.

"What's happened, Lacy?"

She wiped her eyes with the sleeve of her lightweight blouse. "Pastor Obie, I apologize for coming to you like this. I'm not a member of your church, but I don't know where else to go for the help I need."

"Lacy, you can come to me anytime. Membership has nothing to do with it. I'm here to help."

"Thank you. Chet thinks I'm having an affair. It's not true. I love him. I would never do that."

"Why does he think that?"

"I spend lots of time with my band members. We rehearse for our weekend jigs. One band member hit on me, but only once before I put him in his place. I made the mistake of telling Chet about that, and now he thinks the worst."

"How long has it been going on, his suspicions, I mean?"

"About a month, right after he finished the Augustine house. I was stupid enough to tell him."

"It wasn't stupid, Lacy. You did the right thing to put it right out there in the open. That's what marriage partners should do."

"Chet wanted to beat him up, but I talked him out of that. His drinking is the big problem. When he's drunk, he threatens to leave me. He says it's my fault that men make advances."

"Chet loves you very much, Lacy, and I'm sure he doesn't mean that."

"He says we don't need the money from my gigs, but music

is an important part of my life. What can I do?"

"You could make some concessions? Weekends off? Fewer practice sessions? Get him to go with you on some of those weekend gigs?"

"Maybe. But I'll give it all up if it's the only way to keep him in my life."

"Lacy, I'm sure there is a way to keep both Chet and music in your life."

"If only I could?"

"I'll talk to him. Does he go to the Diamond Inn?"

"Every evening, and sometimes afternoons."

"I'll catch him there this afternoon. He'll listen to me. I'll bring Ernie in on this if I have to."

She looked down and tapped the arm of her chair rhythmically. He waited for her to face him before he continued. "I'll do my part, Lacy, but there's something you should do."

"Anything."

"Come back to church, and bring Chet with you." He saw resistance in her expression. "He'll listen to you. You both need the prayers and support of God's people."

"Some of them wouldn't like it."

"Most will."

"I don't know?"

"You'll be welcomed back."

"Are you sure?

"I'm sure." He prayed silently that it was true.

"Alright, maybe I'll try if that's what it takes." He thought he heard a sob. Maybe I will."

* * *

Obie's visits to the Diamond Inn were rare. Throughout his boyhood, he watched his father go in and out those doors with regularity. It was only after he returned to Stafford Rest that he visited it for the first time, and that was to intervene in Chet's drinking problem. Now, years later, he was intervening again, for the same person and the same reason.

As Obie took the stool next to Chet, Chuck Hinky made a

perfunctory swipe with a towel on the bar top and asked, "What's it going to be, Preacher?"

"The usual."

Chuck laughed. "You expect me to remember that far back? It's been a while since you've darkened my door?"

"Well, it's wine ... red. And Cassie and I did come in once to hear Lacy sing. And don't forget that I married Chet and Lacy here. He nudged Chet with his elbow. "Isn't that right?"

Chet's voice came from a deep place, without much strength. "Obie speaks the truth, Chuck," he said. "He's not only a brother in arms but also a minister of the Gospel."

"You don't need to tell me about Obie, Chet. We go way back. We did boy things together, and your dad was part of that."

"Yeah, Dad told me you guys had some adventures."

"Obie's made more of his life than we have," Chuck said.

"Lots of folks might disagree," Obie said.

"That's not true. You have quite a following," Chuck said as he set a glass of wine before Obie. "My establishment is the seat of this community. Everything that happens, or even gets rumored about happening, gets aired over this bar."

"That drink's on me," Chet said. "It's not often I get to drink with you, Obie."

Obie wanted to get to the business for which he had come. "No, Chet. If you treat me, then I'll have to treat you back, and I don't want to do that."

"So, you're trying to interfere with my drinking, then?" The declaration held an edge of hostility. "Did Lacy send you?"

"Yes, she did, but it was my idea. She's concerned, Chet."

"I'm concerned, too," Chuck said. "He spends far too much time in here."

"Lots of people are concerned, Chet. I'm sure Ernie and Francis are."

"Did she tell you what's going on?"

"Some of it." He hesitated. "Chet, this is a discussion that should be private. We may want to go to my office."

Chet pounded the bar with a fist. "Hell, no! We can't talk about much that I haven't already told Chuck. What did she tell you, Obie?"

"She said you thought she was having an affair with one of her band members. But I know that's not true, and you know it, too. That's not who Lacy is."

Chet said quickly, "Of course I know it. I've had time to think about it, and I will apologize for even thinking it. But she's gone for ungodly hours on weekends and sometimes late nights during the week. And none of that involves me. She spends more time with them than she does with me."

"Couldn't you go with her on weekend engagements?"

"Obie, I work hard. You know that. I can't lose that much sleep and still function at work."

He wanted to point out that drinking also interfered with his work, but said instead, "I know it's difficult, but she's a talented musician, and it's the nature of her business."

"Well, I can't put up with it. I love Lacy, but it's asking too much."

It seemed the right time to make his pitch: "Chet, marriages are hard, sometimes. I speak from experience. Sometimes, more is needed than two people trying to sort it out. There's a spiritual element needed to make things right."

Chet said in a raised voice, "Aw, there's the preacher. I knew he was in there somewhere." Then he smiled. "Obie, you're not going to invite me back into that god-awful congregation, are you?"

Obie tried not to be flustered. "Yes, that's exactly what I'm doing. And that element you mentioned is only a tiny part of our church family."

"I suspect you've already spoken to Lacy about this?"

"I have, and she's agreed to give us a try, but she wants you to agree to it too."

"I don't know ..."

"Attend one time. Both of you. And we'll go from there." He prayed silently. *I leave it up to you, God.*

"If Lacy agrees."

"Good. Now, let's get you home. You've had enough to drink."

Chet laughed out loud. "Don't push it, Preacher."

* * *

Jacob pulled with youthful energy on the oars he had taken over from his dad, gliding the boat deftly through a tangle of underwater growth. They were far into the Morass on this fall day that had dawned warm and sunny.

The Saturday morning invitation to go rowing came without prior notice but was not an unexpected gesture from his father; trips into the Morass were familiar and welcome experiences. His father had taken him there often, even before he was old enough to handle the oars.

It dawned on him that there were always new things to see here. Today, the late summer vegetation lay on the surface in a jumbled profusion of greens and browns, in color contrast to dead trees that stood stark against the sky. Jacob pushed with an oar against a smaller tree. "Pretty solid," he said.

"Most of these trees were standing here when I was your age."

A thought entertained during the last couple of trips to the Morass came again, stronger this time. He had held off sharing it with his dad because he had thought it might seem silly. But now, it felt appropriate.

"Dad, did you ever think that the Morass is kind of like life?"

"In what way?" His father was in that raised eyebrow mode. "Tell me your thoughts."

Jacob wanted to say it right. "There are all these things that go on in the Morass, and they're all different."

"Contrasts?"

"Yes. All these dead trees and bushes alongside growing things. And underneath us is all kinds of life that we can't see, the good and the bad together."

His father looked pleased. "Jacob, you're right. Life is like that. This place can represent 'the good' and 'the bad,' but it can also represent 'the different.' I think you've given me an idea for a sermon." They laughed. The whole idea would require further thought.

"Did Grandpa ever tell you how the Morass came to be?"

"He said it was a geological wonder of the ice age and had been here a long time. Our job, according to him, was simply to enjoy it. When I was growing up, he guided high school and college groups through here."

"To teach students about it?"

"Exactly. Dad was knowledgeable about the Morass, just as he was about the woods and mountains."

"How did he learn all that? He wasn't a college professor or anything like that?"

Jacob liked it when his dad laughed. He wished he would do it more often.

"Not at all. He was self-educated, from books, from experience, and from my Grandfather Jacob, who passed along his wealth of knowledge."

"Jacob, the one I'm named for?"

"That's right." There was respect in his father's voice. "Your great-grandfather is someone I must tell you more about. He was a remarkable man in many ways." Jacob saw his father hesitate before saying, "I believe he's partly responsible for what I am today."

"I'd like to know more about him and Great-Grandmother Prissy," Jacob said as he rested the oars on the gunwale. "And there are also things I want to know about you, Dad."

He had not meant to blurt it out so forcefully; he studied his father's face as the boat drifted.

"I doubt there's much more to say about me than you already know."

On one level, that was probably true; he had listened to tales of his father's growing-up years and the difficult times in three wars. He could even recite the names of towns in Italy where some of their ancestors lived. Nevertheless, his father's thinking was what he desired. His statement about Great-grandfather Jacob influencing who he was had whetted the appetite for knowing more.

Jacob was not sure why that seemed so important, but thought it might be because of something Alicia asked last week as they held hands under the table in chemistry lab: "Jacob," she said, "what are you going to be when you grow up?"

"I'll play baseball. I'm really good at that. My coaches say my throw from third to first is phenomenal." He had emphasized that last word.

"Be serious. That's just a game," she had said. "I've heard you talk about things you like to do, but we're almost adults, and we'll soon have to make some decisions ... the kind adults make." It was at that point that the chemistry teacher silenced them with a shaking finger.

They had not resumed that conversation, but he had thought about it. Friends and relatives had probably asked the same question regarding his future. If so, he had given it no consideration. It sounded like Alicia was asking him to make serious decisions, and that caused him to think about what he was good at other than baseball. Sure, his mother told him he was capable of being whatever he chose to be, and his father's sage advice was to "do what you love," but he felt the need to "nail it down," a phrase he had heard Grandfather Ken use.

Her question had prompted a question he wanted to ask his father. Here in the isolated waters of the Morass, it seemed a good time to ask. "Dad, when did you decide to become a minister?"

As usual, his father took time to answer. Jacob waited. A few yards away, a red-winged blackbird sat on a protruding mound of earth and stared at them as though waiting.

"That's not a question with only one answer," his dad said as he stretched out his legs. Jacob thought he heard a sigh. "Had you asked about my decision to pastor Stanford Rest Methodist, that would have been easy because it was within your lifetime. I was asked to take the job, and that was when I decided."

"But it's not just a job. I've heard you say it was a calling."

"Yes, it is."

"Mom said you were once pastor of a church in California."

"Yes, I was, for over two years."

"So, you must have decided to do that?"

"I sort of fell onto it. But yes, I made the decision to take it on."

278

"But, for only two years? Why didn't you stay?"

The expression on his father's face was hard to decipher—anything from anger to annoyance. Jacob knew immediately that he was not likely to get a straight answer.

"Son, there are things you wouldn't understand about my decision to leave that conference." Jacob saw him pause. "You know I was married before I married your mother."

"Yes, to Annie."

"She died, as you also know, but you may not know that we were separated before that. It was at that time that I left."

"And that's when you went back into the Army ... when you became a chaplain?"

"I was a chaplain before, right out of seminary. That's when I went to Korea."

Jacob drew in a breath before asking the question he wanted answered. "Dad, how old were you when you knew for the first time that you wanted to be a minister? I know you made decisions about serving God after you were lost on Algonquin. Was that when you decided?"

"I wasn't lost. I was geographically confused." His father was smiling. "But, to answer your question ... no, I did not make clear decisions about it then. Jacob, you must understand about that time in my life. I was caught in a vortex of conflicting emotions. I remembered my mother's desires for me, and the Catholic Church had cast its image on my young mind. And there's my friendship with my mentor, the then-pastor of Stanford Rest Methodist."

"Charles Lansing. Wasn't that his name?"

"Yes. Pastor Charles. I'm surprised you remember that. He had a great influence on my life."

"Did you want to be like him?"

"I suppose I did, for part of my youth. I used to pretend to give sermons from the same pulpit where I do it now for real. I suppose I thought about it. Charles may have wanted that for me, too."

"Then there was the war and your years in college. Journalism at Berkeley makes it seem like you turned your back on wanting the ministry."

His father was silent for so long that Jacob thought he might not answer. When he did, his tone was somber. "Son, I had some dark years."

"Because of the war?"

"That was part of it."

Jacob waited several seconds before realizing he would not likely hear more about those "dark years." Maybe it had something to do with Aunt Laura and the letters. *Maybe another time?*

But he still wanted to piece together his father's path to becoming a pastor. He said, "I know you went to seminary right after college, but you didn't decide until your senior year. So, Dad, what happened? What changed your mind? Was it because of that dream?" The tale of the "vineyard dream" was one he had heard all his life.

"Yes, that influenced me, and it was when I started planning to go to seminary, but it was your mother who caused me to finalize those plans."

"Mom did?"

His father's face brightened. "Yes, your mother went to Berkeley to see me. Her presence and her faith in me made me decide."

"But then you broke up, and you went on to seminary anyway. That must ..." He stopped. He recognized his father's expression. He would not push the subject further; it could wait for another time. He was happy to have learned more about his father's spiritual path.

He knew he should not say it, but he did anyway. "Dad, your life has been a morass, hasn't it?"

His father looked shocked but soon recovered. "Yes, I guess so. Parts of it."

"I guess we all have our morasses?" He wondered if that was a stupid statement.

His father said, "Jacob, I have my own question for you. Why are you so curious about my pastoral history? Are you interested in the ministry for yourself?"

He was found out. "Yes, Dad. I am interested."

"You're only fifteen. You have plenty of time to make that decision."

"I'm almost sixteen. Anyway, it's only a thought I had after someone asked me what I wanted to do with my life."

"You have lots of career choices, Jacob. But who asked you that?"

A wading blue heron turned its head to look at them. "Just somebody."

"Alicia, was it?"

"She thinks about things like that."

"She's a bright girl." His father was smiling. "You like her, don't you? Is she your girlfriend?"

He nearly choked on the words. "Yes, she is."

There, he had said it to someone; he had said it to his dad. Maybe he would tell his mother, too.

CHAPTER THIRTY-ONE

January 1988

Obie's hands nursed a mug of hot coffee as he strolled from the kitchen to the lounge chair in the study. It was late morning on the first day of January. Jacob and Julie were still asleep, tired from last night's Watch Meeting and midnight fireworks on the town beach.

What was there about the dawn of a new year that stirred the memories? One memory, his September conversation with Jacob in the Morass, came often. Jacob's observation that the Morass diversity somehow resembled the courses of human lives felt like the truth.

Today, that metaphor seemed appropriate, for it brought up images of his own struggles with difficult questions that had no apparent answers. His surface then may have appeared calm, but underneath were all those unseen forces, "the good and the bad," that had acted to change him. *And he had changed, perhaps for the better, despite all his shortcomings.*

He had to smile, for he had been maneuvered into talking about himself. Jacob had opened that door to declare his interest in the ministry. Smart! At sixteen, however, interests were about as permanent as smoke.

Cassie joined him with her own cup of coffee. "You look pensive," she said. "Tell me what you're thinking about."

"About our son. He's matured."

"He's sixteen today, in case you've forgotten."

"How could I forget? I can smell the cake you baked yesterday." *Her smile was beautiful.* "I love you," he said.

"And I love you, Obie."

"Jacob's smart."

"I know that."

"I don't know if he's told you, but he's interested in the ministry."

"Yes, he told me, sort of. What are your thoughts about it?"

"I think the interests of a sixteen-year-old are fleeting."

"That's true in many cases, but Jacob is mature. Speaking as a teacher, there's another quality I've observed. He's dedicated."

"Meaning?"

"When he takes on something, he finishes it. Don't you remember how he organized that group of boys to clean up the town beach last October? And how good was our church Christmas play this year? He pretty much wrote that. He may have your writing genes."

"He does write well. I was proud of him for that article he got into the Quarterly about the Stafford Rest church bells. As for those other things, I'm sure he had help with those endeavors."

"Yes, but he spearheaded them. Our son is a leader. We should take him seriously when he says he wants to enter the ministry."

"Yes, I do take him seriously, but I won't encourage him. I'll help him however I can, but I can't encourage him to become a minister."

"Maybe that's because your ministry has had so many ups and downs?"

"I won't deny that possibility, but it's not the main reason. To be clear, I would be thrilled to see Jacob go into the ministry, but I want him to make that decision himself. I've always told him to do what he loves to do. God plants in us a love for what he wants us to be."

"Like the love of writing?"

"Exactly."

"And my love of teaching?"

He was pleased that she understood. "Now, let's get the rest of this family up so we can have a day of birthday celebration."

* * *

Obie's emphasis on his statement that "God plants in us a love for what he wants us to be" seemed to minimize somehow her desire to improve O'Shane Vineyard. The issue lay between them like an open sore to which neither was willing to apply an ointment.

It was mainly about the wine; he believed she wanted to turn O'Shane Vineyard into a winery. That was not true, of course, but she had made little effort to correct his misconception. The larger picture was that Obie did not value her opinion about the vineyard's future. She was determined to have a discussion. During the birthday dinner, her thoughts often strayed to what she might say to him.

Hours later, after Dan, Ly Yen, and the twins left, Julie retired to her room, Jacob went to the study to read one of his gift books, and Cassie and Obie went to the porch to sit on the glider.

"Sixteen today," Obie said. "How could that be?"

"Does that make us an old married couple?"

He moved close enough to put an arm around her shoulders. She surrendered to that warm feeling that came at his touch.

"Cassie," he said, "We're not old, and we never will be as long as we have each other."

She turned her face up to be kissed. They sat on the glider for several minutes with their arms around each other.

But she must state her case. "Obie, I want to discuss something with you."

"What, Sweetheart?"

The glider squeaked rhythmically as it moved back and forth. "We talked about loving what we do," she said. "But can't we love more than one thing?"

"Of course. We can, and we do. I didn't mean it to sound exclusive. But I believe there's one overriding thing for which we're gifted, and we are supposed to make that the focus of our life."

"And my overriding thing is to teach. "I'll always be a teacher. But, as you know, I've spent years researching ways to improve our vineyard. Obie, it's an important interest of mine."

The glider stopped moving. He said, "I know, and your ideas have made a difference. But I think you want to get into serious winemaking. Isn't that it?"

She forced a laugh. "Not at all. It's more of a hobby ... wine-making, I mean. My main goal is to turn O'Shane Vineyard into a thriving business."

"So, do you mean you aren't as involved with the wine part as you've led me to believe?"

"Obie, I haven't led you to believe anything about it. You've come to your own conclusions."

"Well, you don't tell me much, so what am I to think?"

"You can ask." She had not meant to sound so harsh. "Obie, I'm sorry. I should have explained more."

He was silent for a long time before saying, "I guess we should have talked more. Frankly, I'm relieved you aren't interested in being a wine master. A winery requires experts. I don't know what wine to order in a restaurant, and I doubt you have even the barest knowledge of what it would require."

She would not address his dismissal of her competence in the winemaking culture but said, "It's true that I don't know much, but I do want to educate myself on the subject."

"Well and good, but I can't see it fitting into the future of O'Shane Vineyard."

"Obie, it does have a past. The vineyard made wine on a limited scale before the O'Shanes purchased it. There is still equipment in the basements. Don't you remember that Lyle and Neal showed all that to us?"

Before he could answer, she said, "Anyway, winemaking would be on a very small scale. The important thing is improvements in other areas. We should make several changes and upgrades to improve production and distribution."

"I don't think we should fix something that doesn't need fixing."

"And you're wrong, Obie. You're being shortsighted about this."

"Cassie, the vineyard's future is bleak. Let's examine the facts. Lyle and Matilda have declared themselves 'retired.' Kent is here now, and as efficient as he is at the bookwork, he knows little about the day-to-day maintenance of the business."

"I don't think that's true. He grew up in the vineyard."

"And Joel has no interest at all. He'll probably leave home soon."

"Neal is the one with the knowledge," she said. "He's running the vineyard now, with Lyle in the shadows. He told me that he'll learn what's needed to make the improvements I've suggested."

She felt his body stiffen. "The vineyard has problems, and winemaking would add to them." There was firmness in his declaration.

Responding was pointless; he could not get the anti-winemaking fantasy out of his head. Anyway, something more important needed to be addressed.

"Obie, I need you to respect my role in this," she said.

"Of course I respect you."

"You don't."

He looked distressed as he turned to face her. "Cassie, I can't imagine what you mean, but if I've done or said anything that shows disrespect for you, I sincerely apologize."

She grabbed his hand. "Oh, I didn't mean it in any accusing way. It's just this one thing about me that I want you to understand better."

"Please tell me." There were worry lines on his forehead.

"For years, I've interacted with the Augustines concerning O'Shane Vineyard." She paused a second. "But your participation has been marginal."

"That's not true, Cassie."

"Oh, yes, it is true. Whenever I try to bring you up to date on some issue, you grunt and say, 'It'll work itself out,' or 'I'm not worried about it.' You've left it up to me to solve all the problems."

"Well, that's what you asked me to let you do. You seem to like doing it."

"And that's a point I want to make. I do like it, and I'm good at it. I've learned a lot about the vineyard and how it works. But I want some respect for what I've done ... and what I'll keep doing."

"I do respect you for it."

"That's the first time I've heard you say it."

Obie bowed his head. She waited.

"Sweetheart, if I'm remiss, I'm sorry, but I don't have much hope for the vineyard ever being anything like you imagine. I don't want you to be disappointed."

She made sure to say with emphasis, "Obie, the vineyard has the potential to be much more than it is, and I intend to work to make it so, but I want you to help me more, even if it's only in the form of encouragement."

His grip on her arm was firm. "Cassie, Sweetheart, my biggest concern is that all this is beyond you, that you simply ..."

"Beyond me?" She fought down her anger. "You think this is beyond me? Obie, after all our years together, you should know better. You've just said a stupid thing?"

"Yeah, I'm good at that." She was glad he was smiling. "Cassie, you're a talented woman, and I will never disparage you or your ability to do what you set out to do. But you must accept that some things are beyond our abilities. It's got nothing to do with us. In this instance, it's the resources, time, and distance. I admire your ambition, but what you have in mind is not practical."

As she rose, she wanted to blurt out, "The hell it isn't!" Instead, she touched his arm gently and said, "Maybe? Who knows?"

* * *

Obie surveyed the small gathering in the church office. Those present after the Sunday morning service were there by his invitation. Seated on the couch and in chairs around the room were Staff Parish chairperson Lucille Epps, Frances Boswell, Roland Kilpatrick, Dan and Ly Yen Williamson, Sarah Hill, Chet and Lacy Boswell, Arthur Baines, and Cassie.

As he surveyed the group, he realized he might have picked a better time for this meeting; an early January storm had moved in, and it had already begun to snow. He promised to keep the meeting short so everyone could get home safely.

"Pastor, why are we even here?" Arthur Baines asked. His tone displayed annoyance.

"It's a project I wish to give priority," Obie replied.

"Well, let's deal with it quickly."

Obie had unashamedly stacked the deck with people of his choice, and Arthur was a last-minute inclusion; it was prudent to include at least one potential opponent. He had decided against inviting Amos because of his blatant confrontational nature; Arthur would carry information back to Amos but was unlikely to be as disruptive.

Obie seated himself in a chair that faced the group. "I've thought about this for some time," he said. We need a church store, one that will serve not only our congregation but the whole town."

"And who in town would it serve?" Arthur said. "Are you talking about needy folks, or drunks and drug addicts?"

"Arthur, it won't be a shelter that deals with such problems. We're not equipped for that. I want a little space where people can buy everyday items such as food, clothing, or furniture at severe discounts. It's not charity because those who can afford it will pay, and those who are needy will find some help. I've called this meeting today to discuss the feasibility of such a project and, if you agree, to form a plan."

"Isn't this something for the Administrative Council to decide?" Arthur said.

Roland's deep and authoritative voice came quickly. "Of course, it is. We won't make any final decisions now. We're simply exploring possibilities, taking one step at a time. This group represents a wide spectrum of the church, and if we agree that it's a good idea, we'll take it to the Administrative Council, which will have the final say."

Obie said, "I know you have questions, but first, I want you to know that this idea came from Abigail Hunt." He would not reveal how he had stimulated her imagination.

"How is she?" Sarah asked. "I hear she's bedridden."

"Yes, Sarah, she's very ill, but her spirit is up, and she knows we're meeting today. She sends all of you her love and best wishes." He prayed silently to be forgiven for the slight embellishment.

"God bless her," Roland said. "She and Pinky have kept

this church running." There were nods of agreement.

'As you know," Obie said, "she organized and carried out our church program that brought needed help to several cancer patients in the community, and even beyond our community. But this proposed venture isn't connected to that. It's in addition to it. Abigail saw the need and thus her suggestion."

"I have a lot of questions," Arthur said.

"And I've anticipated some questions the group might have. You want to know who this store will serve, where it will be located, and where the resources will come from? You may have other questions, but I'm certain those are the core concerns."

Heads were nodding. Obie continued. "Let's not forget that one Church duty, beyond saving lost souls, is to help the poor. Our town people often struggle to meet basic needs."

"Sometimes they do not speak," Ly Yen said. "Such a store will let them find help without shame." *His daughter-in-law was familiar with poverty.*

"And don't forget that everybody likes a bargain," Obie said. "For instance, the store might provide the option of purchasing a good used refrigerator instead of buying a new and more expensive one."

"Used refrigerators are a dime a dozen," Arthur said. "People even throw them away."

Sarah said softly, "Pastor Obie, I don't think we have that many needy people in town. It's a small community, and it's full of people from our old stable families. I know some who are poor but not destitute."

"That's a good point, Sarah," Obie said. "We have a stable base, but there are also many new faces, and some come with needs. And as Ly Yen suggested, some needy folks won't let you know about it. A store will provide a space to conveniently find some item you need without running to Tupper Lake or Saratoga to buy it."

"And where will all these items come from?" Arthur said.

"From us, to start with. We have several pieces of furniture in our barn that Cassie has discarded so that we can have something more modern." There was a trickle of laughter. "But it's still good furniture, things someone will cherish. We'll give it to the store, and I'm counting on everyone in our congregation having items they're willing to part with." He was encouraged to see several heads nodding.

"Aren't the other churches doing something like this?" Dan asked.

"Yes," Obie said, "but on a limited scale. They use their church space, which is small in those churches, especially in the Baptist building. I've talked to both pastors, and they will support our efforts. But the organization and maintenance will be ours."

"Where will it be located?" Chet Boswell asked.

Obie was glad Chet had spoken up. Getting him and Lacy back into their congregation was a significant achievement, but getting them involved was essential.

"The church basement has a kitchen and meeting space that might serve, Obie said. "And there's the education wing that we no longer use except for storage. Also, Laura Williamson said she will donate a section of the factory outlet store on Main Street, provided we bear any construction costs. Personally, I think that space is ideal since it will allow us to house larger items."

"Are we talking major funding?" Arthur said.

"There will be some expense, but donors will come forward." He would not reveal that the Love Fund was one of those donors, as it had been for several projects since his return to Stafford Rest.

"Who will run it?" Dan asked. "It will require a 'hands-on' approach."

"Yes, it will," Obie said, "but that's where our members have the chance to serve ... to be practicing Christians."

It was confirmed that he had "bearded the lion" when Arthur said, "Pastor, a Christian is supposed to spread the Gospel to the world, not give us a price break."

"It's not like that at all, Arthur," Obie said. "Remember who Jesus looked out for. He loved the poor, the meek, the poor in spirit. We're commissioned to spread the gospel, and frankly, this seems like a good way."

Sarah said, "Pastor, somebody will have to run it, be in charge, wouldn't they? You're too busy for that."

"Don't worry, Sarah. I have someone in mind. And I've already asked her."

"Who?"

Obie nodded toward the group. "Frances will be the administrator. She has the know-how to run such a project and has flexible time from her library duties. Frances, do you want to say something?"

Frances sat forward in her chair and spoke with assurance. "Only that I'm honored to do God's work. I will do my best to serve."

Lucille, who had been silent during most of the meeting, said, "Amos isn't here today, but we could use his expertise in furniture and construction."

"I'll let him know about it," Arthur said.

The project soon received the group's approval, and the rest of the meeting went by quickly. Arthur left before the rest. Chet and Lacy lingered and were the last in the room. Lacy asked, "Pastor Obie, why did you invite us to this meeting? We've had no part in church work."

"Of course, you have. You've become an active choir member. That's service of a special kind."

"I haven't done anything," Chet said.

"What do you want to do, Chet?"

"Well, if you get that space in the outlet, I can do some construction work."

"Yes, you can. Why do you think I invited you?" Obie smiled to show that it was said in jest.

"I don't do construction," Lacy said.

Obie wanted to nail a suggestion to Lacy's psyche. "My dear, you're a leader, and I have several ideas for you." *Let her chew on that.*

* * *

When the office was clear of everyone except his mother and father, Jacob stepped from behind the auxiliary doorway leading to the basement. He had not meant to hide; he had waited too long and did not want to interrupt the meeting.

"I didn't know you were there," his mother said.

"Nor I," his father added with an eyebrow raised.

He could have retreated to the basement where he had told his parents he would be, but he was drawn to the proceedings. He often watched his father tend to his duties throughout the sanctuary and in the pulpit, but it was a mystery about what happened behind the office door. He said, "I was just curious."

His mother laughed. "I suppose you're gathering information about the duties of a minister?" she said.

"I wasn't thinking about that."

"You could have attended," his father said. "It won't hurt you to see some hard parts of the calling. If you continue your interest, you'll need to know what a minister's job is. Part of it is what you see and hear on Sunday mornings and in our study groups. But that's only a fraction of what it takes to run a church. Today, you saw some more nitty-gritty stuff. And this was an easy group. Launching worthwhile projects, such as you saw this morning, must be accomplished with love and patience, but also with discipline."

"Mr. Baines is a troublemaker, isn't he?"

His father chuckled. "I see you've gained some insight. That's good. But remember that no one is beyond hope."

"It's snowing harder," his mother said. "We need to get home."

* * *

Obie saw Amos at the Stewart's Shop and wanted to avoid him, but the man zeroed in on him. As he got into the car with a bag containing bread and ice cream, Amos caught up and put a hand on the door before Obie could close it.

"What's the big idea, Preacher? I wasn't notified about your meeting on Sunday. Why wasn't I?"

"I guess somebody slipped up. I'm sorry, Amos." *God forgive me.*

Amos leaned in until his face was inches away from Obie's.

"You've got it in for me, haven't you?" he said.

"No, Amos, I don't have it in for you." He still gripped the door. "Look, Amos, it's freezing outside. Why don't you get in? Then we can talk."

Amos walked around the car and got in to sit in the front passenger seat. "I think you did it on purpose," he said. You would like me to leave the church, wouldn't you?"

It would be easy to answer in the affirmative. Amos was like the ingrown toenail that plagued him for months before he had it removed. Amos was not a blighted toenail, however; he was a member of his church.

"No, I would not like that," Obie said. "But you always look for trouble, and I must protect myself and the other members from your anger."

"What anger? I'm not angry. I just want our church to be what it's supposed to be. But if I'm a little angry, I have a right to be."

"I think your anger is of your own choosing."

"You don't know that. You don't know a thing about me."

Obie wanted to lighten the mood. "I know that you can be a pain in the rear."

Obie was surprised that Amos chuckled before saying, "I've become pretty good at it. You give me lots of practice."

Obie said, "You were right, Amos. I excluded you from the meeting. I thought you would try to derail it."

"So, you just now lied to me?"

"I'm afraid I did."

After a pause, Amos said, "Don't you ever get angry?"

"Indeed, I do, but I control it."

"Preacher, you have a lot of stuff bottled up inside you. You'd be a better preacher if you'd let some of it out."

It was not exactly what he expected to hear from Amos. Obie said defensively, "And you should rid yourself of your own anger."

Cold was creeping into the car, so Obie started the engine. Amos said, "People ought to tell other folks about it, but who'd want to listen?"

Was Amos asking for help? Maybe there was hope.

"We have lots of folks in our church who will want to hear your story, Amos. Christians help bear the burdens of others."

"Real Christians do that," Amos said as he opened the passenger side door and stepped out. Before closing it, he said, "By the way, your store idea is good."

Amos had surprised him more than once today. Maybe he was not all bad.

CHAPTER THIRTY-TWO

March–April 1988

From the enclosed porch, Obie scanned the expanse of town and lake through their large southern window, a daily ritual assuring him that all was well. Patches of morning fog still obscured parts of the view. It was Saturday, and Sunday's sermon was already in hand; he could relax before going to the office.

Church matters were quieter now. Everything had fallen into place in the two months since the initial meeting that birthed the church store. Store construction within the furniture outlet was finished, and people were volunteering to run it. Frances Boswell was the ball-of-fire leader he had believed her to be.

Lacy and Chet's involvement delighted Obie. As promised, Chet supervised the construction that separated the store from the furniture outlet while Lacy secured donations at her performance sites. In addition, she was organizing a fundraising event in the village that would attract musicians from around the area. "It will bring in lots of revenue," she promised.

Money was not a worry. He had recently told Cassie, "The Love Fund can handle the whole store startup, but it'll mean more to everyone if they sacrifice a little." He had added, "People need the chance to serve. It promotes spiritual growth."

He finished his coffee and morning devotion and was gathering his notes to leave when the phone rang. It was Lacy. She was crying.

"What's happened?" he asked.

"I'm at the outlet. I came in early. Amos Adams was here. He said terrible things to me."

"Is he still there?"

"He left after I hit him with a broom."

"You hit him!"

"I shouldn't have, but he made me so angry."

"Lacy, I'm coming to see you."

On the drive down the hill and into the village, he speculated on what to do about Amos. He had endured his nonsense for years. *No more.*

Laura was with Lacy, who was still red-faced but not tearful. Laura said, "Obie, you have to do something about that good-for-nothing."

"I intend to, but I want to know exactly what happened."

Lacy said, "I was busy pricing items in this section. He came up behind me and started yelling at me about what a bad person I was. He called me names."

"It's early, but were there other people around?"

"I don't know, Pastor Obie. We screamed back and forth at each other, so others would have heard us."

"I heard it," Laura said. "I had just come in the front door. I don't think there were any customers in the outlet section."

"So, you didn't do anything to make him angry?"

"Nothing. He approached me."

"What, exactly, did he say?"

"That I was a terrible influence on the young people in the church. That I was creating a pathway to Hell. He called me a slut.'"

Obie fought down his anger. "Did he mention anything he thought gave him the right to voice such nonsense?"

"Only that there were others who feel the same way. He said he had spoken to several young people who wanted me to step down from the choir."

"Did he say who those young people were?"

"I asked him to name them, but he couldn't. Pastor Obie, as you know, I've put up with this kind of treatment before, but I won't again."

"Lacy, please don't judge us all for this one member's actions. He's someone I'm always at odds with. There's no vicious circle of young people who want you to leave. They love you, Lacy."

"I don't know ..."

A loud voice came from the front of the store. "There she

is, Sheriff!" Amos was pointing in their direction. Beside him was Tony Atlee, the aged district sheriff who seemed to have trouble keeping up with Amos.

Obie stepped in front of Lacy. "Sheriff, what's this about?"

Atlee was catching his breath. "Reverend Obie," he managed, "Amos says this young lady attacked him. He said she hit him in the head with a board. Is that true?"

"No, it was a broom," Lacy said.

'See, she admits it," Amos said. "I'm having dizzy spells."

Obie could not help himself. "Likely dizzy from the lies you bombarded her with."

"I want her arrested!" Amos yelled.

Obie said, "Sheriff, there's absolutely nothing to this. Amos verbally assaulted her."

"Nevertheless," Atlee said, "I'll need the young lady to come with me to Evergreen. We can sort it out there."

Laura said to Lacy, "I'll call Kent Augustine."

* * *

The matter of Lacy's "assault" on Amos Adams soon became the talk of the town. Those well-acquainted with Amos applauded her spunk, and the few who were his friends wisely persuaded him not to pursue his promised lawsuit.

Obie soon learned that after pouting awhile, Amos had written a letter to the Methodist district superintendent about "A dangerous and immoral woman in our church and a pastor who supports her." He had mustered a small base of malcontents to co-sign.

Obie told Cassie, "It's frivolous, but now they'll surely move me."

"It's not your fault."

"Doesn't matter. This whole thing has caused turmoil. The conference will want new leadership here. Assignments are coming up soon. I'll be out."

Cassie sighed. "And what will you do? You've said you'll not take an assignment that requires us to move."

"And I'll stick to that."

"Obie, a pastor is what you've become. You've put years into it. In your own words, it's how you serve."

"Sweetheart, it's not the only way to serve."

"Well, you could go back into the Army ... be a chaplain again." She was smiling.

He laughed. "Yeah, they would love to take a sixty-one-year-old. Cassie, I have options. Don't forget that I'm a success-ful writer."

"It's been years since you've written anything more than a few articles."

He grinned. "There's my sermons. The Methodist Publishing House will fall all over themselves to get those."

"Be serious. And please be upbeat. I think they'll keep you here. Everybody knows what a troublemaker Amos is."

"Writing was my first real success. Pastoring is what I was given to do in this time and place. Maybe God will want me to return to what I do best."

"Don't decide what God wants. I heard you tell Jacob that just last week."

"I'm open to his will for me. He'll let me know."

Cassie hugged him as she said, "You're so strange."

*   *   *

It was a "warmish" day in early April with spring on the horizon. Obie hoped to leave the office early and take Cassie to dinner in Evergreen, but that plan was interrupted when Lucille Epps called to say she would arrive within minutes. She added that Amos Adams was also invited. The springtime celebration with Cassie was delayed.

Although he suspected that his days at Stafford Rest Methodist were numbered, he had also assumed he still had the support of most of his congregation. *Maybe not.*

Lucille arrived first. "Obie," she said, "We're going to extinguish this fire. I have always sympathized with Amos because he has his troubles, but he's stirred up discontent in our membership, and it needs addressing."

"I agree, but it's likely that I'll be gone, so that will solve the problem."

"No, Amos will cause trouble no matter who's pastor. I've tried talking to the man." Obie heard her sigh. "As for your being moved, I haven't heard anything, although a decision may come soon."

Amos arrived with his usual bluster. "I'm busy today, so I can't stay long. What's this about?"

Obie was in no mood for niceties. "You know what it's about, Amos. We're going to talk."

Amos bristled. "I wrote that letter because it was the right thing to do for our church."

Lucile's tone was softer but direct. "It's the job of the Staff Parish to request pastor transfers. You should not have gone over our heads."

"I have every right, Lucille. Another church member attacked me, and this pastor here told me it was my fault. He sides with her even though she admits to hitting me. And I doubt that I'd get any justice through Staff Parish."

"First of all, Lacy's not a member," Obie said. "She's a potential member. She's ..."

Amos banged on the arm of his chair. "She's a tramp! We don't need members like her. And Chet Boswell's no better. He threatened to beat me up."

"Amos, that's absurd. Lacy is a fine young woman." He added, "And Chet's her husband. What did you expect from Chet after what you said to her?"

Lucille asked Amos, "On what do you judge Lacy's character?"

"Isn't it obvious? She's out in bars and clubs with those music types two or three times a week, and usually without her husband. What do you suppose goes on in those places?"

"I don't suppose," Lucille said. "It's her business. You didn't have the right to accuse her of anything. What does her private life have to do with yours? You don't have a clue about what goes on around you. You shut yourself up in that little store of yours and don't see a thing." Obie was surprised; it was not often that Lucille showed such emotion.

Amos was silent a moment before saying, "We're talking

about the church, Lucille. We must keep our church pure, as the Bible tells us. When we see sin in someone, we're supposed to condemn it. Our pastor can't seem to do that. That's one reason he has to go."

Obie's attempt at restraint failed. "Amos, if I rejected folks because they sin, we would have empty pews. It's my job as pastor to help people become aware of God's forgiveness for their sins."

"Maybe sinners like you, Amos," Lucille said softly.

"I'm not a sinner," Amos responded.

Lucille slapped her notebook shut and said with emphasis, "You're the worst kind of sinner."

"You can't name one sin against me."

"I happen to know that you overpriced Annie Ludwig's kitchen cabinets that you installed last fall."

"I didn't. Anyway, that's different. That's business."

"And I know other things," Lucille said. "You'd better be careful asking us to name your sins." Obie heard her sigh again. "But to argue solves nothing. I called the three of us together to discuss the damage your letter has done and what, if anything, we can do about it."

"What damage?" Amos said. "I did what's best for the church."

Lucille said, "What you're guilty of is trying to convince district leaders that your views are the views of all our members, and that's not the truth. I'm going to call a Staff Parish Committee meeting. We'll decide then if we should write another letter."

Amos said, "Don't forget that I'm a member of Staff Parish, too, and there are others there who think like I do."

"I'm aware, but we have the majority for what we must do," she said. "Amos, I also think we should censure you by letter for what you said to Lacy Boswell."

Amos rose so quickly that his chair crashed to the floor. He stormed from the room and slammed the door behind him.

CHAPTER THIRTY-THREE

April 1988

Obie acted swiftly after Lucille's unscheduled meeting: At the end of the following Sunday's service, he announced to the congregation, "We need a candid discussion about recent events. We've grappled with issues that have distracted us from our Christian mission. Please stay in the sanctuary if you want to participate in this informal discussion."

He had briefed Cassie that morning of his decision to hold an open forum. She said, "Good. Speak up for yourself to let people know you're doing your best."

"Maybe I can do better. Glenda Smith told me once that I was aloof. Am I?"

"No, but you are a private person, and to some people, that can look standoffish." *Leave it to Cassie to be honest.*

Hardly anyone left the sanctuary, except Chet and Lacy, who told him that their presence would make people uncomfortable. Obie brought a chair to the front and sat facing the congregation. Amos Adams moved to a front-row pew. *Amos wanted his presence known.*

To encourage a conciliatory mood, Obie said, "We're doing good things. The cancer relief project has saved lives. Abigail Hunt's work is invaluable. And the store project is right on schedule. You've all made contributions of clothing and other goods to that effort. And don't forget that you can buy products there for yourselves."

"Give it away and then buy it back," a grinning Ernie Boswell said. "Makes a lot of sense." Frances slapped his arm.

"Ernie has our largest collection spot at his marina," Obie explained. "And, I'll bore you again with my often-repeated message that God's work is not only about what happens in this sanctuary but how we act out in the world."

Arthur Baines said, "But it's within these walls that we save sinners."

"And it's out there that we find those sinners," Lucille countered.

Amos said, "Let's get on with it. We're supposed to discuss our problems and whether this preacher will return."

Lucille said, "Amos, whether Pastor Obie will return or be reassigned isn't in our hands. I suspect that decision has already been made. Furthermore, your effort to interfere with a process that belongs to church members in committee is something we will address today."

Amos's face was red. "So, am I not allowed to speak my mind? Isn't this an open discussion? Or is that only for them who side with this pastor?"

Obie had hoped to ease into the discussion, but things had escalated; "Folks," he said, "I believe that honesty serves us best, and I invite anyone and everyone to express their opinions. And that does include you, Amos."

"We'll see," Amos replied.

Obie elected to address the core issue. "Some members think I'm leading us away from our Christian responsibilities."

"Pastor," Lucille said quickly, "Our members don't think that, and I don't think Amos really believes it, either."

Amos said firmly but in a controlled voice, "Speak for yourself, Lucille."

Obie said, "I think most folks would be satisfied if I remain here another year, but since a few don't feel that way, it's important to address the issue with everyone present."

Blain Conners, who seldom expressed his opinion to anyone, stood and said, "You're doing a good job, Reverent Gainsworthy, and I don't understand how anybody can think different." He sat down.

"You're doing just fine," someone from a back pew said. Voices of consensus and scattered clapping were encouraging.

Sarah Hill's aged voice might have gone unheeded had she not raised her hand. "Pastor Obie, I've known you since you were a little boy mowing my lawn. I remember that you never had an easy time of it growing up. But you were still a sweet, polite child." She paused to smile. "You always did an excellent job with the mowing, and you've done an excellent job here in your ministry."

"Will the accolades never end?" Amos said in a soft but audible voice.

If Sarah heard, she gave no indication. "But you do some things differently from what our previous pastors did, and I'm not complaining about that, but you've never told us why."

Sweet, gentle Sarah was putting him on the spot. He glanced at Cassie, but her placid expression gave him no help. *Was he standoffish, as she suggested?* He struggled but said, "All pastors have their way of doing things. We're individuals."

Sarah continued, "Pastor Enslow wasn't here more than a month before we knew everything about him. Obie, Dear, please don't take this the wrong way because we love you, but you've been our pastor for thirteen years, and I still find you something of a mystery."

Arthur Baines was blunt. "You're more interested in doing community work than church work. You neglect what's the most important."

"Amen," Amos said.

"That's not what I meant, Arthur," Sara said.

Glenda Smith said, "You rush right through the sacraments like they don't matter."

"I take great care with the sacraments," Obie said. "They do matter. And don't we observe all the Christian Holy days throughout the year? Glenda, how do I fall short in that?"

Lucille broke in. "I don't see anything wrong with how you conduct church services, Pastor Obie. Everything is done with reverence."

Obie calmed, but still smarted from the negative words. Had he taken certain aspects of his ministry for granted by not understanding their importance to people? Had he so misjudged his congregation that even his beliefs were questioned? *Would this church be better off if he had stuck to his writing as he wanted?*

Amos stood and said, "Preacher, are you a real Christian?"

"I have no idea what you mean by that," Obie said.

Amos turned to face the congregation. "See, he can't even answer a straightforward question."

Roland said, "Amos, what reason do you have for asking

such a question?"

"Well, he seems pretty much a man of the world. He goes to bars. He wrote books that don't have Christianity in them, mostly about stopping wars and such. And there are other things."

"Amos, I'm happy that you've read my books," Obie said, "but do you have specific questions for me that we can discuss openly?"

"Since you're so vague about telling us that you're a real Christian, maybe we need to find out what your real beliefs are."

"Amos, are you finished?" Lucille said. She sounded out of patience.

"I've just started," Amos said. "You all heard about what happened at the outlet store not long ago ... how I was attacked and then told I was wrong to file a lawsuit." He paused as if to take a breath. "And, yes, I'm not suing, but that whole affair was brought about by this preacher's actions, or lack of ..."

"Amos, show respect," Lucille said.

"I wish I could show more respect, but as a real Christian, it's my duty to point out the character of the man who is running down our church."

Obie tried to control his irritation. "Amos, all you're doing is airing your own opinions."

"Alright then, answer this. Have you brought into our church a woman of ill repute who has caused our children and some of our adults to sin?"

There were howls of protest throughout the sanctuary.

"I have not!"

"And have you drained money from our church treasury and from our members to fund silly projects that are not needed in our community?"

"Our projects are beneficial."

He was about to remind Amos that he had once approved the store project, but the man said, "Do you own a vineyard in California that supplies wine to drunks all over the country?"

Cassie said, "Yes, Amos, we own a vineyard." Obie caught her glance, which could signal either apology or defiance. Her voice trembled but was firm. "Yes, we supply grapes to winemakers. And no, we don't make wine ourselves, but if we did, I'm sure it would not be as pure and fine as the wine Jesus made in Cana."

Several people clapped, but Amos said quickly, "Preacher, you were divorced, weren't you?"

"No, I wasn't divorced. My wife died." He hesitated. *Truth was important.* "We were separated when she was killed."

"Your questions are much too personal, Amos," Roland said, not hiding his irritation.

"I'm trying to get at the character of this man," Amos said. "The purity of our church is something I greatly value, as I'm sure most of you do. I did some checking up on the Rev. Gains-worthy. A cousin of mine has a friend who knows someone who attended a big church in San Francisco where our pastor was once the minister. What I've learned is that he was fired from that position."

"Not true," Obie said. "I resigned." He was apprehensive about what was coming.

"And why did you resign?"

Obie's thoughts raced back to the day in Monterey when his emotional separation from Annie led him to a one-time encounter with a woman who seemed, at the time, to be sent for the sole purpose of ministering to his hurt pride. He was ashamed and repentant afterward.

The congregation did not need to know the details, only relevant facts. "I resigned because my emotional state over separation from my wife interfered with my ability to serve. Simply that."

"There was talk, according to my cousin, that there was more to it. And you seem to have lots of secrets." Amos's smile promised evil intent. "Isn't it true that Dr. Daniel Williamson is your son?"

Obie had never been asked that question publicly, nor had he volunteered such information. Dan sat near the front, and Obie studied his face to determine how to answer. There was only a slight twitch in the corner of one eye. *Everyone knew, anyway.* Perhaps it was time to go public. Dan did not care; he had said so more than once.

"Yes," Obie said, "Dan is my son." There were more smiles than shocked faces. He glanced at Laura, who sat with Ben a few pews back. She was frowning; he would have to deal with that later.

Amos appeared surprised, as if he had expected another re-action, but he recovered quickly. "You have some questionable friends. Maybe you'd like to tell us why you haven't condemned those homos?"

The room grew quiet. Obie said, "That's right, I haven't condemned homosexuality. And I won't. And as for my friends, they're simply my friends. It seems that I judge people differently than you."

"God will judge them."

"God looks on the heart, Amos, and not on the human conditions we find ourselves in. Jesus taught us that."

'Amen!" came a voice from the back.

Amos looked slightly fazed but said, "We can do better. This church needs a minister who does what the Bible tells us to do."

Glenda Smith said, "Obie, I've known you a long time, and yes, I think you mean well, but we're an older congregation and set in our ways. Maybe you haven't quite fitted in?"

Obie smiled. "Glenda, I am what I am. I won't … can't change that any more than you can change being set in your ways." He hoped that he had not ruffled her feathers.

At that moment, Obie saw Chet and Lacy Boswell enter through the narthex door. *They must have changed their minds about attending.* They came down the right-side aisle to sit with Ernie and Frances. He was not sure whether to feel pleased or cautious.

Amos, still standing, was not about to abandon his agenda. "Your liberal side lets you bring riff-raff into our congregation, doesn't it?"

Chet stood quickly. "What do you mean by 'riff-raff?'"

Lacy was not hostile, but her words were delivered with a strong, clear voice. "That would be me, wouldn't it, Amos?"

Obie did not give Amos time to reply. "Lacy, do you mind if I call you a 'sinner?'"

Lacy laughed. "I am a sinner."

"Chet was quick to say, "Me too.""

"As we all are. But, Amos, I have a question for you." Obie paused until Amos was facing him. "You say you want to keep our church pure and that you want your pastor to follow the Bible's teaching, isn't that right?"

"Yes, that's exactly what I want."

"Who did Jesus spend most of his time with?" He didn't give Amos time to answer. "It wasn't with the organized religious leaders of the time. He came to call sinners to repentance. Amos, should the Church turn away the sinners?"

Amos looked confused. "Well, no, of course not."

"Didn't Lacy just confess that she's a sinner?"

"Well, yes, but I'm sure she didn't ..."

Obie did not give him time to recover. "So, Amos, what do we do? Lacy is a sinner, and Chet admits to that, too. Can we disregard Jesus' commission to us? Can we turn them away?"

It was one of the few times he had seen Amos speechless. Voices came from all over the sanctuary. "You're in our prayers, Chet and Lacy," someone said. Another said, "We love you." Sarah Hill said, "Welcome to our church," her gentle voice finding more volume. Other people went to shake Chet and Lacy's hands.

After things settled, Obie said, "I'm no saint. No one is. I do the best I can, but I can do better. And perhaps I should be more open. Thanks, Sarah, for pointing that out. So, to that end, and with your indulgence, I'll reintroduce myself right now."

"That's not required, Pastor Obie," Lucille said.

"I believe it is." He looked toward Cassie. "This morning, Cassie told me that I'm standoffish. That's the word she used. I've never thought of myself like that, but maybe it's how others see me. Forgive me if that's the case. I want to make up for that."

Obie prayed silently. *"God, let me speak the truth as you would have me speak."* Aloud, he said, "Everyone here knows me. Many have known me all my life, for I was born and raised here. You know I'm truthful and hard-working. Yes, I went away awhile but came back because Stafford Rest called me ... and I came back because of someone, too." He smiled at Cassie. There were several knowing heads.

"But you already know all that, and most of you accept me as I am, but a few want to know how my beliefs align with theirs. And I respect that. But you must realize that we all have different takes on things. The person sitting beside you doesn't believe exactly as you do. Methodists, even from the beginning in John Wesley's England and Francis Asbury's Colonial America, made room for disagreement."

"That's right," Roland said, "Even the Apostles disagreed."

"And I'm no different. The fact that I'm a minister called to make disciples for Christ doesn't mean I will think just like you or require you to think just like me. Forgive me if it seems I'm talking down to you. I don't mean to do that."

He paused a moment to clear his head. "The *Apostles' Creed* sums up the beliefs that flow through all Christianity, Catholics, Protestants, and even independent churches. It's what binds us together, a core that we can't break."

Lord, let me get this right: "It's the rituals that divide us. We're often critical of things the Catholics, Baptists, and other denominations do, but does it really matter whether we use grape juice or wine in our communion? Baptize by immersion or by dousing the head? What's important is that we commit to God. He looks into our hearts." A few frowns told him that he might have touched nerves.

Cassie's encouraging smile helped. He raised his voice a little for emphasis. "The danger I try to avoid is believing that my way is always the right way, the best way, the only way. I've known ministers who so embraced the rituals of their denomination that they regard them as the only way to salvation. I believe it's arrogant to think we know the mind of God."

He plowed ahead. "We rely on the scriptures to determine God's will for us, as we should. And that serves us well, except that we often limit our views to written scripture and forget who God is. He's the Master of the Universe. His knowledge is infinite, and his mind is unknowable."

Arthur Baines said, "So you're saying we can't really know God? That's a pretty bleak outlook."

"Arthur, I'm saying that we can't limit God to what we know of him in the scriptures. He's much, much more."

"Roland looked glum. "Are you saying that we can't ever get close to God?

"Not at all. God is so close to us that we don't even realize it. Call it the Holy Spirit, if you will. We feel that presence when we pray ... if we're not simply mouthing words. We must actively seek God's presence."

"How can we do that?" Obie was surprised that it was Lacy who spoke.

"Open your heart and mind, Lacy. Be quiet and listen."

With a sarcastic edge, Arthur asked, "Do you do that? It sounds like that transcendental meditation thing."

"It's opening up to God's will," Obie said. "And it's best done alone."

"Yes," Sarah said. "Jesus said to go into a closet to pray."

Obie said, "Arthur, to answer your question, yes, I do that often. Sometimes, it's only for a minute or two at home in my study, or sometimes, it's back in the office before our services. But sometimes, when I have a big decision to make, or something is troubling me, I go to a private place to pray ... and listen."

Sarah said, "Jesus went off by himself like that."

"Have you done that a long time?" Chet asked.

"Most of my life, I guess. My grandfather, Jacob Gainsworthy, played a role in forming my beliefs."

Jacob, who had gone to sit next to Jane Paxton, looked up with interest.

"I'm sure many of you remember Jacob Gainsworthy," Obie said. Several hands were raised. "He had little use for church ritual. But that's not what influenced me. He believed Christianity could be condensed into one word. Love! To him, it wasn't theology. He wasn't that sophisticated. He served God by loving everyone and doing good to everyone he knew." Obie wondered what they would think if they knew about Jacob's Love Fund, which had changed the lives of some who were right now sitting in these pews.

"Grandfather Jacob prayed, but it was like a conversation

with God, as if they were good friends. I once heard him say, 'Me and God had us a good conversation.' He was looking outside the window at a mountain as he said it. I saw that he listened to God, and that realization has stayed with me and influenced my thinking."

"Prissy and Jacob were my good friends," Sarah said.

"Glenda said, "So if I hear you right, you don't think it's important to do all the things we love to do on Sunday mornings? Maybe we don't need to sing hymns, light the Christmas candles, or give testimony?"

"Glenda, I don't mean that at all. All the rituals we observe bind us together as Christians. We need those, and we need the structure of our denomination to keep us on the right path. I'm sorry if anyone has misinterpreted that. But the core of Christianity is what's most important, just as the family is the important part and not the house in which they live. However, it's good to remember that a family needs a house."

He had said enough about his beliefs; he must still deal with the Amos situation. He said, "I'm not changing our rituals or installing a meditation room. But I want us to walk as close to God as possible."

"Thank you for taking the time to tell us this," Lucille said.

Obie said, "But now, we have to discuss the matter of Amos' verbal attack on Lacy Boswell."

Amos jumped to his feet again. "Her assault on me, you mean!"

"Amos, we have to talk about this, and in a civil manner," Obie said.

Roland spoke up. "Amos, you were wrong in what you did. Even if it were true, it's not something you should say to anyone. And it's not true, which makes it much worse."

Amos' expression did not indicate a level of sincere repentance when he said, "I might have used other words, but she's certainly not suited for our church. And she did hit me."

Obie put into words what he had wrestled with during the night. "Amos, we can't allow you to decide who is suited for our church. That must stop."

Amos appeared shocked. "Is this a trial?"

"No, but there may be some consequences ... depending on you?"

"What's going on here? You're acting like this is my fault."

Lucille stood. "Amos," she said, "Staff Parish is censuring you for your accusations against Lacy." Her voice almost broke. "Those accusations were made without any foundation of truth, and some members may have believed them. You've given false witness, and that's a sin."

"So, what will you do, kick me out of my church?"

"No ... but understand that we have that right."

Obie prayed silently. He had not taken lightly his decision to give the matter over to Staff Parish after Amos stormed out of their last meeting. Lucille had called all the members together the next day; she told Obie she wanted leniency but would accept the will of the committee. Obie attended but did not participate; he wanted decisions free of his bias. The anger against Amos was apparent, and, except for a few dissenting voices, it was decided to admonish his actions publicly. At the end of that meeting, Roland summed up the group's general feeling. "We're not excluding him from our congregation, but we want him to shape up."

Frightening Amos was not easy. He roared, "It seems I'm the only one who cares about our church." Obie saw him glance at Arthur and Glenda, who had been surprisingly quiet the past few minutes. "I've defended our tried and true ways, but now you'll see how we'll go downhill as a church that serves God. If you don't get rid of this preacher, it's on your heads."

"We'll always serve God," Lucille said.

"He should be kicked out of the ministry," Amos said. "If Abigail Hunt still chaired Staff Parish, this wouldn't happen. He's her son-in-law, but we all know there is bad blood between them. She would put him in his place. It's too bad she's unable to be here."

Heads turned when a voice came from the back, near the narthex. "It's okay, Amos, I'm here." Abigail walked slowly down the aisle, assisted by Dan Williamson.

People clapped, and Obie was once again awed by the power her presence brought. Roland shooed people over in the front pew, and Dan helped her gently into her seat before sitting beside her.

Amos sounded almost reverent as he said, "Abigail, it's so wonderful to see that you can still come to be with us. And it's at a fortunate time, too. I'm under fire here for wanting to rid us of this pastor who's tearing our wonderful church apart." Amos paused before saying, "Can you tell us something about him?"

"Yes," Abigail said, "I can tell you all about Obadiah Gainsworthy."

"Please do," Amos said.

Her voice was diminished but not weak. "Obie and I go way back," she said as she looked him in the eye. "I can call you 'Obie,' can't I? Rev. Gainsworthy sounds so formal."

"Of course you can, Abigail. Most folks do."

"I first saw Obie when he was three days old," Abigail said. "He and Cassie were born on the same day. Obie's mother, Vi, was our housekeeper. I loved Vi and was devastated when she died at a young age." She turned her head toward Obie again. "Obie, I'm sorry we didn't do more to help you over those difficult years."

The words surprised Obie. He nodded. She continued, "I admit that I didn't realize Obie's potential. And I became angry at him because ..." She hesitated. "I suspect most of you know what happened in our family ... that something bad turned out to be something good."

Obie noticed that she was holding Dan's hand. "But, enough of that," she said. "Anyway, you all know his history after that, his war record, his literary skills, and his pastorate with us for the past several years."

"And that's the part that concerns us," Amos said. Obie had watched his face change as Abigail spoke. Things were not going as he wished.

Abigail's words were not designed to give Amos hope. "Listen here, Amos. I know that somewhere deep inside you, there's a good man, but he's lost in a jumble of hate. Yes, you're being censored, and justly so. Your actions were deplorable."

Abigail paused. Her voice was weaker, but she still held the determination he recognized. "We're not excluding you from our congregation, Amos. We will keep you close so we can find that excellent man inside you. And if you let him, this good pastor will help you."

Amos looked as if he wanted to speak but seemed unable. When he finally did, his tone was subdued but still defiant. "I'll look for another church that does God's work." He walked up the aisle toward the narthex.

Lucille called after him, "Amos, our prayers are with you."

Later, as people left, Obie said to Abigail, who still sat in the pew beside Dan, "Thank you for those kind words. I'm not sure I deserve them."

"Yes, you do, and they were overdue. Obie, let them be my final testimony in the repair of our relationship, and to our God who sees all ... and forgives."

There came to Obie's memory a well-performed play he and Cassie had attended at Evergreen High School several years before. When the curtain was pulled back at the end, revealing the entire cast, cheers had gone up—and then, as the final curtain was drawn, a sense of finality came; there was appreciation in the performance, but sadness that it was ended. Such were his feelings now. He saw tears in Abigail's eyes—and felt them in his own.

Part Three

1988–2024

The Bells

CHAPTER THIRTY-FOUR

May 1988

"Wait. Just wait a minute, Jacob," Alicia said. "It will ring. It always rings."

Jacob held the rope that would ring their bell. He was the bellringer for May, having drawn the lucky number that determined who held the coveted position. He had only to pull the rope to send forth the familiar Sunday morning sound that would reverberate throughout the town, declaring that Stafford Rest Methodist Church was about to begin a service. Alicia was there to keep him company.

"It's been over a minute," Alicia said. "You have to ring it."

Years before, the three town ministers had agreed to ring their bells in a sequence that would not interfere with one another, even alternating the order so that no church bell was always last. His dad said it started as a "fun thing" for the ministers but caught on with the congregations.

Today, the Baptists were to ring first, then themselves. But there had been no bell sound from the Baptist church.

Jacob could wait no longer. He pulled down hard, and the bell rang loud and clear. He held on as the rope pulled him up. As his weight overcame the resistance, he dropped hard enough to ring the bell again. Once rhythm was established, it was easy to continue. Jacob loved the sound; he stopped after about a minute, and the Episcopal bell began a few seconds later. That bell was more resonant because of its larger size.

Alicia found him again after the service. "What do you think happened?" she asked. "I don't remember any of our churches not ringing their bell on Sunday morning."

"Their bell fell once and was damaged, but that was before your family arrived. They fixed it, but it never sounded quite the same. Maybe it's broken again."

"Let's go find out."

During the five-minute walk to the Baptist church by Cedar

Creek, Alicia put her hand in his. That felt good, but he extracted his hand as they passed the home of a baseball teammate. He was glad Alicia did not notice.

The Baptist service was over, and only a few cars were still in the parking lot. Pastor Owens was at the main entrance door shaking hands with exiting parishioners. They waited until those last few members were gone.

"Can I help you kids?" Owens said, motioning them closer. "Jacob and Alicia, what brings you to my door?

Although Jacob had been present a few times when his dad met with the other ministers, he had never had an actual conversation with this pastor, so he was surprised that Owens remembered their names.

"Your bell didn't ring," Jacob said. "What happened?

"It's cracked. It happened once before, but this time it seems to be beyond repair."

Alicia said, "What will you do?"

"We haven't had time to think about it, but we may do without a bell. After all, it's not the most important thing for a church. We'll manage."

"Well, it is important." Alicia sounded resolute, like when she disagreed with him.

Owens said, "Yes, it is important, but bells are expensive in the size we need, and I wouldn't even know where to find one."

"But I do," she said. "I know who has one."

"Who?" came simultaneously from Jacob and Owens. She had not mentioned that fact.

"Mr. Adams has a bell," she said. "I went to his carpenter shop with Dad last summer. There was a bell on a table in the back. I think he was cleaning it."

Owens' face brightened. "Did he say if it was for sale?"

"No, and I don't know anything more about it. We went there for something else."

"Amos Adams is a member of your church, isn't he? You can ask him about that bell."

Jacob said, "Yes, he's a member, but he's disaffected right now." "Disaffected" was the word his dad used. "He's mad at us," he added.

"He's not a nice man," Alicia said.

Owens said, "I'll get my stewards to talk to him."

"I would miss hearing your bell," Alicia said. "Wouldn't you, Jacob?"

He would not say it aloud; his friends had kidded him for his opinion that the church bells somehow created a harmony that bound village people together. Bergen Wolfe, who played first base, had even called him *"Zauberglockmeiste,"* or "Magic Bell Master."

"Yes, I'd very much miss it."

* * *

Jacob thought all week about the conversation with Pastor Owens. The Baptist church was visible from their home, and he watched expectantly for any indication of the bell's replacement. Nothing happened, so he went to talk to the pastor after baseball practice on Friday. Alicia could not go because their family was "entertaining guests."

"Mr. Adams wouldn't talk to us," Owens told him. "It sounds like he's down on all our churches."

Jacob's parents had told him not to talk to anyone about Amos, but now, he said, "He's a businessman, so maybe he'll sell it to you if you offer him enough money."

Owens laughed. "Jacob, 'enough money' is something we don't have."

The broken bell was still in the bell tower. At Jacob's request, Owens took him up a ladder to see it and pointed out the large crack that ran nearly its full height. "It's only valuable for scrap metal," Owens said. "We'll find another bell somewhere if we can't get the one from Mr. Adams."

It bothered Jacob that such a thing could happen to a church. His parents expressed their sadness about it but offered no solutions. It worried Alicia, too, but she dismissed it as a problem they could do nothing about.

It seemed to be up to him. "Rev. Owens, I'll get that bell for you."

On the way home, his apprehension rose. He had made a

promise without thinking it through.

* * *

What had he gotten himself into? He should have told his father what he was doing. And why was he even doing it? The adage that "promises have little to do with actions" became more relevant early Saturday morning as he approached the Main Street building with a large sign over the door that said, "ADAMS CUSTOM BUILDER." Another smaller sign in the window announced "Antiques Bought & Sold."

He would make fast work of it. After all, Mr. Adams was angry at his father, not at him. He tried to keep that thought in mind.

No one was in the cluttered front room, but through a rear door leading into a back room, he saw Amos bent over a wooden cabinet that lay across two carpenter horses. As Jacob entered the room, he recognized the stain scent, like that which came from his father's brush as he refurbished their old furniture. Amos stood quickly and laid his paintbrush on a table.

In what his mother might describe as a "churlish manner," Amos said, "You're the preacher's son. What do you want?"

Jacob fought down the urge to run. The man knew who he was. How could he not? *Remember why you're here.*

"Mr. Adams, you have a bell ..."

"A bell ..."

"Mr. Kent Augustine's daughter, Alicia, said she saw a bell here for sale."

"A bell, eh?"

"A church bell. A big one. You know, like we have in our church."

"What's your first name, young Gainsworthy?"

The man was probably playing some game with him. "It's Jacob, Sir."

"Well, Jacob, I don't know who sent you, but you can carry a message back that I don't have a bell for sale, and even if I did, I wouldn't sell it to your church."

"Mr. Adams, it's not for our church. It's the Baptist church that needs a new bell. Theirs is cracked so badly that they can't use it anymore."

Amos rubbed his chin and said more civilly, "Yes, I heard about that. Too bad."

"Alicia might have seen that bell somewhere else?"

"No, she saw it here. But it's not here anymore. I sold it several months ago. Anyway, it was much smaller than what they need."

Jacob tried to hide his disappointment. *So much for trying to help. But maybe all was not lost.* "You must know a lot about bells, Mr. Adams. You might know where they can find one the right size?"

"Those old bells are scarce and expensive," Amos said, "and I doubt they could afford it."

"They might be able to," was all Jacob could think to say.

He waited for Amos to comment further. When he did not, he turned to leave.

Amos said, "Wilburn Clark, a man over on Temple Ridge has one."

"The right size?"

"Maybe even a little larger than they need."

"Is there a church there?"

"No. Clark owns a wilderness lodge. He looked for years to find the right one for his place."

"Is it inside the lodge?"

"No. The last I heard, he was going to mount it outside in a roofed shelter, but I don't know if he got around to doing that."

"Do you think he would sell the bell to the church if the price were right?"

"I doubt it. Anyway, the Baptist church couldn't match his price."

Jacob had overheard his dad talk to his mother about the "Love Fund" thing used to help needy people. He had asked about it once, and his father said he would tell him about it someday. Maybe there was money there to help pay for the bell.

"Sir, will you speak to Mr. Clark, the owner of that bell, to see if he'll sell it?"

"Don't be foolish, young man. The Baptist church will have to do its own negotiations."

It was difficult to hide his disappointment, but maybe he would change his mind about helping. "Mr. Adams, can you help them find a bell somewhere?"

Amos laughed. "So, am I to use my valuable time to trace down a bell somewhere that might fit into that church's steeple? Did your father put you up to this?"

"No, it was my idea. Anyway, Dad is very busy. Our whole family is upset right now because my grandmother is so sick. Mom spends most of her time with her."

For a moment, Amos appeared compassionate. "Yeah, I heard that she's in a bad way ..." His scowl returned. "She let me down, that woman."

"Dad didn't send me."

I think you're lying, young man. He sent you here just to harass me, didn't he? You tell him to mind his own business and let me mind mine. And you, young man, can get out of my sight right now!"

Jacob fled the store. *The man was scary.* He was nearly home before he regained his composure. *Had he stirred up trouble?* Should he tell his father what he did? It may be best to forget all about the bell.

By the time he reached his own doorway, he had decided. He said aloud, "I'm going to find a bell for that church."

CHAPTER THIRTY-FIVE

May–July 1988

Abigail Hunt died one month after Obie's impromptu church session. At Laura and Cassie's request, he officiated at her funeral, speaking words of comfort to the family and overflowing crowd of friends while at the same time soothing ancient memories.

After a service at the cemetery, where Abigail was laid to rest beside Pinky, the family hosted a smorgasbord luncheon in the spacious banquet room at *Abigail's*. As Obie looked around, he thought that the whole county might be in attendance.

He sat alone at present but searched the room for family members: Obadiah and June Paxton were filling their plates at the food bar; that would be a marriage someday—maybe soon. He would talk to Obadiah; the boy had been admitted to medical school but foolishly planned to take a year off to work in the California vineyard, ignoring the risk of losing his place at school. "Just for the experience," he had said. Cassie approved, however, so Obie needed to walk carefully in the situation.

He smiled at the sight of Jacob sitting at a table with Alicia Augustine. Jacob had admitted that they were "going steady." They were too young for that, but they did look at each other with genuine affection. *God bless them.*

He saw Laurie at a table in a far corner with Cassie and Francis Boswell. Laurie and Francis had become good friends; Francis had taken her under her scholarly wing the previous summer when Laurie volunteered at the Stafford Rest library. She would soon graduate from Buffalo and look for a teaching position. If she had any romantic interests, it had never been apparent. She was an independent young woman and would succeed at whatever she attempted.

He watched Laura and Ly Yen shuttle back and forth between the kitchen and the banquet room. Laura appeared to have assumed a supervisory role for the restaurant. Ben was absent, having rushed back to the clinic right after the church service.

Obie caught Dan as he passed by. "Is it too soon to talk about the future?" he asked his son.

"Not at all. Mom, Cassie, and I have conferred already. We'll have a family meeting soon."

"Dan, I realize I'm not a part of it, and I don't want to be, but I can't help wondering about this restaurant. Who will run it, and do you even want to keep it in the family?"

"Obie, you are family, and you're certainly involved. As for the inn, it was managed in the past by Grandmother's iron fist, but in the past year, she has given more responsibility to Laura and a few trusted employees."

"I'm sure you'll get it all sorted out."

"I'm not sure we'll keep it. It will require a family effort, and most of us have careers without time to manage any of Grandmother's extensive enterprises. Anyway, she has a will that she instructed Kent to keep secret, so we don't know yet who'll get what."

Obie had never given much thought to Abigail's business matters, but now could not help asking, "Just how extensive is her estate?"

"She owns several rental houses on Indian Knob and Blackberry Hill and properties in Evergreen and other towns. And, there's also the Inn and Stafford Rest Furniture with its outlet store."

"What about her real estate business?"

"What a headache that's going to be. The Stafford Rest branch is small, but the Evergreen one hires several people. Grandmother turned the management over to another firm, and that's something we'll soon have to deal with."

"I'm sure it's complicated," Obie said, "but we shouldn't even be thinking about that today. We're here to honor Abigail, not discuss her financial affairs."

Dan laughed. "What would she be talking about if she were here?"

"Yes, I suppose you're right."

* * *

It was several weeks after Abigail's death before Laura, as executrix, brought them together for a "reading of the will" and to discuss the "distribution of assets." Cassie told Obie that she thought it strange that her sister had said little about it before-hand.

July brought warm weather in abundance by the time they met at Ben and Laura's home by the lake. Obie was not inter-ested in going, but Cassie insisted. "You're as much a part of this family as any of us," she declared. "Anyway, I'm sure the whole thing is pretty straightforward." Obie wondered how any of Abigail's dealings could be "straightforward."

The Williamson home was a thoughtful mix of modern and Adirondack architecture. The native stone fireplace, dark today, was almost as large as the one at the inn. In the spacious living area, Obie and Cassie sat on large, fabric-covered couches fac-ing Dan and Ly Yen on another sofa. Kent Augustine and Laura sat in chairs adjacent to the couches. Ben passed out drinks. Laura's organizational skills were evident as she got right to the business of addressing the group.

Dan was not about to let formality ruin the day. "We're here to divide the spoils, I see."

Laura ignored the remark. "Some of you have questioned me about what's in the will, and I apologize for putting you off. I did that because there's so much involved that I had to learn about and understand. Kent's help has been invaluable. Mom wasn't forthcoming with her financial affairs, but she did leave a letter that stated her reasons for some of her choices. Anyway, you'll learn about it all today, and some of it will be surprising and controversial." Everyone was sitting forward, interest ap-parent.

Laura continued, "Kent will read the will to you later and even give you a copy if you wish, but first, I'll cut through the legal jargon and spell it out to you in English. Except for bank and financial accounts, I can't give you the exact values of Mom's real assets since they're subject to market value."

"Perhaps ballpark figures?" Cassie said.

"I can give you those," Kent said, "within a few hundred thousand dollars."

"Mom was exceedingly solvent," Laura said. "I wish Obadiah, Laurie, and Jacob were here. Julie, too, because they're all named in her will."

Obie found himself interested. This distribution was Abigail's last act of giving away the things she valued. Will it provide a peek into her closely guarded personal life? *For whom did she really care?*

Laura said, "Here's the simple breakdown of Mom's assets and where they're going." She cleared her throat. "Dan gets the real estate business, lock, stock, and barrel. In her letter, she said he had worked in it and knew the business better than anyone else." Obie saw a change of expression on his elder son's face that was hard to interpret. "He and Ly Yen also have the Garnet Point House, but that's not in the will since it had already been deeded to them several years ago. Mom writes that it was because of 'their unselfish care of a sometimes 'cranky and sick old lady.'"

"The factory is to be mine," Laura said, "along with the factory outlet. In her letter, she wrote, 'because of her faithful management for the past several years.'" She was silent momentarily before saying, "Thank you, Mom."

"You deserve it," Dan said. Heads nodded, including Obie's.

Laura continued: The vacant land plots and all the houses will be sold, and the proceeds will be divided evenly among Obadiah, Laurie, Jacob, and Julie. Jacob and Julie's share will go into trusts administered by Cassie.

"Mom had a substantial personal banking account," Laura said. "From that account, two million dollars will go into a trust fund for the medical clinic and will be administered by Ben." Obie glanced at Ben, who smiled. "Various charities also get a share from that banking account. What's left will be divided between Cassie and me."

"What about *Abigail's?* Dan asked. "That's a real gem."

Obie knew what was coming; Laura had already leaked

that tidbit to Cassie. "It's to go to Cassie and me," she said.

"I knew it," Dan said, laughing. "This whole thing is rigged."

"Be quiet, Dan," Laura said. "You have your share." Obie was happy to see that a sober occasion could become jovial.

"Actually," Laura said, addressing Cassie directly, "I wanted to talk to you about this, but couldn't because of the secrecy clause in the will. I'm willing to incorporate and divide the restaurant shares evenly among all the family members. It's a family affair, after all. If that's okay with you, Cassie." What choice did Cassie have, Obie thought, although he was sure she would have made the same suggestion.

Kent said, "There are several personal items she wanted to go to individuals. For instance, her Lincoln is going to Ly Yen."

Ly Yen said, "Oh, it is too much luxury. We always have trucks."

"Dan has been keeping you from the good life," Cassie said.

"What do you know, Cassie?" Laura said. "I've never seen you drive anything but a Jeep."

"And they have served me well."

Kent said, "There is one final distribution, that of Abigail's financial accounts, stocks, bonds, and the like. I must admit that I'm stunned at the worth of those."

"Dad managed some," Cassie said. "I remember him sitting at the dining room table, deciding what stocks to buy. Mom got her fortune by leveraging money she had already leveraged several times, but Dad couldn't stomach that kind of investing. I suspect that much of this came from his accounts that Mom inherited."

"Yes, I'm sure you're right," Laura said. "And yes, it's quite a large figure, more than all the rest of the estate combined." She seemed nervous. Could it be that she had been favored over the others?

Obie observed the upturned faces. These were his relatives and relatives by marriage, and they all had similar expressions. If it was not greed, it came close. Although they were already assured of substantial wealth, they were looking for more. Even Cassie was sitting forward, waiting expectantly. Obie allowed himself a moment of feeling superior; *he would never covet wealth.* And Cassie should know better. He made a mental note to speak to Jacob again about the dangers of having "too much."

"But ..." Laura said, drawing out the word, "this distribution will go to only one person."

"What!" came from collective lips.

"Yes, I know," Laura said. "I'm shocked, too. That's why I said this might be controversial."

"It's you, isn't it?" Cassie said. "Mom always liked you better."

"No, Cassie, it's not me. And she didn't like me better."

"Well, dammit, tell us who *is* getting this big pile of money."

Kent Augustine said in what sounded like a purposely theoretical tone, "Obie Gainworthy is the inheritor."

CHAPTER THIRTY-SIX

September 1988

Obie and Cassie had gone to California alone, and August had eased into September by the time they returned. They were back only a few hours when Obie received an early morning telephone call.

As they sat outside on the patio later, he told Cassie, "Carl Enslow informed me that this is definitely my last year at Stafford Rest Methodist." He tried to keep emotion from his voice. "It's certain that I'll be assigned to another church."

"And how does he know that?"

"Carl has contacts in the conference. I don't doubt that his information is correct."

Cassie appeared thoughtful before answering. "You have said more than once that we would never move away from Stafford Rest. So, I must ask, will you resign?"

He had anticipated the question. "Cassie, we must talk seriously about our future."

"Isn't that what I've been saying all along?" He was encouraged that she had smiled as she said, "This is as good a time as any."

"If you remember, Carl chastised me a few years ago. He said I was pampered and given more than I deserved. I hated to hear that, but it's made me think about my commitment, or maybe my lack of it."

"You don't lack commitment. Look at the years you've given this church."

He needed to make her understand. "Sweetheart, I've become too content. I've held things together, but I've also learned. And what I've learned may be useful somewhere else."

"So, you're just what other churches need?"

"No, Cassie. To think that way is egotistical. There's a reason the Methodist Church moves ministers around. Pastors learn from their congregations and carry that knowledge to other congregations. Perhaps what I've learned can be used elsewhere."

"Be like a troubleshooter?"

"My commitment is to go where I'm most needed."

He heard her sigh, "So, we'll be uprooted from Stafford Rest?"

"Not necessarily. We can manage it."

He heard that little clucking noise that often accompanied her thinking process. "How?"

"I'll commute. There's nowhere in the conference that can't be reached in a couple of hours. If God wants me somewhere, he'll make a way."

"Shouldn't a pastor live in the church community?"

"That's ideal but not essential."

"So, you'd travel like that for the rest of your days? That's no life for you ... or for me."

"Cassie, I can retire from pastoral ministry in a few years and then be available for interim work as long as I want. I can choose when and where. I believe God will allow me that."

"You told Jacob not to decide what God will do."

She was sharp today. "Yes, I know. But I can present God with my plan. In fact, I've already presented that plan."

She took his hand. *A good sign.* "And did God approve?"

"I'll have an answer in his good time."

"What about your writing? I know you want to get back to that."

"And I will, in good time."

"If God is willing?"

"Yes, God willing."

"Obie, there's something else we have to clear up.

"Since we're mopping the decks, tell me."

"You've been distant since I expressed an interest in wine-making. So, I want to make something clear. My interest goes no further than enjoyment. It's a hobby. Yes, I've liked learning about the different vines and the processes required to get wine from vineyard to bottle, but my real challenge has been to improve the vineyard overall. I think I've made it better. It's certainly more profitable, and achieving that satisfies some innate part of me."

"Your mother would compliment you." They both laughed.

She grabbed his hand. "But so that you understand, I'll never go to California to make wine."

"I never thought you would, Cassie. I'm sorry you think I've been distant about it. I stepped back to let you do your own thing. Maybe you should actually pursue your interest in wine-making."

"All I've done is have Neal cultivate a few vines to experiment with. Anyway, it's Obadiah who is most interested. That may be more than a hobby."

"He'll be a physician, Cassie. He'll lose interest in the vineyard."

"Maybe, or maybe not. Your grandchildren are smart and talented. They'll succeed at whatever they attempt."

"I'm a lucky man to have such a fine family."

"You are, and do you know what your luckiest thing is?"

"Tell me."

"You have me."

* * *

"Why do you think she did it?" Obie asked Kent as he eased himself into an overstuffed chair in the lawyer's office.

"Who knows Abigail Hunt's deeper thoughts? All we know is what she said in the letter that accompanied the will, that 'Obadiah Gainsworthy will decide the best use of the Hunt family financial funds.'"

"She never seemed to trust me about anything, although that did change somewhat later in her life." Kent did not know their history, and Obie saw no reason to reveal details of those old battles.

"Well, she did trust you, and in a big way."

"And I'm here to discuss my decisions and to start implementing them."

"Yes, let's get to it. We could have had other family

members present."

"I see no reason for that. I didn't even ask Cassie to come. No one seems interested. It's been several months since the reading of the will, and not a single family member has said anything to me about it, not even Cassie."

Kent laughed. "Obie, surely you know they're on pins and needles about what you'll do. They should hear it. If I were in your place, I would already have told them."

"Perhaps, but I'll get everybody together this weekend. Have a picnic, maybe."

"A picnic is always good."

"Kent, we've brainstormed ways to use Abigail's money, but there's one thing we didn't discuss, something I've finally decided about. She left funds to the medical clinic in her will, but the facility is bursting at the seams. The Main Street building is far too small. They need a new and much larger space since they're pulling in patients from all over the area. I've looked into the purchase of vacant land on South Clearwater Road."

Kent nodded. "A larger clinic is certainly needed, and it's a splendid use of those funds. Will you supervise the construction?"

"Oh, no. I'll have a committee for that. We'll secure an architect knowledgeable in the field, but local carpenters and contractors will do the construction. And, of course, you'll handle all our legal matters."

"Abigail would be pleased. It will honor her."

"Yes, her *and* Pinky."

"I bet you already have a name in mind?"

"I do. It will be called 'The Pinkerton and Abigail Hunt Medical Center.' But, of course, the committee will have the final say on that."

"Obie, I can't think of a better use for her money."

"And that's not all. Additional funds in both their names will go to educational scholarships for area students and to the Evergreen and Stafford Rest libraries for expansion in both size and inventory. Plus, select veteran groups will receive support."

Kent seemed in thought before saying, "Your plans are

extensive, but everything costs more than expected. I know that Abigail's accounts are sizable, but are you sure there's enough for all this?"

"I believe so. If not, don't forget that I control Annie's fund, and it can make up for any shortfall."

"Do you still want nothing from Abigail's accounts to go to family members?"

"That's correct. Everyone has already received sufficiently."

"There will be disappointment."

"I don't care. Abigail gave me this task to administer as I see fit. I didn't ask for it any more than I asked for Annie's fortune. But I'll do it my way since it was dumped in my lap."

"Obie, you asked me why I think she gave you this money. Now, I turn it around and ask you why *you* think she did it."

Obie sought to capture the memories from that first night after he received the news of Abigail's unexpected gift. At first, he suspected she might have lost her mind, but quickly replaced that thought with the knowledge that she never did anything without clear and purposeful planning.

"Kent, she was asking forgiveness."

"Yours?"

"No, not mine. She could never express such things to individuals. She was asking for God's forgiveness. She was burdened with all the intrigue, which were surely shady deals in her life, and the questionable things she must have done to amass all this money. Maybe she considered me to be in the best position to advocate forgiveness for her sins. Of course, I'm not the one who forgives sins, but I'll do the best I can to use her fortune for the common good."

"And I'll help in whatever way I can. And while you're here, I want to suggest some changes in your own financial realm, namely, the handling of Annie's funds. You should bring everything into one place. Since I already manage most of your affairs, let's get the accounts from the Hartford firm into one basket."

"Yes, let's do that."

"Also, your Love Fund is a loose entity. It's been run by one person who has exclusive control. It needs to be in a foundation with a board of directors."

"Yes, I've thought about that. Family members can run it. Also, I'm changing the name. How does 'The Jacob and Priscilla Gainsworthy Foundation' sound to you?"

"Splendid idea. I'll begin work on it today. But, were you serious about a family picnic?"

"You bet! You'll come, of course?"

"We will. I want to see the faces when you announce these decisions."

* * *

"You're rich, now," Alicia said as she held Jacob's hand under the picnic table. They sat apart from the rest of their picnicking families. "What will you do with it all?"

He had never thought of Grandmother Abigail as "rich." It had not occurred to him, even as he listened to his parents talk about "dividing the estate," that it in any way affected him.

"It'll help next year when I go to college."

"Help? You could probably buy part of the school?"

Jacob shrugged. It was not that big a deal. Most of it was tied up in property and would be, for a while. He and Dad talked about money. His father had said more than once: "Money does great good, but it's the love of money that harms."

Earlier that afternoon, he had watched faces as his father revealed the decisions about where most of the money was going. It was evident that some did not share his father's views. *Who was right?*

It was another subject, however, that he wanted to discuss with Alicia. "Speaking of colleges, it's our senior year, and we must make applications soon. I've talked to our advisor and know what to do."

"Yes, me too."

"I've read material about schools that appeal to me."

"Me too." She seemed reluctant.

"I want to play baseball, and I might be able to get a scholarship somewhere, but even if I can't, that's okay." He hesitated a moment. "If we discuss it together, we can decide what schools to apply to. We've never seriously discussed it."

"If you want to, but don't forget that we have different interests."

"I want a liberal education. Dad and Mom think it's the best way to prepare for seminary. Why don't we get together some night and ..."

"Jacob, you know that my interest is more in business."

He had not expected resistance. *Maybe she didn't understand.* "We can go to the same school," he said. "Lots of schools have broad electives. And almost all have baseball teams. We can find one that suits us both."

"It sounds more like you want us to choose a school based on your needs. That's not fair to me, or to my needs."

It took a few moments of awkward silence for him to understand her viewpoint. *What was he thinking, putting himself first?* "I'm sorry, Alicia. You're right. It's just that I want so badly for us to be together."

She was quiet for so long that he began to worry. Finally, she said, "How long have we been going together?"

"A couple of years, I guess."

"No, it's longer than that. And you should know that I make my own decisions about such matters."

He could not restrain a sigh. "If we go to different schools, we'd be apart," he said, stating the obvious.

"Yes, but we would see each other during vacation breaks and the long summer periods. And personal computers are making it easy to write letters."

"I don't have a computer. Dad says they're a fad."

"My parents are getting one. My dad wants to keep his records on it."

Enough about computers. "Alicia, if we're not together, we'll meet other people. You'll see other boys, and I'll be friends with other ..."

"No, Jacob! You're my boyfriend. And I'm your girlfriend. I would never be with anyone else." She paused. "Would you?"

"I'd not plan to, but ..."

"Look at Obadiah and Jane. They attended different

schools, and now they're engaged."

"That's true, but don't forget that things nearly fell apart when he went to California for a year to learn about how the vineyard works."

"Well, he's back and in med school, and she'll join him next summer after they get married. See, it all worked out for them."

"That's their lives, not ours." He hesitated; he needed to say what he was thinking. *How would she take it?* He plunged ahead. "We could get married right after we graduate from high school. We'd be old enough."

Her face showed astonishment. "No, we would not be old enough. Don't talk foolishness, Jacob."

"You said you wanted to marry me someday."

"And I do, but I said 'someday.' After we finish college, that's what I meant. It's ridiculous to talk about marriage now. We can marry after college and be together while you're in seminary."

"Hundreds of schools in the country could give us the education we need. Let's at least do some planning together."

"All right." She grabbed his hand again. "This weekend, in your barnroom?"

"I'll reserve it. But so that you know, I won't give up on us going somewhere together.

His parents had a similar objective many years ago, although their plan had failed. *He would not let that happen.*

"Alicia, wherever we go, you'll be my girlfriend. That won't change."

"It'd better not." She squeezed his hand harder. Her hand was strong and yet so soft.

* * *

Jacob had told his father nothing of his "discussion" with Amos Adams about the bell. But now, months later, he knew that he must. There was guilt for not telling his parents, but he also needed to act on his promise to find a bell for the Baptist church.

Village people had noticed the absence of the Baptist bell

that sent out its Sunday morning call to worship. He had told Rev. Owens that the bell Alicia saw was no longer for sale but that another bell was available if the owner could be persuaded to sell it. Telling his father was harder.

"What, you went to Amos with this?" was his father's response as they sat in the study on a rainy day in late September. "Why would you do that ... and without telling me?"

"I only wanted to help. The Baptists need a new bell."

His father's scowl softened. "I know you meant well, and I'm pleased by your compassion, but it's the Baptist church's business and not ours."

"I miss their bell, and a lot of other people do, too. Don't you miss it, Dad?"

His father smiled. "Of course I miss it." He saw a faraway look in his father's eyes. "I grew up here, so I've heard those bells for a long time. But coordinating our ring times did make a big difference."

It seemed a good time to open the discussion he intended. "Dad, can our church, or maybe that Love Fund, help them buy that bell?"

His father rubbed his chin. "I'm not sure we should. From what you've told me, there is likely no bell for sale. And even if the one Amos mentioned can be purchased, it may be expensive. I haven't talked to Rev. Owens about it, but I bet they're looking to find one less expensive."

"Yeah, something that won't sound the same?"

"Yes, there is that."

"People loved the sound of that bell. I saw it, Dad. Pastor Owens took me up in the bell tower."

Jacob knew he had his father's interest when he asked, "Is it like ours?"

"It is. It's nearly a yard across and made of bronze. The crack is big enough for me to put my finger in it."

"That's too bad, Jacob, but I'll have to think about helping them buy a new bell."

Jacob could not hide his impatience. "They've been without a bell for a long time now."

His father was biting his lip. "Do you know that man's

name, the one with the bell Amos mentioned?"

"His name is Wilburn Clark. He has it."

His father's face brightened. "Wait a minute," he said as he went across the room and took a newspaper from his desk. He scanned it a moment before asking, "From Temple Ridge?"

"That's right."

His dad held out the newspaper. "I thought I recognized that name. Mr. Clark had a bad accident last week. His lodge caught on fire, and he was badly burned. This article was in the newspaper, and a couple of parishioners mentioned it Sunday in their prayer requests. The lodge appears to be a wreck. I think that the bell will be up for sale."

Jacob could not be happy about someone's bad luck, but this felt like an opportunity.

CHAPTER THIRTY-SEVEN

October–November 1988

Two significant concerns preyed on Obie's conscience, and he put off making decisions about them until late October. He was bowing to his compassionate son's request to help obtain a bell for the Baptist church, and he would address the matter of Amos Adam's estrangement from their church.

The first seemed straightforward; he had learned from Chet that Wilburn Clark, recovering from his burns in the hospital in Saratoga Springs, was putting his wilderness lodge up for sale. "Damage is too extensive for him to undertake," Chet told him. "He said that he's going to sell everything he can, including restaurant supplies and such, so I'm sure that bell will be for sale."

It remained to inform Owens of the opportunity to accept financial help from the Love Fund, or what would soon be the "Jacob and Pricilla Gainworthy Foundation."

The other matter, that of bringing Amos back into the fold, was also much on his mind. This was his last year at Stafford Rest Methodist, a bittersweet year.

On the one hand, he felt good about his years here. Membership was increased, bridges were built to the other churches and the community, and he had been faithful in adding disciples for Christ.

But on the other hand, failure to solve the enmity with Amos tarnished his image of himself as a "good and caring pastor." How could he leave with that hanging over his head? He had prayed about it often, even going to the ridge twice to plead for answers.

On this Saturday, Obie sat with Jacob in the church office. They had discussed the progress of Jacob's second-grade Sunday School class, but as his son got up to go, Obie said, "You're doing an excellent job teaching the class, but I know you want to talk about that bell."

Jacob laughed. "I thought you would never tell me what you've decided."

Obie was pleased that his son was learning patience. He said, "I've discussed the matter with the Love Fund administrator, and half the bell cost will be paid if it is bought at a decent price."

Jacob was smiling. "Wonderful. When will you tell Pastor Owens?"

"Today. But you can do that yourself. You've earned that right. Jacob, you must understand that there's still work to do, whether by the Baptists or by us. It's still to be determined if that bell is for sale and is the right size. And, of course, if it's affordable. These big bells are antiques, and they're expensive. There is also the problem of installing it in their steeple. If it's as big as ours, it's cumbersome."

Jacob shrugged. "Mr. Adams would know about the bell's size." He added, "If he'll tell us."

Obie said. "We might have to get the information from Mr. Clark, but only after he's well enough to talk."

"We could go to see the bell. Isn't it close by?"

"Temple Ridge is forty miles from here. Chet told me the lodge is in the backwoods, with only a private road to access it. It was a summer lodge for years and closed in winter. We can hike in, though."

"I'm always up for a hike. You know that."

"Fine. We can make it a family thing with Mom and Julie. We'll take a picnic basket."

"And Alicia can go, too."

Obie expected that response; Jacob had included Kent and Cara's daughter in almost all their recent family outings.

Jacob turned back at the door. "Dad, there's something else." Obie saw him hesitate. "I'm not sure how you'll feel about this, but I'm worried about Mr. Adams."

"I worry about him, too." He had not shared his recent thoughts with Jacob and wondered what was coming. "What do you have in mind?"

"I know he's not a nice man, and you don't get along."

"To say the least."

"But he was active in church, and he did useful work, until you kicked him out."

There was obvious pain in his son's words. "Jacob, I didn't kick him out. He attempted to hurt the church, and we disciplined him for it. It was his choice to leave."

"Okay, but he needs to come back."

His son must have listened to his thoughts. "I know that. But what he really needs is to repent, and I fear Amos won't do that. He's too convinced that his way is the only way."

Jacob stepped back into the room. "Dad, in one of your sermons about a year ago, you said that we must be careful how we pull people into the spiritual way of thinking."

"I don't think I said it exactly like that, but yes, we should be gentle with our invitations."

"You talked about 'stepping stones,' like stones placed in a stream to get someone safely across. I asked you about it later at home, and you told me that the way of a good leader was to give people stepping stones. Dad, Mr. Adams needs some stepping stones?"

Obie's tears welled. *Jacob's thinking was more Christian than his.*

He suddenly realized that the two things he had worried about were not separate problems. They were related, with one solution—and he knew exactly what that was.

"Yes, he does need stepping stones, Son, and we're going to give those to him."

* * *

Obie had a plan and prayed that Amos would listen. He first thought about engaging him in conversation at his store on Main Street, but on a mid-week morning in early November, he caught him on neutral ground.

Amos' truck was parked in the Stafford Rest Furniture Outlet parking lot. He still badmouthed the church, but Frances verified that he routinely purchased their bargain-priced furniture and antique pieces.

Amos was exiting the store carrying a small table on one shoulder. "Looks like a good piece," Obie said as cheerfully as he could manage.

Amos frowned as he said, "I suppose you're going to tell me that I don't have the right to pick up furniture here that people are throwing away?"

"Not at all. You have the same rights as everyone. That's what the church store is for. I look for things here myself." He forced his best smile. "Amos, I'd like to talk if you have the time."

"I'm busy, Reverend. Some of us work for a living, you know."

"What I want to discuss with you is work-related."

Amos put the table down. "Well, make it quick."

"There's a bench over there." Obie pointed to a corner of the outlet store and said, "Let's go sit." He picked up the table and placed it on his shoulder, leaving Amos with no choice but to follow.

Amos appeared reluctant as he sat. "What's this about?"

"Amos, do you need work?"

"What do you mean? Of course, I need work. Times are hard, and why would I need to talk to you about work?"

"I'm sure you don't need my help finding work, Amos, but you do have specialized skills for a job I know about. That's what I meant."

"So, what's this job that needs my skills, and who's offering it?" He studied Obie's face. "And what's your interest in this?"

"You know, don't you, that the Baptist church lost its bell? They …"

"Yeah, I know all about that. You sent your son to haggle me about it."

"No, I did not." *He must keep control.* "That was Jacob's idea. He went to you on his own."

"Why does he even care? It's not your church. For that matter, why do *you* care?"

As much as he wanted to preach a lesson on Christian caring, Obie did not want to get sidetracked. "Jacob talked me into getting involved. That's why I'm talking to you about it."

"Well, as I told him, I no longer have a bell for sale. So that's the end of it."

"No, it's not the end. Wilburn Clark lost his lodge in a fire and ..."

"Yeah, I know about that. That's too bad. I like Clark. I understand he's selling everything."

"Yes, and he has sold that bell to the Baptist church."

Amos looked genuinely surprised. "They made a deal?"

"They did, and the bell is waiting to be picked up."

Obie had presented Owens with the Love Fund gift news; the pastor was initially reluctant, but once Obie explained the nature of the Fund, he accepted the gift. That was when Obie nervously floated the idea that an expert was required to supervise the bell's installation in the tower and that Amos was the logical choice. Thankfully, Owens agreed. But there was no reason to give Amos all the background information that had brought them to this point.

The reconciliation plan would fall into place if Amos took the job; working together could create an atmosphere of trust, a condition never shared with the man. Obie had revealed his intention to Jacob, and his son responded with, "Yeah, lead him back, stone by stone."

Obie said, "Amos, they need your assistance to install the bell. I told them that you are the expert they need."

"What's your part in all this? You and me don't work well together."

"Yes, Amos, I know. But for this once, let's put aside our egos and do a good deed. As for my part, I've told Rev. Owens that our church will get the bell to them. It's paid for, so we only need to go pick it up."

"It'll take at least two strong men."

"Amos, will you install the bell for them?" Obie wanted to nail it down.

"How much are they paying?"

When Obie told him, Amos shrugged, but there was interest. He said, "It's for a good cause, so I guess I can. You say you have the job of getting the bell to the church. So, what's my part in that?"

"We need you to transport it. It's heavy, and we don't want to damage it. It will be your responsibility to move it safely to the Baptist church and to install it."

"It's probably four hundred pounds with the supporting frame and wheel. It'll take two or three men to handle it."

"You'll use your truck, won't you?"

"How else?" Amos said, looking disgusted. "Am I going to carry it on my back?"

Obie controlled himself. "We'll help you move it, Amos. Mr. Clark said it was never used at his inn. He had planned to mount it in a new structure, but hadn't gotten around to building that."

"That lodge is isolated at this time of year. The access road will be closed."

"I know. My family and I recently walked in from the main road. We should have driven. It was quite a hike. It's steep, too, so we'll need to get there before it's snowed in."

I have other jobs lined up, so the sooner, the better."

"Yes, let's get it done. I'm free on Saturday afternoon. The weather is mild, and my grandson, Obadiah, will be here for a couple of days, so I'll get him and Jacob to help. Is that enough hands to handle the job?"

"I guess it'll do."

"Amos, thank you. You're performing a great service."

Amos did not answer but picked up the table, placed it on his shoulder, and walked out toward the parking lot.

* * *

Jacob was excited as he waited at the end of their driveway. At last, today, they would have the bell. He was proud to have played his part in its acquisition. Bells were so important in inspiring people. Alicia wanted to go with them to pick it up, but her father had vetoed that.

Obadiah soon arrived, having driven up Blackberry Hill in his father's older model sedan. As Jacob climbed in, he gave his cousin a quick slap-five.

The plan was to follow Amos Adams' truck to Temple Ridge. His dad would ride with Amos. Obadiah's car coughed as they entered the furniture outlet's parking lot. His dad came out to meet them.

"Obadiah, it's good of you to help," his father said. "Your studies give you little time for visits, so to spend even part of a day helping us is very generous."

"Glad to assist, Grandfather," Obadiah said, "but I've never been to Temple Ridge, so we'll follow you?"

"You can, but Jacob knows the way in case we get separated."

Jacob said, "I was there with Dad."

The truck went ahead, and they followed, but they were not halfway up Garnet Point Hill before the engine sputtered, and the car limped forward with only a few starts and stops before quitting altogether. Obadiah pounded the steering wheel in frustration. "I knew it!" he said. "I told Dad it was on its last legs."

"What now?" Jacob said.

"I'll get Dad's other car," Obadiah said, then added, "But that's probably not the best solution. He's on duty at the clinic and likes to keep it handy. What about your mother's Jeep?"

"She's at a teacher meeting in Tupper Lake."

Obadiah snapped his fingers. "I know what we'll do," he said, his voice animated. "I know exactly what we'll do."

"What?"

"We'll fly out there. I talked to Dad last night about that area. He knows it. He said he had landed there on the pond. I'll get him to take us."

"Isn't the floatplane in winter storage?"

"We normally have it bedded in by this time, but Ernie's busy. It's been moved from our dock to his, but it's still in the water. Thankfully, the lake hasn't frozen yet."

Perhaps flying was a better way. Mr. Adams and his father would reach the inn in less than an hour and wonder why they had not followed. It was essential to get help to them.

"Are you sure about this, Obadiah?"

"It's only a ten-minute flight. Dad won't be away from the clinic more than half an hour, an hour at the most. I'm sure he'll do it. It's the best answer. If we hurry, we can even get there ahead of your dad."

* * *

It had been a lonely stretch of highway even before they turned onto the side road that led to the inn. A chain stretched across the road a hundred yards in, halting travel.

The chain had no lock, so Obie removed it and motioned Amos through. "The road is soggy," he said through Amos' rolled-down window, "and it's steep, too."

"Get in," Amos said. "This truck has seen worse."

The vehicle performed well in a lower gear, but for a quarter mile, it was slow-going. They eventually reached a plateau where the road leveled out, and they saw the inn in the distance. The road surface was still soft, with ruts, so they crept along with the engine straining.

Where were Jacob and Obadiah? In the parking lot, he had noticed the heavy exhaust emitting from Obadiah's car. Maybe they had engine trouble? Even so, that car would never make it this far on this road. They would have to walk in. It was two o'clock now, and darkness came early this time of the year. This project would take longer than they had planned.

There was another worry. "Amos, I noticed a big drop in the temperature. A huge drop."

"Yeah, that was in the forecast. Don't you watch the weather news?"

"I guess I missed that. It's been above freezing for several days, so I never …"

"You should have planned better." Amos's voice rose above the engine roar. "It's the same way you run a …"

Obie cut him off. "Amos, we have a job to do. Let's get it done. Then, you can call me out."

Amos grunted. "Reverend, I've got a lot of calling out to do." Their conversation to this point had been affable.

"I'm sure, but right now, we have other worries, like where are Jacob and Obadiah, and can the two of us lift the bell onto the truck without their help? Even if we can, will the added weight cause us to get stuck on the road?"

Amos laughed. "Sounds like you're panicking. This was

your idea, Preacher, so quit your complaining."

Obie remained quiet but felt subdued. There was no real reason to worry. Even if Jacob and Obadiah did not arrive today, they would manage. They could force a door and stay overnight in the lodge.

Amos said, "The temperature drop is actually a good thing. Mud freezes, you know. It'll firm up the road."

They finally reached the inn. The bell sat on a platform beneath a covered patio that occupied space between the main building and a smaller building. It would be easy to back the truck up to it. This would work, after all.

As Obie stepped from the truck, he was amazed by the severity of the cold air on his face. Why had he not watched the weather news? He shoved that thought aside and determined, as he had told Amos, to "get the job done." Somehow, they would load that bell onto the truck bed and get back to civilization with it.

* * *

Jacob was buckled in with his headset adjusted for speaking to Obadiah over the engine noise. On the dock, Dan gave a "thumbs up" as he unhooked a line and shoved the airplane away from the pier. At the same time, Obadiah increased power, and the Cessna moved out into deeper water. He opened the throttle, and the water pounded the pontoons until they lifted off the surface and into the air. The sunlight was brilliant in Jacob's eyes.

Obadiah twisted dials on the panel. "Just setting a course to get us to the pond," he said.

It had taken longer to get going than planned. Dan was with a patient and made several phone calls after that. At first, he was reluctant to release the keys to the airplane, suggesting they use his car.

"That will take too long," Obadiah had argued.

"The airplane has sat there waiting for Ernie to winterize it. And it's getting bitterly cold. If you'll wait a couple of hours, I'll fly you out there myself."

"Dad," Obadiah argued, "we need to help lift that bell onto the truck. Two more hours is pushing it to fly there and back before dark."

Dan had relented, but Jacob saw that he did not like it. Before the cabin door closed, he had said to Obadiah, "Circle the pond a couple of times to see that you have a clear landing area. It's not like the lake. There are a couple of dead trees on the north end and brush in the water on both ends. I trust your piloting skills, but be careful."

It felt like they were in the air longer than the ten minutes predicted. Obadiah said when the pond was in sight, "Help me look for the best spot to land."

They circled the area twice. The log structure looked intact, although Jacob had been there and knew there was severe fire damage inside. He could see the walkway and the dock it led to.

"See that bunch of lily pads?" Obadiah said. "I'll set her down just beyond that. We'll have plenty of room to spare and not be far from the dock."

"I see Mr. Adams' truck by the building."

They circled again. Finally, Obadiah said, "Okay, here we go." The engine became much quieter as they pitched toward the pond. The cluster of lily pads rushed toward them. The impact was light as they touched the water, and there was a sense of slowing.

"No!" Obadiah yelled as the engine roared back to full power. Jacob saw that he was trying to avoid whatever was in the water, and the airplane was straining to lift.

"Get up … get up," Obadiah said in a surprisingly calm voice.

There came a sound of metal and a jolt as the pontoons hit a solid surface. Jacob's body surged forward against the restraints.

They were still moving, and the engine was roaring. Obadiah was trying to lift into the air again, but Jacob saw that they would never clear the trees at the pond's edge.

Obadiah cut the power. Still sounding calm, he said, "Jacob, hang on. We're going to have a hard stop."

Two large dead trees straight ahead came toward them so fast that Jacob felt he should duck. As they struck, the sound hurt his ears, and the impact was violent. The silence came so quickly and was so complete that he thought he might be deafened until he heard the startled cries of a waterbird.

They were nearly face down. Below, he saw the bent prop and the water level several inches up the windscreen. His seat belt held him in place. There was pain in his right leg. Obadiah was pitched forward toward the yoke, but he was not moving. Jacob fought to keep from passing out.

CHAPTER THIRTY-EIGHT

November 1988

"They've crashed!" Amos's voice was shrill with surprise.

Obie experienced fear with each step as they ran toward the dock. "That's Dan's plane," he shouted.

There was no way to know who was in the airplane, but it had to be someone from his family. "We have to help them," he said as his feet struck the wooden flooring of the dock. He could hear Amos's labored breathing.

"There's no boat here," Amos said, "but I saw a canoe back at the lodge. We'll have to go back and get it."

"No one is getting out," Obie said. "They could sink."

"Let's not waste time!" Amos yelled. "We need that canoe!"

Negative thoughts tormented Obie as they rushed back to the lodge and worked frantically to remove the canvas that covered the canoe and a large rowboat. His panic intensified as they carried the canoe back down the pathway to the dock.

"I don't see anyone yet," Obie said as they reached the water's edge.

"Maybe they can't get the doors open."

As they launched the canoe into the water, Obie strained to see any movement from within the aircraft.

The airplane had come to rest about a hundred yards from the dock and looked to be wedged between two trees; its tail was sticking up. As they paddled toward the wreckage, Amos kept shouting, "Are you okay? Answer us so we know you're okay."

Obie yelled, too. There was no answer.

* * *

Jacob's head was spinning, but he tried to focus on the situation. *They had crashed; he was alive.* He saw that Obadiah was bleeding from his nose and not moving.

Jacob shook him. "Come on! Wake up! Open your eyes!"

He punched Obadiah several times on his shoulder and was relieved when his cousin said, "I'm all right. Stop pounding on me."

Jacob tried to stay calm. His father always stressed the necessity of remaining cool-headed in dire situations, and Grandpa Ken had fortified that advice with tales of his adventures gone wrong.

"We hit a log in the water," Obadiah said, his speech slightly slurred. After a few seconds, he added, "I didn't have enough space to lift off."

Jacob cared little for details about what had happened; his concern was their present predicament. "We have to get out!" he said.

Obadiah responded with grunts before saying, "We're not sinking. That's good."

"The water is over my feet."

"It won't get any higher."

"How do you know?"

"We're stable," Obadiah said while pushing and pounding on his door. He added, "At least for now."

Jacob pushed on his own door. "It won't budge," he said. "It's stuck."

"Mine is free. I can get out this side."

"Are you hurt, Obadiah?"

"I'm okay, just a little addled. This damned restraint didn't do its job. He chuckled. "Something got in the way of my nose." Jacob was glad that Obadiah's innate humor was intact.

Jacob's right leg was painful. He ran his hand down the side but could not reach below his knee. His hand came away bloody. *Don't panic.* He put both hands behind his knee and yanked, but his leg would not budge.

"I'm stuck, and I'm bleeding, too."

Obadiah reached across Jacob's lap. After an exploration, he said, "Your leg is wedged. We can get out my side once I get out of this useless harness."

"Should I unhook my harness? It's keeping me from falling forward."

"No, keep it on."

"Do you think someone will rescue us?"

"If the radio is working, I'll send a message that we've had an accident but are okay."

While Obadiah swore at the radio, Jacob continued trying to free himself. Nothing worked. In exasperation, he said, "Obadiah, get out and get help. Dad is out there at the lodge. I saw the truck, but they might not know what's happened."

"Yeah, that sounds like the best plan. This damned radio isn't working, and we have to get you out."

For the first time, Jacob realized that he was very cold. He had worn his lighter jacket instead of his parka. He should have watched the weather reports. Now, he was shivering, and his teeth were chattering.

Obadiah pushed open his side door and slipped through. "I'll get help and return as soon as I can," he said, but a moment later added with despair in his voice, "I can't swim ashore in this weather."

Jacob saw that the water on the windshield had begun to freeze. He wrapped his arms around himself, and that was when he heard voices calling their names.

* * *

Amos paddled, and when the canoe was only a few yards from the airplane, Obie heard and recognized his grandson's voice. "We're okay, Grandpa, but Jacob's stuck."

They glided under a bent wing to the side of the cabin where Obadiah sat in the open doorway. Both wings had collapsed enough to allow the cabin to sink and submerge the lower half of the cabin underwater. "Is there much water inside?" Obie asked.

"Some, but right now, it's not coming in. But the whole thing is unsteady. It could slip into deeper water. We have to get Jacob out right now."

They helped Obadiah into the canoe. His nose was bleeding, but his voice was steady. "I messed up, bad. Dad will kill me."

"You're both alive. That's what matters."

"What happened?" Amos asked.

Obadiah's head was down, but his voice was clear. "We'd just touched the water when we hit a log. Smacked it pretty hard. I tried to get back in the air again, but we ran out of space."

They kept the canoe tight against the cabin area where Obie could see the interior. Jacob looked up at him and said, "It's good to see you. Dad, but I want to get out of here. I'm freezing."

"We'll get you out, Son ... and soon."

Amos looked inside. "Can you move your leg at all?" he asked.

"No. The door is pushed in against my calf. It feels numb."

"What can we do, Amos?" Obie asked. He could not hide his concern.

"Stay calm, Reverend ... one step at a time. I'll climb in and see what it looks like. Then, if I need tools, I'll go back and get them from the truck. But we'll get him out."

Obie was amazed at Amos's calmness. He asked, "What can I do?"

"You and me will take this failed pilot ashore and up to the lodge. I'll get my tools while you search the lodge for something warm to wrap around Jacob to keep him from freezing. But first, I need to assess the situation."

"Amos, do whatever needs to be done."

Amos climbed in carefully to prevent rocking the fuselage. Obadiah sat quietly in the canoe with his parka hood pulled over his head. Obie watched and waited.

Amos sat in the left seat, bent over Jacob, while his hand explored the area between the door and the seat. Then, he sat up and said to Obie, "I need you to get my tools. This thing is unsteady. I'm afraid it'll slip into deeper water if I move around. Here are my keys. You'll need them to unlock my toolbox on the truck."

Obie took the keys that Amos passed through the door. "What tools do you need?"

"A crowbar is the main thing. And shears. There's also a

heavy hammer. Hell, bring the smaller box with the ratchets, too. I may have to take the door apart. You're a smart man. Bring whatever you can carry that you think I might use."

"I'll get back to you as soon as I can," he said while handing his jacket to Amos for Jacob's benefit.

"Hurry up. We're freezing here."

* * *

Jacob tried to be patient and think of things other than the cold and the danger. The man beside him was silent, apparently absorbed in thought. He moved once, reaching for a glove he had placed on the dash. Whether through that movement or by chance, the fuselage shifted slightly.

"Don't worry," Amos said. "We're not sinking. Not yet, anyway."

"What's taking so long?"

"It's only been ten minutes."

It seemed longer. "Sorry. I'm cold, that's all."

Amos's voice was softer than Jacob expected. "Well, just stay tough," he said. "That's the way to get through things like this."

Amos was a mystery. The subdued man in the pilot's seat, so close that they rubbed elbows, did not fit the pattern Jacob had formed in his mind. Their encounter in Amos's store left an impression of someone angry at the universe and unwilling to compromise except for his own benefit. And there was never anything positive in the tidbits of information from his father, either directly or overheard. Jacob wanted to know more.

"Mr. Adams, we never talked before, just you and me, except that once at your store."

After a pause, Amos said, "We never had reason to. I don't talk much to kids."

"Don't you like kids?"

"Sure, I like kids ... if they're not smart-asses."

It was Jacob's turn to pause as he searched for the right words. He managed, "I didn't mean to be disrespectful about the bell."

Amos grunted and mumbled something Jacob could not understand before saying, "No, you did well. Better than your dad, in fact. It's just that I don't talk to kids your age much. I never had the chance."

He waited, hoping to hear more, but Amos was silent. Cold lips made speech difficult, but Jacob managed, "Did you grow up in Stafford Rest, Mr. Adams?"

"No, I'm from Pennsylvania. Coal mining town. I came here in sixty-nine."

"Is that when you joined our church?"

"Yeah, soon after." Amos's calm voice changed to the one he remembered. "And, now, that seems like it was a big mistake."

Jacob would not discuss the rift between Amos and his father. He said, "Why did you come here?"

Amos answered in such a low tone that Jacob strained to hear. "I wanted to get away from there." He turned his head to face Jacob. "Listen here, young man, you ask too many questions. Don't be so nosy."

Jacob had many more questions to ask, but at that moment, his father's voice came from outside, loud and clear. "I have the tools, Jacob. We'll soon have you out."

Amos' baritone input was, "It's about damn time you got here, Reverend."

CHAPTER THIRTY-NINE

November–December 1988

The crash of Dr. Dan Williamson's airplane by his son was big news throughout the area. Reporters came from as far away as Saratoga Springs to interview the rescued and the rescuers. For days afterward, Jacob told and retold his story to classmates, teachers, and church members. His bruised leg healed within a week.

"You just like the attention," Alicia told him.

"I don't," he protested, "and I don't want to think about it. I nearly froze."

"This is the coldest early winter since we moved here."

"And it follows the warmest summer I can remember."

Conditions soon returned to normal for Jacob, but less so for Obadiah, who had initially endured Dan's displeasure at his lack of "horse sense" but was then pardoned when Dan admitted his poor judgment. "I should not have let him go with so little preparation," he said.

The FAA inspected the crash site and interviewed Obadiah concerning the procedures he followed before and during the accident. He told Jacob by phone that he was grounded until they finished their investigation and was "very embarrassed" by the whole thing.

The airplane was a total loss. The pond froze quickly, trapping it in the ice where it would be until spring. Ly Yen told Jacob that Dan was already looking for a replacement.

Despite the difficulties, the bell was finally safe in the Baptist church narthex, waiting for Amos' installation. Pastor Owens predicted that it would ring for Sunday services in mid-January.

In the following weeks, everyone seemed to forget about the accident, and by mid-December, Christmas preparations were in full swing. Jacob met with organizers from the other churches to plan a combined Christmas Eve service. He was busy, but it was work he enjoyed.

Nevertheless, he had pushed aside a topic he wanted to discuss with his father. The opportunity came on a Saturday afternoon after they put away their skis following a brisk trip around the ridge.

"Dad, I want to talk about something with you, and I'm not sure how you'll feel about it."

"That sounds serious. Let's go talk in the barnroom."

It was cold in the barnroom, and they kept their parkas on as Jacob placed firewood in the stove and lit a pile of kindling underneath. His father sat in the rocker, and he sat in the straight-backed chair.

"What's going on, Son?"

"It's about Amos Adams."

His father grunted and scratched his chin. "I had hoped for a quiet and peaceful Saturday afternoon."

"Dad, let's be fair. He helped rescue us. He stayed with me and freed my leg."

"Yes, you're right; he did that and deserves credit. Your mother and I invited him to have dinner with us at Abigail's, but he declined. The newspaper articles emphasized his part, which can only help his business. But why do you want to talk about him?"

"It's just something that needs to be said." *Was that too blunt?*

"Jacob, you know you can talk to me about anything. What's bothering you? Has Amos said something to you?"

He cleared his throat. "Dad, I know you and Mr. Adams have your issues, but ..."

"That's putting it mildly. He's been a thorn in my side. And he was a thorn for Rev. Enslow before me. I daresay it was the same for previous ministers."

"No, he wasn't here before Rev. Enslow. He told me that he came from Pennsylvania in sixty-nine."

"Humm, I didn't know that. I thought he was a longtime resident."

Jacob took a deep breath. "So, if you didn't know that, then maybe there are other things you don't know about him?"

His father stared at him as if not sure what to say. There was that thoughtful pause before he answered questions, a trait his mother pretended to hate. He said, "You've talked to Amos, it seems. What is it about him that I ought to know?"

"We talked some, and for a little while, he was different."

"Different, how?"

"He talked in a quieter voice."

"Well, yes, that is different. What did he talk about?"

"Not much, except for telling me he came from Pennsylvania." Jacob paused; he needed to get a point across. "Dad, it wasn't so much about what he said as it was about what he didn't say."

"And we can't know anything about what he didn't say, can we?"

"I think he wanted to say more."

His father picked up the poker, opened the stove door, and punched aimlessly at logs that had barely begun to burn. "Look, Jacob, I don't know what opinions you've formed about Amos with only a few minutes of conversation, but let me tell you this." The stove door closed with a metallic clang, "I've dealt with the man for a dozen years, and he's never strayed far from being the mean, self-righteous buffoon I'm sure he has always been."

"Except that he helped us get the bell, and he helped me out of that wrecked airplane."

"Humm. Of course, you're right, Jacob. Thanks for reminding me, but you know that he rejects my offers of conciliation."

Jacob disliked the unfamiliar feeling of taking a stand against his father, but he was the one who said, "Always speak up for what you think is right."

"Dad, you're always open with me about the good and the bad of ministry. I know you do that to help me decide about my future, and I also know that the things you've taught me are things you believe in and follow yourself." He took another deep breath. "But I have a couple of questions, and I don't want you to think I'm showing disrespect for asking them."

"Son, you can ask me anything."

"You've said it to me, and I've heard you say it to other people, that ministers should know all they can about members of their congregations. Well, just how much do you know about Mr. Adams?"

"Enough to drive me crazy, sometimes."

"Dad, were you ever in his store before this bell business? He's a longtime member of our church, and you didn't know he was from Pennsylvania. Do you know *anything* about his background or his family? You really should."

He had gone too far. He saw it in his dad's face and heard it in his voice as he said, "It hurts to hear that from my own son." A moment later, he added, "Jacob, you're right. I've neglected my duty as a minister. What can I do?"

It did not seem right, his father asking his advice. "Dad, I'm sorry. It's not my place to ..."

"It is your place. You're taking ministry seriously. I'm grateful to you for pointing out my faults. But I want you to know that my goal has always been to bring Amos back into the fold. That's why I involved him in our bell adventure."

"And do you want him back even though you think he can't change?"

"I've never said that he can't change. I'll do everything in my power to help him."

Jacob was relieved but still needed to make his point. "I only said those things because I think there is more to Mr. Adams than we know. When we were alone in the airplane, he started to tell me something, but held back. Dad, can you ..."

"I'll talk to him, Jacob. I understand what you're saying. I'll dig deeper. Your grandmother said there was a good man in there somewhere. If there is, I'll find him."

*   *   *

Obie endured two soul-searching days before he took his misery to Cassie. "Jacob told me that I've failed to live up to my pastoral duties." He searched her face for understanding. "Sweetheart, am I a bad minister?"

She seated herself in a chair beside his desk. "Our son is coming into his own," she said. "We must listen to him even when we feel it's unimportant."

"Yes, I know," Obie said. "He has become our moral watchdog. Have we made him that way?"

"We've taught him right from wrong, with a Christian perspective. He may measure people's behavior with that yardstick. But isn't that a good thing?"

"It is, but I fear we've failed to make him understand that we don't always live up to those standards ourselves, and that's where grace and forgiveness come in."

"He'll learn that people aren't perfect," she said. "And he'll learn the hard way if he tries to police some of the more cantankerous members of our congregation."

"I don't think he'll do that."

"Of course he won't. Jacob is smart. But, to answer your question ... yes, as I've always said, you are a good minister." She hesitated. "What, exactly, did he say to you?"

Obie took several minutes to relate details of his and Jacob's conversation without downplaying their son's critiques and their effect on him. He finished with, "Should I try to know people better?"

"Of course you should. You should know them as well as you can without appearing nosy."

"I've never liked to pry. Anyway, it's a little late since I'll move on in a few months."

He could almost hear her thoughts. "Sweetheart," she said, "forgive me for pointing out again something I said back in April when you were about to address the church in that open session. You were smarting because someone told you that you were 'aloof.' I said you were a 'private person,' which might have given you the impression that I thought you were uncaring."

"You said it looked 'standoffish.' I still remember that word."

"I'm sorry if that bothered you. But there is some truth in it. Obie, can I be blunt?"

"I expect you to be, as usual." He made sure she saw his

smile. "Hit me with it."

"You are reserved when you speak with people. I mean that you weigh your words carefully before you say anything, and that's not bad ... normally."

"I don't hold back in our committee meetings."

"And you're effective in those administrative details, but I suspect you're more reserved when you talk to individuals."

"You might ask Ernie or Chet about that."

'They're close friends. That's not like talking to Amos Adams."

"Well, I've had many contentious words with Amos."

"Obie, what I'm saying is that to get people to be open with you, you must open up to them. Maybe that's the insight Jacob has about your connection with Amos."

"He's really concerned about the man."

"And he wants you to be concerned, too."

"I am concerned, but Amos irritates me more than I want to admit."

"And that's where Jacob is right again. You must overcome your irritation, or hate, or whatever it is, if you are to discover why Amos is the way he is."

Obie could not stop a sigh. "I don't hate Amos. I dislike what he is, but I don't hate him. But I do understand what you're saying. You think I won't know what drives him unless I get to know him better?"

"Exactly."

"I'd rather skin a rabid skunk."

She did not laugh at the jest this time, and her tone was serious. "Just do what you know you must."

It was not only Jacob pushing him. And Cassie could push harder.

CHAPTER FORTY

December 25, 1988

On Christmas morning, the three church bells of Stafford Rest rang clear and loud, each tolling its unique sound at its scheduled time. Two minutes later, the combined bells sent forth a torrent of sound that, if not resembling harmony, was at least a resounding message of cheer.

Jacob's smile exhibited pride in having played such a large part in finding the new Baptist bell, which, according to him, "helped restore harmonious unity" among the three churches. Obie was sure he would remember that every time he heard the bells. Their son was the "real deal."

Obie considered it a miracle that the Baptist bell installation was completed by Christmas, for the tower had needed extensive repair and reinforcement before the bell could be moved into it. Rev. Owens predicted it would take longer, but Amos hired extra help and soon finished the job.

Obie stood outside the office door and watched people enter the sanctuary. He would soon go to the narthex to join the procession, but first, he wanted to see the faces of the people as they assembled. This would be his last Christmas service in this church, which felt bittersweet.

He did not expect a large crowd; families, especially those with young children, were reluctant to attend when Christmas came on a Sunday. The three churches had held a combined Christmas Eve service in the Episcopal church, so the season was sufficiently observed in most eyes.

He watched Cassie and Julie take their usual places near the front. Jacob had been sitting with Alicia for the past year, often apart from their families; today, they seated themselves on the far side. Jacob was in love, and from all indications, that love was reciprocated. He was okay with it, as was Cassie.

He looked toward the chancel and was reminded again that an era was passing. He remembered the time he and his mother first entered this church. She had violated Catholic rules, and he had entered an unknown world that, for all practical purposes, he would never leave. In his imagination, he saw the Rev. Charles Lansing at the pulpit, with the big black Bible open before him, reading Scripture in his precise way, with exact punctuation and proper accent evident in every word. *What an influence the man had on his life.*

Kent and Cara Augustine came down the center aisle and sat in a pew behind Cassie and Julia. Dan, Laurie, Obadiah, and Jane Paxton entered and approached the front. Ly Yen was not with them because she would lead today's service and was still in the office preparing.

Obie was pleased to see Chet and Lacy Boswell in the choir procession. The couple still struggled with their beliefs, but there was reason to be happy about their progress. Many other faces were familiar. Obie was pleasantly surprised that the sanctuary was filling; people were showing up to support their church—and maybe him, too.

Ly Yen came from the office to stand beside him. "Thank you for waiting," she said. "I am nervous about doing a sermon."

"Ly Yen, you've already helped me with several services. You'll do just fine. People love you."

"But I have never done a big sermon, except for practice at the seminary."

He laughed. "Those are the hardest. Here, you're simply talking to friends and family."

"Yes, Pastor Obie, that is good to remember, but I want to say the right things, what Jesus wants me to say."

He held one of her hands in his. "My beautiful and talented daughter-in-law, you are the most likely person I know to preach God's love to our struggling world."

He saw tears in her eyes and felt them in his own. "I must do what Jesus tells me to do," she replied.

As they walked to the back to join the procession, he was surprised to see Amos in a pew by himself. It was time to have a conversation with Amos. *Maybe today?*

Whether Ly Yen saw him looking at Amos, he could not know, but she whispered, "He is a lonely man. He needs love."

"He's hard to love."

"Pastor Obie, you speak often about love as if it is most important for a Christian."

"I believe it is."

"Then you must love Amos."

He did a stagger-step, causing Lucille Epps behind him to bump his leg. "Ly Yen," he whispered after he composed himself, "You've become a taskmaster."

"I must say what Jesus tells me to say."

* * *

Alicia Augustine had led the committee that brought the harmony of the Christmas bells to the village that morning. Jacob wanted to give her credit: "Ringing all three bells at the same time was a good idea, like a finale," he said as they walked down White Pine Street, "even if we only heard our own bell."

She hooked her arm through his. "I'm sure it was quite a sound out here. It was just a fun thing for Christmas Day. Our committee will experiment with ways to ring for harmony, but it will require exact timing."

The day was mild, and it felt good to be outside. Their destination was the Augustine house on Lake Road. Her family had gone from church to visit the Williamson family on Garnet Point, and his family would join them there. Alicia suggested going to her house for a couple of hours before joining the others. He had not objected; it meant time alone with Alicia. It also provided an opportunity to continue a serious discussion.

She did most of the talking as they crossed the concrete bridge on Main and started up Lake Road. He listened dutifully, saying little but silently rehearsing what he would say later.

The new Augustine home sat above Lake Road within sight of the cemetery. Kent had purchased the land from

Grandmother Hunt two years previously. The house was neither as elaborate nor as large as Aunt Laura's or Chet's, but the homey atmosphere appealed to Jacob.

Alicia made coffee and brought two steaming cups into the living area. Jacob sat on a leather couch, pondering how best to open the conversation about colleges. She had cut him off the last time, saying, "We can talk about it later." *"Later" had arrived.*

"Alicia," he said, taking her hand. He had learned that holding her hand was the best way to get her full attention. "I have a question."

"Yes, Jacob, I await your inquiry." She was smiling. It was often hard to get her to be serious.

He sipped his coffee before saying, "I want to make real decisions about next year. Are you willing to do that?"

"I'm already making real decisions." She shook his arm. "Have you even applied to any schools yet?"

"I'm waiting for us to decide together."

Her smirk revealed displeasure. "I'm a little late myself, but you need to get busy. Don't your parents prod you?"

"Yes, Mom does."

"It seems you've just dreamed about schools we can attend together." She paused. "Jacob, forget about 'together.' That would only work if we had a clear choice for both of us, but I don't think we do. This is a once-in-a-lifetime decision, and you need to look out for your own needs, just as I do."

A fear he had entertained returned. "Alicia, you don't really want us to attend the same school, do you?"

She took his hand again without speaking, which increased his anxiety. She finally said, "Don't you have your own choices of schools you'd like to attend?"

"Well, sure."

"So, why aren't you applying to those?"

"I'm not sure I'd be accepted. That's something you don't have to worry about. You aced the SAT."

"Schools look at writing ability, too, and that's where you excel. And there's baseball. Look at all the write-ups you've had from sports writers, and there's still a season to go."

"Yeah, I have baseball, but it's not a reason to choose a school. You know my ambition."

"I do know, but it might help you get into a really good school."

He knew but asked anyway, "What's your first choice?"

She did not hesitate. "Berkeley."

"Dad went there."

"I know. And I asked him about it."

"You talked to Dad about Berkeley?"

"He's a fountain of information. I could almost smell the eucalyptus trees."

"I'd go there just to be with you."

Her serious look returned. "You're not thinking clearly, Jacob, and that's unlike you. Don't you see, we must make our own choices about this. Otherwise, we might end up resenting each other."

"I'd never resent you, Alicia." He took a deep breath. "It sounds like we're breaking up?"

Her eyes looked damp. "Jacob, we're adults, now, even though our parents don't see us that way. We must be realistic. No, we're not breaking up, but we're reevaluating. And it's for the best. You have your dream, just as I have mine. We must give each other space to grow."

It was hard to speak. "That would mean years apart."

"We have all this year to be together. We'll make the most of that time."

"What if we grow apart? What if you meet someone else?"

Her hand on his arm was firm. "Jacob, right now I love you, and you love me. Let's let that be enough and enjoy it. If our love is real and meant to be, we'll be together someday."

Her words seared, but he knew she was right. Alicia was mature, as his mother had once said. She had seen what he had not.

Even through his pain, a sense of relief came. He could now follow his own dream.

CHAPTER FORTY-ONE

December 25, 1988

Darkness had fallen as Obie backed onto the highway from the Williamson home. It had been a Christmas day overflowing with friendship and good cheer.

"I knew the Augustines would come," Cassie said, "but having all the Boswells with us was a real bonus."

Obie felt it, too, the pleasant feeling of friendship. He said, "It's been an extraordinary year of events, both bad and good, but today was all good." He quickly added, "Except for not having Abigail with us."

"Grandma would have loved it," Jacob said from the back seat.

"I talked with Miss Frances," Julie said, her voice still high with excitement. She had become quite attached while in Frances' Sunday School class. *Only good could come from that.*

"Everything was splendid," Julie added, echoing Laurie's comment before they left.

"Laura looked so beautiful today," Cassie said. "She seems happy. Marrying Ben was a blessing."

"Mom, that was ten years ago," Jacob said.

Ten years? It seemed like only yesterday that Obic had, at Laura's request, sized up the repentant Ben Williamson's fitness for marriage. Ben had changed her life for the better. But he was not going to comment on that subject. His own ties to Laura were real; everyone knew the details, so any comment would be superfluous. Laura was happy. That was the main thing.

He did, however, have something to say to his son. "Jacob, you and Alicia were more than two hours late." Cassie touched his arm; he recognized that as a warning against unnecessary words. "I'm not prying," he said, softening his tone. "We were worried since you had said you were coming."

"We went to her house," Jacob said. "We discussed colleges."

"And did you make any progress on that neglected subject?" Cassie asked. This time, Obie touched Cassie's arm with his own warning.

"We did," Jacob said, but there was not the positive level the words promised. "We made some decisions ... I think."

Obie was ready to make a congratulatory comment concerning Jacob's unstated progress when what he saw caused him to hit the brakes. They were at the center of Main Street.

"What's wrong?" Cassie said.

"Amos, over there."

Amos Adams was on the side of the road, walking with a package under his arm. Cassie said, "Why did you stop? He won't talk to us."

Jacob said, "Dad, have you spoken to him? You know, what we talked about?"

Obie felt a familiar touch of remorse. That was a mission he had not attended to—his promise to Jacob that he would talk to Amos. *God, are you reminding me?*

He rolled his window down. "Amos ..." He was not quite sure what to say. "Merry Christmas."

Amos stopped but did not approach. "Same to you, Reverend, and to your folks."

"Amos, can we have a little talk?"

"Right now?"

"Yes. Well, not here on the road. I'll drive my family home first and come right back. I'll only be five minutes."

"Suit yourself. I live over my shop." The words were said without emotion.

Lucille Epps, who seemed to know more than anyone about Amos, had told him about the cramped apartment over Amos's store, but he had given it little thought. After he had taken his family home and returned, he wished he had asked her more about it.

He climbed the outside staircase and knocked on the door. Amos led him into a room overflowing with antique furniture, some of which looked in need of repair.

He sat on an ancient leather couch to which Amos had pointed. Amos took a chair facing him and said, "Well, Reverend, what are we going to talk about?"

On the drive back, Obie had rehearsed what he might say to open a conversation, but the words did not come easily. "Amos, I know we've had our problems, but I hope that this being Christmas, we might take time to be more sociable."

"Christmas is only one day out of the year. But I suppose we can be sociable, as you call it ... for a day." Amos's voice was anything but smooth, but at least he did not appear combative.

"Did you have a good Christmas?"

"Pretty much like last Christmas, and the one before that."

"Did you spend it with family, or with friends?"

"What friends? No, Reverend, I spent it alone. And that's the way I like it."

"I saw you with a package. I thought it might be a present."

"You thought wrong." Amos talked in a monotone now. "Did you know that Beth's Café stayed open today? On Christmas Day! But I wanted to celebrate Christ's birth with a good meal, so I had supper there. The package you saw was the leftovers that I'll have tomorrow."

"I heard that the Café was open," Obie said, still searching for words. "I suppose that even on a holy day, someone has to care for the needs of others."

"It's more likely they want the profits."

"Perhaps."

"Is that what you're here for, to ask if I've had a good Christmas?"

Obie reminded himself that the objective was to learn more about the man. "Actually, I want us to know each other better. We've never conversed about anything other than church matters."

"That's not my fault, Reverend. I'm ready to talk anytime." His expression resembled a smile. "Well, maybe I am sometimes a little difficult to talk to." *Concession. That's progress.*

"Perhaps that's true in my case, too. Conversation is a good thing."

"I don't talk to anyone much, just business, and only with a few in church. Although there is one ..." Amos hesitated, and Obie waited for any tidbit to help him understand the man better. But Amos said, "I'm curious. Why do you want us to talk after all this time? It's not just a Christmas thing, is it?"

Honesty was best. "No, I've come because of Jacob. He asked me to talk to you."

Obie was surprised at the sudden softness in Amos's voice, a quality seldom heard. "He is a good boy."

"He's the best, although I admit to being prejudiced." Obie leaned forward. "Amos, thank you for caring for him the afternoon of the crash." *Except for offering him a meal, had he never properly thanked the man?*

"He was just scared. All I did was talk to him to get him settled down."

"No, you stayed with him to free his leg from that smashed door, although you knew there was danger."

Amos was quiet for a long time before he cleared his throat and sat up straighter. "You're lucky to have a son." There was another pause. "I had a son once."

The words were startling. "Tell me about your son," Obie managed.

"It's been many years." Amos was looking down.

"Back in Pennsylvania?"

"Yes ..." He looked up. "How did you know I lived in Pennsylvania?"

"Jacob told me. You must have told him?"

"Yes, I suppose I did."

"Tell me about your son, Amos."

"Do you really want to know, or is this some preacherly duty you feel required to do?"

They sat close, and Obie started to reach out and touch the man's arm in a gesture of compassion, but then drew back; they were nowhere near that level of communication. "I want to know, Amos. I really do."

Amos launched into a monologue about his wife, Ester, and his son, Michael. He went into detail about Ester's beauty and charm and how she was "the best mother any child could ever want." And Michael was a "smart boy, destined to do big things."

Amos spoke in a low tone.. "We were a good family, full of love for one another. I had a good business, the same kind I have here. Big house with attached shop and store. We were churchgoers. That little church was not affiliated with other churches or denominations, but it suited my ways. I've always been a believer, even while growing up. I'm a believing Christian." He stopped and wagged a finger at Obie. "Like I was in your church."

It was not the time to debate that issue. "What happened?"

The gravel returned to Amos's voice. "The preacher in that church, with his charming ways, sweet-talked Ester into believing she belonged with him instead of with me." Amos stopped and sat back. "I don't know why I'm telling you all this. You'll just blab it to the whole town."

Obie struggled to overcome the surprise at what he had heard and quickly said, "No, Amos, I'd never betray confidentiality. What you tell me will go no further." He waited, and when Amos did not respond, he said, "Did Ester leave you, Amos?"

"You might say that. She left in more than one way." He stopped.

"What about Michael? Did he go with her?"

"She took him. He was only eleven years old."

This would explain much about Amos's ill temper. Obie wanted to know more, but yielded to compassion. "Amos, I'm sorry. Really sorry."

"It's not your doing, Reverend," he said, but added, "Although I guess I might have it in for preachers in general."

A breakthrough had presented itself. "Look, Amos, I'm not that minister or that kind of man. I would never ..."

"Stop!" Amos held out a hand. "You *are* that kind of man! And that's why I've never liked you."

Obie was shocked. "I don't know what you mean."

"You weren't assigned to our church long before I heard the rumors about how you'd fathered a child by the Williamson woman, but then didn't marry her. And it wasn't long before I learned through an acquaintance about you being a minister in California and how the church members there believed you left because you had an affair. That didn't sound like Christian behavior and certainly not how a minister of the gospel should conduct himself. It sounds more like a minister who'd steal a man's family to satisfy his own desires. That's how I've thought about you."

Obie felt crushed. In a few words, Amos had referenced the periods of his life for which he had prayed hardest for closure. *How could he respond?*

This time, he did touch Amos's arm. "Look at me, Amos. Take a good look. "I'm a man like you. Ministers are people like you and me. We sin. I'm not making excuses for that, just stating a fact."

"But you should stay above that. You should be pure."

"I try to be pure, but I'm also human."

Amos drew a deep breath. "On that day I left this church, you told the congregation about your beliefs. You and me have a lot of beliefs that push up against each other. I know that. But you also talked about 'love' that day, and you talk about it a lot. So, it seems to me that loving people means you'd want to be friendlier. Tonight, you've asked me to tell you about a part of my life that I don't like to talk about. But I've known you for ten years. Why haven't you asked me anything about that before?"

Obie shrank back into the couch; the scent of old leather was strong. Jacob had voiced that same shortcoming. He now understood better what was driving Amos. This conversation should have taken place years before. All the harsh words that passed between them might have been prevented.

His voice felt weak. "You're right, Amos. We should have talked years ago. I should have gotten to know you better. I'm at fault."

"There are others you need to know better, too."

"And I'll take care of that." *A long prayer session lay ahead.* "Amos, I want you to come back to church services."

"Do you, now? You kicked me out! And now you want me back?"

"You left on your own accord."

"Humm ... it has some bad tastes, but I'll consider it."

"I'll see that you're warmly welcomed."

"We have big differences, Reverend. You're a liberal who condones mountains of sin."

Obie smiled. "Maybe we can discuss those issues together in a civil manner."

He was not sure, but Amos may have smiled. He remembered a question he had meant to ask. "What happened to Michael? Do you ever see him?"

Amos lowered his head a moment, and when he looked up, his eyes were moist. "After they left with that poor excuse for a preacher, they hadn't gone more than ten miles before their car hit a truck head-on. They're all dead."

Obie bowed his head. Amos's burden was now his to share.

CHAPTER FORTY-TWO

January 1, 1989

The fireplace cast back heat and embers as Obie tossed on another log. He made sure no sparks reached beyond the hearth before he went to sit on the couch beside Cassie, who had just arrived, sleepy-eyed.

"It'll die down later," he said.

The lit fireplace was unnecessary because the weather was mild, but he had fired it up anyway; it seemed the right thing to do on the first day of the year. It was nearly noon. He had been up for two hours.

"Are the kids still asleep?" she asked as she cupped her hands around her coffee mug.

"Julie is, but Jacob left right after I got up. He's meeting Alicia. If the ice on Cedar Creek is strong enough, they'll go skating." He patted her hand. "Sweetheart, I apologize for not coming back last night to greet the new year. I just meant to take a short nap."

Cassie yawned. "That's okay. I should have joined you. We're too old to stay up so late. Julie wanted to see the Times Square ball drop, so we watched it together."

Obie stretched out his legs. He felt relaxed, unlike the days following the Christmas Day talk with Amos. Questions had nagged his mind: Why had he not shown more compassion toward Amos? Had he not loved enough? A sense of "liberation" came only after hours of prayer and meditation, one spent on the cold and windy ridge trail.

Cassie roused him from his reverie. "Don't you feel guilty this morning?"

It was a rare Sunday morning without a church service. Two weeks before, he had declared this Sunday a holiday free from services. There had, however, been an early service the previous evening. That placated most people, but Arthur Baines spoke up for the disapproving members: "How can you have a Watch Service at eight in the evening?"

"No guilt," Obie said. "Not in the least. It's time people get used to new ideas."

"Wow! You're living dangerously."

"And relishing it." *This might be the right time to share his new insights.* "Cassie, Sweetheart, I've been thinking."

She laughed. "It's about time."

He set his mug on an end table. "I've told you some details about my talk with Amos."

"You didn't break a confidence, did you?"

"Oh, no. I just wanted you to know that he's a hurt man, and that's the reason for much of his bad behavior."

"Well, he's back in church. You must have influenced him."

"Maybe, but here's the thing. I should already have known what troubled him. It would have made a world of difference in how I treated him. I wasn't compassionate."

"Obie, you didn't know."

"That's my point. I should have known." He grabbed her hand. "Cassie, I'm going to change. I won't be an administrator who makes things happen just to have a smooth-running church. I've been so tied up trying to make it all work that I lost sight of the fact that the church is made up of people ... all kinds of beautiful, wonderful, and flawed people. Amos isn't the only one I've failed." He took a breath. "Our people aren't only church members. They have lives. In the time I have left here, I'll get to know every one of them better."

"You're too hard on yourself. You've done good things."

"At a cost. You told me once that I need to care for the little things instead of trying to save the world. That's advice I intend to follow."

"Obie, I've meant to say something to you but haven't." She took a breath. "I think your feelings of shortcomings stem from the fact that you can't forgive yourself for your own sins ... sins that God has forgiven. Doesn't that mean you're questioning God's ability to forgive?"

He felt tears gathering. "Honey, that's something I'm dealing with. Carl told me much the same thing some time back. But it's only lately that I've confronted it. I do accept that I have been forgiven. I know it beyond a doubt."

"I'm truly happy about that."

"But that doesn't mean that I don't need to fix my people skills."

"People love you. And there's no fault in being a private person."

"Standoffish," he said, trying to smile.

"Obie, I see your zeal in this, and I admire it, but you're only here for a few more months, and you probably won't take another pastorate, so why punish yourself?"

He needed to make her understand. "Cassie, I've seen something lacking in myself. I've preached love but haven't practiced it as I should have. I want to fix that."

She patted his hand. "Well, in my view, you're punishing yourself needlessly."

"Sweetheart, you love me and don't see my faults."

She laughed. "Oh, you think not? If you like, I'll name them for you, maybe even make a list to attach to the office bulletin board."

He laughed, too. *Thank God for Cassie. Her good humor had smoothed many hurts.* "Sweetheart, I'm determined to make changes. I'll make the little things my priority, as you suggested. I'll be closer to people. I'll do more home visits, hospital runs, private conversations, and maybe even more visits to the Diamond Inn."

"You're already close to many people. Look at how you defended Lacy. She would do anything for you."

"That's just it. I have a few close friends who happen to be church members. And, yes, I've served them. But I've chosen my friends, and I fear I've shut out many. That's what I want to change."

"Amos is back in church. That's a positive change."

"It is, although there is still work to do there."

"He's changed. He's quieter. Other people have noticed it. Camilla Landry told me she thinks he's seeing someone."

"I find that unlikely, but it would be a good thing."

"He's not a bad-looking man when he keeps his mouth closed. God does work in mysterious ways."

"We've talked, and without the bluster, but with honesty. I think he sees that we both want the best for the church. We've named our positions: he charges like a bull, and I move with stealth. I'm hopeful we can find a comfortable place to work together." He added, "I believe Amos and I have learned something from each other."

"I'm sure you have."

"We've even prayed together. At first, he didn't want to do that, but I reminded him that because Jesus paid the debts for our sins, God has forgiven us, and that we should give thanks in prayer."

"I repeat, God works in mysterious ways."

He took a deep breath in preparation for delivering a decision over which he had agonized. "I won't be leaving the conference," he said. "I'll serve wherever they appoint me."

She surprised him with her familiar little giggle. "I thought as much." After a moment, she said, "But what about your writing?"

"I've had it backward, Cassie. I'm a pastor first and a writer second. There aren't nearly as many writers who are ministers as there are ministers who write. It seems I'm destined to be a writing minister."

"Are you sure, Obie? I don't want you to have regrets."

"I've weighed the sacrifices. But frankly, I've worried more about what I'm asking of you. There could be household upheavals."

She turned to face him. "We'll handle whatever comes. Don't forget that I'm a minister's wife. We're a special breed. We'll manage."

They put their arms around each other and sat like that for several minutes. Cassie broke the silence. "Could you have imagined seventeen years ago today that we would be here on Blackberry Hill, celebrating Jacob's birthday?"

"I was numb with joy that day. It was the most wonderful thing that had ever happened to me."

"And to me."

"And we have all these relatives coming to celebrate with us. What time will they arrive?"

"I said four o'clock. Dan and Ly Yen are always on time, but I'm unsure about Obadiah and Laurie. Laura and Ben will be late, as usual."

"We'll miss Kent and Cara," Obie said, "but I'm sure they are enjoying themselves with Lyle and Matilda."

"It's Jacob's good fortune that Alicia stayed home this year."

Julie appeared in the doorway at that moment. "Mommy, I'm hungry," she said.

"Honey, I'll make pancakes in a few minutes. For now, go into the kitchen and make yourself some toast."

"With butter and jelly?"

"Of course. Everything you need is there."

Obie said, "I think Jacob suspects."

"I'm sure he does. After all, we've had a party for him almost every birthday." She sighed. "Obie, have we spoiled our son? Have we made life too easy for him?"

"Certainly not. He's a responsible and mature young man. And he's making serious plans for his future."

"He's been applying to some excellent schools. What if he gets accepted to one of those? How can we afford that?"

Obie laughed. "There's no way he'll get into one of those."

Her voice rose. "Why on earth would you say that?"

"Only that they are very hard to get into. But, to be clear, I'll be delighted when he gets into any good school. And we'll worry about the cost when the time comes."

She gave him a forgiving nudge and said, "And he's seriously in love. Don't forget that?"

"Yes, he probably is, but he's young, and so is she. Look at our own history. Young love doesn't always work out as we imagine it should."

"I know, but it's different with them. Their lives are stable, unlike how ours were. They love each other, and I'm happy with that. They'll work out the college thing between them."

"Maybe. But four years apart? A lot can happen."

"It turned out well for Obadiah and Janet."

"It will be what it will be, according to God's will, of course."

Cassie sighed and moved closer before saying, "Obie, do you believe in miracles?"

"I do."

"We'll have all our family members around us in a few hours. We'll celebrate, feel good, and show love to one another." Her eyes sparkled. "But have you ever stopped to think that you, Laura, and I are responsible for all these people who will be here today? Isn't that a miracle?"

"It is. And every family member is a miracle. We're all miracles. We're all part of God's plan."

"Is that the pastor speaking?"

"It's a morally feeble and repentant man speaking."

She laughed that laugh he loved so much and said, "Enough religious and philosophical chatter. We must get ready to entertain. But first, let's make pancakes. Julie's hungry, and so am I."

"I love you, Cassie."

"And I love you, Obie Gainsworthy."

They went into the kitchen holding hands.

CHAPTER FORTY-THREE

May 15, 2024

Dear Rabbi David,   *May 15, 2024*

I received your letter yesterday. Handwritten letters are rare nowadays. Although it is good to hear from you again after several months, it saddened us all to hear of your father's passing. Living past one hundred years is not only an arduous thing, it's a privilege. (That's a quote from Dad, although probably not original.) He is taking it hard on one level but accepts it on another. Adam was a special friend.

As you know, they served together in the Second World War and are members of what we now call "The Greatest Generation." Dad was also a chaplain in two wars after that. I believe your father served in the Israeli army, as well. Their sacrifices have made it easier for their sons, grandchildren, and great-grandchildren. <u>We must not forget that.</u> Even so, it seems there is never an end to wars. Our prayers are with you and your country in this latest problem. May peace prevail.

It has been several years since our visit to the Holy Land, but I'll never forget the gracious way your family hosted our family. Your four grandchildren got along famously with our three children. Some of them correspond to this day.

It was a great surprise and a meaningful experience when you and Adam went with us to Italy after we left the Holy Land. Seeing those two old soldiers retracing their footsteps is something I will not forget.

I don't remember if I told you, but the beautiful lady who joined us in Italy, Rosa Turmack, has since passed away. I do not often see Dad cry, but he did when he received that news from Matthew, Rosa's son.

As for your inquiry about our families, all is well. Dan, my older brother, has completely retired from his practice, leaving it to his son Obadiah and granddaughter Samatha. Samatha is Obadiah and Jane's daughter, and also a physician. The clinic has become essential in our area, serving more than just our village. Dr. Ben Williamson started it back in the seventies, and it's a shame he died before he could see its greatest growth.

Dan is in good health for his age. He still flies, but usually with Obadiah. They mourn the death last year of Ly Yen, the wife and mother. Dan, especially, grieves. And I have to say that, from my perspective, Ly Yen was a remarkable woman; she rose from humble beginnings to become an important and beloved leader in the Methodist Church. She is buried in the family cemetery next to Laura, her mother-in-law. Laura is Dan's mother; I once tried to explain our family relationships to you, but it's easy to get confused.

My cousin, Laurie, and her husband make short visits and come in the summer for longer vacations. (Laurie is Dan and Ly Yen's daughter, and a professor at Brown).

My mother (Cassie) sends her best wishes and condolences, and I'm sure she will write to your mother. Mom still pursues her many interests, although she depends on some of us to cart her around since she no longer drives. A lot fell on her in recent years because of the Napa Valley property and the Hunt family interests, the latter especially after Aunt Laura's illness and death. The factory is finally sold, and Abigail's (the inn) is the only surviving Hunt interest; it is now under non-family management. As for the vineyard in California, it has long been leased out. Mom and Dad still talk about selling it outright, but that never happens. Obadiah will be very unhappy if they do that; I won't be surprised if he ends up owning it. Family members still go to the Napa House for vacations, although Alicia and I have not gone there for three years.

Dad has also given up driving and is mostly content to stay home on Blackberry Hill, spending his time writing and painting. Painting has always been a hobby, although his canvases are quite good in the traditional sense. However, his writing has been his truest focus since he retired from the Methodist Conference a few years ago. I write, too, and have published a couple of books that some people pretend to read, but my output is nothing like Dad's.

Mom and Dad want to stay on Blackberry Hill as long as possible, although they know they can come and live with us whenever they like. They have lots of help with their house and garden. Anna Adams, especially, has been a big help even though she cares for her aged mother, Lucille.

David, you've told me about your parents' positive influence on your life. That is my experience, as well. Mom spurred me on to be the best I can be. Without her, I might never have applied to the better schools. Her wit and sparkling humor have helped Alicia and me through some difficult places. She also keeps Dad on his toes with her little needling comments about events in their life together. They love each other fiercely.

Dad has been my inspiration throughout my professional life. I knew from an early age that I wanted to be a minister. I watched him, what he did, what he believed, and how he followed God's calling even though it was not always pleasant. Writing was his great love, and he is good at it, but he put that aside for many years to answer what he determined was his "calling."

He is not perfect, of course, as none of us are. He once asked me to name his greatest fault. All I could come up with was that he worried too much about his own abilities as a pastor instead of just going on doing what he was led to do. I think he listened. As a pastor in the same conference, I have seen the esteem people have for Dad. He could have had greater leadership in our conference, but chose to stay true to his goal of simply teaching "love" as the essential element of Christianity. And that also became the focus of his writing as he moved away from his early scholarly genre to a more relaxed and down-to-earth one. Although he and I go in different directions on some doctrinal and social issues, the "love" element is most prominent in both our ministries.

David, I've seen you in your environment doing your best to enlighten souls, and despite the differences in our cultures and religions, you and my father are much alike. You meet on a field where understanding dwells. Don't we need more of that?

Now, as for my immediate family: I am in perfect health except for a slight limp left over from a broken leg of many years ago that ended my college baseball career. Alicia is healthy also, but we had a scare a few months ago about a lump on her breast; it turned out to be nothing, but it frightened us. She's the love of my life, and I don't know what I would do without her. She's thinking of retiring from her business enterprises and spending more time at home, but I have doubts about that.

As for our children, all are well, health-wise. The twins, Daniel and Kenneth, will turn twenty-nine next month. Dan lives in Florida, is an attorney, and is unmarried, although there is a relationship that looks encouraging. Ken, now retired from Army chaplaincy due to wounds received in Afghanistan, pastors a church in Atlanta and is married to Donna. We are blessed with two grandchildren, Elizabeth and Alexander, who come to Stafford Rest for Christmas and for two weeks in the summer. I want to believe that Alicia and I draw them here, but it's more likely they come to see their great-grandparents and the two Boswell grandchildren down the road to whom they have become much attached.

Abigail, our youngest, is a teacher in Schenectady, so we see her often. She has an apartment near her work, but owns a house here and spends most of her weekends and summers here. She is unmarried, but there is hope because she brought a "friend" home the last few times she came.

David, I want you to know that you and Clara are welcome to visit and bring whomever you wish. We have a big house with plenty of room. Alicia inherited it from her parents. It overlooks Diamond Lake.

As you know, I pastor a small church only a few miles from here. I commute right now, which is a drain on energy sometimes, but it's what Dad did for several years in the area. We moved a couple of times early in my ministry and will have to move again if I'm assigned somewhere farther away. I don't have quite the moxie for what Dad did one time when he was to be assigned to a big church in Albany; he sent the conference a letter of resignation, which the District Superintendent *promptly sent back shredded into many pieces. He told me that he wouldn't really have resigned, but because he was led to serve in a "mountain ministry," he had to protect that mission. I keep hoping that I might someday be assigned to Stafford Rest Methodist, but so far that has not happened. It's a healthy church after many years of "up and down." In fact, all three churches are doing well. The tolling of their bells is something I have always loved.*

I had better bring this epic to a close. But one last thing: Today is my parents' birthday. Yes, they were born on the same day, coming into this world only a few minutes apart. I have often listened to heated arguments about who is older.

Alicia and I are going to Dan's home on Garnet Point this evening for the birthday party. For some reason, my parents prefer that location and insist on using the patio. I suspect it brings back some shared memories. Even with all that we know, I am sure there is much they have not told us, and I bet it would fill a book. Take care, and I look forward to hearing from you again soon.

Your Friend,
Jacob Matthew Gainsworthy

* * * * * * * *

This ends the

WINE FOR TOMORROW trilogy.

A LAST WORD

All characters in the *Wine for Tomorrow* trilogy are works of the imagination and not meant to resemble any person or persons, living or dead. A few prominent personalities are mentioned, but they have no interaction with the fictional characters.

My characters navigate this period in history (1931–2024) against the backdrop of real-world events that are sometimes highlighted, sometimes not, but never intentionally altered.

Except for the imaginary villages of Stafford Rest and Evergreen and a few unnamed settings throughout that are composites of real places, these books are as true as possible to geography and topography; I thought that especially important in the war chapters of the first two books.

I have taken some literary license in portraying the Methodist Church hierarchy and procedural matters. I do not mean to elevate that Christian denomination over any other; I chose it simply because I know it better than any of the others, having been a "Methodist" all my life.

I included the author-generated charts and maps at the back of this volume to facilitate readers' navigation of the numerous characters and to orient them to the physical layout of the Stafford Rest area. The charts were the idea of my good friend, Barbara Woodrum Harvey. I drew the maps for my own use, but I thought readers might be interested, despite their amateur quality.

While I admit to endowing some of the main characters with theological beliefs similar to my own, I resisted making my characters overly preachy, although some readers may consider them so. I believe I have adhered to the theme I established in the beginning, that love and hate cannot exist side by side. Thank you for reading the *Wine for Tomorrow* trilogy.

Rupert Pratt
2025

ABOUT THE AUTHOR

Rupert Pratt grew up on a small farm in Salt Rock, West Virginia. He graduated from Barboursville High School in 1951, and after an enlistment in the United Air Force, earned a BA degree from Marshall College (now Marshall University) in 1957 and a MA degree in 1959. He married Mildred Mereness from Schenectady, New York, and taught in the Schenectady City School District for thirty-six years. Rupert and Millie have two sons, Gregory and Jonathan, and three grandchildren, Elizabeth, Nathan, and Andrew. Millie passed away in 2013.

In addition to the *Wine for Tomorrow* trilogy, he has authored two non-fiction works, *Touching the Ancient One: A True Story of Tragedy and Reunion* (2006, 2021) and *Tri-State Heroes of '45: Together With a Year in the Life of a West Virginia Farm Family* (2020). Information about Rupert Pratt's books and other related subjects is available on his website: https://www.touchingancientone.com.

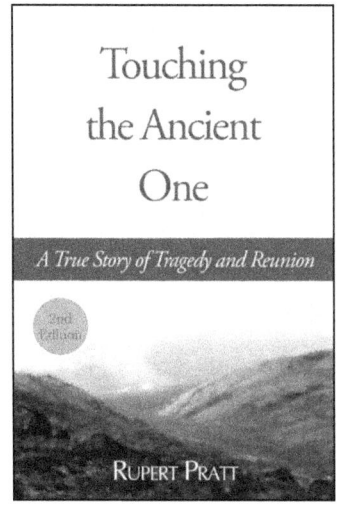

Touching the Ancient One–A True Story of Tragedy and Reunion is my story of a 1954 Air Force C-47 crash on Kesugi Ridge in South-Central Alaska that took the lives of ten military service members; I was one of six survivors. It's also the story of a reunion forty-two years later bringing together crash survivors, their families, families of the victims, and civilian and Air Force personnel from that time. There followed other reunions, the erection of plaques honoring the men who perished, a high military honor for rescuer Cliff Hudson, and a 1998 return to the mountain crash site.

This is a reprint of the 2006 edition with some updated information.

Touching the Ancient One
was awarded a Silver Medal from
Military Writers Society of America.

https://www.amazon.com/Rupert-Pratt/e/B002BMD2DM

Tri-State Heroes of '45: Together With a Year in the Life of a West Virginia Farm Family resurrects selected local, national, and world events of 1945, but hangs on a framework of diary entries of Pratt's mother, who was thirty-seven that year, while Pratt himself was only twelve. The daily life on their little farm in Salt

Rock, West Virginia, presents a unique mosaic that tells an unforgettable tale of faith, family, and hope on the home front. Pratt honors military service members of the Tri-State area of West Virginia, Ohio, and Kentucky with 'mini-stories' from Huntington, West Virginia newspapers of that year [1945 Huntington Herald Dispatch and Huntington Herald Advertiser]."

There are over 8,000 personal names in the index.

Tri-State Heroes of '45 was awarded a 2021 *Military Writers Society of America* <u>Silver Medal</u> in Memoirs/Biography.

Tri-State Heroes of '45 can be ordered on Amazon:

https://www.amazon.com/Rupert-Pratt/e/B002BMD2D

Love and hate battle for control between two Adirondack families: One family enjoys wealth; the other struggles for survival. Obie, a child of the Depression, loves two sisters: Cassie is his best friend and confidant; Laura is the one he's determined to marry. Abigail, the girls' mother, will do anything to prevent that. Suffering bitter betrayal, Obie is cast into a world ravaged by war. This story plays out over the diverse areas of the New York Adirondacks, the boot of Italy, and the Bay Area of California. Above all, it's a story about a young man's loss of faith and his convoluted journey to reclaim it.

Wine for Tomorrow can be ordered on Amazon: https://www.amazon.com/Rupert-Pratt/e/B002BMD2DM

Blackberry Hill

A Novel

The Sequel to
WINE FOR TOMORROW

Rupert Pratt

Obadiah (Obie) Gainsworthy, a gifted writer and highly decorated soldier and chaplain, struggles to regain personal stability. He's lost Cassie, his great love, and is estranged from his activist wife. War-weary and failed at pastoral ministry, he fights despondency. Friends call him "a good man." He calls himself "unworthy . . . a writer who doesn't write and a preacher who doesn't preach." Reclamation may come through a place he's spurned for many years, but has remained a subtle whisper in his ear—Stafford Rest, a little village in the Adirondack Mountains.

Blackberry Hill can be ordered on Amazon:

https://www.amazon.com/Rupert-Pratt/e/B002BMD2DM

WINE FOR TOMORROW Trilogy Characters

Ancestors and descendants of the Gainsworthy, Petitucci, Hunt, and Augustine families.

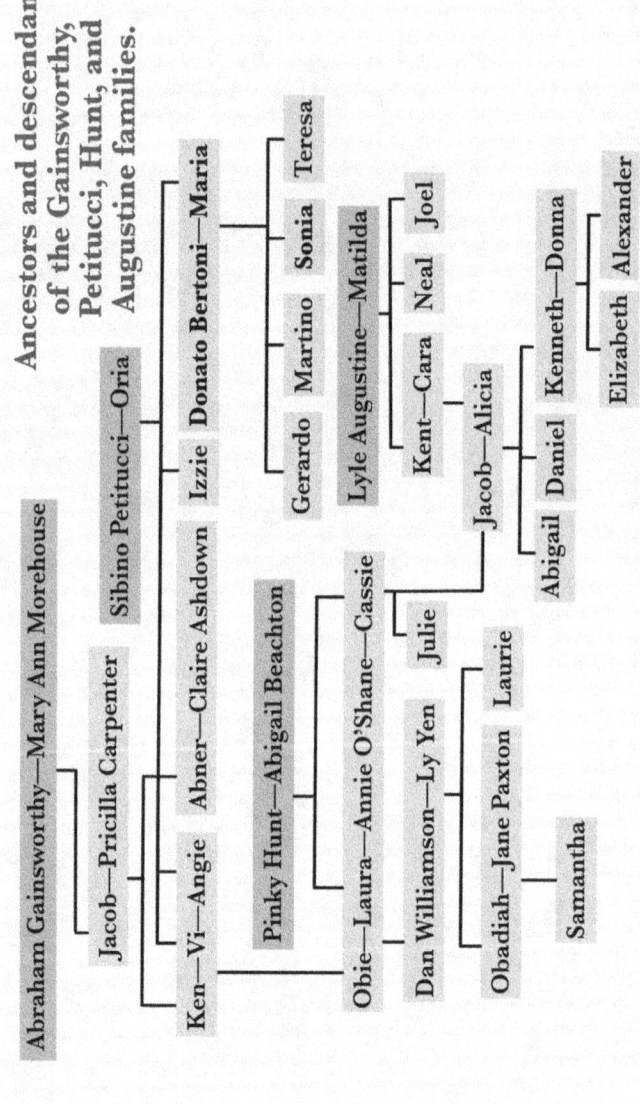

The Silverman Family

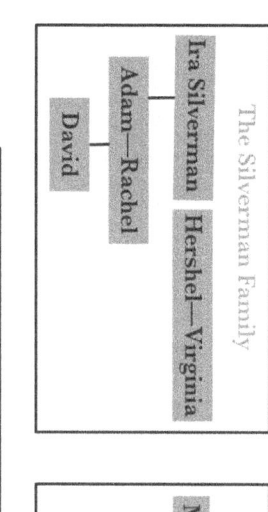

Ira Silverman — Hershel — Virginia

Adam — Rachel

David

The Burroughs Family

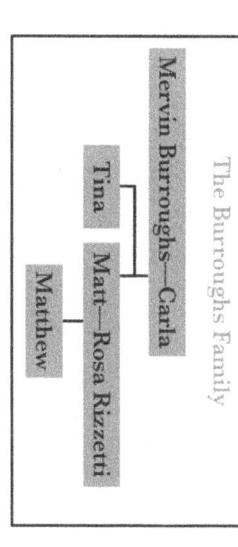

Mervin Burroughs — Carla

Tina — Matt — Rosa Rizzetti

Matthew

Sgt. Silverman's Squad Members

Maxwell Burke   Matt Burroughs   Edward Grugs

Ted Clemons   Christian Meinard   Harold Perkins

Leander Deboise   Thomas Rivera   Paul Aimes

Timothy Copland   Obie Gainsworthy

WINE FOR TOMORROW Trilogy Characters

Characters who are not necessarily members of the Gainsworthy, Petitucci, Hunt, or Augustine families.

Other Pivotal Characters

Bernadette Simon

Dr. Ben Williamson

Ed Jackson

Methodist Church Officials

Anthony Gladstone

George Delany

Other Village Pastors

Father Curtis Parker

Rev. Ernest Owens

Obie's Boyhood Friends

Chuck Hinky   Ed Baumgartner   Tommy Mathews

Ernie Boswell—Cora Stringer—Frances Gibbons

Chet—Lacy Grandcastle

Pastors and Members of Stafford Rest Methodist Church

Rev. Charles Lansing   Rev. Carl Enslow   Sara Hill

Lucile Epps   Roland Kilpatrick   Amos Adams

Arthur Baines   Glenda Smith

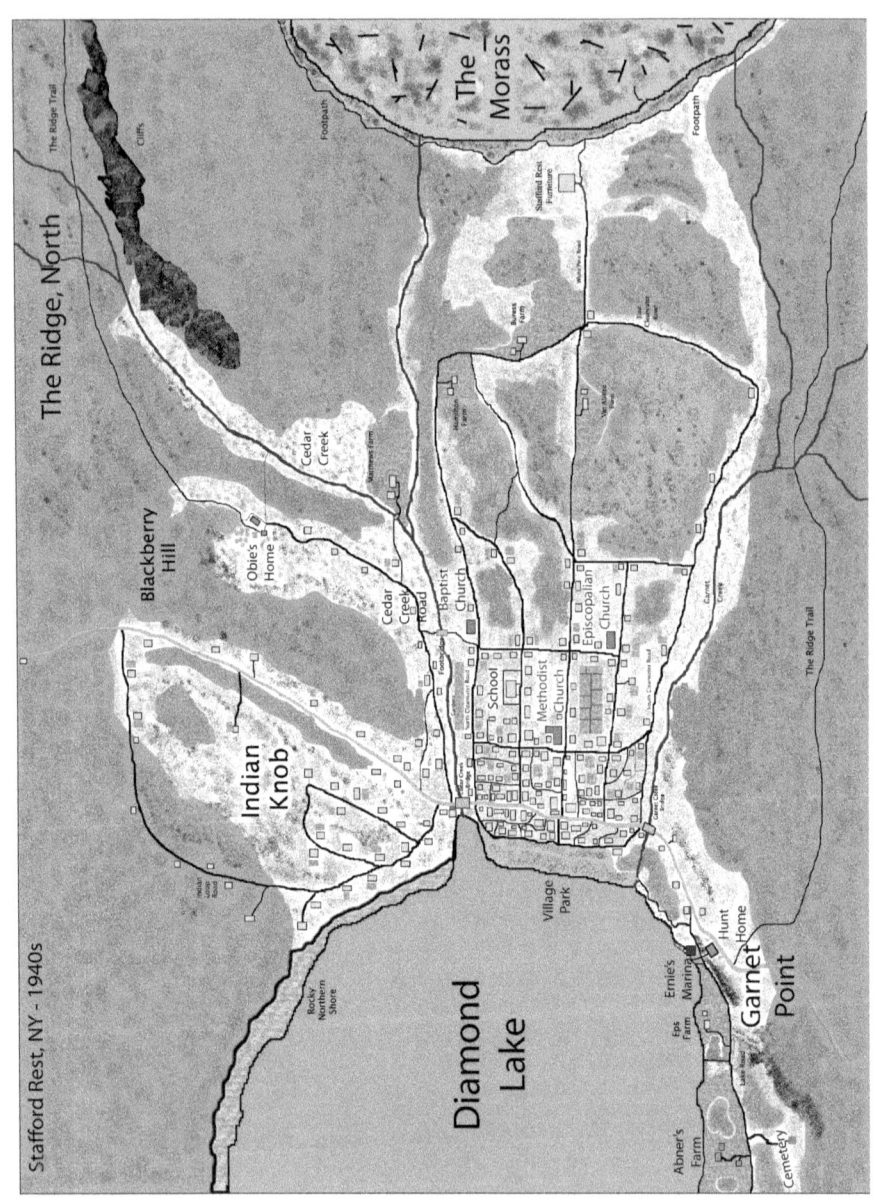

Stafford Rest, NY - 1940s

The Ridge, North

The Morass

Blackberry Hill

Cedar Creek

Obie's Home

Cedar Creek Road

Indian Knob

Baptist Church

School

Methodist Church

Episcopalian Church

Village Park

Diamond Lake

Rocky Northern Shore

Ernie's Marina

Eps Farm

Abner's Farm

Hunt Home

Garnet Point

Cemetery

The Ridge Trail

396

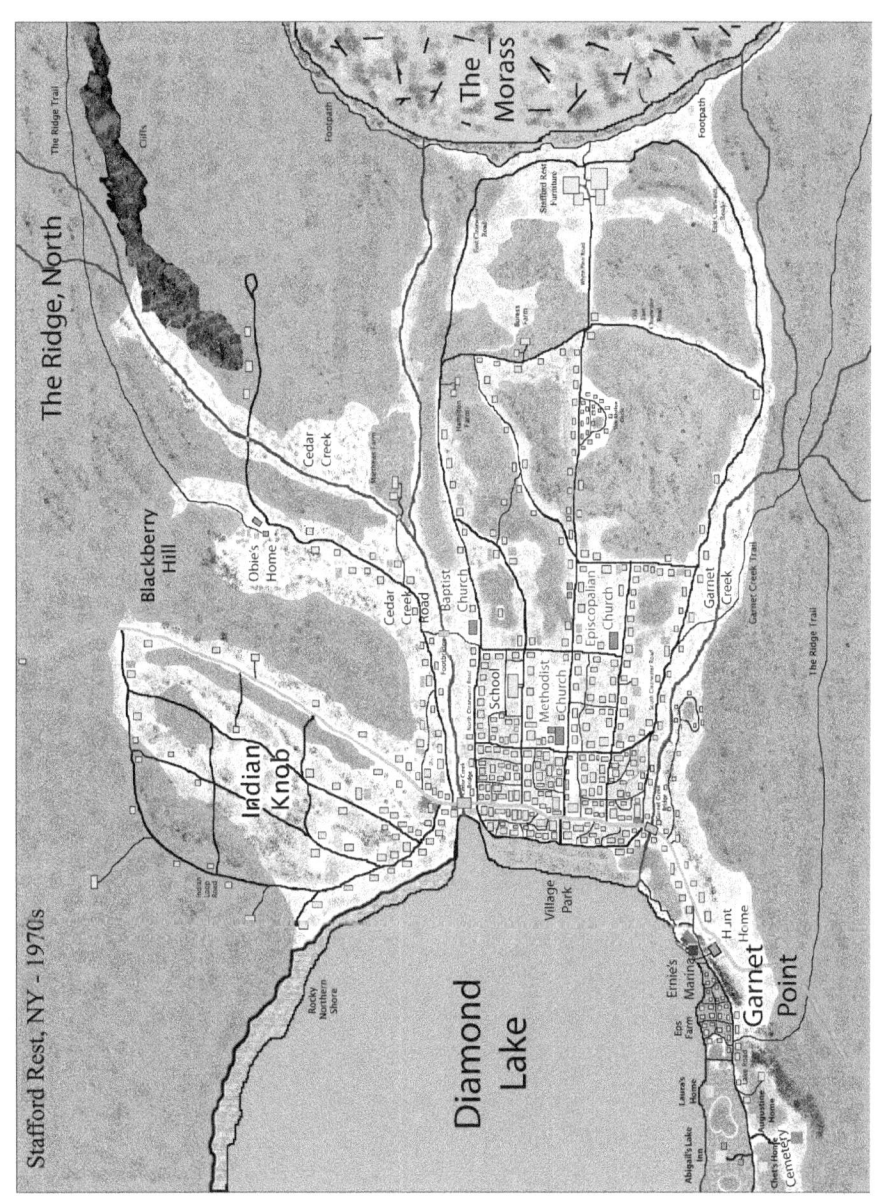

Stafford Rest, NY - 1970s

The Ridge, North

The Morass

Diamond
Lake

Indian
Knob

Blackberry
Hill

Cedar
Creek

Garnet
Point

Rocky
Northern Shore

Village
Park

Obie's
Home

Cedar
Creek
Road

Baptist
Church

Episcopalian
Church

Methodist
Church

School

Garnet
Creek

The Ridge Trail

Footpath

Stafford Rest
Furniture

Footpath

Ernie's
Marina

Hunt
Home

Eps
Farm

Laura's
Home

Abigail's Lake
Inn

Chet's House
Cemetery